I0825394

ENCHANTMENT
OF
DARKNESS
SHANA J. CALDWELL
ENCHANTMENT
OF
DARKNESS
SHANA J. CALDWELL

Enchantment

Of

Darkness

SHANA J. CALDWELL

Enchantment of Darkness

Paperback ISBN 978-0-646-82984-5

Hardcover ISBN 978-0-646-83288-3

Editor *Tara Routley*

Cover design by *CoverDungeonRabbit*

*

Hardcover Edition: MARCH 2021

For the women who strive to take their lives into their own hands.

Your life is yours, this one is for you.

Rain belts down around me as I trudge up the muddy path towards the centre of the village of Elderview, people mill about unfazed by the rain as they continue their daily chores and jobs. My dark green dress sticks to my slim body, my boots flick mud that tangles with the hem. I haul the full wheat bucket beside me, the contents threatening to spill over each time the bucket crashes into my legs. The lid does little to keep out the rain, and dread fills me as I realise we won't get the full price for the contents of soggy wheat grains. The crop this summer had been poor, wheat had struggled to grow with the little rain we'd been granted and the two weeks of spring were full of rain, which drowned any progress we'd made, until we were thrown into a cruel winter.

Life in the mountain gully was miserable, the crops barely grow, the sun hardly makes its way here and when it did it burnt everything in its path and the town was riddled with poverty. Few notice me as I keep my head down, eyes focused on the sloshed path in front of me covered in multiple boot prints. My long black hair sticks to my back and the sides of my face, doing well to hide the few centimetre long scar that runs just underneath my right ear. I don't dare remove a hand from the bucket handle to move it out of the way.

Each person around me looks just as miserable, heads down with equally soaked clothes. The rain drowns out the sound of the village chatter and the misery each person feels, it drowns out the cries of the hungry children and the dying animals. It is a blessing and a curse we all feel too well. Wooden and wire fences begin to come into view, protecting small wooden cottages that had been well worn down over time.

I catch my breath as the path finally levels out to flat ground, the village around me thrives with life. Makeshift rain catchers are spread out on the paths as people collect the clean water, filling bottles and buckets as they come and go. I make my way to a dry patch under the shade of a large tree that sits between two buildings and set the bucket down, my arms shaking with the effort. Although I spent most of my days carrying heavy buckets, I had no muscle and still struggled with the basics. Lack of food stopped me from growing any form of real muscle. If it wasn't for the rain and the river that ran down behind the mountain our village would die, they're the only source of water, the walk from town to the river took almost half an hour and double coming back. Most days in summer I spent walking to and fro, collecting as much water as I could until my body collapsed with exhaustion. Luckily, there was always baked goods for me once I'd returned home.

My mother is one of the best local bakers while my father is a farmer, tending to the crops that grow behind our home. While my aunt sews clothes and blankets, she also looks after my little brother when he isn't at school. After I lost my little sister ten years ago, my parents wanted to take every precaution they could with my brother, he's six now and my twentieth birthday is only a four days away. I'd been working for my family from the moment I turned twelve and I envied my brother for the six years of freedom he still had.

"Ravynne Morgan, is that you?" I turn to the sound of my name, pushing the wet black pieces of hair behind my ear. I narrow my eyes as I see Jester Cornrow coming towards me, the local news reporter. We went to school together and he was always the one to start drama with his words of nonsense and lies.

"Jester." I clip, I squeeze my hands together as he comes to a stop in front of me. He pushes the wet orange curls back from his face as his blue eyes trail over me, his brown overalls were drenched as well as his newspaper bag.

"I haven't seen you in ages. How is everyone?" he asks, leaning against the tree. He looks out towards the crowd, his pale cheeks are flushed pink and covered in a scatter of dark freckles.

"They're well, thank you for asking." I look away from him and study the people around us, a few glance our way with questioning eyes; the scowl on my face doesn't keep them staring for long. This village is small, and I did well to keep to myself. I had no use for friends, and I hardly had the time for myself these days so I doubt I could handle sharing that with others.

"If you're looking for a story, you're looking in the wrong place." I say clearly. I feel his eyes focus on me. I stare out of the village and up between the large forest between the looming mountains. Sitting above us is a large cobblestone castle, housing the most ruthless faerie King ever known to exist. Apparently, according to the whispers of the villagers.

"Why do you think I'm looking for anything?"

"Because no one talks to me unless they want something or want to get something out of me." I look back down to my bucket and pick up the handle, I'd already taken too long standing here wasting time on Jester.

"Rav."

I scowl as I turn my head towards him, "*Do not call me that.*" I launch myself back into the rain, it muffles out his reply. Good riddance. I haul the bucket across the village until the familiar wooden building of the farming shop comes into view. I walk up the few rickety stairs and open the screen door, it rings a cow bell and announces my arrival.

I set the bucket down inside as the door shuts behind me. A short thin man comes out from a back room, adjusting the straw hat on his head. I offer my best smile as I walk up to the wooden counter.

"Ravynne, how are the crops?" he asks, looking over to the wet bucket. I can't recall his name.

"Not the best this time of year, but this is the last lot we have until the rain slows down. Da' is still out sowing, but the quality of those crops will wane. I don't know what we're going to do for the winter, it seems everyone in the town is just as worse off as we are." I shake my head as I retrieve the bucket, I use all my strength as I sit it on top of the counter that just reaches my waist.

I peel back the lid, a few wet patches are noticeable but apart from that the rest of the wheat had survived the trek. I sigh in relief as he mixes the contents with a wooden spoon.

"Yes it's not good at all, if that damned useless faerie actually gave a rats ass about us we could flourish down here." he shakes his head as he takes the bucket and places it under the counter, he pulls out a brown money bag and begins to count out a few gold coins.

"That's true, I haven't seen him yet," I say idly, looking out the dusty window at the rain coming down. It was forbidden to talk about the King in such a way, but we had no guards here. No one who could reprimand the folk for speaking ill of him. The King faerie hadn't left his castle in over twenty years apparently, just before I'd been born. The stories as to why he hadn't come down since were too muddled to know the real truth, although there are whispers he comes down through the nights to make sure we're still in line with his ruling.

The man coughs up phlegm and spits it on the ground beside him, I try not to cringe as I scoop up the ten gold coins. "You're lucky, he's a cruel looking thing. You have safe travels now, aight?" I nod my thanks and stuff the gold coins into the secret pocket of my dress, it weighs down comfortably as I take to the rainy streets again. I spare yet another glance towards the castle, an anger so severe threatens to take over me as I see the distant flicker of golden lights. He sits up there in his royal castle and did as he pleased while we were left to starve and die down here.

I struggle to think of anything else as I head back through town. I move through the crowd like a shadow as I wedge myself between the cluster of people. Once out I quicken my pace, heading down the slope towards my farm. Our home sat at the base of the slope that reaches the village, with a few rare neighbours around us. The ground is slush with mud and I struggle to keep my footing, I try and slow down and my boot connects with a slick rock.

My arms pinwheel as I fall backwards, my feet fly out from under me as I land hard on my back. I groan as I blink black stars out of my vision and feel the mud soak into my hair and clothes. As I do a shadow falls over me and blocks out the rain and sunlight. A shadow with pointed ears.

A faerie is standing over me.

I don't move as I watch him, his unnatural deep violet eyes study me while his head is cocked to the side like an animal. His short raven black hair is a wet mess on his head, sticking to his sharp jaw line, forehead and the side of his throat. His pale ears jut out on both sides, one pointed tip is donned with a silver ring.

His blue tunic is shielded from the rain by a dark blue cloak, a golden pin holds it together at the base of his throat. I push myself up on my elbows and wince, "If you're going to stand there you can offer to help me up or go away." he blinks slowly and holds out a hand clad in leather gloves for me. I take it hesitantly as he lifts me up; as if I weigh no more than a feather. If he thinks I'm going to treat him differently because he' a faerie, he's going to be in for a surprise.

I pull my hand from his as I adjust my dress, not thinking about the lingering warmth that it's left with; my back aches with the small movements. I feel his eyes study me as he takes a step back, his black boots are caked in mud and I have to wonder how long he's been in town for. Was he the King they all talked about? He looked far too young to be a King.

"Th-"

"Do not thank me, unless you would like to be in my debt, then you may proceed." his voice is deep and takes me by surprise, I frown as I swallow my words. I ring my hands out in front of me, unsure of what else to say.

"What is your name?" he asks.

"Ravynne." he nods slowly as he looks away from me, my eyebrows raise as realisation sets in, I am talking to a real faerie.

"You seem like you've strayed far from home." I look back towards the castle and back to the man in front of me, he licks his lips as he sighs and looks back towards me. I keep my head high as I hide my hands in the sides of my dress, I shiver involuntarily as the rain begins to beat down harder.

"May I accompany you to your home?" he asks, his violet eyes seem to swallow me as I look into them. I struggle to tear myself away from him and his unearthly beauty, he is so beautiful it hurt to look at him for too long.

"Why do you wish to?"

"Because I would like to see that you get home safely, since it's apparent you cannot on your own." he raises an eyebrow as he pointedly looks at the mud stains. I hold back a retort.

"Yes you may." I turn and head back down the path, he keeps in step beside me easily, standing a few inches taller. The rain and muddy path seem like they don't affect him, his steps are light and calculated and I struggle to keep my balance as we go down the slope.

"You never told me why you're down here."

"Visiting."

"Why?"

"My father ordered me to." I turn my head towards him at the mention of his father, my King. It shouldn't have surprised me that this is his son, but it does. Although if his father looks anything like him, he would look far from cruel even if it was his nature to be cruel.

"Oh. Did your visit satisfy you?" I keep my voice even, not wanting to give him any emotion to hold against me. I see our small two story wooden home come into view and my nerves stand on end. A wooden fence runs along the outskirts of the house, going further down to the farmland, a lemon tree sits plump in the front yard. If anyone was home and saw me with a faerie they'd flail me alive. I was told two things from birth, never trust a faerie and never speak to one, for they twist your words to their bidding.

"They never do, until I saw a pretty young woman slip in the mud. That was a first." I try to hide my frown as I look back up at him, he was only a few inches taller than I but it still caused me to tilt my head back.

I snort. I was not pretty. "You're very funny, you know that?" I say, looking away from the smile that tugs the corners of his mouth. Maybe he is charming me to think I found him attractive.

I hate to think it might be working.

"I have not been told that, no. But that is kind of you."

We walk the last part of the trip in silence, the rain turns to a light hail as we reach my home. I unlatch the wire on the gate and rush up onto the wooden patio, he stands outside the gate and watches me.

"Are you mad? Get up here, it's hailing! You'll get hurt!" I call to him over the crashing sound of hail hitting the metal roof. He walks into the yard and up the stairs, shaking wet droplets off of him.

"I didn't know if I was going to intrude or not." I roll my eyes at him and pull open the screen door, then push the wooden door open. I hold it open as he walks inside, I lock the doors behind us and take my muddy boots off.

"Pass me your boots." I say, pointing to them. He frowns but pulls them off, handing them to me. I sit them on the steel rack that sits under the coats beside mine, half admiring the quality of their leather. "It's so you don't trek mud through the house, my mother would be furious."

I'm conscious of how small our home is now that he's inside, the small entry way opens to the living room on our left. The small three seater couch is tethered at the edges, the once bright yellow is now dull and sad. He stuffs his hands into his pocket as he looks around.

Across from the couch we have a large open fireplace, a window overlooks the patio with white lace curtains my aunty made us a few years back. The floorboards creek under my feet as he follows me into the kitchen, I turn the stove on and fill a pan with water.

"Would you like a cup of tea before you go?" I ask, placing the lid on it.

He takes a seat at the round wooden table, his body seeming to take up the entire space, "Yes please, that would be splendid."

"Right, well I need to change. I'll be down in a moment." I leave the kitchen and hurry up the stairs into the room I share with my aunty. I peel myself out of my sodden dress and catch my reflection, my white bra and undies are drenched and the sun hits the shadow of my hip bones and my ribs. My narrow face is all angles, I nibble my bottom lip as I take in my grey eyes. No one in my family has eyes like mine and I always feel alienated because of them. I push the self-loathing thoughts aside and pull my muddy hair up into a bun, frustrated I can't bathe right away and get rid of it. I slip into a pastel pink dress and head back down to the kitchen, I keep my steps light as I enter.

"You never gave me your name," I say, coming to stand in front of the boiling water. I reach into the cupboard above the sink and pull out two chipped white mugs. I grab two tea leaf bags and the cup of honey, sitting them on the bench.

"I can't give you my True name, but you may call me Nyx."

"Well Nyx, how many teaspoons of honey do you have with your tea?" I turn and raise an eyebrow at him. Why couldn't he tell me his True name? Was there some unknown rule I didn't know about?

"Two."

I turn and scoop out the honey and fill the cups with boiling water, turning the stove off as I manoeuvre around the kitchen. I drop two dollops of cream into the cups and hand him his. I hold mine in my hands and relish in the warmth it brings them. I take a seat across from him, keenly aware of the warmth radiating from his legs.

"I'm sure this wasn't what you were expecting." I say at last, taking a sip of the tea. He does the same, watching me with those unsettling eyes. I turn my head to the side and look out over to the kitchen window, already feeling heat climb up my neck.

“How did you get that scar?” my head snaps back to his, instinctively my hand goes up to the right side of my throat. I narrow my eyes at him.

“Why do you care?” he blinks slowly.

“I’m curious, is all.” he sips his tea innocently. I lower my hand and wrap it back around the cup, but itch to let my hair down once again.

“It’s…it’s not important.” I sigh, looking down as the cream swirls with the dark water.

“I would say otherwise,”

“Then it’s none of your business. What is this? Twenty one questions?” I groan, looking up to him.

“What’s that?”

“A game.” a faerie prince, know all tell all but yet he knew so little of our world? A thin line forms on his forehead as he frowns, it’s rather painful to watch really. I wave my hand.

“Don’t worry about it, we’re not playing it. You can stop thinking about it, it’s disturbing me.” I give him my best queasy look, and to my surprise his chest rumbles with laughter.

“I disturb you?” his eyes sparkle as he looks over me, and his smile widens at my obvious discomfort to his question.

“No.”

“Ah, how humans lie,” he muses, sipping his tea contently. I press my lips into a thin line, he knew the bare minimum about me and still pushed my buttons. Why on earth had I thought this would be a good idea? I barely liked communicating with my own people.

"Faeries deceive," I retort.

"We're more alike than we realise," he coos.

We are nothing alike.

"Tell me another lie, let's entertain the idea. Go on, why did you invite me inside?" he rests his elbow on the table and rests his chin on his palm; his fingers tap at his cheek as he watches me.

"Because…" why did I invite him inside? "I felt sorry for you."

"You lie easily, too easily I shall say."

"Yes well we're not all born into a good life are we?" I grumble, bringing my cup to my lips.

"You should know better than to judge others by what you see, Ravynne."

I desperately need to steer this conversation in a different direction. I stand from the table and decide to lean against the sink, feeling immensely better with the small amount of distance between us.

"Do you come to the village often?" I ask, sipping my tea. He raises the cup to his lips, I watch as his Adams apple bobs as he swallows. I bite my bottom lip.

"Only when my father sends me, apart from that I'm never home to begin with for him to force me to visit more. It holds no interest for me, this is his village after all."

"Do you not care for all the humans starving here?" I ask, my words come out sharper than I intend.

"It… is not in my nature to care."

"Yeah and it's not in my nature to invite a faerie prince into my damn home," I snap, fingers tightening around the mug. I felt foolish now, if my family knew who was in their house right now I would be shunned, as if I had no respect for them or myself. He is a part of the problem.

"I feel I have upset you?" he asks, placing his cup down. I clench my jaw, and look out the window over the kitchen sink. The hail has relented and the rain is only a soft drizzle now.

"I think it would be best if you left." I say softly, the chair scrapes and the floorboards groan. He hesitates.

"As you wish. Be well, Ravynne." I hold my breath as I hear him leave the room, pull on his boots and hear the doors close. I release it once I know he's gone, I put my cup and his in the sink with shaky hands. I brace myself on the edge of the sink and take a deep breath, he is nothing but trouble.

There is no way I would let myself be so foolish again.

"Ravynne, can you come in here and help your brother please? We can't get these damn buttons to clip." I groan internally as my mother's voice finds me in the kitchen. I sit the newspaper down on the table and enter the living room. She sits on the couch, trying and failing to do up the small black buttons.

He stands there, shoulders back and head high. His short black hair had been combed back from his round, soft face. His pale green eyes pierce mine as he watches me walk over. It is his first day of school and he wants to look as neat as he possibly can.

He turns to me as my mother's hands leave his white shirt, I tuck his collar down and do the buttons up with nimble fingers. I help him tuck his shirt into his black pants and adjust the black suspenders over his shoulders.

"Do you think he'll need his jumper today? I just can't predict this weather lately." I turn to where she sits and silently grab his black jumper from the arm of the chair; he pulls it on and zips it all the way up.

"You look adorable," I coo, standing over him. He grins as he runs from the room, back up into the bathroom no doubt to gloat at himself.

"If it wasn't for the different eye colours you and your brother would have been a spitting image of each other at his age, you just had longer hair."

"Yeah, and I wasn't boy." I cross my arms over my chest, picking at the sleeves of the blue emerald dress I'd chosen to wear today. I'd pinned my hair up in a loose bun, letting strands fall around my face. I'd barely slept a wink last night, my thoughts consumed by Nyx. I had a nagging sensation that he might have put a spell over me, or glamour, whatever those damn faeries do.

"Can you take him to school today? I'll be able to pick him up on my way home this afternoon. I think your father needs your help today." I look at her soft features that are so alike to my own, she'd cut her chocolate locks up to her ears and had the same green eyes I'd so dearly wished I'd had growing up. Wrinkles were beginning to age her face around her eyes and her forehead. When we lost Cece, she seemed to age an extra twenty years.

"Yeah, that's fine. Do you know what Da' needs help with?"

"Most likely with cleaning up the crops, you'll have to wear something more appropriate for that though." she raises a delicate brow as she appreciates the dress, Aunty Mana had made it for me as an early birthday gift.

"Yes Ma' you know I will." I roll my eyes and fight the smile, as much as I like helping with the farm I like wearing my dresses more. Call me selfish.

"Are you ready Kalin?" I call, peering up the stairs. Small footsteps pound on the wood as he comes running down with his school bag in tow.

"Have a good day my boy, I'll get you this afternoon and have your favourite lemon cookies ready." Ma coos as she comes over to us, peppering his forehead with soft kisses.

"Mum." he groans, but stands and takes her affection. I feel a twinge of jealously as I watch them, my favourite cookies as a child had been wild berries. After my sister passed they cut the tree down, I didn't know if it was to rid them of the memory of her or punish me for not watching her better.

"Come on, we'll be late." I slip into my boots and open the front door. He follows behind quickly, saying goodbye one last time over his shoulder. I take his hand in mine as we begin the small trek up into the village.

Today the weather is much nicer, the sun beats down and warms my skin while birds chirp and sing in the trees and shrubs. After rain the village always flourished with wildlife, which meant more taking for the hunters.

"Are you nervous?" I ask, glancing down at him.

"No." he says, swinging his small hand with mine. My chest aches, I'd never have this chance with Cecilia. I squeeze his hand tightly, until he moans in protest. He never liked holding hands, that was for *girls* apparently.

We enter town and I lead him to the small school, it sits on the outskirts of the forest. Apart from the church it is the second largest building, having two stories and a small oval out the back. It was for all ages, but I'd stopped going once I'd turned sixteen and had decided to help tend to matters at home instead.

Other parents are dropping their kids off as well, Kalin spots two boys that he'd been friends with for years now. He waves at them and catches their attention. Their mothers look over, quickly looking away once seeing me. They never discriminated against my brother, but to the eye of everyone else I am a child murderer. I let them gossip and hold my head high, any retaliation would just stain my name even more.

I kneel down and brush a few strands of hair back from his forehead.

"Have a good day, and don't get into trouble. Okay?" I say, straightening his shirt. He stops my hands and holds my face in his own hands, smooching it together.

"Yes sissy, now go." he runs off before I can get another word in, I watch as he and his friends head through the gate and into the large red building. I stand and turn to leave. Someone bumps into me;

nearly sending me sprawling.

"Watch it." I snap, regaining my balance.

"You're a murderer and a faerie whore now too, care to warm my bed?" a young man says, smirking as he stands with two of his friends. I don't recognise them, though they don't look much younger than I.

"Don't you have school to be attending?" I growl, wringing my hands in the skirts of my dress. My heart races in my chest, if they knew then surely it wouldn't be long until my parents found out.

"Don't you have a faerie to be fucking?" he spits back. I supress the anger as I turn and flee back towards the crowd of the village. I ignore the rest of their taunts, getting the odd look or two from the other folk.

I storm down the path, letting my feet pick up speed until I'm racing back towards the house. I'd been taunted and jabbed at for the last ten years. It wasn't something new but it still hurt.

Old wounds never really heal. And if they do, it's never the same.

I see the safety of home and relax, their words can't find me here. I enter the yard and walk around the back of the house, whistling a tune to myself as I go. Our goat, Millie, baas at me from the green shrubs, the bell on her neck clanks as she turns to watch me.

"Hi Millie." she turns back to the shrub and carries on. We'd gotten her two years after Kalin had been born, mainly for the Christmas roast that year but when the time came none of us had the heart. She'd become a part of the family. The back yard behind the house is fairly simple, Millie has a large goat pen towards the left of the yard that consists of wood fencing and wire mesh that she'd be locked into at night time. The rest is covered with green grass, which she kept from overgrowing. We didn't have a back door so whenever we wanted to come out here we had to go from the front. The wooden fence around the back yard stops and I open the silver gate, locking it behind me. I walk down the dirt path, avoiding the puddles as I head towards the farm.

I look over the fields on both sides of me, the three fields to my left are dirt, while the three on the other side are overflowing. My father had three more to sow until the season was finished for us. Wheat, corn and barley. Once winter came we'd focus on lettuce and tomatoes, all the things that would make a perfect salad.

At the end of the path we have a large, rickety wooden barn. We'd tried to keep Millie in here once, but after we'd come out the next day to find half the lettuce field eaten we hadn't been so foolish the second time.

I enter the barn, welcoming the cool breeze as I breathe in the scents of wheat and hay, tinted with the sharp tang of metal. I find father bent over a bucket, his weathered calloused hands are banging on the lid.

"Hey Da'." I greet him, coming to stand beside him. His short black hair is drenched with sweat, his blue overalls in no worse state. He wipes the back of his hand over his forehead as he turns to me, the lid still half on and off. His steel blue eyes pierce mine as he smiles, it lights up the shadows under his eyes.

"Hey pumpkin, did Mum send you?" he asks, his voice deep and rusty. He is a well-built man, harbouring more muscle than most of the men in town. He's slightly taller than I am, reminding me of Nyx.

Stupid faerie.

"She sure did." I grin back, I'd completely forgotten to change out of my dress. I didn't mind though, I'd just have to scrub it dearly tonight with the other mud stained dress I hadn't dared touch yet.

"Good, we need to make a trip to Orrinshire. I need to buy some more equipment and seeds." he turns back to the bucket and slams the lid on with a bang. I perk up at the sound of visiting the city. It was a two day journey if we took the carriage, it would just mean we'd need to borrow one of the Densley's horses.

"You know the Densleys charge far too much for the horse." I frown, crossing my arms over my chest.

"Yes, but I need these seeds otherwise we'll run out through winter. You know how rough the last winter was, and how rough this one will be. I can't rely on the few we have to get us through, not with your mother's business waning." he doesn't need to delve deeper, we both know the villagers are scared to go to mother's bakery for fear they'd be tainted by death.

"How long will we be gone for?"

"Six days, I was thinking we'd spend an extra day there. In case you were interested in browsing through a few of the shops there, it'll be your birthday after all." he stands up and rubs his hands on a dark rag before wedging it back in his pocket.

"Thanks Da'. When did you want to leave?" the journey to Orrinshire meant crossing the river that protected our village from the rest of the world, with the large amount of rainfall last night I'd have to hope the river hadn't swelled too much.

"After I clean up here, can you be a sweetheart and go to the Densley's? Two gold coins should cover the costs of the six days."

"No worries, I'll bring him down here." I turn and hurry back to the house, needing to retrieve the gold coins I'd forgotten about in the pocket of my dress in a haste to primp myself. Getting them is easy enough, facing the Densley's is another task in itself. They lived across the road from us, renting out their stables and their horses. They'd been the first to know when we'd lost Cecilia and although they'd been helpful, they hadn't associated with us too much to avoid the gossips of town. I go across the path and pat down my dress out of habit.

They didn't have a fence that protected their front yard, only from the back of the house and onwards. I rap on the door three times before taking a step back, idly making myself look busy with the gold stitching.

"Hullo Ravynne." I look up to see Mike Densley standing behind the screen door, I force a smile as he opens it reluctantly. He was as tall as I was, with broad shoulders and an unruly amount of golden hair on his head. His deep honey brown eyes watch me, waiting.

"Hi Mikey, Da' and I were needing to borrow a horse for six days," I say. When we were kids we were inseparable, both our parents always thought we'd wed once we reached adulthood but that too wilted away with everything good in my life. He was an attractive man, no doubt. But I couldn't handle the kindness he had given me.

"We have Gallion available, although he's three golds," he says, rubbing the back of his neck. I twist my mouth, far too expensive but I couldn't argue.

"That's fine, I need him today. Like now." I feel my cheeks redden as I look away, it's harder to shut myself off from him. He knew me, more than the rumours in town and I know he didn't see one bad bone in my body.

"Sure, I'll bring him out." he closes the door and disappears, I sigh and tread back down the steps and wait. A few moments later he enters from the side of the house, leading a chestnut gelding. He was already saddled with the right gear to attach him to our cart. Mikey stops in front of me and silently passes me the lead. I give him the three golds and pat the white strip of fur that ran down the horses face.

"Hey boy, you're a beautiful boy," I coo, scratching behind his ear. He knickers softly and nudges me with his large nose. I smile.

"You were always good with animals." Mikey says, trying to dissolve the tension that had silently built up between us.

"Probably why Millie has stuck around as long as she has." I look up to see his lips twitching towards a smile, although the rest of his body language is closed off.

"Be safe, Ravynne." he offers before heading back inside, whistling to himself. I lead the horse across the road and back through the yard, Millie comes over and investigates. Her brown and white fur is stained green from rolling in the grass.

I shoo her away as we go through the gate and towards the barn, where Da has managed to pull out the white chipped cart. He'd already packed a few bags into the back of it. He'd made a wooden roof for the back of the cart so when it rained or the weather was against us we'd be safe under it.

"Thanks pumpkin, go grab your things. I'll meet you out the front, I've already sent word to your mother." He takes the horse from me and begins to ready him. I leave and go back to the house, taking my three finest dresses and boots with me. I throw in some pyjamas as well. I fold them into my brown leather saddle bag, grabbing my toothbrush and mint paste from the bathroom as well as my petunia perfume.

I sit the wide brim straw hat on my head. A black ribbon is tied around the hat and flows down my back with my hair. I look myself over in the mirror once more before hurrying out of the house. It had been months since we'd left town and I valued spending these few days with Da.

I find him sitting astride the carriage, reins in hand with a straw hat on as well. I climb up beside him, throwing my bag into the back as I get settled.

"Are you ready?" he asks.

"As ever."

He whistles as he cracks the reins and the horse begins to walk the path leading away from the mountains and the village. Not many city folk knew our town even existed, which helped with the minimal amount of tourism and prying eyes.

I settle back in my seat, folding my hands over my lap and watching the mountain wall begin to grow lower, before finally staring over flat green terrain. In the distance, mountains cover the horizon, casting shadows over the valley. Ahead I hear the low roar of the river, I close my eyes and let the unsteady rhythm of the cart carry me.

3

Two days pass by in a blur, we'd camped out both nights under the stars and left before the sun had broken. We'd taken this road enough to know the best stops for fresh water and edible fruit, and the best places to camp. I'd been coming on these trips since I'd turned six, and soon Kalin would most likely take my place. I wasn't entirely sure what *I'd* be doing once that time came, but I knew both parents were hoping I'd find a young man soon.

That is one thing I'd happily disappoint them with.

Orrinshire comes into view, the loud noises from the city folk are the first thing that draws your attention; the next is the overwhelming amount of people. We'd reached the city late afternoon, even as the sun began to set people crowded the streets. We ride through the wide dirt street, people chatter all around us as they go about their afternoon. Lights and candles begin to flare with life as the sun sets, casting a golden ray over us. I pay no attention to them as I watch the shops go by, all similar due to the same wood being used to build them all. We reach the middle of town and head down a side street, Jarrod's Tavern comes into view sitting on the corner of the intersection. The black paint on the sign hanging above the door has been freshly painted, the doors are propped open with a large rock.

"Wait here while I go and rent a stable and two rooms." Da jumps down, passing me the reins. I hold them loosely as he goes inside, emerging moments later with three sets of keys. He passes me one as he climbs back up.

"Room three, take your things upstairs and I'll meet you in the tavern." I give him a quick kiss on the cheek before reaching over and grabbing my bag, I climb down with more grace than he had and walk inside.

Sweat and mead overwhelm my senses as I walk through the open doors, a bar sits in the middle with small circular wooden tables littering the open space with no real order. Towards the back right are the stairs that lead up to the rooms, I take two at a time as I go. I find my room easily enough and unlock the door.

A single cot sits in the middle of the room, a small brown dresser opposite it. I sit my saddlebag down before walking into the small joint bathroom. I splash water on my face before undoing my now wavy hair, letting it flow around my shoulders.

I grab the seven gold coins and put them in my pocket, I'd keep one for myself and give the rest to Da once I found him again. I head down stairs, locking the room behind me and stuffing the key in my bra.

I find an empty table towards the front of the tavern, save for a few half empty pitchers. I take a seat and move them to the side, a small plump woman wonders over; wiping her hands on the white apron.

"How may I be helpin' ya' tonight lassy?" she asks, collecting the empty pitchers. Beads of sweat drip down the sides of her forehead.

"Two glasses of mead, please and two bowls of the special soup." I give her my warmest smile as she bolsters away, here I was just a country girl exploring the city. None of these people knew of the things that haunt me at home, none of these people knew a thing about me.

Da' enters, running a hand through his hair as he shrugs the baggage higher up his arm. The movement draws a few looks from the women, who stare with no shame. He heads upstairs oblivious, appearing moments later and coming to the table. I pass him the six coins once he sits down.

"Did you order dinner?" the weariness is evident in his words. He'd rest well tonight, whereas I'd be a pile of nerves and excitement.

"Yes and two glasses of mead."

"Don't drink too much of that stuff, it'll go straight to your pretty head," he says, leaning back in the chair. I roll my eyes and look back around the tavern, I know the city had a few others which were mainly for drinking and dancing. The others times I'd visited I'd been too full of fear to venture to them on my own, and I couldn't drag father along with me. Tonight felt…different. Somewhere in the tavern a young man begins to sing, the band begins to follow his lead. I tap my foot along.

"You know I never do." I raise my voice over the music.

"I know, do you have any plans tomorrow while I go get the few things I need?" I think it over, on the trip here I'd wondered what I'd do. Usually I follow him to the farm supplies but tomorrow I was thinking of going to the library, to see what sort of lore I could find on faeries.

Nyx had definitely put some sort of enchantment over me.

"I was just going to take a look around town, see if there're any new shops or something I might find interest in," I say casually, drumming my fingers along the table. He doesn't argue, only yawns.

The waitress brings back two cups of mead and steaming stew, I thank her before digging in. Deer and tomato basil soup, delicious. Da has the same thinking, we both power through the soup before turning towards the drinks.

I drink mine quickly, while Da takes his time. Once finished I stand from the table. His eyes follow me.

"Where are you off to?" he asks, sipping.

"I want to have a look at the night life, I'll be back shortly," I say, feeling over eager to venture into the night. I hadn't changed from my dress but I assured myself it wouldn't matter.

"Be safe pumpkin."

"Always." I kiss the top of his head before hurrying out of the tavern, gulping in the fresh air of the night. I walk down the dark street before entering the main one. People walk to and fro, lost in their own worlds. I walk along, keeping to the well-lit areas from the lanterns. I'm not looking for anything in particular, but a small part of me is looking for adventure.

To my right, down another side street I spot another tavern. Music blasts from the open doors and I find myself drawn towards it, I let my feet take the lead as I walk up the few steps before heading into a thick rowdy crowd.

I gently push through the people, finding the bar. In the back left corner a man is on stage, playing some type of guitar. Each time he plucks at the strings my body moves, as if drawn to the sound. I can't get a good look at him from back here.

"Two cups of ale please."

The bartender fills them up and slides them to me, I pass him a gold coin and get eight silvers in return. Pricey. I stuff the coins back in my pocket and pick up the two frothing glasses, excusing myself as I find an empty seat near the front. Three girls sit at a table, one seat is left.

"Is it okay if I sit here?" I ask, drawing the attention from a girl with a long brown plait. She pats the seat and smiles warmly up at me, her eyes glassy from one too many glasses.

"Of course, I'm Sal. Lillia, Olive, a friend." she shouts over the music, I settle in between her and a girl with a blonde bob. She smiles at me, "Lillia, nice to meet you."

"I'm Olive," the dark skinned girl says, her corn rows gleam with small golden flowers that have been weaved into the hair and I'm momentarily awestruck by her golden eyes.

"I'm Ravynne, thanks for letting me sit here." From here I can see the musician better. His dark blue cloak and hood conceal most of his features, save for pale fingers that move smoothly along the guitar.

"You're not from here, are you?" Sal says, sipping from her cup. I take a deep gulp before answering.

"No, two days journey away actually. We're just in town to get some supplies for the farm."

"Oh that's cool as, my step father works on a farm too," Lillia says, drumming a ring laden hand on the top of the table towards the music. My foot taps involuntarily, as if in a trance.

"What sort?" I ask, genuinely intrigued. We really only had crop farms in my village, but outside of our small world the possibilities would be endless.

"Dairy, I don't have much to do with it though."

"You don't have much to do with anything if it doesn't involve Mason," Olive smirks, a glint in her eyes.

"So not true!" Lillia says, but we all end up with the giggles even though I don't have a clue who Mason is or the importance of them to her.

The musician comes to a stop and I frown, disappointed.

"Don't stress, he's just getting a glass of mead. He comes here every other week to play, he's the best and very handsome as well." Sal mutters to me, raising a plucked brow. I nod a few times before finishing the first cup of ale, I'm beginning to feel the tipsiness and know after my second cup I'd be ready for bed. If I had more than that I wasn't sure where I'd be waking up tomorrow.

"Look, he's starting again." She looks back towards the small stage and I do as well. A microphone sits near his face this time, he adjusts it and clears his throat.

"Alright ladies and gentleman, one last song for the night before I hand it over. I call this 'the call of a fair maiden.'" His voice is familiar, but I can't seem to place it. Or piece together where I may have heard it from.

"Come on, let's dance!" Olive declares, gulping down the last of her drink. We all do the same, and a wave of light-headedness wavers me momentarily. Lillia weaves her small hand into mine and Olive's, I take Sal's hand as we push through the crowd, making it to the open dance floor in front of the stage. He'd begun to pick at the strings, starting slow.

We link arms and I follow their lead, soon enough we're laughing as we dance along spinning each other like lovers. I try to make out the words from his soft voice, barely audible over the guitar.

"Her hair as dark as night, can put a raven heart to fright."

What a coincidence, I muse to myself.

"Her skin as pale as the fresh flakes of snow."

I spin towards him, pausing to glimpse under the hood of his cloak but only his lips show. Moist from licking them between lines.

"Eyes as grey as thunder clouds, erupting at my words."

I frown before being spun back into the crowd, it was as if this song was almost about me…surely I can't be that naive. The alcohol must have gotten to my head and muddled up the words.

"The call of a fair maiden, the sorrow sound is heard."

"Losing a sibling, losing a friend, losing herself in the end."

I can't stop myself from spinning but my heart is beginning to thunder in my chest…they *know.* This had to be about me, there was no other possibility. No other person who could be as unfortunate as I.

"The call of a fair maiden, her loneliness has come to an end."

His words rattle me as I leap with the crowd towards the front, paying no mind to the girls or others. What did they mean by the last line?

No, I must be foolish. Or drunk, or very well both.

The cloak falls back from his face as he shakes his head backwards, and I freeze in the crowd as they begin to cheer and sing even louder. Nyx sits there, his violet eyes as bright as ever as he pays attention to the guitar.

Sweat beads run down his temple and his eyebrows are furrowed slightly with concentration. My eyes trail up through his dark mass of hair to find no sight of his pointed ears.

Had I imagined him being a faerie?

No, those boys had been cruel mentioning me being a faerie *whore.* I hadn't imagined it, he'd used some sort of glamour to conceal them.

His eyes drift up, although his fingers still pick out a complicated sad tune on the guitar that pulls at the heart strings in my chest.

His eyes widen slightly as he spots me, his only sign of recognition. Before I can curse him out or give him a vulgar gesture I'm dragged back into the dance. He keeps his eyes on me as I'm spun around and heaved through the air by a pair of rough male hands.

I force myself to at least try and give him the cold shoulder, to avoid glancing back up at him. I don't want to give him the satisfaction that I recognised him. I dance my way through the crowd, spotting the three girls I'd befriended earlier.

"Let's get a drink! My shout!" Olive says, swaying slightly as she grabs my hand. Sweat drips down the back of my neck as we follow her towards the bar. The song comes to an end and I focus on my stepping instead of his words, a few moments later another song begins. This one doesn't have the same pull as Nyx's song, but nevertheless I found myself bopping my head along.

We didn't have taverns like this in Elderview, considering a small portion of the towns people were my age. A crowd like this would overwhelm the elders that resided there, and no doubt cause more trouble than it's worth.

Olive hands me a glass of mead and does so with the other girls, I know I shouldn't be having more but it is so much fun. I also want to drown out the sour feeling the song had left me with, mead seems like a reasonable solution right now.

"Cheers!" Sal cries, raising her glass in the air. We all clink glasses before throwing back the drinks. It burns my throat as I gulp it all down, before slamming the empty cup onto the bar.

"Let's dance!" I shout, they follow me back through the crowd and onto the dance floor. There's no sign of Nyx, and I relax momentarily and give way to the intoxication that is beginning to consume me.

I don't know how long we dance, or how many times I let myself fall into the arms of strange men with mead strong on their breaths. My dress clings to me from the sweat, and my thoughts are a jumbled mess inside of my brain.

I hadn't seen Nyx again.

I tell myself I *don't want to.*

I find myself in the arms of a strong man, I look over my shoulder to try and grasp a better view of his face but the tavern lights momentarily blind me. I'm stumbling towards the entrance of the tavern, with his arm wrapped around my shoulder tightly.

Sweat and alcohol make me cringe as he belches while we stumble down the stairs. I try and pry myself from his arm, but find my arms too weak to move the weight. He's leading me down the darkened street, where no one can see what he truly desires to do to me.

"St-stop." I mumble, trying to gather my wits about me. My hands flail weakly on his arm, trying once more to move it.

"It's okay, I'll be gentle," he slurs. Finally coming to a stop, he crushes my body against his large one and the building of the tavern. A nail digs sharply into my spine and I hiss, arching into him to try and stop the nail.

"I knew you wanted this." He trails sloppy kisses down my throat, his beard scratches at the soft skin. I wedge my hands onto his chest and try to heave him off of me.

"Stop, please." My heart has begun to race and the panic is beginning to rise. His hands grab roughly at the skirts of my dress, dragging them up to expose my thighs.

"Stop!" I cry out, although my voice slurs slightly and my attempt is weak. His hand skims the lace of my panties and I whimper, although he mistakes it for pleasure. His fingers fumble with the material and I feel hot tears begin to course down my cheeks, dripping onto my chest.

"I believe the woman told you to stop." The voice is deep and full of a cold rage I'd never heard before, not even Da had ever been this angry. The man on me pauses and his head swivels to the man. My breathing is coming in gasps.

"This is none of your business," he says, his hand grips my thigh roughly. I push my hands against his chest and lean back into the nail, biting my lip when it breaks the soft skin and tears at my dress.

What a disaster this night has turned into.

"It is when she's telling you to stop. Now remove your filthy hands from her." The stranger steps out of the shadows but I close my eyes, not wanting to face them. I can't pin point their voice, and all my senses are focused on the trickle of blood that is beginning to run down my back.

"Or what?" The man on me challenges, he releases my thigh and I open my eyes to see him take a step towards my new found saviour.

"You don't want to know." The stranger growls, unearthly and full of power. It vibrates to my very core, and I force myself to look at the man. Only his glowing, violet eyes are visible.

Sensing the fight and finding me not worthy of it, the drunken man grumbles under his breath and stumbles back towards the pub. I almost fall to my knees as I pry myself from the nail, but the man catches me in his strong, warm arms.

"You're hurt," he says, frowning down at me. He holds me gently in his arms, careful not to apply pressure to the pierced skin. I reach up with a hand and run it down his soft cheek, before reaching further and feeling his pointed ears.

"You're a faerie." I giggle, forgetting how much danger I'd been in only moments ago. But in his arms, I have never felt safer from anything that could harm me in this world.

"You're drunk." A smile twitches at his lips, although the slight frown still shows even in the darkness. I huff out a breath and let my hand fall back down to his chest.

"Well I suppose you're right, considering you can't lie." I wince as he helps me find my footing. I reach around and touch my back gingerly, it had got me just above my left buttock. My hand comes back with blood on the tips of my fingers.

"Come, I'll clean your wound," he says, helping me put my arm over his shoulders so he can carry a majority of my weight. I don't stop him as I stumble forward, walking beside him. He doesn't complain when I lean on him, a part of me wishes he'd pick me up and just carry me.

We leave the street, no one pays mind to us as he walks towards the entrance of the city. I close my eyes and sigh, wanting to savour the last remains of happiness the intoxication had given me, next time I would not be so foolish.

He helps me up a few stairs before opening a door, only then do I open my eyes. We're in a small tavern, although this one is deserted of any drunks. Finery graces me as I take in the satin curtains, rich deep red carpet and the dark oak desk. To the right are stairs, which he helps me with again. We enter a small hallway and he uses his magic to open a door to my right with a symbol of a crescent moon engraved in the middle of the door.

Golden lights flicker on as we walk into his room, the door shuts and locks on its own behind me. A queen sized cot sits in the middle of the room, a royal blue wyvern seal is stitched into the golden doona. The Faerie King's seal, his father's seal.

"Here, take a seat." He lowers me to the bed, I hunch over and rest my elbows on my knees, hanging my head down. My black hair flows around me like a curtain, concealing most of the light. I hear running water and a slosh of a cloth in the water.

"I have to take a look at the wound." I force myself to look up, sweeping my hair out of my eyes. He stands there, rather awkwardly as he studies me. A brown bowl and a blue cloth are clasped in his hands. Boldness overtakes me, a boldness I will no doubt regret in the morning.

I stand and pull the dress over my head, bending over to pull the folds of fabric over my head until the dress is a blue pile of material on the floor. I stand straight and look at him, a blush stains his cheeks. His eyes stay on mine. My undergarments are of white lace, rather simple and revealing for such an occasion.

I turn slowly and crawl onto the bed, collapsing belly down. I rest my hands under the pillow and shut my eyes. I hear him sigh as he comes closer, I open my eyes and tilt my head towards him; he leans over the bed and looks at the wound. I don't really think it was this bad, but I'm not objecting.

Warmth dances and lingers against my skin as his hand gently glides my hair off of my back and out of the way.

"This may sting."

True to his word, my back stings as he presses the cloth to the wound, gently wiping the blood from around it. I hiss as I watch, half fascinated in my pissed state by the focus on his face.

His tongue sticks out of his mouth slightly with concentration, moving about his lips as he goes. Is he currently using his magic to heal it? Would he walk me back to my tavern, or would I be forced to walk alone?

"What is a faerie doing in a human city, entertaining the human folk in disguise?" I mutter, eyes half hooded from the drowsiness that is starting to settle in.

If I could just close my eyes for a moment…

"I told you when we first met I don't stay home, if ever," he says, his eyes slip to mine before focusing on my back with sheer determination.

"I remember, I just didn't think this is what you'd be doing with your spare time princeling. I thought it wasn't in your nature to care." He's silent for a moment.

"Just because it's not in my nature to care, it doesn't mean I can't care," he snaps back, a little more aggressively than I'd have thought.

"Finally some bite about you." I grin lopsided, my eyes struggling to stay open as I look at him.

"You are truly tiresome. How much have you had to drink tonight?"

"Maybe four?" I try to recall if I'd had more, but come up empty handed.

"You don't carry your mead well." he muses, a smile etches into his lips.

"I don't do a lot of things well, faerie." I murmur, letting my eyes close. A warm darkness embraces me, wanting to carry me away. I open my eyes before I let it take me.

"Why did you write that song about me?" I ask, finding the courage and pushing my ego and naivetés aside. He stills, hand pausing mid-air.

"You weren't meant to be in the crowd tonight, or hear it."

"Doesn't answer my question," I grumble, sighing as I sink lower into the mattress. The wound has gone numb and not feeling anything is making me feel even heavier.

"I didn't say I was going to. Your wound is healed, so you may put your dress back on." The warmth of his lingering presence evaporates and leaves me shivering while he retreats into what I assume is the bathroom.

"Can't I just sleep here? It's so comfy," I complain, burying my head into his pillow.

"No, you may not. I'd rather not be flayed alive by your father once he awakens to find you not in your rooms, instead in mine." I roll onto my back with a groan and prop myself on my elbows. He leans against the bathroom door frame, arms crossed over his muscular chest. He'd lost the cloak, only wearing a thin white button shirt that is rolled up at the sleeves, with dark green pants.

He is an image of pure beauty, a new toxication all in itself.

“Are you going to make me walk back alone?” I question, dragging my eyes away from him and down to the blue dress. I feel the key digging into my breast, relieved to know I hadn’t lost it.

“Of course not.” He raises an eyebrow as I pull myself up, I sway slightly but grab the bed sheet to steady myself. I cast my shyness of my thin body aside, he’d never have to know he’d been the only man to ever see me wearing so little.

I grab the wrinkled dress, slipping it over my head with effort, the coins clink together in my pocket as I pat down the skirts. I pull my hair back into a low bun, using the elastic band around my wrist to keep it in place.

“Alright, let’s gooo.” I drag the word out as I stumble towards the door to leave. He swoops in and links my arm with his; steadying me.

“Would you like to sober up a bit first?” he asks, looking down at me. I tip my head back and lick my lips, watching as his eyes trail my tongue.

“I mean, yes, it would be nice but I don’t think there’s a remedy for this.” I groan, knowing the hangover tomorrow would be enough punishment for dabbling with such enticement. Da could not know of the man groping me, or the faerie prince who swopped to my rescue.

“May I kiss you?”

“Kiss me?” My mind goes blank.

“Hold still.” His hand tilts my head to his and holds it in place, I don't know who he surprises more, me or himself when he grazes his lips across my own.

A tingling sensation passes from his lips and down my throat as he breathes into my mouth, flooding my veins with warmth and clarity. The fog over my brain clears significantly, but enough to keep the guard I'd built down. His lips linger for a moment longer than necessary, before he pulls away. His hand drops from my face and I feel my own reach up and touch my lips.

Did he just *kiss* me?

"Don't think anything of it, mortal," he says, reminding me it is not what I was thinking it to be. I hold my head high and turn away, pulling him alongside me and to the door so he can't see my reddening cheeks. We walk in silence to my tavern, the effects of the mead wearing off with each step, leaving sober regret in its path.

I reluctantly savour the warmth from his arm against the chilly night, regretting not having a hot bath before I'd gone out tonight. It would have to wait until morning, I'm sure I could sleep a night with sweaty skin and his touch still lingering on me.

My street comes into view, and he pauses at the entrance of it. I look down to see my tavern in darkness, the doors open for their late night drunk patrons to stumble on through. I'm relieved to know everyone has gone to bed. I drop his arm before he can drop mine, wanting a small victory to come out of tonight, as if his lips against mine weren't enough.

"Enjoy your human entertainment, *faerie*," I mumble, beginning to walk down the poorly lit street.

"Where's my thank you?" he calls softly after me, a challenge in his words. I pause and look over my shoulder, clenching my hands into the skirts of my dress.

"I wouldn't thank you unless my life depended on it," I call back. Holding my head up I turn and walk the rest of the way in silence and defiance. Only once I reach the stairs of the tavern, do I allow myself to look back. He stands there, watching.

I slip into the dark room, finding the stairs with small difficulty. After I lock myself into the confines of my safe room, pulling the dress off once more and sliding into the covers, I convince myself he was only watching to annoy me. Not to protect me from other dangers that could whisk me away into the night.

"How's your head feelin' pumpkin?" Da' asks, amusement in his voice. I groan as I look up from the table, I'd been resting my head on my crossed arms for the past half hour now. I'd woken to my brain thumping against my skull, as if it had grown and no longer fit. Nyx had made me sober up, but it did nothing to help the hangover.

"Ugh," I groan out, but keep my head up. A waiter places a glass of water down for us both, along with two plates of bacon and scrambled eggs.

"I did warn you." The knife dragging across the plate makes my ears ring. I dig into the oily, crispy bacon, savouring every piece in the hope it'll cure me.

"Happy birthday, Rav," he says again, much softer this time. I flinch at the nickname, but force myself to look up at him. After Cecilia died, we'd all changed; even with Kalin coming along and being the beacon in a stormy night.

Rav was her nickname for me, because she struggled to pronounce my full name. Cc was mine for her, because I wanted to have something more in common with her.

"Thanks Da'," I say, moving the eggs around the plate uncomfortably. No one wanted to talk about her death, and a few days after it happened it was almost like she wasn't even here to begin with. Even now, the topic of her is hard.

"Would you like to come to the markets with me?" He asks, clearing his throat.

"Yes actually, that would be nice. But I'll need my hat."

He waves me away with a hand, "Go get it then, if you're finished eating."

I look down at the plate, I'd eaten the bacon but hadn't touched the eggs. I move it closer to the centre and head upstairs to retrieve my hat, I put it on and look in the small bathroom mirror.

I'd chosen to wear a soft, pink dress today. It had white lace stitching of flowers along the hem, and a white ribbon that separated the bodice to the skirts that trailed down the front. It was sleeveless, with only thin straps that could be adjusted. I pull the hat down, shading my face. I'd welcomed a warm bath this morning, scrubbing away any traces where Nyx had touched my skin.

I find Da waiting outside the tavern, I link arms with him as we head down the street and take a left, heading deeper into the city. Each time we've come here, it has been different. Some days they have their markets on, or festivals, or days dedicated to their gods.

There are multiple gods to worship and praise. Sheeba, the goddess of the sun and life. Tonika, goddess of the moon and reincarnation. Lastly there's Aryan, the god of darkness. Sheeba rules over the summer months, Tonika rules over the winter months. Aryan is a more devilish god to worship, and his name is hardly spoken in my village or in Orrinshire. He is the god of death and darkness and it is said those who worship him invite the devil in through their front door.

The gods have always fascinated me.

I refocus back on the street, smiling as a little girl runs past me with her sister in tow.

Today we've been lucky enough to miss all of their festivities or days for the gods, and few people mill about the dirt streets. Da' whistles a tune to himself while I observe everything around us, the shop door in each place has been propped open, the strong aroma of coffee whisks its way over to us.

"Do you want a coffee?" I ask, halting us to a stop. He squints at the small coffee vendor, they'd turned a cart into the small takeaway coffee shop, decorating the outside with green leaf vines and bright yellow marigolds.

"Alright, I'll get a long black. I'll continue heading up." He drops my arm and continues on, nodding greetings to the others with his hands stuffed into his pockets. I walk up to the counter and push my hat back, the young girl behind the counter smiles.

"May I have a long black, regular and a tea with two sugars please." I hand over two silvers.

"Course ma'am, won't be too long." She begins making the coffees and I take a seat on the wooden chair beside the cart, fanning my face with my hand.

Orrinshire is sweltering with heat this time of year, with no mountains to shade the sun rays from the city. Its weather isn't temperamental and moved through each season smoothly. When I was young I use to dream of moving here once I was older, starting a new life for myself. Now that just seems impossible, even though a fresh start would be the best thing for me and my family. They wouldn't move though, not when the farm had been passed down from generation to generation.

"Here you are ma'am, have a gooden." She sits two brown cups on the edge of the counter. I sip mine as I continue on, holding Da's in my hand even though it is beginning to turn my palm pink.

The farmer's square sits snug on the outskirts of the main part of the city, right along a large river that supplies the city with most of its clean water. I finally reach the stretch of open grass with the river flowing soundly to my right, ahead I spot Da talking to a man dressed in brown overalls, a leather hat on his head.

Small shacks have been built along the creek, with a thin path running between them for easier navigation. Kids run along, with the occasional dog following. I walk down the thin path, looking at all the leather saddle gear, different seeds and grains, farming tools I'd never seen before. I breathe in all the various smells, leather, grain and the familiar stench of sweat from a long day of work.

"…and then I was like, woah there boy, I only wanted ten seeds!" The man finishes, cackling as he slaps his knee. His face is covered in a thin layer of dirt, while his tanned arms are contrasted darkly against his stained brown shirt with the sleeves rolled up past his elbows. Da' chuckles along, I silently pass him his coffee and smile politely at the man, even though his cackle makes my brain ring even more.

"This your daughter now?" He asks, his light brown eyes scan over me, he gives me a gap tooth smile. I feel Da's arm wrap around my shoulder and pull me to him with a soft squeeze.

"She sure is, beautiful, isn't she?" There's a hint of pride in his voice and it causes my cheeks to flush. The man continues to pack various tools into a hessian bag.

"Yes, she is, last time I saw her she was only yee' big." He gestures with his hand, half way up his large gut. "How old are you now?" he asks, flickering his gaze up to me.

"Twenty sir."

"No need to call me sir darlin'," he chuckles, shaking his head. I stay quiet, unsure of what else to say. I didn't remember him, but Da seemed to be friendly with him. Da's arm drops from my shoulder and I take a step away, looking back around the square.

"I'm going to go and look around, just find me," I say, looking back to Da.

"Alright, be safe pumpkin," he says, smiling my way.

"Always."

I leave the square, lingering on the edge of the shacks. I walk down the small slope and look over the edge and into the water, orange and white fish as large as my palm swim mindlessly around. All rivers and creeks ran clear wherever you went in our continent. If the water was dirty it was apparently an indication of corruption.

"Hey there, you dropped this."

I turn around to the sound of a soft male voice, standing before me is a man a few years older than I. His straight light brown hair just reaches his shoulders, with his hazel eyes piercing mine. I look down at his hand, outstretched towards me.

My black, dirt stained ribbon is held between his fingers.

"Oh, thank you. I hadn't realised I'd dropped it." My cheeks heat as I take the ribbon from him, deciding to tie it around my wrist instead of my hat. He rubs the back of his neck and gives me a half smile.

"That's alright, I thought I'd be a gentleman and return it."

"Well, a gentleman you have been." I bow slightly his way, jokingly. I can't help the smile that spreads across my face, he is by far good looking, with a contagious smile.

He is wearing what most of the farmers I'd seen around here wear, brown overalls with white shirts rolled up at the sleeves, his brown pants are rolled up at the ankles as well.

"Are you from around these parts?" he asks.

"No, I'm from..." Do I tell him, and risk him finding out what everyone in that place had to say about me? "It's a two day journey, some little town no one's ever heard of. Do you live here?" I brush it off, waving my hand awkwardly in the air.

"Born and raised here, I can't say I've ever seen you before. What's the reason for your visit?"

"I'm with my father getting some supplies for our farm, we don't have a famer's square where I'm from." I walk up the slope, with him beside me. We begin to stroll back towards the city, slowly.

"You must have to make the trip often then?" He questions, looking down at me. I twist my lips a few times, is he asking all of these questions because he's curious? Or is there a deeper purpose?

"A few times every six months, we usually stock up."

"Well if you'd like to send word before you come next time I can get the cottage behind my parent's house ready. Won't cost you a dime." I giggle at his offer.

"I don't even know your name!" I exclaim, tapping his arm lightly. Impressed with the muscle I feel. He smirks down at me, "Matt."

"Well Matt I'm—"

"Ravynne, there you are." A cool, collected male voice says from behind us. Matt's eyebrows shoot up as we come to a stop and turn around. Nyx strolls towards us dressed in finery. A black cloak billows out behind him, clipped at his throat with a golden wyvern pin, while his dark green tunic is tucked nicely into his pants. His eyes pierce mine before dragging to Matt. The air around him ripples with authority, so *intense* it takes me a few moments to collect my scattering thoughts.

I hold in my groan as I plaster a smile on my face, remembering last night's escapade. Nyx stops in front of us, slightly looking down at Matt. I have the urge to scream and rip at my hair, what is he doing here? Out of all the times he could bug me, he chooses now.

"Hi Nyx." I grit out, clenching my fists in my skirts.

"Uh hello your highness." Matt bows slightly with respect and I snort. They both look at me, Nyx smirks.

"I was just looking for you, Ravynne."

"Why?" I ask, crossing my arms over my chest. I feel hostile, and had no idea how to be nice to him. He had saved me last night and helped me. I was no fool to forget what I had done last night, and I remember quiet clearly stripping down to my undergarments in front of him. His hands slide into his pockets, his beauty had been dulled slightly and there was no trace of his pointed ears.

"That isn't really a way to talk to royalty." Matt whispers, leaning down slightly. I give him a quick, pointed glance before looking back to Nyx.

"My apologies, your *highness*, what ever may I help you with on this splendid morning?" I bow low, almost snapping myself in half and grazing the ground. Each word said dripped with sarcasm, and then I realise my mistake.

I'd offered to help him.

As if knowing this, he straightens and smiles again, this time it's more wicked and slightly cruel.

"I'd like you to take a walk with me."

"That's it? A walk?" I ask, almost not believing it.

"It's alright. I'll catch up with you later?" Matt asks, half turning my way. I look up at him and struggle with a decision, why did I care if Nyx is there? I am a grown woman.

"That would be lovely actually, if you're free tomorrow morning would you like to grab breakfast before I leave?"

"Yes, of course. I'll pick you up." He looks visibly relieved, and I smile up at him.

"I'm staying at Jarrod's Tavern, I'll be ready around ten." He looks hesitantly back to Nyx, who looks rather annoyed, before walking back up to the farmer's square. He looks over his shoulder once, I offer a small wave. Once he's out of hearing range I drop the smile.

"What do you want?" I hiss, coming closer. I don't know if I wanted to strangle him or slap him or kiss him.

"Did I interrupt something?"

"Yes, you did." I snap, I forcefully link my arm with his and begin tugging him back down the way I'd been previously walking. Cursing myself to find I really like the muscle I feel, and the warmth that seeps into me.

"Woah there, why are you so grumpy?" he asks playfully, I look up to see a softer smile on his face and feel my annoyance waver.

"I don't know, maybe it's the fact I nearly got naked in front of you last night, or the fact you kissed me, or the fact you wrote a damn depressing song about me, or to top it off you saved me from that filthy man so now I feel in debt to you. It's my birthday and I just wanted a nice day, stress free and faerie free." I grumble, ticking each one off on my fingers to emphasise my point.

"It wasn't a proper kiss," he points out, slowing us down to almost a stop. He turns me towards him, looking me over.

"Yes, thanks again for pointing that out." I look away, feeling slightly embarrassed. I'd kissed other men before, but it stings to think I was unworthy of *him* kissing me. Which only works to fuel my annoyance with him even more.

"Happy birthday Ravynne," he says softly, I look back up and my lips part slightly as he closes the distance between us. My heart thunders in my chest, and I feel the world around me begin to fade into the background. All I can see are his violet eyes.

"Stop working your faerie magic on me," I whisper, out of breath as though I'd been running. A small line forms on his forehead, a slight frown.

“I’m not.”

“I wouldn’t stay here, this close, if you weren’t,” I say again, feeling my words come back to me. Confusion flickers in his eyes, but he steps away. And…I still feel the same. Odd.

“Rav, there you are! I’ve been looking all over for you!” Da calls out, we both turn to see him walking down towards us. Arms full with bags of supplies. I drop Nyx’s arm and take a healthy step back, putting a reasonable amount of distance between us.

“Let me help,” Nyx offers once Da reaches us. Da gives him a suspicious look before unloading three bags onto him. Looking to me in question, I shrug.

“Da, this is Nyx. Nyx, this is my father, Darren,” I introduce them, Nyx nods his head slightly.

“It’s nice to make your acquaintance.”

“You too. Do you know Ravynne?” Da asks, looking at me before puffing his chest out to look at Nyx. I roll my eyes, could this day possibly get any worse?

“No.” I say.

“Yes.” Nyx says at the same time, we share a glance and I throw my hands in the air, “Yes, sorry, we’re…well actually I just met him, and he was just accompanying me on a walk.” I hurry the words out, if Da knows I’m lying he doesn’t point it out, he huffs and begins walking back to our tavern.

I walk a few paces behind with Nyx, taking a bag of seeds from him.

"You know I can carry them all, right?"

"Yes, but I like to at least feel like I'm helping," I answer, annoyed once more. For once, I'm going to be glad to leave and head home. Nyx never really visits the village, so I'll be safe there.

"You're very snappy today," he says, low enough so Da can't hear. I shoot him a glare full of daggers.

"Yes, well." I don't really *know* why I'm so snappy, maybe the kiss last night had meant more to drunk me than it did sober me…and possibly hurt both my feelings.

Stupid faerie.

"What are you doing after this?" he asks.

"Going out for lunch," I say, keeping my eyes trained on Da's back. We'd nearly reached our tavern, walking faster than usual. Da was never one for being a fast walker, neither was I.

"Would you like to do something afterwards?" he asks again, looking down at me. I hold in my sigh and reluctantly look up at him, why is he being so kind? He had no trouble with sending me home last night.

Yes, I'm definitely annoyed about last night.

"Uh…" I struggle to find an excuse, because a small part of me secretly wants to see him, maybe get to know him a bit better and ask about the King and why he never leaves his castle.

"It's okay, I understand. If you become free, or change your mind, you know where to find me. Tomorrow I leave though, so you might not see me again for a while." He looks back ahead as we turn down my street, I study his face before turning to see the tavern.

"Where are you going?" I ask, getting the better of myself.

"Oakwood, you wouldn't know where it is."

"Why not?" I ask, wanting to know.

"Because it's in Faerie." He smirks down at me, light dancing in his eyes. I groan and walk ahead, swaying my hips slightly as I go. I am not in the mood for games. Da waits outside, the few bags sit on the ground beside him.

"Want help carrying them to the cart?" I ask, sitting the bag down at my feet.

"No, it's fine. Go freshen up, after this we'll grab a bite to eat." Da nods thanks to Nyx as he places the bags down, he rubs his hands on the back of his pants.

"Well, I'll see you later Ravynne. Don't forget my offer. Darren, it was nice meeting you. Have a well afternoon." He nods to my father, his eyes lingering on me a moment longer before he turns and strides down the street, his long legs carrying him with inhuman speed. I watch him go, unable to take my eyes from him.

"There's something about that boy I don't like." Da mumbles, picking up the bags. I cross my arms of my chest, fiddling with a strand of my hair.

"I agree."

☾

We sit in a booth outside, the chilly breeze ruffles my hair as I take a sip of my tea. We'd chosen a well-known, family friendly café. Da had insisted on shouting me, so I'd chosen a blueberry muffin and a ham and cheese croissant. Above us is a star shaped canvas, with small white flowers hanging delicately underneath it.

"Did you get everything you need today?" I ask, sitting the cup back down. The sun just reaches the right side of my body, warming my right leg and arm. To my right, a small boy squeals playfully as he runs around the wooden table his parents sit at, his older sister chases him.

"Yeah I did, hopefully it should last us until next season," he says, taking a sip of his mead. The thought of drinking almost makes me gag, I felt a million times better, but I wouldn't be drinking anytime soon.

"If not, I could always make the journey here," I offer, looking back to Da. He runs a hand roughly over the stubble of his beard, eyeing me suspiciously.

"What? I could." And I could also see Matt if I so wanted to. I raise an eyebrow, I was old enough to be able to make the journey, and it wasn't like I do anything much at home anyway.

"Well, I suppose so." He tosses the idea around in his head and I smirk at him, sometimes he was such a dad. The little boy squeals again and I look over, watching as his black hair flows with the breeze, his small legs threaten to give way on him. He'd only be three or four, his parents talk to each other, not paying much attention to him or his sister at all. My vision begins to blur at the edges and a queasiness takes control of me.

His sister chases him around the table, paying no mind to her mother's hand that comes into her path to slow her down. She stomps her foot on the ground as she has an outburst at her mother, but the little boy has continued to run.

He leaves the safety of the small, wooden fence that shelters the café and giggles as he reaches the dirt road that was mainly used for carriages and riders, ahead a man shouts warning.

But it's too late.

His giggles turn to screams, and then to silence.

I am frozen and I cannot move.

The horse rears up, snorting. People are screaming, a dark red liquid has begun to trickle into my view of the road. His mother stands and screams, rushing out to the road. The man on the carriage is off as fast as lightning, pulling the little boy out from under the carriage.

The father holds the little girl back, stopping her from looking. Her

mother is wailing, and wailing. No one knows what to do but stand and watch, I want to move. To help. But I can't.

I can't.

I can't.

"Rav? You alright?" Da says. I blink furiously, the little boy is running around his table with his sister in tow. I turn to look at Da, my hand had been clenching my cup of tea. I let it go, it clinks the plate.

"What happened? What about the boy?" I ask, looking around half frantically. What had just happened? What about the little boy? I turn back to him, watching as the mother and father talk to each other.

Something isn't right.

"You zoned out there for a moment, are you sure you feel alright? Your eyes are blood shot. What about the boy? What boy?" Da asks, reaching out a hand for me.

"The boy, is he okay?" I stand on unsteady feet as I watch the mothers hand go down to stop the little girl, and the little boy begins to head for the fence.

"I don't know what you mean Rav."

This can't be happening.

"Stop! Stop him!" I scream, pointing frantically and beginning to run towards him. I have no idea what I was doing, but I have to do something. The mother and father look over and I hear the mother shout out for him. He's fast, but I'm faster.

He giggles as he runs towards the road, I sprint fast, I look to the side to see the man in the carriage, shouting out at me. I look to the boy and take the only chance I might have to save his life.

I leap, in a flurry of the skirts from my dress with my hair streaming out wildly behind me. My hat flies off as I wrap my arms around his small body. I spin in the air, cradling him to my chest.

We land with a hard thud, the right side of my body takes the majority of the blow from the ground and ignites with fire. My teeth rattle in my head as it connects with the ground. I keep my arms tight around him, waiting for the impact of the horse.

But it doesn't come.

I open my eyes, forcing myself to sit up but not letting go of the boy. A woman collapses on the ground in front of me and wraps both of us into a sobbing hug. I see the others from the café looking at me, mouths wide open. I find Da and feel the blood run from my face.

I look up, reality setting in. The man in the carriage is calming his horse down, he'd just managed to stop in time. If I hadn't leaped for the boy, he wouldn't have made it.

"Thank you, thank you, thank you," his mum mutters to me, she sits back with him now wrapped in her arms. Her blue watery eyes search my face, her ginger hair stick out wildly from her bun.

"That's okay," I say absently, looking back towards the horse. Large black hooves stamp at the ground, it snorts as it looks down at me. I shiver, a man offers his hand to me. I take it, steadying myself. I brush my skirt off and retrieve my hat.

Did that really just happen?

"Miss, thank you," a small female voice squeaks. I look down in time to see the little girl wrap her arms around my legs, resting her head on my thigh. I brush a hand over her head, "That's quiet alright, make sure you keep your eye on him at all times. Can you promise me that?" I ask, she looks up me with the same eyes as her mother's and nods her head vigorously. She lets me go and runs back to her family, where her little brother is now crying.

"Ravynne, how did you know?" Da asks, running up to me. He takes my right arm, it's grazed from my forearm up to my shoulder, it oozes blood slightly and has gravel and dirt sticking to the open cuts.

"I don't know," I mumble, looking at my arm as well. I'd have to clean it up. On the outside I must seem cool and collected, but on the inside I am freaking out.

How did I *see* that happen before it did?

Did Nyx do something to me?

"Come on, let's get you to the tavern and cleaned up," Da says, wrapping my good arm over his shoulder. I cradle my other to my chest, still feeling like I'm in a dream.

The walk back to the tavern is a blur, and suddenly I'm sitting at a table in the tavern with a bowl of warm salt water and a washer. One of the female workers cleans up my arm, rubbing an aloe vera ointment over it to help with the healing. She peppers the cloth along the side of my face near my eyebrow, I wince as she applies the ointment above my brow.

"Thank you," I say up to her as she wraps my arm in a soft gauze from my wrist to shoulder. I feel ridiculous for going to such measure over a graze, but with the worried look on Da's face as he leans against a pole, I don't complain.

She nods and offers me a smile before taking the now dark water and dirty cloth away with her. I stretch out my arm and see what sort of mobility I have with it, thankfully it doesn't stop me from moving normally.

"Well…I didn't see that coming," Da says, taking seat across from me, I let out a nervous laugh and rest my hands on my lap.

"Trust me, I didn't either." *But I did.*

"How did you…?" he asks, but I can see the wariness in his eyes.

When he was my age, our town had grown up to fear witchcraft and everything involved with it. Even though it was ruled by a faerie now a lot of those beliefs are still in place.

If I openly admit to seeing what happened before it happened, it could possibly be worse for me and put me and my family in danger. I bite my tongue, I hate lying to him, but I have to.

"I don't know, I was watching them play and I thought I saw him leave the area so I went after him, anyone would have done it." I avoid his eyes as I look at the stained table top.

"They would have but no one but you seemed to notice."

"Yes, well lucky I'm observant." I mumble, looking back up to the stairs. I didn't want to talk about what happened anymore, the little boy is safe and that is all that matters.

"I might head up to bed for a bit, I don't feel too well," I say, rising from the chair. Da beings to rise, no doubt to help, but I shake my head.

"I'm fine now, I just need some rest. I'll be better come dinner time, I promise." I reassure him, giving him a knowing smile. He relents and sits back down in the chair.

"Alright Rav, I'll see you for dinner then."

I head up the stairs and lock myself in the room. I begin to pace, trying not to freak out. It was so much easier said than done. I pause in the middle of the room, throwing my dirty hat on the bed. I run a hand roughly through my hair, before throwing it up in a high bun.

I have to find out what had happened, *if* it happens again I need to be more prepared. No one can know what I am about to do. Although being knowledgeable isn't treason, what I wanted to know is.

I pull my dress from myself and look into my bag, I have two options, a soft beige one or a white one. I go with the beige, wanting to look less noticeable. Its thin straps are similar to the other dress, although this dress is one material that reaches my ankles and shows off my boots.

I head out, carefully treading down the steps. My bandaged arm might draw some stares and questions, but they could wait. I spot Da talking to a man behind the bar, and I bee line towards the front door, moving fast with my head down.

I run out head to the main street, once there I slow to a fast walk and head into the centre. There is a large library tucked away in one of the side streets, and I'm sure I'd find some answers there.

If not, Nyx would know something, if this wasn't of his doing, and if it was he would be a dead faerie.

I find the library easy and slip in through its glass doors. Silence weighs heavy in the air as I pause, struck by the beauty of the hundreds of books lined in large, dark oak cases. A man raises his head from the desk that sits in the middle of the large space, raising an eyebrow at me before looking back down at whatever he is doing. I walk in, seeing no one else in the library. Did no one come here?

I wander through the aisles, reaching out and running my left hand along the book covers. I had no idea where to really begin looking, there was so *many* and I only had until the sun went down.

I head down a darker aisle, where dust had collected on the spines of the books and the smell of worn leather and paper hangs in the air. I pause in the middle of the aisle and read the first few covers I spot, *The Do's and Don'ts of Faerie, Beasts of Akrania, The supernatural and superstitious.*

Somehow, I'd lead myself to the right section. Or something had lead me here. I shake the thought off. I didn't want to scare myself even more. My hand hovers over the faerie book, if I knew more about them maybe I'd be able to stave off Nyx for a while.

I choose the third book I'd come across, it's a thin volume with a brown leather cover. I wipe the dust from the cover and crack it open. I swear I can hear it creak as I open it, flicking through the dark yellow pages with black, cursive ink for the hand writing.

Goblins, gouls, ghosts, werewolves, faeries, pixies, vampires. I can't find anything that might tell me what I could be…but why think I'm anything other than human? I shut the book but keep a hold of it as I head back to the librarian, I press the cover to my body so he can't see the title of the book I carry.

"Excuse me, may I ask a question?" I stop at the desk, he peers up at me from behind his large glasses.

"What is it?" he asks, hands flickering over a typewriter.

"Um, it's for a project for school and I've forgotten what it's called. What is it when someone can see the future before it happens…?" I ask hesitantly, sucking on my bottom lip. He looks at me suspiciously, but sighs.

"All you young kids are going to get yourself in trouble delving into topics like this, but nonetheless, what you may be thinking of is a seer. Someone who has premonition into the future, they can also see into the spirit realm and so forth." He waves his hand as he pauses his writing.

"Oh, yes, I think that's it. Thank you." I nod once before heading to an empty table, I set the book down and flick through the pages, going through each category it may have.

Finally, I find the page.

Seer. Prophesier.

My heart beat fills my ears as I hesitate over the page, this could be an explanation as to why I had seen what I had before it had happened, but it could also make me lean towards this being the possibility.

I give in and decide to read the small amount that had been inked down, deciding it was worth knowing it rather than leaving empty handed.

Seer- a person with the ability of supernatural insight who has the power to see visions into the future.

Prophet- a person regarded as the teacher or proclaimer of the will of god.

Seer is a broad term commonly used, some seers can see events before they happen as time is not static and outcomes can change with small or large alterations. Prophets and seers are two streams in the same gift, prophets can know events in the spirit before they happen in the physical, whereas seers can see the events in spirit before they happen in the physical.

I pause reading, holding my finger over the next line I'm on and look at the drawing on the left page. It shows a thin female, with long black hair and no eyes being burnt on the cross. I gulp.

A seer is also referred to as a witch, they can unlock many other abilities and powers if they know how to correctly use their gift. This includes but is not limited to this list below:

- spell casting

-potion making

-telekinesis

-healing

-divination (ability to protect the future)

Suddenly the writing ends, and nothing but blank page is left. I flick to the other page, desperately wanting to know more, to read more, but it continues down the list.

I re-read the small passage multiple times, allowing it to stick itself into my brain. I shut the book with shaky hands, a sick feeling has begun to settle inside of me. If I am a seer, and chose to acknowledge that and act on it, it would make me a witch.

If anyone is suspicious of me in my town, or had some small proof of witchcraft against me, they would kill me like they did in the witch trials. I put the book back in its normal place and flee from the library, the sun is just beginning to set and I have to be back in time for dinner.

I'm not just Ravynne anymore.

No one could know the power I now possibly possess.

I pick at the golden thread of my white dress, the last clean one I'd taken with me on this trip. It was still early morning but I was waiting for Matt to come, needing some normality more than ever right now.

I have dark circles under my eyes, I'd barely been able to sleep a wink last night and when I did my nightmares were plagued with the little boy being trampled and his blood all over my hands.

"You've been out here a while Rav, what're you waiting for?" Da asks, coming up behind me. I let the thread slip through my fingers, crossing my arms over my chest. I lean back on the post and look his way, he'd freshly shaven and ran a hand through his wet hair.

"A friend is picking me up soon for some breakfast before we leave," I say, watching as he comes to stand still beside me.

"Look Rav, about yesterday…" He begins, rubbing the back of his neck. I raise a hand to cut him off.

"I don't want to talk about it, and we can't talk about it when we return home. Ma' can't know, please Da." I turn to him, almost begging. I didn't want to scare Ma' or the rest of the family, I'm already scared enough as it is. This is the last thing they need to worry about, I am the last thing they need to worry about.

"Fine. But you know I'm here if you need to talk." He relents, shoving his hands into his jean pockets. I turn back to the street, finally seeing Matt walk around the corner and towards the tavern. Butterflies flutter in my stomach as I walk down the few steps, "I'll be back in an hour or two Da!" I call over my shoulder, he waves in return before heading to the tavern stable.

"Hey, I thought I'd be late," he says in greeting, smiling down at me. I smile back as we walk back into the main street, the air between us is clear.

"Morning, you're just in time. I was just early."

"How was yesterday?" he asks, leading me towards the edge of the city. People are more spread out here, and it's nice not to be breathing in sweat and bad odour every second.

"It was…alright. Boring for a birthday," I say, forcing a smile and squashing the memory down.

"Next year we'll do something better, you ever hiked a mountain before?" he asks, stopping outside a small eatery. I peer in through the dust covered windows, holding a hand against the glass to see better.

"No, I haven't," I answer, taking a step back and looking back to him. He smirks as he opens the door, bowing and gesturing for me to walk in.

I do as he says, taking a few hesitant steps into the small shop. Inside the white and black vinyl floor is spotless, three people sit in booths, all alone. Matt walks up to the small wooden counter, leaning against it. I follow, peering around to take in more detail, inside the light is dull but each booth that runs along the left wall holds a lantern.

"Two milkshakes please, strawberry and…" he pauses.

"Vanilla, thank you," I say without looking over my shoulder. I walk to the empty booth closest to us and slide into the red seat, it seems to sigh as I sit down and lean back.

Matt slides into the opposite side of the booth, moving the lantern out of the way so he can get a better view of my face.

"I'm sorry if you don't like milkshakes, Dad would bring me here when I was a little boy and I just…love it here." He clasps his hands together on the table, tapping his thumbs.

"It's so, old school in here? If that makes sense?" I giggle a little, unsure if that made sense. He cracks a smile as he leans back, relaxing.

"Yeah it does. Are you ready for the trip back?" He asks. I lick my lips, supressing a yawn. My eyes are beginning to grow heavy from the dim lighting and the scent of burning oil.

"Yes, I can't wait until I'm in my own bed again." I groan, stretching my arms above my head. His eyes flicker to the bandages on my arm.

"Oh, that. I totally forgot." I say, holding it out to look as well. I'd changed the dressing this morning, the grazed skin still red and a little pussy.

"What happened? You seemed in one piece when I left yesterday." He leans in again, reaching out before pulling his hand back and shoving it in his lap. I lower my arm and tap my fingers against my wrist.

"I fell over, I'm very clumsy when I want to be. I went down on my whole side." I scrunch up my face to lighten the situation, he chuckles as he shakes his head.

"I shouldn't have left you in the hands of the royals, they're never nice people."

"He visits often?" The topic of Nyx piques my interest and I curse myself for it. I didn't want to know more about him than I already did.

"Yeah a fair bit, always plays at the taverns. Sort of feels like a mockery sometimes, I've seen him do some pretty nasty things to people." I open my mouth to reply but the waitress comes over, sitting the glass milkshakes down in front of us.

"Thanks." I offer a small smile before taking a sip, savouring the thickness of the dairy.

"You won't see him much though, it's a big city," he assures me, taking the squeamish look on my face the wrong way. I nod and smile around the red straw before focusing back on the milkshake.

We spend the hour talking, sharing stories from our past with each other. I tell him about my little brother, and he tells me about being an only child but living with his uncle's kids. He'd earned a nasty scar on his abdomen from when the oldest brother slipped while they were farming and stabbed him with a machete.

The horror story shocked me, even more when he pulled the hem of his shirt up and showed me the deep reddish pink scar that ran from his belly button and to the right side for about ten centimetres.

We walk back to the tavern in silence, he'd written down his address and handed it to me so I could write if I chose too. I wanted to, but I had more important things to concern myself with.

Currently, why Nyx is waiting outside the tavern talking to Da. I stop and halt Matt, putting my arm against his chest. They hadn't spotted us yet, as we'd just reached the street.

"What?" He asks, looking at them.

"I just don't want to cause any trouble for you," I say and I mean it. If Nyx is connected to whatever the gift I had was, then I didn't want someone as kind as Matt to be caught up in it.

"I'll see you next time, thank you for breakfast, I really enjoyed myself." My words are rushed and I keep sparing a glance at Nyx, his tall muscular frame is helping Da load the carriage with bags, his dark hair waves with the slight breeze.

"Yeah, I enjoyed it too. Be sure to write Ravynne, it was nice meeting you." I reach out and give him a quick hug, not paying attention as he hugs me flush against him. I ease out of his grip, giving him an apologetic smile before heading down the street.

Nyx looks up with mischief in his eyes when I grow closer.

"Hey Da, hi Nyx," I say, bowing slightly. I catch him smirking before I cross my arms over my chest, raising an eyebrow. He shakes his head with a chuckle.

"Hey pumpkin, Nyx here was just looking for you." Da puffs, throwing the last bag into the carriage. He wipes his hands on his jeans before shaking Nyx's hand. He climbs up onto the carriage seat, "I'll wait at the end of the street for ya."

"Alright Da." I watch as he goes, feeling my anxiety beginning to rise. I thought I was doing a good job of being calm and collected… but around Nyx, there is no such thing as calm.

"Hi." I say again, feeling a light blush come to my cheeks.

"Yes hello Ravynne, leaving already?" He asks, his eyes run over me and I hold my head higher and straighten my back.

"Yes, we weren't really supposed to stay today but Da' thought it would be for the best." I shrug, looking back to see Da chatting with some folk.

"What happened to your arm?" He asks, taking my hand in his and surveying the bandages. His hands are soft, his fingers gentle as the brush over the skin of my wrist just before the bandage.

"I…uh fell over." He chuckles.

"Will you ever stop lying to me?"

"No." I say pointedly.

"How did you feel the other morning?"

I look back to him, confused.

"What"?

My heart is a stallion galloping in my chest.

"After your little drinking stunt the other night, how did you feel the next morning?" He muses, a smile tugging at his lips.

"Horrible, but not as bad as I think I could have felt if you hadn't…" *kissed me.*

"Ah yes, I'm glad you pulled up well then." He drops my hand, "I, um, got you something actually. For your birthday, I just wanted to give it to you before you left," he says, opening his cloak and pulling a small black bag from his pocket.

I watch as he pulls out a black leather chain, a half crescent moon pendant hangs from it, the deep purple stone reminds me of his eyes.

"I can't possibly take that!" I gasp, my hand flutters over my heart. Crystals are expensive, and in our village extremely rare. I was sure to get looks from the other folk if I wore this around.

"You can, really. Please." He holds it out, his cheeks turn a slight pink as it dangles in the air for a moment. I hold out my hand, letting him drop it in my open palm. I curl my hand around it and bring it closer to me, running my fingers over the smooth crystal.

"Wow…you shouldn't have." I say, looking back up at him. Two emotions flicker across his face; sadness and confusion. I gulp and slide the necklace into my dress pocket, patting it down to look normal.

"Well. I should probably go…" I trail off, nibbling my bottom lip. He runs a hand through his hair, avoiding looking at me.

"Right, of course. Good day Ravynne, safe journeys," he says, taking a step back, shoving his hands into his pockets. I hold back my eye roll as I quickly close the distance between us, I stand on my tip toes and press a soft kiss to his cheek, "Thank you, Nyx."

I step back and turn, walking up to Da's carriage.

We set out for home and Da decides he now likes Nyx and that I should have taken him up on his offer yesterday. We bicker back and forth, mainly because if Da saw *who* Nyx really was, he wouldn't be so eager to match me with him.

As I watch the mountains in the distance and the thickening forest around us, I only then realise my mistake.

I'd thanked a faerie.

Da and I sit around the crackling fire, the half crescent moon is high above us with hundreds of stars spread across the sky like paint splatter. I roast a piece of meat on a stick, twisting it around in the fire. Tomorrow we'd return home, and hopefully my life will return back to normal.

Da sits beside me, roasting his own piece of meat. A few metres away we have the gelding tied to a tree, he grazes at the grass; not minding the rest stop.

"Thanks for bringing me along Da." I say, watching as the golden and orange flames cover the meat and turn the red flesh brown.

"Always pumpkin, it just also happened to be your birthday," he points out. I pull the stick out of the fire, blowing away the flame that had decided to cling to the wooden stick.

I sit back on the log and begin to take small bites of the meat, savouring the warmth it brings. Da had given me a jumper to wear to keep out the cold chill of the night.

"I wonder if Ma' will have anything waiting for me when I get home," I muse, looking over to him.

"Yes I think she will, something you'll like," Da hints, raising a dark brow. I grin around the food before we lapse into silence. I start cooking a second piece, grabbing it from the small white ice container.

"What did Nyx want?" Da asks, I grip the stick tighter as I shove it into the fire.

"Just to say happy birthday." I half shrug, consciously aware of the weight the necklace makes in my pocket. I hadn't had to the heart to wear it yet, and I didn't have the heart to get rid of it.

"He seems nice, although at first I wasn't too sure what to think of him."

"He is nice, just isn't for me," I state bluntly, resting my chin on my free palm. My hair falls down and nearly catches in the fire.

"I think he's fond of you, more so than you may think." Da point his stick at me before piercing another piece of meat with it.

He was not fond of me, that was the last thing I'd picture Nyx being towards me. He was nicer, sure, but that's where the friendliness ended. He probably thought me weak after I'd stripped down to my undergarments.

I snort, "I don't think so, you should have met Matt. He seems fond of me." It's my turn to point my stick at him, raising a brow in challenge.

"Another one?! How many others do I not know about!" Da teases, grinning at me. I grin back, there were only two but I like to believe he'd wonder if there'd be more men pining after me.

I grow some courage and ask a question I've been waiting to ask since Nyx was out of earshot.

"Da, what do you know of the faerie king that rules over our village?"

"Why do you want to know that?" He asks, biting into his meat.

"I'm curious. No one really talks much about him in village of fear of what the repercussions will be. But he's our leader and yet I know nothing about him." I finish the last of my meat before tossing the stick into the fire, I watch as it catches ablaze and burns down to nothing. Da grunts, debating.

"Now that you're of age it's probably best you know the traditions, especially since you'll have to offer something this year as well." He sighs, loading another bit of meat onto his stick.

"What do you mean?" I ask, clasping my hands between the skirts of my thighs and turning towards him. He holds the stick in the fire, his blue eyes seem to glow as the reflection of the fire dances off of them.

"Once a year, when the moon turns blood red, the adults of the village make the short journey through the woods to the offering place. Sometimes the king is there, other times he isn't. We offer him the goods we make, in hopes for his guidance and his blessings.

"This year you'll have to come as well, and offer something of yours that will grant you blessings. It has to be handmade, it can't be stolen and it can't have magic laced into it," he says sternly, looking over at me. I nod my head once, I had heard whispers about what they did at the offering place, but the young ones aren't supposed to know the business of the village.

"It's in a few weeks, that should be long enough for you to make something."

"But Da, I'm not good at anything. I only lend a helping hand where

I can," I say, shaking my head. It was true, all the talent had skipped me and settled with Cecilia. She had an eye for art, and would sculpt the loveliest little trinkets. Whenever I tried to sculpt something, it always broke or came out looking the opposite of what I'd hoped.

"You'll find something Rav, you're a smart girl," Da assures me. His eyes look upon me intensely and I'm too afraid to ask what the consequence would be if I had no offering to give, if I showed up empty handed.

"When we return home look into things you can make, simple things, any offering works as long as it's made by you. Don't worry about it, nothing bad has happened in the last few years."

"What had happened?" I ask, imagining my eyes would be as wide as saucers by this point. He looks back to the fire, avoiding my question.

"Nothing you need to worry about pumpkin."

"You can't protect me forever Da." I sigh, standing up. I yawn as I stretch my arms over my head, feeling the beginning of a headache blooming in my left temple.

"I can try," he says sadly, and I feel myself flinch. How could he still want to protect me after I didn't protect Cecilia?

"You never told me how the king came to be," I say, pausing before going to the bedroll in the carriage.

"Faeries once conquered our continent, Akrania, hundreds of them plagued each town and city and village you can think of. We even had them here, but this was before my time. Your grandpa and grandma were around when they lived amongst us, and then one day one of them decided he wanted to rule over our village, and try to rule over the rest of the continent. Soon enough the other faeries fell into line, and if they didn't they were slaughtered.

"He didn't get very far, as the human royals were firm with their rulings and had an army of their own. It's said he has a son, but his wife went missing twenty years ago. Word reached our village that she'd disappeared. I've never seen the son, but I do know he visits our village, although that is rare too. The Densley's said they saw him last week actually, milling about," he says, stopping his story. I look away, trying not to give the guilt of lying to him away, as I'm sure it's plastered on my face for everyone to see.

"Dark creatures plagued the earth when the faeries were around in greater numbers, creatures they'd brought with them from wherever they came from."

"What happened to the faeries?" I ask.

"They returned to their own homes, bored of humans. Most of the creatures followed in tow, but some remained behind. There's one that lives in the mountains around our village, although I haven't seen it since I was a little boy. Who knows where it is now." He throws his stick into the fire and closes the lid of the empty container. He stands, wiping his hands on his pants.

"Thanks for telling me Da, I might get some rest now," I say, beginning to move for the carriage. It was sitting in a darkened shadow under a tree, and a silly part of me was scared. As if speaking of the creatures had brought them to life, and to us.

"Night pumpkin, be ready to head off at the break of dusk. Sweet dreams." I wave over my shoulder before climbing into the carriage. I hop into my bed roll that sits beside Da's and zip it up. I roll on my side and rest one hand under the small pillow and one hand over the pendant Nyx had given me.

My dreams are plagued with creatures and faeries, Nyx leading them all.

I sit at the kitchen table, cup of tea in hand as I flip through some designs my Aunty had been thinking of working on. For the offering next week she'd been working on a cloak, blending the blue and green dyes together to get a splashed pattern for the fabric. I still had no idea what I was going to offer, or make. Ma was going to give up six of her best lemon cakes, Da was going to give up a bucket of wheat which he hoped would grant more blessings for us and Aunty was making the cloak.

It's not like I hadn't tried to make something, I definitely had. Everything I tried to bake burned, the crops I'd tried to harvest were bad and I couldn't sew to save my life. I couldn't think of anything, the only thing I was good at was helping others.

I shut the design book and lean back in the chair, sipping my tea.

Aunty Mana rushes in, two different fabrics are splayed out on her open arm. Her dark brown hair is a wavy mess that has been pinned back in a large bun on her head.

Her green eyes sparkle as she looks at me, she was so similar to Ma but so different at the same time. Aunty was older than Ma by three years, and had been the reason Da and Ma had come to date. Her face was aged like Ma's but still held some strands of her youthfulness.

It was in the way she held herself, and the pride she took in her work. The dress she is wearing was one she'd made, a mixture of all different fabrics sewed in into one large piece. It was more casual than all of her other works.

The gold bracelets dangle on her wrist as she sweeps her hand over the two designs.

"Which one do you reckon?" She asks.

The one on the left looks coarse, with small brown dots of fabric scattering the rest of it. The one on the right is more smooth, shining in the afternoon sunlight. It would be perfect for a cloak, reminding me of the one Nyx had worn the first time we'd met.

"The second one." I point to it, putting the now empty cup down.

She nods as she rushes out of the room, back to our room where she did some of her sewing. Other days she went to the bakery with Ma and had her own small section there, that's where most of her fabrics and designs lived. Nearly everyone in town had something made by my Aunty.

"You're welcome," I call up the stairs, shaking my head. I get up and put the cup in the sinks, it clinks against the metal as it slips from my hand.

My eyes grow wide as my vision goes hazy, only for it to appear a moment later.

I stand at the edge of the river, the once clear water was now running blood red. A faint metallic scent wafts from it with the breeze, the other village guests were standing at it as well. All wondering the same question.

I crouch down and dip my hand into it, pulling it back to confirm it wasn't just red water; it was blood. The folk scurry away from me, pointing and shouting at me.

"I didn't do anything." I say slowly, standing up once again. I see Da pushing his way through the crowd to me, shoving people back.

"Witch!"

"Witch!"

Their shouts all combine into one as I squeeze my hands over my ears, not caring that the blood is on my face or in my hair. I just want their shouts to stop.

I look up the river to see a large beast like creature, hiding in the foliage. It grins at me, its white teeth gleam and its large golden eyes are slit like cat's eyes.

It disappears into the forest of the mountain.

The creature had returned, and I had become its target.

"Rav, Rav, are you okay?" Aunty's voice breaks through the illusion. I look down at the sink, taking a gasping breath. My hands clench the side of the bench, my knuckles had gone white from the strength of it. I drop my hands and wrap them around myself.

I turn slowly to find Aunty standing in the doorway, a worried look sketched onto her face. She holds the piece of fabric I'd chosen in her hand, adding violet wild flowers to it.

"Why did you choose violet?" I ask, before I can stop myself. Her worry turns to curiosity as she comes to the kitchen table, spreading the fabric over it.

"Because it's a pretty colour," she lies, motioning her hand over the cloak. Or I am being paranoid. The vision still clings to me like a second skin, and I can't get the large white teeth or golden eyes out of my mind.

When is this going to happen? Now? Tomorrow? Next week? I'd been caught off guard again. I check my pockets, looking for the necklace Nyx had given me. It isn't there. I frown.

"Looking for something?" Aunty asks, watching me.

"Yes, a necklace a friend gave me." I say, looking under the table. I don't know why I feel it should be so important if I had it or not, but now I didn't want to not have it on me.

"Is this it?" She asks, but there's an edge to her voice. I look up to see her dangling the necklace from her hand, the moon swings back and forth slightly.

"Yes. Where did you find it?" I ask, knowing full well I always had it on me. Nyx would never know that, and I didn't mind keeping it like that.

"It was under your bed, you must have dropped it. Who gave it to you?" I go to reach for it but she pulls it out of reach. I frown at her, wondering why she's being so reluctant.

"A friend."

"Which friend?"

"Why are you asking me so many questions? Just give me my necklace back please," I snap, breathing heavy through my nose. She stares me down, a challenge.

A kid runs screaming through the house, up the stairs and into his room. I hear Ma close the door behind her as she mumbles to herself.

"Afternoon girls," Ma greets as she enters the kitchen, she pauses as she look at us. Aunty stands on one side of the table, necklace in hand and I stand on the other; no doubt looking furious.

"What's going on?" She asks, sliding into the kitchen and going into the fridge. She'd start doing test batches for her lemon cakes today, and would do so every afternoon after work up until the morning we had to make the trek half way through the forest to the offering place.

"She won't give my necklace back," I whine, looking to Ma.

"Mana, give it back," Ma says over her shoulder, arranging the ingredients on the kitchen bench. I look back to Aunty, she is stubborn like I am.

"She won't tell me who gave it to her."

"I already told you it was a friend," I exclaim, throwing my hands in the air. Why did she want to know so bad?

"Which friend?"

"Ladies, is this really such a trivial thing? She probably got it from one of her friends in Orrinshire. Mana give her back the necklace please." Ma turns and crosses her arms over her chest. Although she is younger than Aunty, she is the woman of the house.

"Fine." I walk around the table and grab the moon in my hand, feeling a strong sense of relief wash over me. Aunty eyes me with suspicion as she lets it go.

"We will be talking later," she whispers, low enough so Ma can't hear her. I nod once before fleeing out of the house, necklace still in hand. I finally decide to wear it. I clasp it around my neck, the pendant sits just above my breasts and the edge of the neckline of the dress.

Today I'd chosen to wear something more gloomy, the dark grey dress hugs my chest and waist and spreads out to thin skirts once it reaches my belly button. I'd worn my black boots underneath and had decided to let my wild hair down, it is wavy from washing it the night before and catches the sun in the most spectacular ways.

I head into the village, not thinking about where I would go or what I am doing. I don't want to go home yet, or any time soon. I trudge up the slope, liking the burn in my calves from the steepness. How Ma did this every day is beyond me.

I make it to the village, few people mill about as they finish doing the last chores of the day. I walk mindlessly whistling a tune to myself as I go. I go to Ma's bakery, wanting to look through the window at the things she'd created today.

Her bakery was a few shops down from the farmer's one where we delivered the wheat. I walk up onto the small brown patio and look in through the large window that sat on the right side, if I looked through the left window I'd see all the dresses and outfits Aunty has been working on.

In the window a small wooden counter sits, and beside it a large glass counter. Cakes, muffins and pastries sit nicely on the black shelves in all different colours and shapes. My other favourite were the pecan danish Ma made, I could devour a batch of them in one sitting.

"Thinking of breaking in are we?" A male voice muses behind me, I squeak as I turn around, startled. Nyx stands there, arms crossed over his chest and a small smirk on his face.

"Oh you buffoon you scared me!" I exclaim, rubbing my hands over my face. Today he let his faerie show, his earring catches the low rays of the sunlight.

"It's never my intention to scare a pretty lady, although it did look like you were thinking of breaking in," he says, peering around me to see through the window. I ignore his compliment and turn back to the bakery window.

"It's my Ma's bakery, I wanted to come here and look at what she'd made," I grumble. I feel him come up behind me, he leans over me and peers in; trapping my body there with his own.

I try to keep my breathing steady even if I can't keep my heart from bursting in my chest. He smells like the forest, and it's a welcoming smell.

"Why is that?" He asks, finally taking a step back. I turn around and lean against the window, looking around to see if anyone notices me with him. A few people stare, but with a pointed glance from me they quickly look away.

Word hadn't reached Ma or Da that I'd been with a faerie, so I could only hope the same would be kept from them now.

"Do you really want to know?" I ask, finally bringing myself to look up at him. He leans against the wooden handrails and tucks his hands into his pockets, he fixes his eyes onto me.

"Yes, surprisingly enough."

"I don't know what to make for the offering. I can't make things, but I know how to destroy things. I tried baking, and it was a disaster." I sigh, shaking my head.

"You're attending the offering?" He asks, sounding intrigued.

"Well yes, I'm a recently fully fledged adult now so Da said I have to start attending. But I can't make anything and I was too cowardly to ask what would happen if I showed up empty handed." I feel my cheeks heat as I confess, I knew I shouldn't be talking to Nyx but I found it so easy. His lips twist and turn as he thinks, finally he raises a brow.

"There isn't one thing you can offer?" He asks.

"Well…no. Not really. I've never really made anything in my life, I only have myself to give but I don't fancy giving my maidenhood to your father." I joke, his cheeks turn a light shade of pink as I overshare yet again. "I'm sorry, you've just caught me off guard today."

"No, it's fine. You're wearing the necklace?" He asks, his head falls to the side as he looks at it. I stuff down the urge to fiddle with it, a nervous habit I hadn't shaken.

"Yes, originally I just carried it around in my dress pockets but my Aunty somehow managed to get her hands on it. We had a small fight about who exactly gave it to me, so I decided wearing it would be my best bet at having no one take it from me again," I say smoothly, coming to stand beside him. I lean against the railing and look at the mountain, the sunlight breaks over the mountain casting half of it in light and darkness.

"Why did she want to know?" He asks. I look up to see him looking down at me. My eyes flicker to his lips before I look away again.

"I don't know, she told me she'd talk to me later but I'm not in a mood for a lecture. I said a friend gave it to me, and apparently that wasn't enough for her."

"Awh, so you think I'm your friend? Here I was thinking my

presence only worked to frustrate you," he coos, bumping into my side playfully. I stifle a laugh as I regain my posture, but find myself smiling up at him.

"It still does that," I tease, poking my tongue out. His eyes sparkle as he rubs his face thoughtfully.

"You know, it's funny you say that, because I feel the exact same way about you." I smack his arm lightly and burst out laughing, the sound is rich to my ears and I'm momentarily distracted by the fact I hadn't laughed in so long.

"I think you're funny," I say, finally regaining myself.

"You said that the first time we met as well."

"Do just have like an amazing memory or something?" I ask, leaning my hip against the railing. One hand is holding the bar and the other dangles down at my side.

"It's a bonus of being a faerie," he says, shrugging. Already I can feel the moment we had ebb away back into something more formal.

"Why are you here anyway?" I ask, it had grown darker and the village was almost empty of the last few folk that were out. I'd have to head home soon, still feeling haunted by that thing I'd seen in the vision.

"Just checking in."

"Yes, but I thought you didn't visit often," I point out. I push off from the railing and walk back down the few steps and begin to head for home. I hear him follow behind, keeping up with me easily enough.

"I don't," he says, hands in pockets.

"Yet here you are, walking home a village girl," I say, cocking my head to the side and looking up at him. His lips twitch into a smile, for a moment I feel a hot electricity fill the air between us.

Then I slip over, on a loose rock in the slope.

I yelp as my legs slip, my hands go up and I feel strong warm ones grab my arms. Nyx pulls me to him, my back presses into his muscular chest as I find my footing again. His grip is loose on my arms but it fills me with warmth.

"Thanks. God damn it, these rocks always get me," I groan, letting my head fall back onto his chest. I look up to see him looking down at me, with a curious expression on his face.

"You thanked me," he states.

"Yes well I've already done it once, where's the harm in doing it again?" I say, my words coming out more confident than I feel.

"You shouldn't thank a faerie," he says slowly. I roll my eyes and turn in his arms, slightly shocked he hasn't let go of me yet.

"What's the worst you thing you could possibly make me do? Kiss you?" I ask, raising a brow. I rest my hands on his chest and feel his heart beating wildly beneath my palm. I'm glad I am not the only one affected when we seemed to collide.

"Yes," he says softly, his breath tickles my nose and I finally realise how close we've been standing. I clear my throat and step out of his grip, the sun had almost set now and dinner would be ready.

"Nothing I haven't done before. I have to get home though," I say, looking at the distant lights from our house. They'd left the porch lantern on for me.

"I'll walk you." He offers me an arm, and I slip mine into his. Mainly so I don't slip again, that's what I tell myself anyway.

"I won't be able to bring you inside this time," I say as we grow closer. The night's chilly air bites at me. I find the only warmth from Nyx's arm and find myself leaning into him.

"It's alright, I wouldn't expect you to," he says.

"Not because you're a faerie, but because you're a pain," I tease, wanting to lighten the mood before I had to leave him out in the dark. Did faeries see in the dark? Could he see me now, licking my lips stupidly?

"I could only hope that's the real reason," he muses, glancing down at me.

"Obviously."

We lapse into silence, and before I'd like to we reach the front of the fence. I can just hear my family in the kitchen talking back and forth, most likely about how their day has been.

"This is me." I say, absently reaching out and running a hand over the metal gate.

"I'm glad to have escorted you home safely," he says, but doesn't drop my arm. I can't say I want him to drop it, which annoys me.

"I am too. I guess I'll see you around?" I ask, reluctantly letting my arm slip from his. I'm immediately chilly and cross my arms over my chest, rubbing my biceps.

"Yes you will. If not, I might see you at the offering. Have a good night Ravynne." He nods once, licking his lips.

"You as well Nyx," I say, before being trapped by the needs he's seemed to have awakened in me. I slip through the gate and walk up to the patio, once there I turn back and wave.

He waves back and I slip inside, I shut the door and turn. A stupid smile stuck on my face, I walk into the kitchen to find my place ready and my plate full.

"Oh good, you've arrived in time to say grace." Ma says, gesturing for me to come over and clasp hands. I do as she says and I shut my eyes, finding the only thing I can think about is Nyx.

I scrub at the menstrual rags in the river, down near the end of the stream so it won't contaminate the rest of the water. It was the bleed week of all three of the women in the household and I got lucky enough to be the one to clean the rags every afternoon. At least I wouldn't be so moody once the offering came, as I only had two days left and then the offering was two days after that.

I dunk the rag down and scrub with the wire brush, I still hadn't thought of what I could make, but soon I'd have to scramble to make anything.

Or maybe…I could offer something else entirely.

What if, I wrote down the vision of the creature? That would count as an offering, and it was something I'd created.

I finish scrubbing the rest of the rags quickly, ringing them out before placing them back in the wooden basket. I take off for home, I still remembered every detail of the vision and found myself constantly on edge; waiting for it to happen.

As I'm walking up to the farm, Mike is walking down towards me with a bucket swinging in his hands, most likely to go to the river for fresh water.

I give him a polite smile, thinking it would suffice.

"Ravynne, hey," he says, coming to stop in front of me. I stop and watch him, keeping the smile on my face.

"Hey Mike, how are you?" I ask, watching as the morning rays catch his golden hair and seem to ignite it. Ma was so disappointed once I stopped hanging around Mike, she was hoping we'd have cute little Mikes running around the house by now.

Most of the girls my age found a partner and started their wedding ceremonies and then their bedding ceremonies. I was never a fan of learning about them at school, why would I go straight into a marriage as soon as I'd left school?

"Yeah I'm good, how was your trip?"

"Yes it was…pleasant, thank you." I nod, wringing my hands around the basket handle.

"That's good…I have to ask though, what were you doing with that faerie the other night?" His question takes me by surprise, I almost drop the basket.

"I'm— I'm sorry, what?" I stutter, I avoid looking to the ground.

That would be the first sign of me being guilty. He runs a hand through his hair and looks over me, towards the river.

"I saw you and him, he walked you home. I didn't mean to spy, I was just turning the horses in when I heard talking and took a look."

"Why are you asking me this?" If he told his parents…if his parents told mine. I bite my bottom lip and feel the panic begin to form in my gut.

"Because regardless of what you may think, I still do care for you. I never stopped. I just want you to be careful, I've heard the stories and I know their tricks. I just don't want you to end up at the other end of the stick." He sighs, shaking his head. His words are thoughtful, and it means a lot to me to know he still cares.

"Thank you. It was nothing, I can assure you that. He offered to walk me home and I obliged," I say, feeling some of panic dissolve. Maybe I could keep this secret with Mike.

"I hope so Ravynne, I really hope so. How is your offering coming along?" He asks, changing the subject. Which I find strange, this is the most me and Mike have spoken in months, if not years.

"Terrible, I can't make anything to save my life. What about you?" I ask, sighing. He smiles and the tension of the other conversation saps away.

"A bridle, carved with real leather and decorated with golden trimming. It's simple but looks good to the eye, faeries like things that appeal to their eyes," he says, and I feel his words have deeper meaning.

"Maybe I'll just glue a heap of nice rocks together," I joke, wanting to steer away from deeper faerie talk. He grins, strikingly.

"That could work, do you remember when we were kids and you used to make us those crowns out of leaves and flowers? Maybe you could do one of those?" He suggests. I'd forgotten about that. When we were little I would grab twigs and leaves and the prettiest flowers and make crowns out of them, and we'd run around the village thinking we were royalty.

"Oh my, I forgot about those! I could, couldn't I?" I fiddle with the basket handle and look back down to the river, I'd been stalling. Aunty waited at home for me, and she was determined to have that conversation.

"Well, I have to get going. It was nice chatting," I say, nodding once.

"Of course, be careful Ravynne." He strolls towards the river, not giving me a second glance. I shrug it off and head home, storm clouds begin to cluster in the sky towards the castle and a rumble runs down the valley.

I head inside, sitting the cleaned rag basket in the living room. I make quick work of pinning them up on the rope that now hung from one end of the room to the other. With the weather being so unpredictable, Ma had thought it would be best to hang the clothes inside to dry.

"There you are," Aunty says, coming into the room. She moves as swiftly as water, her bracelets don't make noise today. I pin the last rag up and turn to her, her eyes narrow on the necklace.

"Sorry, I ran into Mike on the way home." I leave the basket on the ground and head into the kitchen, breezing past her. She follows, not giving me a moment alone.

"Can you please tell me who gave you the necklace?" She asks again. I reach into the cupboard and pull down two mugs and the tea bags and sugar.

"Does it really mean that much to you, for you to know?" I ask, not looking over my shoulder as I make us a cup of tea. Aunty and I were close once, but once Cecilia died I put distance between everyone. I couldn't risk losing someone else I loved.

"Yes, it does Rav," she says softly. I hear the chair slide against the wooden floor boards as she takes a seat.

"Nyx," I say bluntly, I didn't want to share him with anyone, even though Da had already met him. I *liked* having my own secrets and life outside of the death that seems to still cling to the house and the people in it. To Nyx I was a human girl to annoy, and to me he was a good distraction from my life here.

"Nyx…a royal, yes?" She questions. I turn around with the two mugs in my hand, I place one down in front of her before settling in across from her. I watch her over my cup that sits snug between both hands.

"Yes."

"And what else is he?" She takes a sip, giving me a knowing look. I gulp. She'd heard. Surely she'd heard the gossip in town and had come to confront me.

"You would already know if you're asking me such a question," I whisper, one hand instinctively goes to the necklace. I trace the crescent moon absently. If Aunty told the rest…was the friendship with Nyx really worth it?

Yes. No. Maybe.

When had I begun to consider him as a friend?

"I wanted to hear it from you before I made my own assumptions. Do you know the purpose of that necklace?" She asks, sitting her mug down. I shake my head, I thought it had just been a nice gift.

"It's to stop the sight," she says matter of fact. I clench my hand over the pendant. This was going from bad to worse before I could stop it.

"Aunty it's not—" I blubber, trying to grasp the lies that are just out of my reach. She shakes her head with sad eyes, she looks out the window over the kitchen sink.

"You don't need to lie to me child."

"But—"

"No Ravynne, don't lie to me. When I first glimpsed you carrying it around, I assumed you knew what it's purpose was since you didn't let it out of your sight…so I took it, to test out the theory I'd been working on." She waves her hand in the air, eyebrow raised. I feel the blood drain from my face.

"When I came in yesterday, I watched. From start to finish when I intervened. I had to know, and I'm sorry but you wouldn't have told me yourself," she states, leaning back in her chair.

"Why?" I ask, my voice barely a whisper.

"Because I'm sorry to say my…gift has passed onto you. The necklace is a blocker, and whoever gave it to you must know you have the sight and if they don't they suspect it. That is why I wanted to know, because that knowledge in the wrong hands is dangerous."

"You're…you're a seer too?" I ask, unbelieving. If she was, how had she kept it hidden so well for so long? How had I not picked up on it?

"Yes, although I didn't pursue it. I have the visions, but I don't act on them. I let them come and happen as they play out and I leave it at that. It's dangerous to dabble with them if you're not sure what you're doing. How many have you had?"

"Two, one while in Orrinshire and one the other day," I whisper, tracing a pattern on the table. I was finding it hard to look at her now, she was the only person who would fully understand me.

"What were they?"

"In Orrinshire me and Da were out for lunch, and the vision came to me of the little boy beside us running out to the road and getting hit by a carriage…a moment later I saw him run, but I ran after him. I wasn't sure what was happening, but I saved him. I had to, I didn't have a choice." I look back up to her warily, she looks at me with sad eyes.

"I know it's hard, wanting to change the fate of others, especially when they're so small and still have their whole lives ahead of them. We always have a choice. What was the second one you had the other day?" she takes me by surprise and reaches across the table, holding my hand in her own.

"I was at the river, and the water had turned to blood. Everyone began screaming that I was a witch, but when I looked up to the forest above the river a…creature was there, grinning with golden eyes. And then I came back to reality." I shake my head, this is a vision I did not want to come true. If they thought I was a witch…I'd be burned no doubt.

"Did you see anything else?" She asks, more intensely.

"No, just that. I haven't had any since, most likely because of the necklace." I glance down at it and feel my heart tug, was Nyx trying to protect me or did he have a darker intent on keeping the visions from me?

"You must leave it on until the offering is complete. If the King knows you have the sight…" Her eyes cloud over as her mouth twists with worry.

"Why?" I ask, feeling my heart pick up in my chest.

"Because, since his wife died he has been on the hunt for a certain seer. He seems to believe his wife and this seer are connected. I don't know the true intent behind it, but I've heard whispers he has his son looking. I'm worried for you Ravynne, you need to be careful of that faerie." She lets go of my hand and sits back, before I can reply the front door opens and Da comes strolling in.

"Well, I better get back to my dresses," Aunty says sweetly, she twirls to the sink and places her cup. She nods to Da as she leaves the kitchen and heads back into town. Da gives me a puzzled look but I shrug him off.

I finish the cup of tea, trying to process everything Aunty had said. I decide against leaving a note about the vision, and decide to make a tiara.

I say bye to Da and leave home with an empty basket, heading to the forest near the creek. It was the best spot to retrieve things for the crown I'm thinking of making.

I can't find it in me to whistle a happy tune, so I welcome the silence, hoping something more comforting will come to mind. All I can think of Nyx…and him betraying me.

The offering ceremony comes far quicker than I would have imagined, everyone in the house had spent the morning finishing their final touches to their piece and I had added the last few dandelions to the tiara.

Compared to the rest of the family, I felt my offering was the least valuable one. It wasn't outstanding, or breathe taking. I'd twined green leaves around a twig and tied them with small bits of rope. I'd added red rose petals and a few walnut shells, and finally twined dandelion flowers through it. Rather simple, but I thought it was cute. It was also better than showing up with nothing.

As late afternoon begins to fall upon us, the adults of the village begin to form a line in the centre of the village. Me and my family stand at the outskirts, Kalin had gone to a friend's until we returned.

"Ma, what happens now?" I whisper, eyeing the growing crowd.

"We get into line and follow." She links her arm with mine and leads us to the forming line. Da and Aunty follow behind, and I feel Aunty reach out and give my free hand a squeeze.

Ever since she'd revealed she was also a seer, I felt a small weight lift from my shoulders. I hadn't realised the pressure I had felt in the few weeks until it was on the table for her to know. I'd taken the necklace off and stuffed it into the pocket of my pants.

For once I'd decided on wearing my brown three quarter pants with a loose, white button up shirt. I'd rolled the sleeves up to my elbows and had the top two buttons undone. It felt weird not getting around in a dress, but for the trek I wanted to make sure I was comfortable.

The moon had begun to turn a dull red, even though the sun was still in the sky. It hangs low near the forest, taunting us. Da had assured me with confidence the offering was nothing to be afraid of, but I couldn't help but feel scared.

Ahead of the line, the leaders hold two lit lanterns that now cast a shadow on the ground as the sun slowly begins to dip behind the mountains. The anticipation was thick in the air as a lot of the new adults hadn't attended before. I felt discouraged, after seeing so many beautiful things crafted. I kept my tiara in a basket, so no one would tease me for the poor effort I'd made.

Someone at the front shouts something, and the line begins to move forward. I squeeze Ma's arm as the forest continues to grow closer, there was a wide path beside the school that lead to the offering and it was forbidden to enter the path on any other day.

I stay close to Ma as the forest engulfs us, the large trees block out the last afternoon sun rays and red moonlight spills in through the gaps instead; casting everything with a red sheen. I shiver momentarily, thinking back to the vision.

Most of the girls my age had decided to stick together, not bothering to stay with their families. I received a lot of pointed looks from them, but with my head held high I assure myself their stares mean nothing.

The walk is short but seems long and I have the suspicion the faerie magic has something to do with it. Up ahead I see the people begin to turn right and left in a clearing. I stand on the tips of my toes to try and catch a glimpse of what is to come but struggle to see over the other heads and glaring light coming from the clearing.

I give up, and wait for my turn. Once we get there I'm herded to the right side with the rest of my family following. I gasp as I look around the clearing; it is huge.

The ground seemed to have been burnt out in a large circle, with only dirt and a few green sprouts bursting through. In the centre of the clearing sits a large stone throne, on the armrests lily flowers were carved with a vine weaving between them with large thorns sticking out. Upon that throne, sits the faerie king. His dark green tunic is matched with dark green pants. His unnaturally long fingers drum against the arm rest, the rings gleam in the lantern light and the red moon.

I trail my eyes up to see his narrow eyes watching every single one of us as we file in, his pointed ears hold no jewellery but his raven black hair flows around him straighter than I thought hair could ever be.

To his left, standing just behind the throne is Nyx. He keeps his eyes forward, he's wearing the same outfit as his father but in a deep blue. His hair sticks out, as if he's combed his hand through it one too many times.

If I didn't know any better, I'd say he was avoiding looking at me.

"Welcome, folk of Elderview. It is an honour and a pleasure to grace you with my presence on this fine evening, and I cannot wait to see what you have to offer." The king's voice fills up the space around us, his eyes finally find mine. I freeze as I feel his magic seem to spin around me, wrapping me in a lovely cocoon.

His deep blue eyes pierce mine, trapping me there. I feel an unusual itching sensation cover my skin and I have the urge to scratch, but find my hands unable to move.

He smirks, and there's nothing nice about it.

"Father." Nyx's voice breaks his spell, and I sag slightly. His father's eyes flicker to Nyx before he faces the first few offerings. He waves his hand. "Proceed."

One by one each person goes up to the base of the throne, they sit their offering at his feet and bow low. If he says nothing they stand

and return back to their spot, if their gift doesn't suffice they're sent into the now dark path to take leave home without blessings.

As my turn begins to grow closer, I feel the same panic emerge. I try to catch Nyx's eyes, but he refuses to acknowledge me. If Da recognises Nyx, he doesn't say so.

Ma goes up to the stone, placing her lemon cakes at the base of his polished black shoes. She bows low.

"I'd like to try one," he says, gesturing for her to pass him one. I hold my breath as Ma reaches a shaky hand into the basket and pulls a yellow pie out. She passes it to him while keeping her head still bowed. He plucks it from her hands and takes a bite, munching on it slowly.

"Delicious," he says, finishing off the last of it. She stands up, visibly relieved before coming back to us. Da and Aunty go next, all giving me reassuring smiles as I begin to walk up.

I take slow steps, keeping my eyes focused on the ground in front of me.

I don't want to pull the tiara out, not when the gift is so bland and boring. I stop in front of the throne, focusing on his polished shoes and not on the multiple, nice gifts that had been displayed around for him.

"What do we have here?" He muses, reminding me too much of Nyx. It was frowned upon to look him in the eyes when giving your offering, but I found myself looking up regardless.

He's leaning forward in his seat, far closer to me than I'd like him to be. Out of the corner of my vision I see Nyx tense, jaw clenching as he watches the interaction.

"Well, girl? What do you have?" He asks again, more forward.

"Oh um, sorry your majesty. I find myself no good at making things, so I do apologise if what I've crafted is not to your standards," I say clearly, I hear a few people gasp in the crowd. I look back down and open the basket with slow movements, I pick up the tiara from the red cushion I'd placed it on and hold it with both hands as I show him what I'd made.

"Son, would you please try it on?" He says calmly, taking me by surprise. I look up as Nyx comes out from around the throne and stands beside his father. I turn slightly and make eye contact with him, a pained expression flashes across his face as he takes the tiara from me.

He places it on his head, it rests perfectly behind his ears. With a small dose of his magic it comes to life. The green leaves shine bright and the dandelions burst with colour. I watch in awe as the tiara is transformed into the most beautiful thing I've ever laid my eyes on.

"That is rather nice," the king says, looking between his son and I. Did he know that I knew Nyx?

"It will suffice. You have my blessings," he says, waving me away with a hand. I scurry back to my spot in the line, earning a smack from my Aunty. I supress the urge to hiss at her and instead focus on the ground.

If I look up, I won't be able to take my eyes away from Nyx and that is the last thing I want to do.

The offering comes to an end, the red moon has begun to ebb back to its normal grey colour and most of the lanterns are nearly snuffed out. My legs ache from standing for so long and my neck could use a good massage. I finally dare to look up. Nyx stands back with his hands clasped behind his back and my tiara still on his head.

It suits him, rather nicely.

"Thank you folk, for once again coming and offering me your goods. You all have my blessings. I hope that the crops you sow will be nutritious and the dresses you weave be of the finest material." The King waves a hand lazily and everyone begins to mill out of the clearing, back down the path we'd come up.

Once out of earshot Aunty grabs my arm, squeezing rather painfully.

"Are you stupid girl? Do you want him to have an eye for you? Is the son not enough?" She hisses, causing Ma to frown at her. I pull my arm out of her grip and rub it.

"Of course not, I just didn't know what to do," I snap back. She rolls her eyes and throws her hands in the air. I stomp forward, pushing my way through the crowd. It was well after midnight now, I am ready for bed and do not have time for her attitude.

I arrive home first, slip into a nightgown and decide to spend the night on the couch. I didn't fancy spending a night in the same room as Aunty. I clip the necklace back around my neck and grab my pillow and blanket from the bed.

Once I set it up on the couch the others return home.

"Where's Kalin?" I ask as Ma hangs her coat up.

"Staying at his friend's the night, they'll be going to school together tomorrow." Her voice is full of exhaustion.

"Goodnight Ma and Da," I call as they all head up the stairs. I make a point not to say goodnight to Aunty. I slide under the blanket and rest my arm over my face as a leg hangs off of the couch.

The house falls into deathly silence as I toss and turn, finding it hard to sleep. I give up the fruitless attempt and pull on a coat that hangs above the shoe rack. I slip into my boots and head down to the river.

A cool breeze rustles through my hair as I walk along, pulling the coat tight around myself and stuffing my hands into the pockets. In the distance an owl hoots, and I hear the occasional stick break in the shrubs that surround the road.

I reach the river and sit at the bank, crossing my legs. I watch as the moonlight reflects the water, making it look magical. I reach out a hand, welcoming the bite of it.

How had this river turned to blood in that vision? Was it magic, or was there something dead at the top of the stream making it run red?

I swish my hand back and forth, not paying attention to my surroundings as I get caught up with the way the water seems to move with my hand.

"I thought I'd find you here." A male voice startles me. I yank my hand out of the water and look over my shoulder. Nyx stands there, cloak concealing everything but his head. Nestled in his raven black hair is the tiara I'd crafted, although there is no magic entwined with it now and it looks extremely sad.

"Are you following me?" I ask, turning back to the water. I don't dip my hand in this time, I shove it back in my pocket. Nyx takes a seat beside me, leaning back on his arms as he looks up at the stars.

"No, I didn't feel like returning home and this seemed like the next best place. Father is in quite a mood. I did stop by your house though," he says, giving me a lazy smile.

"It's good to see all fathers seem to be the same, regardless if you're human or faerie. Did you look through my window mister?" I accuse him, I lay down beside him and look up at him. He keeps studying the stars, but I watch as his tongue runs over his lips and the way his eyes seem to take note of every detail.

"Do you expect me not to?"

"Well obviously, it's a bit creepy if you do." I take my hands out of my pockets and place them under my head. I look up at the stars and the moon, trying to find the constellations.

"Lucky I didn't then," he says, looking down at me. I resist the urge to reach up and trace the outline of his ear as the moonlight hits it. Instead I run it through my own hair roughly.

"I wasn't in my bedroom anyway, I decided to sleep on the couch tonight. Such a brilliant idea." I groan.

"Why's that?" He asks, resorting to laying down beside me with his head propped up on his hand. I roll on my side and watch him.

"Aunty and I had a little spat…she knows I'm—" I freeze, remembering he doesn't exactly know that I'm a seer. If Aunty was right, and he was looking for a seer…could he just be using me?

"Knows you're what?" he asks, puzzled.

"She knows I'm looking for a…partner. She didn't want me drawing the eye from you or your father in case your father got better ideas." It was the easiest lie that came to me, and I felt bad for it. Shock flashes across his face.

"You're looking for a partner?" He asks.

"Yes. But the options here are rather poor and boring, I just don't want to be tied down to this village. I want to travel and see the world, to experience everything I can. Good and bad." This is a truth that I'm glad to share with him, with someone who may understand how it feels.

"You find me poor and boring?" He teases, smirking at me. I grin at him.

"You're the only one who I *don't* find poor and boring, I find you rather painful instead." It's my turn to smirk as he bursts into rich laughter. It sends a new sort of warmth through me and moments later I find myself laughing along with him.

"Well Ravynne Morgan, I don't find you poor or boring either," he finally says, once the laughter has subsided. I smile shyly up at him, unsure if it was a good thing he thought that.

"Nyx, would you consider us friends?"

"Yes…I would," he says slowly. He looks at me cautiously, "Why do you ask?"

"Oh, because I was thinking about it the other day. I was trying to figure out when I began to consider you a friend and not a stranger," I say idly, picking at a piece of chipped nail. I resist the urge to chew at it.

"Hmm, probably from the moment you stripped down to your…you know. You remember." He coughs lightly. I grin up at him.

"Oh do enlighten, I don't think I recall?"

"Why are you being difficult?" He groans, looking down at me.

"Because it's fun."

His eyes flicker up the top of the river and his body goes rigid. He stands slowly and I frown up at him. "What are you doing?" I ask, sitting up.

"Shh. Come here," he whispers, reaching out a hand to me. I take it and don't complain when he pulls me behind him, crushing my body to his back. I wrap my arms around his waist and peer around his arm.

At the top of the river, in the faint moonlight I glimpse a set of golden eyes. The hair on my arms stands on end as I grip his shirt.

"This can't be happening," I mutter, jaw slack. This wasn't how the vision went, this wasn't even close. Had I missed something while wearing the necklace? Was there something I didn't know?

"Stay still and be quiet. It hasn't spotted us yet," Nyx whispers, leaning down so his breath touches my cheek. I clamp my mouth shut as we stand there, watching the large black creature move from one side of the river to the next, before it finally disappears into the thicker part of the forest.

We stay there for a few minutes, he stares intently at the space the creature disappeared.

"It's clear," he says, heaving a sigh of relief as he turns to face me. I loosen my grip on him as he does, coming face to face with him while my arms are still wrapped around him.

"What did you mean when you said this couldn't be happening?" He asks, looking down at me.

"I just meant that…" I try to think of something believable, and feel the blush already rising to my cheeks before the words even come out of me.

"I just thought that maybe we were having a moment before, and whatever that thing was ruined it…it was terrible timing on that creature's behalf," I say, fluttering a hand nervously between us. He gives me an amused look as he takes hold of my jittery hand, holding it in his own.

I watch in amazement as he winds our fingers together, squeezing lightly.

He could be using your affection to get the truth out of you, be careful.

"What was that thing?" I ask, diverting the attention back to a lighter subject. I wanted more than anything to hold his hand all night, because it was so warm and welcoming, but I knew better. I'd been raised better than to give in so easily.

"A babunook. They're a creature that never returned back to Faerie, and decided to dwell in the mountains. I'm surprised to see it here, it's been many moons since I've last sensed one here." He frowns, watching our hands.

"What do they eat?" I whisper.

"Children."

My blood runs cold, and my vision seems a hundred times more daunting now. Was the river red from the dead children? Would my brother be one of them?

"Gods," I whisper, looking back to where it had last made its presence known. Nothing disturbs the trees now, and in the distance the wildlife has begun to fill the night again. It was almost as if it had never been here.

"It's a horrid creature, terribly hard to kill as well." He shakes his head, the frown not leaving his face.

"Could you walk me home at all?" I ask, drawing his attention back to me. He lets go of my hand and I let my arm drop from around him, feeling far too cold now.

"Of course, come on," he says, offering me his arm once again. I take it, even though I think better of it. I stay close, and keep my ears open for any unnatural sounds as we make the walk back to the farm. But nothing happens and everything is still.

We reach the farm, and pause for a moment, both watching the house sit in darkness.

"Ravynne, don't feel like you ever have to be tied here. The word is far larger than you could imagine, don't settle for a village as small as this one," he says softly, looking down at me. I twist my lips but don't look up.

"I'll see you later Nyx, I appreciate you walking me home." I let go of his arm and slip into the yard without looking back. I trudge up the steps, suddenly extremely tired. I look back before I go inside and give him a small wave. He nods once before heading back up towards the village. I sigh as I lock the door behind me and strip the coat off.

I collapse onto the couch, having fitful dreams of Nyx and dying children.

In Elderview, everyone has the same routine day in and day out. For example, Ma goes to the bakery every morning a few hours after the sun rose with Aunty, they spend their entire day there and pick Kalin up from school on their way home in the late afternoon.

They do this every day of the week, the same routine and hardly ever break it. It has been a week since the offering, and everyone has gone back to their usual life.

Da is the same, he'll go out at the break of dusk and spend the day farming, only returning for lunch and once the sun has gone down.

Everyone in my village apart from me seems to have a routine, and now I sit on the couch thinking about this. No, I wasn't good at making anything. But *maybe* I could try and use my gift for the better.

Aunty never said I couldn't dabble with the visions, and what if it was something I was actually good at?

I unclasp the necklace and sit it down on the couch beside me, watching it, almost expecting a vision to assault me the moment it left my skin. But nothing happens.

I grab the necklace and head into my bedroom. I stuff it under my pillow before heading back downstairs. I whistle a tune as I make myself a cup of tea, adding a teaspoon of honey instead of sugar.

I stir the hot water as I think, I needed more information on the babunook and I had no way to contact Nyx and ask him for more information. I couldn't let the last vision I'd had come true, I had to try and prevent it.

I can't recall seeing any information in the book I'd read at the library, but since it's a faerie creature they might not be in any human folk lore books.

I was due to go into town today for Da, maybe I could convince him to let me go to the city on my own, I'm sure I'd be able to come up with a suitable lie. I could even meet up with Matt again, if he wasn't too upset over me never writing in the weeks I'd been home.

But if Nyx found out I'd be meeting with Matt, would he be mad? We were friends, and Nyx never mentioned anything more than that.

I finish the cup of tea and open the front door, finding a full bucket waiting for me. I slip into my boots and head into town. It has just reached midday, and clouds have begun to cover the sun. The start of winter wasn't as cruel as I'd thought it'd be, and maybe this winter might not be as bad as the last ones.

I trudge up the road, hauling the bucket beside me.

"Ravynne, may I ask you a question?" I look up, immediately annoyed as I see Jester coming towards me, note pad and pen in hand.

"What do you want?" I groan, sitting the bucket down once I reach even ground and the start of the village. I wipe the sweat away with back of my hand over my brow. He comes to a stop in front of me and has his pen ready to write.

"Word of mouth is you've been seen with the King's faerie son, can you confirm these rumours?" He asks, eyeing me.

"No," I snap.

He jots something down in scrawled writing, too messy for me to read but far too many words for that to be the answer to his question.

"Why did you talk at the offering?"

"Because he asked me a question and it felt rude to stay silent," I say, clenching my fists at my side. He ums and ahs as he writes more notes down.

"Is it true you've been conspiring with the son?"

"No! For goodness sake where is this rubbish coming from?" I say, resisting the urge to stamp my foot. Why was I always on trial for something in this village?

"Everyone. I've had multiple people come up to me with suspicions about you. I finally felt the overwhelming urge to know myself."

I feel my temples begin to thud, and my vision begins to go blurry at the corners. He gives me a puzzled look as I reach up and rub my left temple.

"Are you alright?" He asks. The thudding begins to grow worse, and my vision sways slightly and an image begins to appear ghost like over Jester.

Of all times, did I really have to get a vision now?

"I have to go," I mumble. I pick up the bucket and stagger away, swaying slightly with the energy it takes to keep the bucket in my hands without spilling it.

"Ravynne I'm not finished with you!" He calls. I shrug it off, needing to find a safe place to go, and fast. I find the tree I usually stop at, sheltered from the prying eyes of the village. I go around to the base of it that hides in the shade and sit down, keeping the bucket between my legs and my hands on the handle.

I look ahead and stifle a groan as the forest disappears and is replaced by something far more sinister.

Nyx paces back and forth in the tavern bedroom where he'd taken me when I'd had a few too many to drink. He runs his hands vigorously through his hair as his long legs carry him from one end of the room to the other.

Various pieces of furniture lay broken around the room. I am merely peering into this vision. I'm not here and he can't sense me.

"God damn it, I've been so blind," he growls to himself. He finally comes to a stop and takes a few steadying breaths. He looks towards

the ceiling and pinches the bridge of his nose with his thumb and forefinger.

"I can't let her do this, she's mad. Utterly mad, and she'll no doubt be killed in the process. I can't let her walk to her death, no matter how much she may think she deserves it," he mumbles.

"What will you do?" A reedy voice comes from the bathroom, as the door creaks open a small creature looks out. Its long white fingers wrap around the frame of the door as it pulls it open.

It was only half a metre tall, its nose as long as a parsnip and skin as saggy as my grandma had been once she'd reached a ripe age. It looks at Nyx with large green eyes, far too big for its almost bald head; having only a hair or two sticking out on the top.

"I have to help her, obviously," Nyx replies, looking down at the creature. Its long arms are skinny, but as twice as long as its body. It walks on feet that face the wrong way as it goes over to him, resting a hand on his shin.

"You would be foolish to do that for a mortal human, boy," It says sympathetically.

"I've learnt that maybe being mortal is far more of a luxury than we think it is," he replies, sighing.

"You could very well get killed as well, you know this, correct?" The creature asks, looking up at him. He looks down at it, more determined than I'd ever seen him.

"If it was to save the girl I love, I would go the ends of Earth and

back to keep her safe."

I blink, shading my eyes against the now bright sun. I'd grown accustomed to the dim room and the darkened corner I'd been planted in.

Was Nyx talking about me to that thing?

If so…what sort of trouble am I heading for?

I try and shake the thoughts off as I pull myself up from the tree, grabbing the handle of the bucket. I move out and mingle with the crowd, relieved that no one gives me a second glance.

I go into the farming shop and sit the bucket down on the counter. The same man comes out and gives me a crooked smile.

"Ravynne, how are you?" he asks, opening the lid and grabbing his wooden spoon.

"I'm good sir. How are you?" I ask politely, keeping a small smile plastered on my face.

"Good, good. Did you hear about the new teacher at the school?" he asks, looking up at me. I frown slightly, Elderview isn't a village where we have 'new' people arrive. We don't have new people, we have the folk that had grown up here and that is it.

"No…when did they arrive?" I ask, crossing my arms over my chest. Ma would hopefully know more and I could pry her for details once she returned home, maybe even Kalin could give me some information.

"The day of the offering actually, was as if the King blessed us with him. Seems like a good lad." He nods a few times, but I can tell he doesn't quite believe it. I can't blame him, the King has never sent us a blessing even though he may say he will.

"Have you spoken to him?" I want to delve into more questions, but he gives me a slightly annoyed glance before sitting the bucket down on his side of the counter.

"Twice, he came in looking for wild berries. How weird, right?" He snorts, wild berries didn't bloom in Elderview, and if they did it was extremely rare and hard to come by. You'd be more likely getting wild berries in Orrinshire.

"That is weird," I mumble, gathering up the twelve gold coins. I pocket two for myself, Da could make it work with ten. I nod goodbye as I slip out of the shop and head home.

A new vision and a new person in the village…what are the gods trying to tell me?

☾

I finish washing up the last dishes from dinner, my tummy swollen and warm from the roast chicken and vegetables Ma had made. It is a cooler night tonight, and I'd dressed in wool pants and a long sleeve tee.

I sit the tea towel on the bench and head into the living room, happy to find the smell of the roast had decided to cling to the air in here as well. I find Ma and Aunty on the couch while Kalin does his homework on the mat. I squeeze in beside them, resting my head on Ma's shoulder.

"Where's Da?" I ask, watching as Kalin colours something in furiously.

"Just locking the goat up," she says, nibbling at a cookie from a batch she'd made at the bakery that hadn't sold. I steal one off the plate in her lap and take a bite. Aunty sits beside us in deep silence as she concentrates on knitting a sweater.

"I heard there's a new teacher in town," I say coolly, not wanting to give my curiosity away.

"Yes there is, I met him a few days ago actually. He seems nice, rather funny he arrives when the King gives us his blessings, maybe he's come through for us this time," Ma muses, leaning her cheek on the top of my head.

"He's really nice," Kalin says, looking up at me.

"How so?"

"He comes from a village in mountains far from here, and said he would bring his dog to class this week for us to see!" He exclaims, his legs swing back and forth in the air and he goes back to his drawing, sticking his tongue out in concentration.

"Hm, fair enough I suppose," I mumble, feeling slightly tired. I was surprised I hadn't heard of him sooner, but considering I've become quite the hermit it shouldn't be a shock.

"He's rather nice looking, if you don't mind me saying." Ma says.

"Maaa," I groan, sitting up on the couch. Aunty snorts a laugh but says nothing more.

"What? He is! Dark hair and gold eyes, I have to wonder which town he's come from because he certainly isn't from around here. I could imagine half the girls in the village would be swooning after him." She chuckles, finishing off her biscuit. I steal the last one on the plate and take a bite, I'd have to meet this new teacher and prove to myself I had nothing to worry about, that it was a normal thing to move to a different town and start fresh.

That reminded me.

"Ma, is it alright if I go to Orrinshire for a few days? I was thinking of leaving tomorrow," I ask, looking at her. She frowns as she looks over at me, "What on earth do you want to do there?"

"When I was there last I really took a liking to the library, and I was going to see if there was any way I could maybe make something out of it." The lie slips off my tongue, although I most likely would be visiting the library while I was there. I had to see what I could find, and see if there was some way to learn more about my power. I had a feeling I'd need them.

"Does Darren know?" Aunty asks, the clicking of her needles stills as she finally looks up at me.

"No, but I'll tell him tomorrow. I don't see why I can't go by myself, I am of age now." I point a finger at both of them. Ma sighs and Aunty gives me a warning glance.

"I know you are Ravynne, but it just worries me. What of the men there? You would be all alone in that large city," she says, resting a worried hand on my own.

"I know Ma, but I can't stay cooped up here forever. I'm no use here and if I can find something to do with myself that I enjoy, I want to try it. And there also might be a love interest for me there, if I wish to pursue it," I say, immediately thinking of Nyx but actually meaning Matt.

"A love interest? Why didn't you say so sooner!" She gasps, slapping my hand lightly.

"Because I didn't think it was a big deal, he's a farmer's son and I met him at the markets actually. He's really nice, and cute too." I hear Aunty mutter something under her breath, so I reach out and pinch her arm when Ma looks away.

She slaps me in turn, which makes me swing my leg into hers.

"Gah!" She shouts, giving me a frustrated look. She repositions herself on the couch, not touching me.

"Well, make sure you're careful Ravynne and remember you don't give your maidenhood away to anyone who—"

I jump up, not needing to have this conversation for the billionth time since I'd been of the age where kissing had become a big thing.

"Yes Ma, trust me I know. It's still mine to keep," I assure her, feeling my cheeks go red. I yawn before reaching back and pulling my hair up into a high bun. It was only early into the night but if I was to leave tomorrow I'd need as much rest as I could get. I wouldn't be taking the cart, which meant I'd have to try my hand at riding.

"Good girl, Rav. Make sure you tell Da, I'm sure he won't mind sparing a gold for a room if you ask nicely. I'll cook up a batch of cookies and a few danishes." She rises from her seat and gives me a quick hug, I wrap my arms around her thin form.

"Thank you Ma," I say, giving her cheek a kiss once she lets me go.

"Of course honey, anything for my girl. Now go and get some sleep." She shoo's me away as she heads into the kitchen, singing softly to herself as she begins to bake. I reach down and plant a kiss on Kalin's head, ruffling his hair up as I stand back up.

"Goodnight. Love you."

"Love you too sissy," he says, not looking up. I turn to see Aunty staring at me.

"Be careful on your journey Ravynne, you might find answers you're not ready for yet." She looks back down and continues to knit, as if she hadn't said anything to me. I nod once and climb up the stairs, "Love you Ma!" I shout down once I reach the bedroom door.

"Love you too, Rav!" She calls back up.

I click the door shut behind me and pull the wool pants off, enjoying the coolness of the sheets on my bare legs. I get snuggled in and reach under my pillow, holding the necklace in my hand.

I may not be ready for answers, but I was going to get them regardless.

I head downstairs, dressed in a white button up shirt with black skin tight pants, mainly used for riding. I'd thrown my hair back in a high bun and had the necklace clasped around my neck. I had my saddle bag ready, with a few dresses, a change of undergarments and the few toiletries I'd need.

I'd seen Da in the early morning and told him of me leaving. He'd given me two golds for the trip which was more than enough if I was smart with the money.

On the kitchen table I find a bag of cookies and the dried leftover meat from last's night's roast. I put them in the bag and head out of the house, slipping on my boots and a large wool coat as I go. I head across the road to the Densley's, hoping they'd only charge one gold for the few days.

I go to walk up the stairs when I see Mike talking to a man I haven't seen before. His dark hair is combed back, set with some sort of cream. At the sound of my approach they both turn around, and the stranger pins me with his golden eyes.

I falter a step, those eyes. Where had I seen those eyes before? Regardless, he's quiet handsome. This must be the new teacher.

He is taller than Mike, and has a crisp black suit on, with his white undershirt peeking out.

"Ravynne, what're you doing here?" Mike asks, looking around the stranger. I draw my eyes away from him and look at Mike, he has his arms crossed over his chest and is on guard.

"Hi, I'm needing a horse for a few days again but with a saddle as I'll be riding," I say, gripping my hands together in front of me.

"My apologies my lady, if I had known such a beautiful young woman was waiting I would have taken my leave much earlier," the stranger says, half bowing as his eyes rake over my body. I feel my neck begin to burn from his stare, I wave him off.

"That's alright, no need to apologise. You were here before me," I say, offering him a smile. His lips twitch as he looks back to Mike.

"Well, it was nice to meet you. We'll discuss matters other times," he clips, giving Mike's hand a hard shake. I take a few steps back so he can step past me. As he pauses in front of me, lavender and crushed mulberries assault my senses.

"Ravynne is it?" He asks, taking my hand gently in his.

"Ye-yes it is," I stutter, looking into his eyes dumbfounded. He's charming, handsome, but there's something *off* about him. As if this skin isn't his own.

"It's been lovely to make your acquaintance. I wish you safe travels and look forward to your return." He brings his lips to the back of my hand and plants a warm kiss there. He lets go of my hand and nods once to Mike before heading back towards town, striding with his shoulders back.

"What on earth just happened?" I ask, looking back to Mike.

"He was hitting on you, Rav," Mike says, rolling his eyes. I brush it off, avoiding looking back towards where he had gone.

"Did you get his name?" I ask, shaking the weird feeling from my mind. My hand where he'd kissed still burns, as if he'd left something on my skin behind.

"Yes, it was something weird though. Do you mind which horse you take?" He asks, wiping his hands on his shirt.

"Whichever is cheapest. I only have four golds and it has to last me while I'm away. I should only be gone for a week, if not less," I assure him. He nods and nibbles his bottom lip.

"Alright, I'll bring the mare out." He disappears into the house and I walk down to the yard and wait.

The stranger still lingers in my mind…I'd need to get to know him better before I made any final judgements about him, but his compliment did have me blushing like a new teen again. How absurd.

I hear the familiar snort of a horse and turn to see Mike leading a white mare towards me. In the middle of her forehead is a black patch of fur that is funnily in the shape of a crescent moon.

"She's so stunning," I say, coming up to her. She sniffs my hand before nudging it, I scratch behind her ears. She's wearing a black bridle with silver star decorations, the same as her saddle.

"She's a good one, I'll only charge you one gold for her. I'd rather you be safe than sorry," he says. I dig into my pocket and pull out the gold coin as he hands me the reins.

"Need help getting it on?" He asks with a smirk. He pockets the gold coin and comes around to the left side of her. I sigh in defeat.

"How will I possibly get on her without you?" I coo. I wrap my hands around the horn of the saddle and slip my foot into the stirrup. Mike gently places his hands on my hips as he shoves me up, I swing my other leg over easily and get comfortable.

"I'm not sure how you've lasted this long without me honestly." He says, with a hint of longing in his voice. I give him a tight lipped smile as I adjust the saddle bag. Some days, I didn't know either.

"Thank you Mike, I'll return her in one piece."

"Be safe Ravynne. Return in one piece as well."

I kick her into a walk and head down towards the river, she answers easily and a little more eager than I expect. She must want to get out of this village as much as I do. I look over my shoulder once more and stare at the castle. Would Nyx be there now? Would he be in the city?

This journey is also going to help me get over the crush I'd formed for him, it would never work between us. We came from two different worlds, literally and although I'm fond of his company, I could never fit into his world.

"I'm going to name you Luna," I say down to her, giving her neck a quick pat. She knickers in response and moves her head up in down, as if agreeing.

"Well Luna, it's just us. And it seems I've forgotten my sleeping bag so it's going to be a rough two nights." I sigh, but don't feel too upset about this. I can use the saddlebag as a pillow, and I'd dressed warmly. I'd be fine.

As the day goes on, the view gets more breathtaking. We canter along the dirt road, and I watch the snow-capped mountains in the distance with awe. It had snowed a few times in the village, and the mountains on either side always had the tell-tale snow caps once it was cold. That's how you knew it was winter, and that it was going to be a cruel one.

I pull Luna into a walk. The sun is on the brink of the horizon, casting purple and pink hues throughout the sky. I walk her over to the familiar spot where Da always stop, hop down and tie her to the tree. I walk over to the old fire pit and use the few tools I have with me to start a small fire, once comfortable I lay down and watch as stars begin to cover the night sky.

☾

The two day journey goes quickly, as it always does. We arrive in Orrinshire on the second day as the sun goes down, a few of the city folk give me an odd look as we ride through. It was a rare sight to see a young woman travelling by herself, not that the city was full of crime, but there had been too many incidents to just brush it off.

I ride through the city, not wanting to stay at any of the taverns I'd previously been to before. I wanted something new, and somewhere away from all the bluster and noise. I head towards the farmer's market, hoping something would catch my eye near the river.

"Ravynne?" A hesitant voice says from behind me. I pull Luna to a stop and turn her around, Matt walks towards us with a lantern in his hand.

"I thought it was you, but wow this horse is a beauty," he says, coming to a stop in front of us. He lowers the lantern and looks up at me. I feel a small amount of shame for not writing.

"Hey Matt, how are you?" I ask, fiddling with the reins.

"I'm good, what are you doing back here so late?" He asks, peering around looking to see if I'd been accompanied by anyone.

"I only just got here and I'm looking for a place to stay. I'm planning on staying a few days, mainly spending my time in the library really." I swipe my hand over my left ear automatically as if I had a strand of loose hair annoying me.

"Oh that's lovely, have you found a place yet?" He queries.

"No not yet, but I'm sure I'll spot something soon. I didn't want to stay in the usual taverns." I sigh, the sun's beginning to set and the buildings are casting dark shadows along the ground. Luna is cautious, snorting nervously as they grow with each minute that passes. I'd have to get off her soon and lead her around.

"You could stay at mine? I insist actually, and if it's horrible you can go to a tavern," he declares, smiling up at me.

"Are you sure? How much did you want?" He did mention last time I was here that his parents had a cottage at the back of their house, that would be prefect if I was planning to bring back books to read.

"Free of charge. You're a friend and I wouldn't charge a friend. Come, follow me. It's not far from here." He begins to walk to the wooden bridge that sits over the river.

"Thank you so much," I say, clicking to Luna. She follows grumpily, swiping her tail up to whip me as she goes. Such a moody thing.

"How did you know it was me?" I ask, focusing on the muscles that move under his shirt as he walked.

"The hair mainly, I haven't seen a girl with hair as long as yours in the city before."

"I'm going to take that as a compliment." I laugh, he chuckles along.

"Of course it is."

"So, where are you taking me exactly?" I ask as we reach the other side of the river. On this side of the city it is way more overrun by nature, there is more grass and more trees and shrubs. We begin to make a trek slightly up hill, reminding me of home.

"To my house. If you'd like tomorrow I can set you up in my parent's cottage. It isn't far from here either." He says, looking over his shoulder at me. "It's nothing fancy, but it is cosy and there's a small paddock you can keep your mare."

We come to a stop outside of a small cottage. Vines cover the wooden fence and gate. I stop Luna and hop off, holding her reins in my hand. He opens up the gate and I walk through, Luna whinnies gently as she pushes against me.

"We'll take her out the back first," he says. We walk across the grass and down the side of the cottage. When we reach the back yard he opens a metal gate. In the paddock sits a water trough, a round bale and shelter.

"Thank you." I pass him the reins as I undo her saddle. I swing it over the gate and take the bridal off next. I give her a pat before she walks over to the bale.

"It's alright. Let's go inside, it's getting chilly out here." I follow him to the back door of the cottage. He puts the lantern out as he opens the wooden door. I slip past him and look around. We're in a small hall lit with a lantern.

I walk deeper into the house, finding the living room and kitchen connected as one. On the left side there's a brick fireplace with a wood holder beside it and a dark brown couch, while opposite it is a small oak varnished kitchen.

"Wow, it's so nice in here," I say, turning back to him. He goes over to the fire and begins to load wood into it.

"I built it myself actually, I was never a fan of huge houses." He gives me a crooked grin as the fire ignites, under the couch is a large red mat. He stands and walks into the kitchen.

"Are you hungry? I can get a dinner ready?" He asks, opening the fridge.

"Um yeah, that would be lovely actually. Is it okay if I just sleep on the couch?" I ask, looking back over to it.

"Oh I was going to give you my room, it's just down the hall on the right. The bathroom is connected to it." His blonde hair falls into his eyes as he pulls out a few strips of meat and some salad.

"I couldn't take your room. I'll be fine on the couch," I say shyly, not feeling a hundred percent comfortable sleeping in a man's bed.

I go to the couch and shrug the saddle bag off, resting it against the side. I strip out of my coat and lay it over the couch, it would work well as a blanket and with the fire so close I doubt I'd be cold.

"So, how has everything been?" He asks. I roll the sleeves of my shirt up and sit down, pulling my boots off.

"Busy. I'm sorry I didn't have the chance to write, everything just seemed so full on when I got back and we had a ceremony to attend and everyone went half mad getting prepared."

"Oh that's no good, what sort of ceremony?"

"A silly one." I leave it at that and lean back, letting the plushness of the couch half consume me. Ma's couch wasn't half this comfortable.

"Fair enough, I hated being dragged to things similar to that when I was a kid," he says as he comes over, carrying two plates of cooked meat and salad. I nod thanks as he passes me a plate and fork, opting to sit on the floor and lean his back against the couch.

"So did I, you're lucky you live alone here," I say, digging into the salad. Outside the wind picks up, roaring through the small gaps in the two windows that sit beside the front door.

"In a few ways. It gets lonely though. I should have added another room to it." He shakes his head.

"Could always expand," I say between chewing. It was so nice to have some fresh food, and a comfy place to sleep.

"One day, maybe. Do you live with your family?" He asks, looking over his shoulder at me.

"Yes I do. I wanted to move, but I'm no good at anything. I just help with the farm wherever I can." I say, finishing off the last bits of meat.

"I'm sure you're good at something," he says, pointing his fork at me.

"Trust me, I wish I was." I feel a laugh bubble at my lips, and he grins in return.

"Riding a horse. That's one thing." He raises an eyebrow and I wack his shoulder softly. He stands up and takes the empty plate from me, going into the kitchen.

"Thank you for dinner." I look over at the kitchen as he washes the dishes up. I can feel the exhaustion setting in, and my legs have begun to ache. I hadn't ridden a horse for so long in my entire life.

"That's alright, I'll just grab you a pillow." He flashes me a smile before going into the hallway, returning a moment later with a dark blue pillow. He passes it to me and I fluff it up, resting it at the base of the couch.

"I'll probably crash and burn now, thank you again for this," I say, settling onto the couch. I rest my hands on my stomach as I look up at the roof.

"Sleep well Ravynne," he says, turning the lanterns off. The fire crackles, its light dim around me. I turn on my side and tuck my hands under my head, my eyes flutter shut as I begin to grow sleepy.

Only then, do I realise my hand was still warm from the strangers kiss.

11

I head into the same section of the library from when I'd first been here, and I'm pleasantly surprised to find Nyx standing there with a leather book in his hand. He flips the yellow pages back and forth, skimming the pages with his hand. He hasn't noticed me standing there yet, and I don't make my presence known. He lets out a frustrated sigh as he closes the book, shoving it back in the small space of the bookshelf. Butterflies erupt in my stomach as I watch him concentrate, the fringe of his hair falls over his eyes and I itch to push it back from his face.

"Do you always shove things into small places roughly like that?" I ask, cocking my head to the side. He jumps slightly and looks at me, half startled.

"Ravynne, goodness you scared me," he says, before eyeing me.

"What are you doing here?"

I shrug, "Probably the same thing you are." I point to the books he'd been looking at. I was technically here to get more information on how to unlock my other abilities, but I could also have a look for that creature.

"What's wrong with your hand?" He asks, frowning at it. I lower it and look at it, the burning had stopped and turned into a tingling sensation, as if I'd sat on my foot for too long.

"Oh, nothing. I think I brushed up against poison ivy or stinging nettle." I brush his concern off and walk over to him, the dark blue skirts of my dress swim around me as I stop beside him and scan the books.

"What are you doing here?" I ask, pulling out a random book. I rub the dust off the cover, *A Tale of the Mountains.*

"Research," he says, looking over my shoulder and reading the title. I suck at my lip before putting it back on the shelf. I run my hand over the other titles, it'd be silly to have hope there'd be a book solely for seers.

"Like wise."

"Is something wrong?" I look over my shoulder and find him right behind me which causes me to tilt my head back. I pout my lips, I feel fine, but I was trying to stop feeling these fleeting emotions when I was around him.

"Nothing, just tired from the journey." Which is a half-truth, and

I'm glad that humans can lie in this moment. It's a downfall being able to, but also a blessing.

"When did you arrive?" He asks, his eyes look over my face as if searching for something and suddenly the air begins to fill with static electricity. This was far more than friendly.

"Yesterday," I say, breathlessly.

"I didn't think I'd be seeing you for a while," he says. Out of the corner of my eye I see his hand twitch, and wonder if he wants to stroke my cheek.

"I didn't either, but somehow the universe has a way of pushing us back together," I say softly. I break his stare and look back at the books.

"Indeed it does." He mumbles, taking a step back. The electricity in the air evaporates. I pull down a few books that look promising and turn to see him studying a book on the other side of the aisle.

"Care to join me?" I ask, he gives me a warm smile as he grabs the book from the shelf.

"Would be my pleasure."

He follows me to a table in the back, and I'm thankful it's once again empty here. Did no one use this library, did the city people even know it exists? I sit the books down and take a seat. He drops into the chair beside me, spreading his legs out casually.

"What would the city folk think of a nobleman dallying with a village girl like me?" I tease, reaching out to bump my foot against his. He's wearing finery, like usual. His hair had grown slightly, and curled at the base of his neck now. The collar of his white shirt had a golden wyvern pin in place, representing his father's royal seal.

"What they think wouldn't concern me," he says, leaning in close to me. I watch in awe as his fringe falls against his forehead and the light strikes it perfectly, illuminating the darker strands from the lighter ones.

"Well it should," I say, looking back down to the books. He huffs as I grab the first one off the pile and open it. A book of fairy tale creatures.

"There's a new person in town," I say casually, flipping through the texts and images. His shoulder brushes mine as he leans his elbow against the table, I move the book in the middle of us so we can both read.

"Why does that seem important?" He asks, stopping on a page. The illustration says 'bogs', with a picture of an ugly creature underneath it.

"Because Elderview doesn't just get new people, we never get new people actually. Not in my whole twenty years. He seems nice enough though." I sigh, wishing I could shake the feeling he'd left on me off.

"What's he like?" He asks, flipping pages again.

"Um, nice? He kissed my hand when I first met him, which was when I rented the horse for the journey here. It was sort of weird, I've never had a man do that before." I feel the frown form on my forehead as my eyes wander down to my hand, the one he'd kissed.

"That is weird, I should have done that the first time," he says. I bump his shoulder as I break into a smile.

"You did a step better, you helped me up."

"That's only because you asked me to." He huffs, blowing the hair from his forehead.

"Oh please you *wanted* to. Why else would you stand there and just look down at me?" I ask, holding my hand out on a page that's caught my eye. *Faeries*. Under the title is an illustration of a faerie, with fangs and hollow eyes and long claws.

"Because you took my breath away, and no we do not look like that," he muses, pointing at the picture. But all I can think about is the first part of what he'd said. I look at him, mouth half hanging open. He looks up at me and leans his head to the side, a smile playing on his lips.

"What?"

"You confuse me," I finally say, I heave a breath and look back down at the faerie. The first part of the text begins with a warning about faeries.

"So, what exactly are you looking for? You never said." Nyx asks. I half shrug.

"Something to do with that creature obviously." I huff, scanning the text of what a faerie's attributes are. The one in the photo is terrifying, but Nyx didn't resemble it in any way, was he a different type?

"If you say so."

"I do." I continue to flip through the pages, now slightly irritated at him. I'd have to take some of these books back to the cottage with me and read them after Matt has gone to sleep.

I stop the page when I see the title.

Seer.

Nyx goes still beside me, and I run my hand down the page gently. The photo was of a young woman in robes, with black depthless eyes and a moon pendant around her throat. Similar to the one I am currently wearing.

My hand goes up to the drawing, I skim over the bits of information I already know and hesitate on the pieces I don't. I can feel Nyx staring at me, so I flip the page as if unbothered and continue on.

We sit in the library for hours going through each book we can find in hopes it might hold something worth our knowledge. I slam the final book shut, shoving it away in frustration.

"This is never going to work, why would humans have information on a faerie creature? If we want to know more you need to go to your little fairy land and find a library." I join my hands in the air and flutter my fingers out like wings, pushing them in his face to annoy him. He swats my hands away, half scowling at me.

"It isn't as simple as just going to fairy land," he whispers, looking around cautiously before looking back to me with warning. I lift my gaze to see three men of nobility talking to the librarian, one of them has their eyes on us.

"What is it?" I whisper back, I grab the closest book and open it between us, leaning far too close to Nyx. He loops his arm casually over my shoulder as he leans in, causing my heart to pick up speed as I'm swallowed with the scent of fresh forest and vanilla.

"They've been looking for me all morning and I find I'm not in the mood to deal with them right now."

"Who are they though?" I look back up, the man still looks through squinted eyes. He taps the man beside him and mutters something, causing them all to look our way.

"Members of the royal guard here, they associate with the ruler of this city and well let's just say they're growing agitated with my frequent visits." He drums his fingers against my shoulder, as if listening to music and going along with the beat.

"Why do you visit so much? Secret lover?" I ask, tilting my head away from his so I can look at him. He raises an eyebrow at me.

"Wouldn't you like to know."

He doesn't answer the question.

"Gentlemen, what a lovely surprise," he says, looking up with a cocky grin on his face. I look up to see the three men standing in front of our table. They're all dressed in black uniforms with golden stitching on the cuffs.

"Nyx, we've been looking for you all morning, your presence is requested," the one in the middle says, his eyes flicker to me and I keep the scowl from my face; they must be wondering what a person of nobility is doing with someone as unworthy as me.

"As you can see, my presence is also needed here." He leans back in his chair but keeps his arm around me. I reach up for his hand and intertwine our fingers together, liking how they fit.

"I'm sorry, I do apologise for keeping him from you. He did promise to spend the day with me here as he's quite busy tomorrow," I say softly, giving an impish smile in Nyx's direction before looking at each of the men.

"Where are my manners? I'm Maia, lady of Oakhold." I extend my free hand, the man in the middle hesitates before giving it a shake.

"Oakhold? I've never heard of that city before," he says, dropping my hand.

"I like my women unique, as you can see for yourself." Nyx looks over me slowly, taking each inch of me in and I find it hard to believe the wanting in his eyes is all for show.

"Of course, but what shall we tell his majesty?" The guard asks, looking back to Nyx; who half shrugs and waves his hand in the air.

"I'm sure you'll think of something, now hurry along please, I have important matters to get back to." He keeps his eyes on mine as he says this, not paying the guards any more attention. I find myself caught up in his stare and I'm vaguely aware that the guards grumble something before leaving reluctantly.

"Important matters?" I question, licking my lips slowly. His hand tightens on mine.

"Yes, convincing you I don't have wings and if I did I certainly wouldn't flap them like you tried to." He teases, he lets go of my hand and runs it through his hair. I feel the sweet taste of disappointment and look back to the open book, embarrassed. My neck begins to heat up, as do my cheeks and my goodness it is suddenly hot in here.

"Yes well, I actually have to get going. I'm only here until tomorrow, so I might see you before I head home." I stand abruptly from the table, wanting nothing more than to flee.

"Are you okay?" He asks, looking up at me and half reaching out. He stops himself before he does and lowers his hand. I force a smile.

"Yeah, of course. It was nice seeing you again." I gather a few random books and hold them to my chest, I don't look back as I begin to walk up to the librarian.

Outside, rain pours down. I'd been too caught up in my own world to realise, I sigh as I sit the books on the counter. Looks like they'd be staying here.

I push through the doors and walk straight into the rain, I don't bother to try and shield the wild droplets or the cold wind. It helps ground me, almost wakes me from the hot fever Nyx had seemed to put me in.

"Ravynne, wait!" I pause and look over my shoulder. He takes a few steps out into the rain and stops, breathing heavy.

"I'd like to redeem one of your debts you owe me," he declares. I frown at him.

"Now?" I ask, waving my hand in the rain.

"Yes, if you wouldn't mind."

"Try your best." I lower my hand and watch as he silently debates with himself for a moment.

"Kiss me."

I feel my jaw go slack.

"What did you just say?"

He takes a step towards me.

"Kiss me."

I feel the battle of wanting to stay and to leave begin, if I did this it wouldn't be because of a debt I owed him. On the other hand, I could convince myself this is solely because of the debt and it was one less thing that could tie me to him.

"Okay," I whisper. It was just going to be a kiss, and mean nothing. I can't let it mean anything. I close the distance between us and look up at him, water droplets run down his face and drip from his eyelashes as he tilts his head down towards me. I reach up and rest my hands on the side of his face, gently rubbing my thumbs across his smooth skin. He looks down at me with wonder in his eyes.

I close my own as I reach up and press my lips against his, they're soft and warm and this kiss is different to the first one we'd shared.

His hands go to my waist as he pulls me to him, before he reaches up and holds the back of my neck with his hand.

Our lips move together gently, cautiously.

He pulls back and we're both breathless and my legs are trembling, my hands would be shaking if they weren't holding his face.

"Thank you." He lets go of me and I feel all the warmth leave my body. I step back and run a finger across my lips. He clears his throat before averting his eyes to the ground.

"Safe travels, Ravynne."

I keep my head high as I turn and head for the cottage, letting the rain wash away the hot tears that now slide down my face. How am I meant to convince myself that was only a kiss and nothing more?

12

"I would really rather not," I groan, leaning my chin on my palm as I watch Matt fix the buttons up on his blue long sleeve shirt. "Come on, it's your last night in Orrinshire. Let's go have a few drinks and a dance, you're dressed for the occasion." He looks up and his eyes trail over the dress I'm wearing. I look down at it, the waist is tight and flares out at my hips. Its straps are off my shoulder, and the white lace design of the bodice exposes more of my breasts than I'd care to admit. It's a lovely dress, although for someone more daring than I.

"You think me, getting drunk in this, is a good idea?" I ask, tapping my fingers on my cheek. He grins as he looks at me with a new shine in his eyes.

"Well, we're going to find out. Now come along, the night is fleeting!" He comes over and links his arm with mine, swinging me towards the door. I laugh as I grab onto his arm, I had a gold coin in my dress pocket in case I needed it.

We walk into the thicker area of where all the taverns are, an area not even I had dared venture too. The music from each tavern drifts out into the crowded street, a muddled harmony.

"Which is the best?" I ask, looking from each open door to the next.

"Big Sal's is the best," he says, smiling at people as we walk by them. I keep a small smile on my face, I just had to hope Nyx wasn't going to be here. Ahead of us, a large red sign is propped in the street reading Big Sal's.

We go up the stairs and through the door, a thin layer of cigar smoke hangs in the air along with the stench of mead. I scrunch my nose up as he takes my hand in his and leads me towards the bar.

"Two meads please!" he shouts over the music to the bartender, I look over to my left to where a man with a banjo plucks out a tricky tune. A man with a flute begins to play and the other band members join in. I tap my foot along to the fast beat, the other people in the tavern begin to do the same. A few dance at the front of the stage, swinging and skipping and kicking their legs out.

Maybe tonight isn't going to be so bad after all.

Matt leads us to an empty table, with a clear view of the band. I take a sip of the mead, thankful for the cool drink.

"Thank you for this," I say, sitting the cup down. The band begins to play a new song, singing along this time to the flute and banjo.

"It's no worries, I just want you to enjoy your last night here. How are things at home?" He asks, watching the band as well.

"Yeah they're fine, some man moved into town and I don't know…this may sound silly but there's something off about him," I say, looking over at him.

"If it's a gut instinct it might not be a bad thing to trust it, usually your body knows before your mind." He smiles at me, drinking.

"Mm that's true I suppose. Do you think I could just be overthinking it?"

"You don't seem like the type of person to over think, if he worries you just try to avoid him. You might have a reason to fear him." He sculls the rest of his cup, "Do you want another?"

I look down at my half empty glass. "Yes please." He stands and leaves, and I quickly finish the rest. I didn't feel any better after mentioning the stranger. What if Matt's right? What if there is something to fear about them?

"Here's one for milady," he sings, setting the glass down. I roll my eyes and we clink cups, taking a few deep swallows.

"Do you do this often?" I ask, gesturing around the tavern.

"Not often, but sometimes I do come here with a few of the guys from work after a long day. Do you drink much?"

"Ah no, the last time I was in Orrinshire I had one too many and Nyx actually rescued me from a rather scary situation." I look down at the cup and run my finger around the rim of glass.

"Oh, so that's how you know him." He frowns.

"What is it?" I ask, curious.

"He just walked in…with a woman." I immediately look in the direction Matt is looking to indeed find Nyx moving through the crowd with a rather stunning woman on his arm. Her long blonde hair curls at the ends as it swirls around her.

My heart jams itself in my throat.

"Good for him," I grumble, bringing the glass to my lips. Nyx finds them a table and holds a seat out for her, she smiles shyly as she takes it; tucking her hair behind her jewelled ear.

Her red dress hugs her chest nicely, with puffy cupped straps hanging onto the edge of her shoulders. She laughs at something he says as he sits down, facing my direction. I look down with a frown, I can't let this ruin my night. We were friends, and that's all.

I hadn't expressed feeling anything more and neither had he.

But the kiss.

No.

The kiss was simply repaying a debt.

"My shout," I say, forcing a smile on my face. Matt gives me a sympathetic one as I slip away from the table and make my way to the bar. I lean against the counter.

"Four meads please," I say sweetly to the man behind the bar. His eyes flicker to my cleavage and back to my face; his cheeks go a light pink as he hurries to make the drinks.

"Two meads please," a very familiar male voice says to my left. I force myself to keep my eyes on the stained bar mat, paying extra attention to the red stain.

"Are you just going to ignore me?" Nyx asks, moving closer to me. Out of the corner of my eye he leans against the bar, resting his chin on his palm as he watches me.

I say nothing.

"What have I done to earn a cold shoulder?" He prods. I look up from the mat to were my bartender finishes making the four glasses of mead. I smile with relief as he comes towards me; sitting them on a black circle tray.

I slide my gold coin over.

"Oh no, no ma'am. The drinks are on the house," he says, blushing furiously again. He can't be older than me, and certainly seems younger.

"Oh. Well thank you, that's awfully kind." I give him my warmest smile as I slide my coin back into my pocket.

"So you'll talk to him and not me? And four glasses of mead, we aren't going to have a repeat of the last time you had too many to drink are we?" Nyx muses. I bite my tongue to stop a reply and swiftly turn away from him with the tray in hand, I head back to where Matt sits; another two men now sit at our table.

"Ravynne, this is Nic and Tom." He gestures to the two of them.

One reaches out a hand towards me. I sit the tray down and take his large hand, feeling the callouses on his palm.

"I'm Nic, it's nice to meet you." His pot gut rests against the table and strains the buttons of his red and white checked shirt. His brown eyes are kind, and nearly hidden beneath his bushy eyebrows. He runs his hand over his bald head.

"Lovely to meet you as well," I say, taking my two drinks from the tray.

"Obviously I'm Tom," the other says, grinning at me. His green eyes are glassy from drinking, and the smell of cigar clings to him but I pay no attention to it. His brown hair seems long, but it's hard to tell as he's pulled it back into a low bun.

"We work together," Matt clarifies. I zone out and as they launch back into conversation about work, I feel the heat of Nyx's eyes. I force myself not to look in the direction of his table, the band changes to a much faster beat song.

I pinch my nose as I scull my first mead. I clamp my hand over my mouth as I slam the cup down. Nic roars with laughter while Matt and Tom smile.

"Finally a girl that can keep up!" Nic bellows, all three of them follow my lead as I down the second glass. Already I begin to feel queasy and that tingling feeling of being light headed.

"I'm going to dance." I point to where others had begun to dance.

"We'll be out soon," Matt reassures, turning back to Nic. I stand shakily and move through the crowd to where the dancing area is. A female is on stage, bellowing out a tune.

"We are here to drink your beer."

Someone grabs onto my hand and I'm dragged into the crowd, the lights dance around me as I'm spun through the crowd. I smile with glee as the skirts of my dress flare out as the man spins me out.

"And steal your rum at the point of a gun."

The violin begins to jump from each note, I gather up my skirts as I follow everyone's lead; kicking our legs out. I laugh as a girl links arms with me and we skip around in a circle, she joins in and in no time we're swinging from one another.

Others begin to join in, our laughter contagious.

We're separated and I find myself in the arms of a man I hadn't met before, a rather good looking man. He twirls me around and I glance up to see Nyx staring at me with a frown, the girl talks mindlessly to him but his eyes stay on me.

I could use this to my advantage.

I fall back into the man's arms, pressing my back into his chest. His arms snake around my own and he intertwines our fingers as we rock from side to side.

"What's your name?" He breaths onto my neck.

"Ravynne," I say softly, my tongue feels heavy and thick and my throat is dry.

"I'm Noel."

His hands leave mine as he runs them down my sides, I gasp in surprise. He grins down at me as he takes my hand again, we dance back and forth. Changing partners frequently but still, somehow ending up together again.

As we switch partners, my hand goes into another man's. My skin ignites with fire as I look at our clasped hands. My eyes travel up to meet Nyx's eyes.

He brings me to him, rather forcefully. I slap my hand against his chest.

"Dance with me," he whispers, leaning down. I lick my lips and nod, still wanting to hold my vow of silence.

Dancing with Nyx is far smoother and nicer than dancing with a drunken man I didn't know, he moves like liquid as we dance and twirl around the crowd.

"Still ignoring me?" He growls as he twirls me into his arms; his head rests next to my own, his breath tickles my cheek. He spins me out again before I can protest and picks me up at my waist, holding me up as he goes around in a circle. The crowd erupts with applause.

I can't help grinning as my hands hold onto his shoulders, he smiles up at me as well. He lowers me back to the ground, leaving his hands on my waist.

I relent as I lean my head against his chest, listening to the rhythm of his heart beat.

"Where are you staying tonight?" He asks.

"At Matt's," I mumble, closing my eyes. Downing those drinks has finally caught up with me, my limbs are heavy and my words are thick.

"Oh."

"You're staying with the pretty blonde," I say softly, peeling my eyes open to the bright tavern lights. I spot her sitting at the table, talking to another woman.

"Is that what you think?" Nyx tilts my head up to him, I find his eyes as his hand goes back to my waist.

"What else am I meant to think?" His hands tighten on my waist but he only sighs and shakes his head softly.

"You're foolish Rav, jumping to conclusions like this." I rest my head on his chest, his chin rests on the top of my head as we sway together slowly.

"I don't know what you expect me to say, I feel foolish enough as it is."

"What do you mean?" He asks.

What did I mean? I'm not sure.

"I…I think I like you Nyx, more than I've liked another man before. I don't like the feeling I felt when I saw you with that other woman." I squeeze my arms around his waist as I bury my face even more into his shirt, taking a deep breath.

"I only invited her out to dinner as she's the leader of this cities sister and he wouldn't take no for an answer. She's a nice girl, but it was only dinner. And where have I ended up?"

"In my arms., I whisper.

"Exactly, so stop stressing your pretty little head about it."

"You think I'm pretty?"

"I think pretty barely begins to describe how I see you." He whispers into my ear. I feel my insides warm at his compliment, and I find myself beginning to half fall asleep. I'd have to leave soon.

"I'm sleepy," I grumble. Nyx stops swaying us. I finally open my eyes, I unwind my arms from around him and rub my face. Goodness I was going to have an awful time tomorrow morning, no doubt with a nasty hangover as well.

Matt walks towards us, with Nic and Tom behind him talking back and forth. He smiles as he sees us, no malice to it.

"Rav, I thought you'd be occupied. We're about to head to the next pub for a few more, you're welcome to stay here or head home if you like," Matt says, nodding to Nyx. I straighten, but Nyx keeps his arms around me.

Over protective faerie.

"Do you want to stay with me the night? I was about to leave," Nyx says softly, looking down at me. I suck my bottom lip, nothing would be happening as the moment my head hits a pillow.

"Yes please." I turn to Matt, "I'll stay with Nyx, but I'll be back tomorrow. Be safe boys, have fun." I wave weakly to the three of them as they head back into the crowd. Nyx wraps an arm around my shoulder and also leads us out of the crowd. I keep my arm around his midsection, hand clenched in his shirt.

The walk to his tavern is quick and I don't remember any of the trip. We stumble up the stairs, no thanks to my sluggish feet. A light dims the room as I find myself back in the same tavern room Nyx had first brought me too, the one where'd I'd also seen the vision.

"Now, did you want a warm bath before bed?" He asks as we walk into the room.

"Yes please, I promise I won't drown in it but if I'm not out in five minutes you might want to double check," I say, half smiling as he leads us into the small bath room.

He runs the hot water, feeling it to make sure it's not too hot before squirting some sort of soap into the water. He wipes his hand on his pants as turns back towards me. I lean against the sink, staring at myself in the mirror.

My hair is slick against my neck from sweat, my cheeks are flushed red and my eyes are blood shot. Indeed I was going to be feeling this tomorrow.

"Alright, I'm undressing. Get out." I meet his eyes in the mirror, he rolls his eyes with a smile as he leaves me alone. He leaves the door open though, and I'm too tired to argue with it.

I strip out of the dress and bathe quickly, ducking down to wet my hair and rid myself of the sweat. The steamy water begins to make me feel better, I lean back against the tub as the water laps at my neck.

"It's nearly been five minutes," Nyx calls. I groan as I open my eyes, I pull myself out of the tub and wrap a towel around me. I walk out into the room, leaving watery footprints in my wake. Nyx is laying on the bed, which he'd turned down. He's wearing a pair of loose brown pants and no shirt.

He looks over to me and his eyes widen.

"I don't have any pyjamas," I state, holding the towel close to my body. He springs into action and grabs one of his shirts from the drawers. I let the towel drop and pull the shirt over; thankful that it reaches my thighs.

I climb onto the other side of the bed, pulling the sheet up. I rest my head on the pillow as I face him, he hops back in beside me; letting his leg rest against my knees. I move closer, resting my head against his arm.

I let my eyes close, winding my arms around his.

"Rav, how did you get the scar below your ear?" He whispers.

"After my sister died I tried to…well…I tried to join her. That's as far as I got until my dad burst into the bathroom and stopped me," I whisper. My chest doesn't ache when I tell him. It doesn't feel like the end of the world sharing it with him.

No one but my family knew what the scar was from, and until Nyx came along I doubt no one else would have ever known. If I wasn't drunk, I don't think I would have shared it with him.

"I'm glad he stopped you when he could. I'm sorry you had to go through that," Nyx whispers. He unwinds my arms and pulls me onto his chest. I don't argue as I nestle into him, resting my hand on his bare chest.

"Don't apologise. It was a long time ago."

"I'm glad you're alive Ravynne, for a world without you in it wouldn't be a world worth living in." He presses a kiss to the top of my head, and I'm vaguely aware of the room plunging into darkness. He wraps his arms around me, not letting go.

It's almost as if, if he holds on tight enough I won't slip away again.

For my last day in Orrinshire, I decide to steer clear of the library and anything that holds books. After I'd woken up in his arms this morning I'd nearly suffered from heart failure, the last thing I remembered was getting into bed with him.

I couldn't stop thinking about the kiss, and the little charade we'd played for the guards of being *together.* I couldn't stop thinking about the way we danced together, the way he held me. I hate to wonder what it would be like if there was no charade, and we were like that all the time. I know I'd only give him my heart for him to shatter it.

These were the thoughts that would put me in a foul mood, the thoughts Ma' warned me about when I was a child growing up. I only had eyes for Mike our entire childhood, and then the loss I felt with Cecilia just drove the final nail into the coffin.

I've thoroughly tried to convince myself that Nyx is bad for me, that we're bad for each other. I'd woken this morning to a cold, empty bed. My dress had been folded and sat neatly on the pillow beside my own. No explanation to where he'd gone, it has left me with a bitter feeling in my mouth. I'd confessed I'd liked him more than I should, and he leaves me alone. I was more than determined to figure out what things I could do with my new found power, and if that creature began targeting Elderview I was going to slay it, with or without help.

I couldn't let it harm any children.

I stroll through the markets that are on in the main street, stalls of all shapes and sizes have been set up by travellers from across the continent of Akrania. I let myself relax, throwing my braid over my shoulder.

I take a deep breath and savour all of the herbs and spices that hang in the air, along with cooking meat. It causes my stomach to rumble involuntarily, and I find myself walking to a wooden stall with a cloth shade covering the stone oven.

"Hi there, may I get one of those?" I ask, pointing to a kebab with various vegetables added. He grunts once as he makes it for me, I pass him four silvers and take the kebab from him.

I rest the handle of the empty basket in the crook of my arm and begin to eat as I continue to walk through the crowd, looking into each stall as I pass. A lot of the merchants carry materials for sewing and I grab a small roll of gold thread for Aunty. I come to a stall that causes me to stop in my tracks, a lot of the other people in the crowd don't give it a second glance but I'm fixated by it.

It's closed off, the dark part inside is lit by a few lanterns while there's dreamcatchers hanging out for everyone to see. I finish the kebab and slide the stick into the basket before I walk through the narrow entry. In the middle sits a large table, small cauldrons and various items sit on it with crystals of all sorts.

I run my finger along a few of the leather bound note books, tracing a pentagram. This stall is for magic, which is a brave act of defiance.

"May I help you?" A feminine voice asks, startling me. I look to the back of the tent to see her standing there, layered in purple, pink and green robes. She pulls back the hood and brown ringlets group around her shoulders. Her bright green eyes are unusually…*magical* compared to the rest of her.

"Oh um, maybe?" I look back to the books, and then back to the table with ingredients for spells. I could always grab a few things, but I had no idea what to do with them? Would I need a cauldron as well? That would be even harder to hide from my family.

"This shop isn't for the curious." She says, crossing her arms over her chest.

"No, I do want something, I just don't know how to say it." I defend myself, half offended. She watches me steadily and I feel like a lamb in front of a lion.

"Well…I need help with creating potions I suppose, not like black magic or anything, but things that people can take that can help them." It's somewhere to start, even though I wasn't entirely sure this would be of any help to me.

"Who gave you that necklace?"

"A friend."

"So, you're a seer?" She walks over to me, inspecting me more closely. I touch the moon and take a step back, my eyes widen and I feel the horror plaster itself on my face. She waves it off.

"Oh please girl, I know that type of moon when I see one. And your eyes! They're the elephant in the room." She muses.

"My eyes?"

"Yes, they're the eyes of a strong seer. Only the strongest are born with the grey eyes of sight, although if you're here I assume you have no idea about what you are. Correct?"

"Well, yes," I say. I fiddle with the handle of the basket nervously. Apart from my Aunty, she was the only other person I'd told this too. A complete stranger.

"I have a book that can help you, but why do you want to dabble with potions? Seems folly." She turns and I follow her deeper into the tent, I get the weird feeling that there's magic involved as it keeps unravelling in front of me, but when I look over my shoulder the exit is right there.

"I…it's the first thing I could think of learning that is probably easiest and would help others too. My village burns witches." She comes to a stop and rummages through a stack of books. I pick up the skull of a small animal and flip it over between my fingers.

"Yes it's a good skill to have, but you should focus more on the telekinesis side and the divination." She grabs a book and brushes the cover off, it's as big as her hand and the dark red leather cover has no title.

"This will help with potions, how to make them and what you need to use and the properties of the ingredients you add in case you decide to make your own. You'll need a rune ring to help you hone your ability, so it's more under your control." She heads deeper into the tent, and the light begins to dim and disappear in places. I sit the skull down and hurry to catch up with her, I sit the book in the basket.

She stops in front of a glass case, multiple silver band rings sit on display with a single circle stone of every colour under the sun. She unlocks the door with the swipe of her hand and it slides open on its own.

"What one calls to you?" She asks, looking over her shoulder to me. I look at the rings and step closer, breathing in her lavender and sage scent.

I scan the rings, and they finally snag on a ring that sits towards the bottom. I reach out and pluck it from the cushion, the stone is a grey that's similar to the shade of my eyes.

"Perfect choice." She gestures for me to put it on, I hesitate. What am I doing? Am I really going to do all of this and take this information from a stranger?

Yes, yes I am.

I slide the ring on to the middle finger on my left hand and it fits perfectly. I run my thumb over the stone before flexing out my hand, it nags at me but I'm sure I'll get used to it.

"Start small with your potions, you don't want to over load yourself or do a potion wrong, as you'll have to be the one to try them." She begins to walk back to the front of the shop, I fumble with the coins in my pocket.

"How much do I owe?" I ask, grabbing out the two golds I had left. She stops and looks at me, with pity in her eyes. It takes me by surprise.

"Child, you're in debt to your gift or curse, whichever you like to think of it as. You don't owe me anything, but you must be gone. If you need any help, I'll be back in a month for the full moon markets."

"Thank you, honestly," I say, taken aback. She takes my hand in her freezing one before waving me off, busying herself with the ingredients on the table.

"Now go."

I don't hesitate as I step back into the light. I take a few steps before turning around; only to find her stall gone and replaced by a food stall. The merchant gives me a puzzled look before getting back to work.

My heart beats so hard I feel it'll crush my ribcage as I walk through the rest of the market. I'm extremely aware of the ring and I fear any minute a passer-byer will accuse me of witchcraft.

The ring is going to be harder to explain to Aunty.

I shake the worry off as I begin to leave the markets, satisfied that the journey here had been worth it. I pause, debating whether to get another kebab.

People in the crowd bump into me as they move out of the way for someone, I turn in time to see a guard shoulder me aside. I stumble and drop the few gold coins.

I shoot him a dark stare before bending down and picking the coins up, muttering to myself.

"I'm sorry about that, they're quiet animalistic when they like to be." A rich, smooth voice says above me. I tilt my head up to see a man slightly older than me peering down, a gold crown sits in his brown curls. He pins me to the spot with his honey brown eyes, my grip tightens on my coins. A lot of the more populated cities have human leaders or rulers, whereas our small village has the faerie king. Most travellers don't know about our village or it's ruler, as we're a few days or weeks away from any big city.

"I-I apologise your majesty, I should have moved out of the way." I stand slowly, content to find he stands the same height as I.

"No need to apologise, are you liking the markets?" He gestures around with a ring clad hand and I catch a glimpse of his sword attached to his belt.

"Oh yes, they're lovely." I nod, wiping down the skirts of my dress.

To my surprise I see Nyx stroll up to the ruler's side, hands in his pockets. Today he wears his usual dark green tunic and dark green dress pants with brown pointed shoes. His hair is tussled and unruly, and when he sees me his cool demeanour falters.

My eyes widen momentarily.

"Good, I'm glad you enjoy them. I do have to say, I haven't seen you around my city before?" He rubs a hand against his beard thoughtfully.

"Oh, I'm not from here. I travelled for the markets." I force my cheeks to redden slightly, and lower my head coyly. To my surprise the ruler takes my hand in his, giving the back of it a kiss.

"Well I bless you and thank you for visiting my city." I must look shocked, because he laughs heartily before letting my hand go.

"Thank you sir." I bow slightly and keep my head down, not wanting to draw any other attention to myself, already people were beginning to stare and I hate being stared at.

"Isn't that the girl you were with yesterday?" A guard says, pointing to me with a meaty finger. I recognise him, he'd been the one to stare at us in the library.

"What?" I ask, feeling fear begin to creep up.

"Do you think I'd dabble with peasants?" Nyx looks to the guard with a cocky smile, "You know I only chase finery, and you've been witness to that."

"Aye I have sir, she just looks familiar."

My heart twists in my chest at his words, and even if they are for show, they're cruel. I feel the skin on my neck heat up with embarrassment and this is worse than the time Mike had witnessed me trip over and rip the bottom of my dress off.

"She isn't *too* bland for a peasant. Pretty eyes," the ruler says, looking me over again.

"Too bland for you, sir." Nyx looks away with a tight jaw and begins to walk down the empty path that had opened up for them. I control myself, wanting more than anything to hurl my basket at the back of his head.

"Mmm," the ruler says, he gives me one last glance before following Nyx. The guards follow and the crowd that had formed meet into one once again.

I storm out of the markets and head right to the cottage, I was not spending another night in this city. I'd do something stupid, like commit murder.

I return to the cottage to find Matt brushing down Luna, I pull my coat on and shove the book into my saddlebag. I grab it as I walk out the back, heading for them. Matt sees me and waves, lowering his hand moments later when he notices my sour expression.

"Hey, what happened?" He asks, pausing.

"I'm leaving now, I can't stay in this city any longer. There's been trouble at home and I've just gotten word." I walk past him and grab the saddle and bridle. I struggle to carry both but I manage, the anger fuelling my strength.

"When will you be back?"

"Hopefully never," I grumble, throwing the saddle onto Luna's back. "I'm sorry, that was mean. Probably in a month if everything at home is okay." I sigh, letting him take the bridle from me.

"Well bring Luna out the front and I'll grab some dried meat for you to take for your travels."

I wait until he's inside to climb onto Luna, which is awkward and nowhere near as smooth as it had been when Mike had helped me. I kick her into a walk and enter the front yard. We wait at the gate. She paws at the ground impatiently. Moments later Matt comes out holding a grey cloth in his hand, tied at the top.

"Here, it should last you until you return." He passes it up to me, and I put it into my saddle bag. I dig out a gold coin and place it in his hand.

"Thank you, for this." I force his hand to close over the coin before I hold onto the reins. He sighs and shakes his head as he moves to open the gate, "You're so stubborn."

"I know." I half smile, but the fleeting moment doesn't last.

"Be safe Matt, and find a roommate while I'm gone yeah?" Luna walks out the gate and begins to prance in place. I feel her nerves as good as my own, and maybe she's picking up on my anxiousness to leave.

"Can't promise anything."

I nod once before clicking my tongue and squeezing my heels to her flank. She takes off down the empty road, whinnying softly. I take a deep breath as we go through the city, I avoid the main roads in fear of seeing Nyx again and once we're on the main stretch we fly across the land like a shooting star.

I return to chaos.

After I sadly return Luna to the Densley's, I go home and hide the book in my mattress, making a cut on the side that presses up against the wall. No one would find it there. I keep the ring on.

The two days journey had given me time to collect myself, and compose myself for everyone. I couldn't return a blubbering, heartbroken mess. Did Nyx mean those things he'd said? If he did, why kiss me? Was I really a peasant in his eyes? He couldn't lie.

I shake the growing anger off and head into the village. Once I reach the centre I'm overwhelmed by the panic that hangs in the air. I begin to fret as I rush to Ma's shop. I find her and Aunty on the patio talking to each other in hushed voices.

"What's going on?" I ask, stepping to stand beside them. Aunty shakes her head as she looks at the people rushing around, some are even crying.

"There's been…a death. One of the kids." Ma whispers, wringing her hands on her flour caked apron. My heart jumps to my throat as my vision spins.

"Where's Kalin?" I ask, half panicked already.

"Safe with Da' at the farmer shop," Aunty assures me, giving a sad, knowing smile. The panic calms down, but doesn't leave completely. The creature has begun its hunt.

"What happened?" I ask. Ma pales as Aunty wraps an arm around her shoulder.

"From what we've heard, their little boy left through his window in the middle of the night and never returned. They found him this morning by the river." Aunty wipes under her eyes as she looks away. I'm half stumped, I came over the river and saw nothing?

"He was in Kalin's class at school. No one's sure what happened, or why he left the house. Mike found him." Ma grabs my hand tightly, looking at me with blood shot eyes and tear stained cheeks.

Mike had been with me when we'd found Cecilia too.

"I'll go and see him soon, he wasn't home when I dropped the horse off. Does anyone know anything else?"

"You shouldn't be asking such questions Rav, not when you've just returned." Aunty whispers, more in warning than anything.

"Why not? How are we meant to solve it and stop it from happening again?" I say, shocked.

"It's the council's job to do that, and if not, it's the king's job. He has magic and I'm sure he'd be able to figure it out and who is behind it with the swipe of his hand, but the council members are stubborn and want to solve it themselves." Aunty makes a sour face, as if she's just eaten lemon. I already know what is behind it, but figuring out how to kill it is going to be another task.

"I'll stop my questions for now, but if they don't do something I will." I let go of Ma's hand and head back down into the crowd, no one glances twice as I head down to the river. If I was going to start somewhere, it would be there. The next place would be the boy's home, but I couldn't do that in broad daylight.

As I get closer, there's a large cluster of people standing in a line to hide the scene. I see Mike, pale faced and teary eyed standing not far off. His arms are caked in blood, and his shirt and pants are covered as well.

I walk closer, peering through the gap of the people. They'd moved the body, but the blood is still covering the river bank.

"Sad, isn't it?" A man says behind me, startling me. I turn around to see the new teacher standing there watching me with those unnerving golden eyes.

"Yes, it is," I say slowly, watching him warily.

"Funny you return when this happens, convenient timing," he says casually, but the point is implied so I cross my arms over my chest.

"What are you trying to say?"

"Oh nothing, just an unusual coincidence." He winks as he says this, and I grow unsettled.

"You know, it's funny this happens a week after you arrive. You're not from here, you're the most likely suspect so I would be careful if I was you." I say, narrowing my eyes at him.

"And I wonder how your village folk would feel knowing they have a faerie sympathiser amongst them?" He muses, grinning at me. I don't let him see my surprise, instead I go over to Mike. How on earth did he suspect that? Had he seen me with Nyx?

"Hey," I say softly, stopping in front of Mike. He looks from the river and down to me, he wipes away the few tears that escape.

"Hi." His voice is hollow, and I look back to the river as well.

"I think I know what's doing this, maybe, but I need to ask a few questions about…what you found." I whisper, so no one else can hear.

"What?"

"Mike, please, can you tell me what you saw?" I turn and look at him, nibbling my bottom lip. If more children died and I stood around and did nothing, I'd never forgive myself.

"Do you really think you know what's doing this?" He looks at me sharply, almost accusingly.

"Yes, I do. But if I don't have the details of what happened I might be misled and I want to do everything I can to help." I reach out and take his hands, some of the blood crusts off.

"Does it have something to do with the son?"

"No, I haven't spoken to him since that night you saw him walk me home." I say, giving him what I hope is a truthful expression. Nyx was technically involved, but not on the level I needed to be on.

"I really don't want to relive it, Rav," he whispers, lip quivering. I rub my thumbs over his palm, feeling my own tears gather. A loss of a child, regardless if you knew the child, is something that affects everyone.

They're innocent, and I think that's why this creature likes them so much.

"I know you don't and I'm so sorry I have to ask this of you."

"Doing this…won't bring her back." He says, his words hit home and I know he's right. I can't resurrect the dead. But I can stop more children from joining her.

"I know, but it can stop others from going down that path as well," I assure him. He sighs, and sits down. He leans against one of the large rocks that sit on either side of the river and gestures for me to sit with him. I do, taking his hand in mine. The late midday sky is covered in clouds, building rain. I'd need to check out the scene before it rained.

"I found him this morning, I was going to collect water just as the sun broke the horizon. Everything seemed normal, fine. There was no noise, nothing.

"I came down and when I went to scoop the bucket into the river I noticed there were ribbons of red swimming down it. When I looked up…I saw him."

He takes a steady breath, squeezing my hand in his.

"He was…he was naked. Sprawled out on the bank, and there were so many deep gashes Rav, his arms and legs and stomach were covered in them. Blood was everywhere, and when I went closer…" He stops, shaking his head.

"Please," I beg, looking up at him.

"His heart had been cut out, or eaten out. Something fucked up happened to him, Rav and it terrifies me." He looks down at our clasped hands. I sit there, silent. I know we are both thinking of Cecilia, of how we'd found her mangled body half sticking out of the river.

I had no doubt in my mind it was the babunook. It had to be, I just had to find some solid evidence. If the babunook is behind this murder, could it possibly be the reason for my sister's death?

"Thank you Mikey."

"Find what's doing this Ravynne. If anyone can stop it, it's going to be you."

I just hoped he was right.

I spend the afternoon with Mike, I finally encourage him to go into town and eat something and after that we spent the time with the horses and reminiscing about old times. Once I'm satisfied that he's not as sad, I leave his home and head straight back down to the river. The sky has darkened and the sun is beginning to set, I had to act now.

The line of people are gone, and there's only flowers left in their wake. My heart squeezes in my chest as I get closer, this is all too familiar and it felt like Cecilia all over again.

I stop in front of the flowers and survey the area.

The blood has dried and is in a wide sloppy mess. There are gouge marks full of blood around where I assume the body had been.

I walk around it slowly, there is a stream of now dried blood leading to the river from the slight slope of the bank.

He'd been killed here and why no one heard anything disturbs me. I struggle to see more details as the sun sets and casts shadows over the land, but I do notice two odd things. One set of tracks leading to the blood are animalistic with deep claw gouges; but the set leaving are boot prints. They're beside the claw marks and I'm thankful no one had disrupted them.

Animal to human.

Could the babunook do that? Or was it from Mike? Had he gone to follow the path as well?

I sigh and turn from the river, heading back home. I felt like I've found something but nothing all in one, it's extremely frustrating.

I open the front door and pull my boots off, shrugging out of my coat. I find Ma and Aunty on the couch with a glass of mead in their hands.

"Where's Da?" I ask, noticing Kalin isn't there either.

"Helping with the funeral," Ma replies, looking over her shoulder to me.

"Kalin?"

"Upstairs," Aunty answers. I trudge up the steps and go into his small room, it was half the size of my own but perfect for him. I tap on the closed door before opening it. I find him lying on his single bed that's pushed up against the side wall.

"Can I come in?" The lantern on his desk illuminates the few toys he owns scattered on the floor.

"Okay." He looks over as I shut the door behind me, I walk over and take a seat on the side of the bed. He tucks his hands under the pillow and I brush his hair from his face.

"I won't let anything happen to you, I promise."

"Sissy, if you had a secret but couldn't tell anyone, would you tell me?" His question takes me by surprise.

"Yes, I would. What secret…do you have?" I say slowly, my hand rests on his shoulder as he looks way from me and twists his lips.

"Do you promise not to tell anyone?" He whispers.

"Yes, I promise."

"Roger knew he was going to be taken. He told me at school." He looks back up at me with wide eyes. I go still on the bed.

"He knew?" I ask, trying to wrap my head around it. If he knew, why did he go? He nods fast.

"Yeah he did. He said something had come to his window and wanted to play, but the thing dropped the ball and when Roger picked it up, his hand touched the creature and it burnt him." Kalin's eyes are wide and terrified and the urge to protect him consumes me.

"The thing said he'd get a new ball and be back to play and well…I guess he got the ball." Kalin begins to cry, and I pull him to me and wrap him in a fierce hug. I rock him back and forth as I stroke his hair.

"Promise me you won't talk to any strangers, or go anywhere? Okay? You trust no one." I pull him back and tilt his face to mine.

"I promise." He sobs, reaching up to wipe his nose.

"I'll find what's done this and I'll solve the problem. Tell your friends to be careful, okay?" He nods a few times and pulls himself from my arms; climbing back under the covers and resting his head on the pillow.

"Get some sleep." I plant a soft kiss on his forehead before I stand, reaching to turn the lantern off.

"No sissy, leave it on. Roger told me it doesn't like light," Kalin whispers. I nod once, leave the room to go into my own.

I had the bare minimum to solve this, but it was better than nothing. Without Nyx's help.

15

The next day, I have my head in the book I'd been given. I'd read a quarter so far to great lengths and even re-read most chapters. Currently I know the basics for simple potions, how purple meant poison and blue meant happiness but adding them together would mean only temporary happiness. There are so many plants I haven't heard of, and I highly doubt they'll be in my village.

I did want to make something for a burn.

I'd mulled over what Kalin had told me last night and I'd gathered two things out of it; the creature touched its victim and left a mark behind to track it and was afraid of light.

If I make a potion that could heal a burn, or to chase away whatever the creature puts on its victim it's definitely a start. I know the basics for healing, so I just need the ingredients.

I close the book and hide it back in the mattress, I unclasp the necklace and hide it there as well. If any visions could help me, I needed to find out. I roll off the bed and pull denim overalls on over the yellow top I'd been wearing. I grab my basket and head down stairs.

I head down to the river, if I can get a sample of the blood left behind maybe I'll be able to test the potion on it. Otherwise, somehow, I was going to have to find whatever is doing this and test it on myself.

At the river I find the dark patch still there. I look around to make sure I'm alone before I crouch down. I pull out a handkerchief and lay it open on the ground, I grimace as I begin to pick at the dirt covered blood. After flaking off a large amount I tie the handkerchief up and put it in the basket.

Healing. Light. What else represents these things?

I wander along the river, looking at the flowers that bloom there. Maybe something yellow would be ideal, or white. I sigh as I continue down the path, heading closer to the neighbouring mountain.

It was early morning still, and everyone had been gone once I'd woken up. The funeral for Roger is at midday in the small cemetery that sits near the school. I planned to go; if only to see if anyone acts suspicious.

I don't like funerals.

I hum to myself as I enter a thicket of shrubs and then I spot them.

Gold, yellow and white lilies bloom in the open expanse in a patch of sun. Perfect.

I crouch down and pluck two of each colour and put them in the bag. I find some aloe vera and break a few pieces off, Ma always used this for soothing sun burn when I was little, spreading the sticky paste the leaf produces over the burn.

I leave the shrubs and go back to the river, seeing if there's anything else I could add while I'm here. I decide on some bug shells, maybe their shells could help with protection. It's a weak theory but the only thing I have.

I return home to a quiet house and immediately get to work. I begin to boil the river water over the stove and lay the ingredients out in front of me. I pull out two cups from the cupboard, I'd need to water down the dirt and blood to see if anything would happen when combined.

I tie my hair back from my face as the water begins to boil, I crush the bug shells up into dust and tip it into the water, I then add the chopped up pieces of aloe and shred the flowers into the water.

Most concoctions take a few hours to brew, so I put the lid onto the pot and turn the heat down to a simmer. I'd come back after the funeral and see if I'd made anything or if it is just flower flavoured water. If anyone in the family asked, I'd tell them I was trying to make a perfume.

I go back into town, eating an apple as I go. The sky's begging to grow darker again but I doubt it will rain, as it didn't last night.

I see the crowd on the other side of the school on the outskirts of the forest, most are dressed in black. I realise too late I hadn't changed from my overalls. I hurry over, spotting Ma and Da lingering at the edge of the crowd.

"Am I late?" I ask, coming to a stop. A few people glare at me before turning back. I can just see the priest dressed in all white standing upon a make shift platform in front of the freshly dug grave.

"On this fateful day we bury one of our own with heavy hearts, this isn't the first time we've done this and they will join a special place in our hearts along with Cecelia." His voice booms around the silent clearing, only a few sobs can be heard and the loudest comes from his mother.

I wince at the mention of my sister, and out of the corner of my eye can see Ma wiping her eyes. The priest continues, but I feel an overwhelming itch consume me. I look around the crowd and try to supress the nagging feeling.

I cross my arms over my chest and try to focus on the ceremony once more, they've begun to lower the wood coffin into the ground. I wipe away the few tears that fall as I watch it disappear into the ground.

My vision begins to go black around the edges and it's too late for me to hide as I'm overcome with a vision.

"*Witch!*" everything launches into oblivion.

"What are you doing?" I ask, looking around the dark clearing. Nyx kneels down and draws a white circle and sprinkles red mushrooms around it.

"It's protection for you, once it arrives it won't be able to touch you in the circle." He stands and shoves the chalk in his pockets. I look up at him and clench my jaw.

"What about you?"

"I'll be fine." He sighs, watching me. I step into the circle and cross my arms over my chest. As I look around the dark clearing, the moon breaks the clouds and illuminates me.

"I would feel better if you were in here with me," I say softly, looking back to Nyx. He tugs his bottom lip between his teeth before reluctantly taking a step into the circle. As soon as he does the world around us seems to go still, not even the crickets chirp.

I reach out and grab his hand, squeezing it tightly. I keep my eyes focused on the darkest part of the forest that sits in front of us, I hear a twig snap.

"Don't move." Nyx whispers, slowly stepping in front of me and holding me behind him. I hoped he knew how to kill this creature, because I sure as hell didn't.

The shrubs move away as a tall, dark figure comes towards us. It's hunched back is covered in black thin skin as it walks in the shadows and watches us with those taunting golden eyes.

"You will leave this village alone," Nyx says, staring at it. Its head

seems to tilt to the side as it stops moving. I feel my heart beating as wild as a rabbit in my chest, and this small circle didn't help my worry.

"Raine Nyx, why it has been so long since I've feasted my eyes upon you." Its voice croaks, as if in desperate need for a glass of water. Raine Nyx? Was this his True name?

"You aren't welcome in this village," Nyx says, tensing in front of me.

"I am not welcome in either worlds, this one has a better source of food." It doesn't blink as its eyes focus on me.

"The children aren't a source of food for you," I say, stepping out from behind Nyx but still within the circle. It chuckles deeply.

"Anything is a source of food if only you put it in your mouth."

"I won't allow you to kill any more children." I raise my chin and put my shoulders back, trying to look as daunting as I possibly could.

"A soul for a soul. You would willingly sacrifice yourself for children that aren't yours? To never bare your own? That is, if you manage to kill me." It finally stalks out of the shadows and stands in the moonlight.

The babunook stands taller than Nyx, with black matted hair hanging from its thin long arms. It holds its clawed hands in front of it, while its wolf-like skeleton face bobs gently. Its gold eyes sit in the dark hollows of the eye sockets, magic in their own right.

"That is why I've come. I won't let Ravynne die for a creature of my world."

Nyx steps out of the protection.

I am screaming.

I cannot stop screaming.

I am screaming for Nyx.

"Ravynne, Ravynne! It's okay, you're okay. I'm here." Hands are over me and shaking me, soothing me. Bringing me back to reality. I open my eyes and to my surprise see Nyx leaning over me. I'm lying down and my cheeks are damp. His shadow falls over me and blocks out the sun. His violet eyes capture mine, but they're wild and untamed.

"It's okay Ravynne, I'm here now," he whispers, wiping the hair from my face. I take sobbing breaths as I try to calm my anxious heart.

I couldn't let Nyx sacrifice himself, no matter what feelings I had for him.

"Ny—Nyx," I stutter, grappling my hands wildly at his shirt. He leans down and pulls me to him. I wrap my arms around his chest and breath him in, now wasn't the time to be marvelling over the muscle in his back or how good he smells.

"Shh. It's okay." he whispers into my ear, I feel a wave of calm wash over me to drown the last of the panic. I was sure he was using his magic, but right now I couldn't care.

"She's a witch!" someone shouts. I feel the rise of the panic wanting to come back, but the magic taps it back down. I lean back out of the safety of Nyx's chest and look up, everyone at the funeral had stopped and now gathered around us. Nyx stays crouched by my side protectively, holding his arms around me.

"What?" I ask. I find Ma, Aunty and Da staring at me gobsmacked. Ma breaks from the crowd and rushes over, she crouches next to me and her hand butterflies over my arm.

"She's not a witch, she had a seizure. She's had them since she was small," Aunty snaps, glaring around the crowd. She stalks over to us with Da in tow.

"Her eyes!" someone else shouts.

"Witch!"

"Burn her!"

"She's the one that's killed the child!"

The shouts blur into a muddled mess that I can't depict and I hide my face back into Nyx's chest. My body has been sapped of any sort of energy, and I couldn't stop reliving the vision.

"Enough!" Aunty shouts, raising a hand. The voices stop, but people still murmur back and forth.

"You will not speak ill of Ravynne, you have no evidence and you will not be burning anyone at the cross." Her voice is strong and holds every inch of power I know she possesses.

"We will find evidence." The priest's voice reaches my ears and I shiver, if anyone had sway over the village people it would be the priest.

"Good luck," Aunty spits.

Nyx holds me tightly as he lifts me from the ground effortlessly. I wrap my arms around his neck and bury my face into his shoulder, not wanting to look at anyone. The burning cross sat deep in the forest, and is where they'd burn the witches long ago before I was born.

"What happened?" I whisper.

"You…you had your thing." Nyx whispers back, but I feel him tense slightly as he does. I sigh, I couldn't stop him from knowing now.

"I've known…I'm a seer for some time now. When I went to Orrinshire and you had to escort me home, the next day I had my first vision. I looked into it when I was there last, and I found a book that could help me." I whisper back, my hands tighten on his collar.

"I suspected that much, that's why I gave you the necklace. You aren't wearing it?"

"I thought, I thought I could receive the visions and see if they could help with how to catch the babunook. They've killed a child Nyx, I can't just sit around and do nothing." I can hear my parents whispering back and forth as they follow behind us, I assume Nyx is taking me home.

"You have an amplifier ring on, whenever you have a vision it will make it a hundred times stronger. Your eyes glossed over a milky white and glowed. What was the vision? Why were you screaming and crying?" He asks, his hand moves down to open the latch on the gate.

"Don't worry about it, I assure you that vision is not going to happen," I murmur, already feeling drained. It explained a lot. As we go up the stairs I bolt up in his arms, I look over his shoulder to see my family stop and give me a worried look.

"Nyx, I'm making a potion inside…they can't come in," I whisper. I wiggle myself out of my arms, but I'm thankful when his hand rests around my waist to steady me. I lean against the front door. "Get rid of them." I look over to them warily. He sighs.

"As you wish."

"Leave and occupy yourself with work, do not return until sun down." As he says the words I can feel the static of magic in the air, weaving its way around my parents and Aunty. Their faces go blank as they turn and head back into the village.

"Will they be okay?" I ask as he turns back around.

"Yes, they just won't come home until the sun is setting. Is that enough time?"

I nod slowly as I turn and open the door, I walk into the kitchen and take a seat in the chair. I rub my temples with my thumb as I try to ease the skull splitting headache.

"Any way you could kiss me and take some pain away?" I remember him taking away the intoxication, maybe he could do this as well. He walks over to the pot and looks through the clear glass lid. A sweet smell now surrounds the kitchen.

"I could, but I will not. You should learn a lesson from this." He turns back to me and crosses his arms over his chest as he leans back against the sink. I drop my hands and look at him with a sour expression on my face.

"That's just rude," I grumble.

"I never claimed I wasn't."

"I still haven't forgiven you for what you said about me at the markets," I say quietly, feeling my heart clench again in my chest. I'd have thought by now I would be over it, but apparently not.

"I didn't mean to hurt you with those words. I didn't want the human ruler to be paying more attention to you than he needed too. He's not a good man Ravynne and I'd struggle to save you from him and keep the peace between us." I look up to see Nyx running a hand through his hair, the top buttons of his white shirt were undone and the sleeves were rolled up.

"I can protect myself." I look back to my hands and pick at my fingernails. This wasn't helping the growing thudding behind my eyes.

"Yes well, I can protect you too."

"Could you grab my necklace please? It's in my mattress in a hole on the closest side to the wall."

"Sure."

He leaves the room quickly and the silence gives me a few precious moments to think. I can't help thinking, does he not find me bland? It shouldn't change anything, but in my heart I feel that it does.

He returns and sits the necklace on the table before rummaging through the cupboards. I clip it on and rest my head on my hands as I watch him.

"What are you doing?" I mumble.

"Making you a drink to help with the headache." I watch as he pours some of the potion I had made into the cup, before adding more water and sprinkling in what seems to be his magic. He stirs it with a spoon before coming to the table and placing it in front of me.

Pieces of flower swirl around the cup and I can faintly make out the bug shell pieces.

"You have to drink it all and this way you'll know if the potion you've made is any good." He sits down across from me and leans back in the chair. I sit up and grab the glass, I take a small sip.

It has a strong sweet taste, but nothing foul. I finish the glass with a few large mouthfuls and sit it back down, my stomach grumbles as the warm liquid churns.

"It'll only work because you put magic in it."

"Not necessarily," he shrugs. He looks tired, and worn out.

"Nyx, where have you been?" I ask, feeling a seed of worry begin to form. Whenever I'd seen him before he seemed prim and proper, and seeing him dishevelled caught me off guard.

"I was trying to get clearance to a book that will help give me more information on the babunook but it was denied, faeries can be hateful creatures." He scowls as he looks out the window, the muscle in his jaw ticks.

"It's alright, we'll figure it out," I assure him, mainly because I knew one of the main things to kill it. A soul for a soul. If I killed the babunook I would die with it. That was the only reason I could assume it would die.

"I don't want you to go anywhere near this. But since I know you, and you will, please do not take your necklace back off. That amplifier in your ring is the strongest I've come across in the human world." He leans in and I freeze as he takes my cold hand in his warm ones. He fiddles with the ring and I relax slightly.

"But what if it can help us?"

"I don't want you to get confused with the vision and reality. It's not uncommon for a seer to descend into madness not being able to tell reality from a dream." he stops fiddling with the ring and rubs his thumb over the back of my hand.

"What does your True name do?" I blurt, thinking about what the babunook had said. *Raine Nyx*. That had to be his True name, a name I was not supposed to know…but a name that can now work to my advantage.

"It gives you control over me to an extent. If you knew my True name and asked me to stand as still as a statue for twelve hours I would have to do so, as my name binds me to the power. Why do you ask?"

"No real reason…can other faeries use it against you?" If they couldn't, that meant the other creature wouldn't be able too.

"No we can't. That's a strange question to ask Ravynne."

"I am a strange person, if you haven't figured that out." I look up from our clasped hands to find his eyes already on me. I feel my heart begin to pick up pace as the familiar warmth of him rushes through me.

"Oh I have, it's admirable."

"Well I'm glad someone in this world admires me." I nibble my bottom lip but feel the hint of a smile on my lips, I don't know when we crossed the line from friends to flirts but I loved it.

"I'm not the only one with my eyes on you." His voice is soft, but plucks each string in my heart that had been hurt by his words of me being bland. I was bland for the king, but I wasn't bland for *him.* God, faeries are confusing.

"Oh yeah, who else?" I entertain the idea.

"That city boy…Mike?" Nyx raises and eyebrow in thought and I burst out laughing. "What? Is that not his name?" He asks, confused.

"No it isn't, his name is Matt." I giggle, the headache had begun to go away and I barely noticed the throbbing. Surely this could work on the children.

"Yes, well him. He definitely has eyes for you."

"I never even see him," I point out. I tap my fingers against his palm. I could honestly hold his hand forever and I am so glad he can't read my mind.

"Did you stay with him for your visit?" I stop tapping his palm. We'd kissed, truly kissed each other. Debt or not, it was more to me than that.

"Yes." I feel guilty, why do I feel guilty? I wasn't with Nyx and he wasn't with me. His open expression closes and I feel his warmth pull away from me, sucking the warmth out of the room.

"I slept on the couch, and he slept in his own bed. I mainly stayed because it was free. I wasn't going to sleep in another man's bed," I say quickly, wanting to grab the last pieces of warmth and yank them back around us to take us back to a few moments ago.

"No I understand, you don't need to explain yourself to me. But give me this, what do you mean by another man's bed?" He asks coolly. I swallow hard.

"I've never slept in any man's bed before…apart from yours and that night you healed my back." I pull my hands from him and shove them into my lap, how embarrassing. I feel my cheeks go scarlet as I avoid looking at Nyx, deciding everything else is far more interesting.

"I can't give you what you need Ravynne."

"Why are you here then?" I force myself to look at him now. His lips twist as he thinks, I feel his mind working as he tries to figure it out.

"Because..." I hold my hand up, not wanting to hear it. Not wanting to break my heart yet again.

"I actually would rather not know. Once this creature is gone we'll both go back to our respective lives and that will be that." I stand up and wring my hands together in front of me.

"Do you really want that?" I feel his eyes burning holes into me and I force myself to meet his gaze. His violet eyes are intense and pull me in all the same, how they had the first time I'd seen him.

Which is why the next words on my tongue are like poison.

"Yes I do. After this thing is gone, you won't see me again."

His faces closes down and he stands from the table, as if angry. I should be the one that's angry, he just told me he couldn't give me what I needed. What did I need though? Would I wait forever for him to come around, if he ever decided too? This is too much for one day.

"As you wish," He grits out. He shoves his hands in his pockets and straightens himself. Only moments ago I'd been holding those same hands, why did our interactions always come to this?

"If you want to help me figure out how to get rid of this thing, meet me tomorrow by the river where the boy died in the morning. If not, I'll know not to be disappointed when you don't show up." I walk over to the sink and rest my hands on the ledge. I clench it until my knuckles go white. He has to go, I need air without him in it.

He leaves without saying a word, as silent as he possibly can.

I look out of the window and over the mountains, I wipe a few stray tears away as I do. We have to stop ending things this way.

I trudge down to the river bleary eyed, the sun was about to break the horizon and I had barely slept a wink last night. I'd put the potion I'd made in a container and hid it under my bed, that night I forced Kalin to drink a glass of it. I was hoping it would work to keep away the babunook and keep him safe.

I was wearing a dark red wool jumper and a pair of black leather pants, I was in no mood for finery today. I'd chosen to wear my hair up in a messy bun, too lazy to brush it or do anything with it. I had more important things at hand.

I find Nyx standing there, dressed in his cloak and usual attire. He hasn't heard me approach so I pause, watching as he stares over the river and into the land beyond this small village.

In this moment I can fool myself to think everything is okay, but the illusion is shattered when he turns and sees me. The emotion on his face disappears as he takes me in.

"I'm surprised you've come," I say as I stop beside him.

"I'm surprised you're not wearing a dress," he retorts. I hit his arm without malice.

"I can't charm you-" *all the time.*

I don't finish the sentence. I clear my throat instead.

"Anyway, this is where the boy was killed." I walk over to the dark patch, the gouge marks were still there but the footprints had vanished. Had I imagined them?

Nyx crouches down and sweeps his hand over the area, in a ghost like manner the body appears again. I squeal as I take step backwards. I didn't know he could do that sort of magic.

"Yes this is the babunook," he declares, standing up.

"How can you be positive? I mean, I know it is, but confirmation based on evidence is always handy." I prop my hands on my hips and feel the last few strands of sleep leave my mind. The early morning sun casts a golden glow over us and the valley.

"The babunook feeds on children's hearts. It's the purest piece of a child and when the babunook eats it allows him to walk as a man amongst us."

"What did you just say?" I feel my blood run cold.

"It can shape shift if it's eaten, but it has to eat regularly to keep whatever form it's taken on." He looks down at me. "Why do you ask?"

"Uh…" I lose my words, how could I explain it? If the teacher was the babunook, maybe I could get close enough to kill it without losing my soul in the process.

"Yes?" He persists.

"Nothing, forget it." I wave him off and walk up towards the gouge marks, they lead right into the forest.

"Do you think they go anywhere?" I point at them, looking over my shoulder.

"Only one way to find out."

Like that, we're walking into the darkest and deepest part of the forest as the sun casts light over land but shadows plague us into darkness.

☾

We walk for hours and find nothing. The gouge marks had vanished into thin air about an hour ago, and we'd just been wandering forward hoping to see if we could find something, anything.

We spend most of the walk in silence, occasionally Nyx will point out certain berries or mushrooms and let me know if they're poisonous or not and what potions they can enhance. I was glad I'd worn my jumper and jeans, as the chill of the air is biting and freezing whatever piece of skin I have exposed. I don't think Nyx is as uncomfortable as I am, but if he is, he has a good way of not showing it.

The green grass withers as we step into a clearing, leaving only brittle yellow land. I look up to see a large wooden cross standing in the clearing, the thick foundation is charred and has gouge marks in the side.

The burning pole, used in the witch trials.

"What on earth…" he walks over, looking at the stack of wood that has been freshly placed at the base of the cross. I shiver, and take no further steps, afraid if I did, I'd find myself tied to it.

"The burning pole, used before I was born to be rid of witches. It's a tale told to us from the moment we're old enough to talk." I whisper, shivering at the phantom breeze that caresses my face. I can almost feel the others here that have died at the hand of the priest.

"You've got to be joking. Do those people not understand that I am magic? That the king is magic?" Nyx turns to me, shocked. I fiddle with my earlobe as I watch him.

"Yes, they do. This is why it's dangerous for me now, if they have evidence of witchcraft I will end up here. That's why I need to kill the babunook before it comes to that."

"I won't let them kill you."

"Yes and I won't let you die in the process, so this argument is void." I snap back, taking a step back from the clearing. The air here feels wrong, sour, tainted.

“Humans can lie,” he counters. He walks back to the cross and runs his hand over the wood. He whispers words that don’t quit reach my ear. I see a ripple come from his hand and cover the cross.

“What did you just do?”

“None of your business. Now shall we keep walking?” He comes back towards me.

“We’ve found nothing. Maybe we should meet again tonight and see if we can find something?” I suggest, I tuck my hands into my pockets and begin walking, feeling better with each step between me and the cross.

“You want to find it when it’s in its most dangerous state? Are you mad?” His voice carries to me as he follows.

“You’ll be there to protect me and you said it eats children and I’m not a child.” I purse my lips as a small part of me wants to put him in his place.

“Yes but… you’re…pure. Innocent.” He chokes on his words as if they’re hard to say and I feel horrified. I hadn’t given myself to anyone, and hadn’t wanted to until I’d met Nyx. I stop in my tracks and turn to him.

“So what? I’m a virgin. What does that have to do with anything?” He stops in front of me, his cheeks scarlet as he avoids meeting my eyes.

“It means you’re innocent and that your innocence can be taken from you. It’s like a child’s heart, it’s pure and they feed off of it.”

"So you're saying I have to be intimate with someone before we can look for it at night time? You do realise how stupid that sounds. Virgin or not, it can still kill me if it wants." Is he idiotic? I will not let something so small stop me from catching this thing or finding where it lives.

"Yes it can, but I would rather it not take your soul and your purity in the process of that," he snaps, surprising me. I step back.

"You confuse me, so much. One second you want me, the next you don't and then you decide you want to protect me? Make up your mind Nyx because I am sick of it," I retaliate. I want to throw something at him, or shake him with my frustration. This is unfair.

"We can't be together," he states, finally making eye contact with me.

"Why can't we? Who are you to tell me what I can't want or need." I feel my bottom lip beginning to tremble and he sucks in a sharp breath.

"If we were together, and my father found out exactly who you are, he would use you against me for his own gain. You'd have heard the rumours of him seeking a seer. They're not wrong and I will not let him have you, even if it means I can't have you either. It's a sacrifice I'm willing to make." His words are like a slap in the face and a hug at the same time.

"So while we work on this, do we just pretend everything is okay? This is unfair Nyx, for us both. We shouldn't be around each other, it's a temptation. It's not a sacrifice I want to make." My anger shrivels to sadness and I sigh, I finally find someone who I'd like to be with and to share each moment with and I can't have him. Why is my life so unfair?

"I can't leave you alone. It's not easy for me either, so stop acting like it is." He takes a step towards me, and then another. His hands find my face and he tilts my face towards his.

"You're a pain in my ass," I whisper, feeling a few tears fall. His face winces with pain as he wipes them away with his thumb.

"I know I am. I am sorry that I've hurt you. I didn't mean to fall for you." He leans his forehead against mine, I wrap my arms around his waist and clench my hands into his cloak. He is warm and safe, this is home.

"You're not the only one that fell." He sucks in a sharp breath.

"Can we have this moment to pretend we're okay and that this is possible? I know it's foolish but I need to know what it is I crave so much. To know what I'm missing out on." It sounds far sadder when I say the words out loud, but it would be worth it in the end. Even if we did manage to both go our own way, we still had this moment.

"I think you're the most beautiful woman I have ever laid my eyes on, you're stubborn and smart and caring and I couldn't keep my eyes off you from the moment I saw you. I wrote that song about you to clear my head of you and when I saw you dancing…" he shakes his head, breathing out deeply. His lips twitch into a soft smile, "It was the most enchanting moment I have ever had in my hundred years of life."

"You're a hundred?" I ask, feeling slightly shocked. He's enchanted by me and wants me the same way I want him. How could I make this work between us?

"Is that seriously all you took out of that?" He chuckles, shaking his head.

"Well duh." I feel my lips twitch upwards and he pulls his face away from mine. His lips twist and turn as he looks down at me, his thumb traces my cheek gently.

"We should get going, your family will wonder where you've gone. Are you going to tell them what you are?" I don't pull away and neither does he.

"My Aunty already knows, but it would probably be best if I did." I bite my bottom lip, if they knew would it put them in danger's path?

"If I can't be here to protect you, they will be." He leans down and plants a warm kiss on my forehead, lingering a moment.

"Fine. Let's go." I pull away, but intertwine our fingers together. He comes up beside me and leaves our hands intertwined. It's such a small gesture of affection and I never want to let go.

"I had a sister once," I say, not sure why I feel the need to tell him.

"A sister?"

"Yeah, her name was Cecilia. She was younger than me and it was my job through the day to watch her while everyone was working." I remember her black short hair, as soft as silk. She had freckles sprinkled across her face with large sky blue eyes and a gap tooth smile. Nyx stays silent.

"One day, it was around lunch time and she wanted me to take her swimming. I was only ten at the time and I had only just figured it out myself and I thought it was a good idea. I could teach her." I take a steadying breath.

"We went down to the river and Mike came with us. We were best friends as kids, but he hated the water. He couldn't swim but wanted to hang out with us regardless. When we got there it was swollen from the rain a few nights before and the current was stronger, I could see it rippling in the middle but I didn't know any better.

"I jumped in, paddling out towards the middle. I would swim to the other side and back, but it was so strong that day. I barely made it to the middle so I turned around and went back, by this point I'd already been washed down the river. I'd felt something swim past my legs and try to grab onto my ankle, and it only scared me more." I feel hot tears fall down my cheeks and run down my chin and throat. It has been a long time since I'd told this story to anyone, as no one seems to want to talk about what had happened. Mike knew what happened that day.

"When I pulled myself out I heard a splash and when I looked up I'd seen her lips part in a scream but the water washed it away. She didn't appear again. Mike was screaming and I jumped back in, I couldn't not try to save her. I searched for so long and by the time the adults arrived with Ma and Da I hadn't found her. It took two days before the river washed her body up. She was…unrecognisable. Her stomach had been disembowelled, her skin was all blotchy purple and her jaw had been ripped off." Nyx wraps an arm around my shoulder and pulls me closer to him, we don't stop walking and I allow myself this time to cry.

"It wasn't your fault Ravynne, you're not to blame," he says softly, squeezing my shoulder gently.

"I am though, if I would have said no, or had hopped in downstream more. If I had yelled warning about what I'd felt touch me, maybe…" These are what if's that ran through my mind for years after we'd lost her, and they still did now. Losing someone you loved and being responsible is one of the hardest things I have ever had to go through in my life.

"You couldn't have known she was going to jump in without you, you couldn't have known the river was unsafe. You were only a child as well."

"I was meant to protect her and I couldn't. I can't let this creature kill the kids of my village. If they label me a witch then so be it." I wipe away the tears furiously, I couldn't let a mother go through the same pain as mine is, even after so many years and a new son.

"Some things are meant to happen Ravynne, even if they are terrible things. You can't control the things that happen to you, but you can control how you grow from these experiences and how you feel about them. I've been around long enough to know loss, but I've been around long enough to know that you can heal from it. You are strong, stronger than you could ever imagine." Nyx's words sooth me, even if I slightly disagree with him I stay silent and save the argument for another day. The sun has reached the middle of the sky by the time we leave the forest and find ourselves back at the river.

I slip out of his arm and walk a few steps ahead, wrapping my arms around myself. I feel extremely exposed, after sharing such a personal piece of myself with him. This felt far more intimate than anything physical that we'd done.

"What's the plan now?"

"My plan is to get some food from Ma's bakery and go to the school. I have to check on a few things there. You need to go and get more information on how to kill the babunook," I say over my shoulder, not looking back as I walk up past home and towards the village. I hear the crunch of dirt as he follows behind me.

"Would you like me to accompany you to the bakery?" He offers, catching up beside me. I loosen a breath as I look ahead, focusing on putting one foot in front of the other.

"If you'd like, I'll be helping Da on the farm after I do these few things so I won't be free until tonight most likely." As we reach the village multiple heads turn our way, people actually scurry to put distance between themselves and us and I'm pleasantly surprised to find it doesn't bother me. I've never fit into their mould they've made for everyone and if I want to kill the babunook ,the less casualties the better.

We go into Ma's bakery in silence, a few people mill about looking at Aunty's designs while a few people my age buy some cakes from Ma. I wait until they leave before I step up to the glass display cabinet. The selection is bleak today.

"Hi Ma," I say, finally looking behind the counter to see her.

"How are you feeling?" she asks. Worry creases the skin on her forehead as her eyes flicker from Nyx to me. He stands near the front of the shop, hands tucked into his pockets as he nods to Ma. She gives a tight lip, polite smile back.

"Better, but we'll need to talk tonight. Can I just grab a blueberry muffin please? There's none at home." I tap the glass to where the last few where left, I look over to Nyx in question, he shakes his head.

"Oh, tonight Mr Kaliya is joining us. He's bringing over his famous meatloaf in good hopes for your health." I frown.

"Who?" I take the muffin from her, crinkling the brown bag up slightly.

"The new teacher at school, he was very concerned about you after the little…incident. He's offered to bring meatloaf and pray for us." She wipes her hands on her apron and I look back to Nyx.

"He can't come over for dinner." I say, looking back to her.

"Ravynne can you please not be difficult for one moment of your life? He's a nice man and you will be polite when he arrives."

If he comes tonight…does that mean he isn't the babunook? Could it stay a man even at night, or did it have no choice? On one hand, this is the perfect opportunity to get closer to him and find out as much information as I can.

"Fine, but he's not sitting in my seat." I grunt. Ma gives me a relieved smile as she leans against the counter.

"I'll see you this afternoon."

"Bye Ma, love you," I call over my shoulder as I exit the bakery with Nyx on my heels. Once we're far enough away I take an angry bite of the muffin. I hadn't told Nyx my suspicions of the teacher and if he knew there was no way I'd be able to get as close as I needed too.

"Why are you annoyed now?" He asks as we begin to walk back to my home.

"Because he annoys me and I don't think he likes me."

"He'd be a fool not to like you."

"He'd be a fool *to* like me." I roll my eyes as I stuff more of the muffin in my mouth, forgetting my manners as crumbs cover my cheeks and fall to the ground. He grins as I poke my muffin covered tongue out at him. It was such a strange thing, feeling so happy after a moment with him over something so small.

"Maybe I can charm him with my good looks and witty humour," I tease, swallowing the last of the muffin. I stuff the brown packet into my pocket and wipe my hand over my lips.

"He'd be far too distracted to eat the meatloaf if you did that."

"Think I could work on making myself less innocent then?" I jab at him, still slightly annoyed he'd suggested such a thing. He sighs heavily and runs a hand through his hair but doesn't answer.

We finally reach the gate and I spot Da sowing the crops, I open the gate but hesitate a moment before taking a step over the threshold.

"I need you to get information on the babunook before you return, do you have any idea when it might strike again?" I ask, looking up at him.

"I'll try my hardest for you, but it won't be an easy feat and will cost you a price, both of us a price. It depends how much innocence the child's heart held, it could be a few days or a few weeks." He looks over me, as if trying to guess what sort of plan I'm formulating.

"I'll pay whatever, just be quick. Please." He nods a few times, the muscle in his jaw ticks. Was I meant to hug him bye, or just simply leave?

I chose the latter. "Bye Nyx, be safe. I'll be waiting for your return." I say softly, finally walking into the yard and shutting the gate behind me. He looks down at the gate and me, I feel like this symbolised more than me closing a gate so the goat won't escape.

"Be safe Ravynne, don't do anything foolish while I'm gone."

"Always."

I push the meatloaf around the plate, the light brown pieces did not appeal to me at all. I had tried meatloaf before, but this one had an odd flavour to it. It didn't tastes horrible and smells exactly how meatloaf should, but with my concerns I'm automatically put off it. I pierce a potato and plop it into my mouth.

Aunty and Kalin had taken to sitting on the couch to eat dinner, while Da and Ma and myself sit at the table with Kalyia sitting opposite me. He digs into the meatloaf, but I've noticed when he swallows he winces.

"So, how are you liking the school?" Ma asks him, batting her lashes a few times in his direction. I stop myself from rolling my eyes, everyone but me seems to be under his charm. If I didn't think he was the babunook I feel I would be as well, but fear keeps you wary and on your toes.

“It’s wonderful, and the children are great. Your boy excels in each subject and is always pleasant.” He smiles warmly at her before looking to me. “What do you do with yourself Ravynne?”

“For now, nothing. I was considering taking on an apprenticeship in Orrinshire but I’m unsure yet.” I lower my fork and pick up my glass of raspberry water.

“You’ve never mentioned this before,” Da says, looking over at me.

“That’s because I’m undecided. So until I make up my mind, I’ll help here wherever I can,” I assure him. It would hurt to be away from them but I wanted to see the world and all the beauty it has to offer me.

“Well, you’re young still so you’ll have plenty of time ahead to make those choices,” Kalyia says, looking over me coolly. After our little confrontation at the creek when the child had died, I had tried to avoid him. We both knew something was going on, but I refused to let him get the better of me.

“Yes, plenty.” I eat the rest of the vegetables but don’t touch the meatloaf again. They talk back and forth about little things, and I find myself wondering why he’d even wanted to come over for dinner. The conversation is boring and Kalin was busy with Aunty.

“I’m going to go and check on the goat, take the leftovers out for her,” I declare, rising from the chair. Ma doesn’t look over at me, instead is transfixed by the story Kaylia has launched into. Da nods once before joining the conversation again.

I gather the leftovers on my plate and head out the front door, so far I had found no real information to tie Kaylia to the murder. The moon is hidden by thick clouds tonight, so much so I'm barely able to make out the goat in the distance pacing in her pen.

"Hey girl, I brought you some food," I whisper. She bleats as I open the cage door and move inside. I shut it behind me and scrape the leftovers onto the ground near her water bowl. She nudges my thigh, not eating.

"What's wrong? You never say no to food." I frown as I crouch down in front of her. I feel over her for any signs of an injury but find none.

Was it because Kaylia is the babunook and she can sense the beast beneath the skin?

The only way I could know for sure, was to follow him back to wherever he lives and see for myself. Maybe there'd be something at his house that I could use against him, although going without a weapon wasn't ideal.

I leave the pen and go back inside, Ma and Da are cleaning the dishes while Aunty, Kalin and Kaylia are playing a game in front of the couch. My heart picks up its pace as I see Kaylia casually brush his hand against Kalin's arm.

Sensing me, Kaylia looks up sharply, narrowing his eyes at me. I rush into the kitchen and place the plate in the sink.

“I’m going over to Mike’s for a bit.” I tell them, loud enough for everyone in the house to hear.

“Alright, be safe and don’t return too late. They still haven’t caught whoever killed that boy,” Da says, planting a warm kiss on my forehead.

“I’m always safe.”

I turn into the hallway to see all three of them laughing and I clench my hand. Why was I the only one immune to this man?

“Thanks for dinner, but I must be off. It was a pleasure having you over,” I say into the living room, batting my lashes. Kaylia grins up at me and I swear I can almost see the beast lurking behind his mask.

“Of course, I do hope you enjoyed it.” His voice carries over to me, and as I turn away he says “Be safe tonight Ravynne, there’s still a murderer on the loose.”

I hurry out of the house and cross over to Mike’s. I stay silent as I slide up beside the house and press myself against its wall. I wasn’t sure how long I’d be waiting until he left, but I had to make sure no one saw me either.

I lie on my stomach and sit my chin on my hands as I watch the front door, in the distance crickets chirp while an owl hoots somewhere in a nearby tree.

I don’t know how long I wait, for when Kaylia leaves I’d begun counting the grass stems I could barely make out in the moon’s light. He leaves my house in what seems to be a hurry.

I perk up as he heads down towards the river, his jacket flies out from behind him. I stand slowly and begin to creep along the tree line that sits on the side of the path. I'm careful to not stand on any branches or shrubs, vaguely I can hear him mumbling a string of words but can't strain my ears enough to hear what he's saying.

Once he reaches the river I watch as he heads up the path where'd I'd seen the footprints go from the murder scene. It can't have been a coincidence.

I follow after, holding a large stick between my hands as I head into the forest. It's a lot harder to see here, but he doesn't do well to hide as he barges through the undergrowth.

I pick up my own pace as I follow, my heart thunders in my chest as I begin to hear half strangled sounds from what I can only assume is him. I have to know what is about to happen.

Finally I see a light, the flame from a torch illuminates a medium sized hut and the broken gouged earth around it. I stop at the edge of the forest and peer through the shrubs, holding a hand over my mouth to stop any surprised noises from escaping.

Kaylia stumbles out of the hut, wearing nothing but a gold bracelet around his right ankle. He makes a choking noise as he falls to his knees, digging his hands into the soft dirt.

A loud crack echoes around us as his back snaps upwards, the bones of his spine press against the tight skin as they begin to move and grow. I watch in horror as his face begins to flake away. A large wolf like skull breaks through the last of the skin as a large black tongue hangs out of the exposed jaws.

For a moment the eye sockets are an endless black, moments later the golden eyes spark to life and look around the clearing. The rest of his body breaks into place as he tears from the mask he's been using as a disguise.

The babunook stands in its terrifying glory. It heaves as its arms hang by its side, claws hang low enough to touch the ground. The matted hair that hangs from its arm is clumped with what I can only assume is blood.

I must have forgotten to breathe. Suddenly I'm wanting to gasp for air. But I can't, not unless I want to die tonight.

The babunook hunches over as it turns and stalks into its hut, huffing and grunting as it does.

Now is my only chance to escape.

I crawl back from my hiding place. Only when I can't see the light of the torch do I stand up slowly and turn towards the forest, darkness seeps into every corner and shadow. The moon doesn't reach this place.

I am lost.

I am *lost* with a monstrous creature only a few feet away.

I run straight, my feet fly beneath me as I move branches out of the way, a few snag at my clothes and break off in my hair. I hear my heart beat thundering and can only hope the babunook hasn't heard me yet and if he has, hopefully I'm too ahead for it to catch me.

I regret admitting it, but I should have waited for Nyx.

The forest around me looks the same the deeper I go and I fear I've been running in circles. Panic is a wild animal inside of my chest and I can't think straight, only move.

I break a clearing and face plant on dead grass and dirt. I hold my breath as I listen to the forest around me. I hear deer nicker to each other in the distance and the occasional bird chirping. I am safe.

I sigh a breath of relief and roll onto my back with my arms spread out. A shadow of a cross towers over me, I tilt my head back to see the burning pole.

How much of a coincidence is it that, of all the places, I've ended up here?

I pull myself up on shaky legs and walk over to it. I put my hand against the wood, waiting for something magical to happen. Nothing comes, no visions or magic.

I shiver involuntarily as I take a step back, so many women had died in this very place, for being the same as me. It had been so long since our village had heard the word *witch*. With me in the mix now I'm afraid this pole would be getting used far sooner.

I'm close to the village though and if Nyx and I had found this in daylight I'm sure I can figure out how to find it in the dark. I walk across the clearing and head into the forest, hoping I was going in the right direction. I have no idea what time it is, or how long I've been trying to get home for.

If Ma or Da decide to visit the Densley's to see when I'd be coming home, they're in for a big surprise.

I walk for what feels like hours, surprised to find myself emerging beside the school. I stand there, dumbfounded. The village is silent around me, not even the crickets chirp here. It's too silent.

Dread begins to seep in as I walk through the open clearing, the few houses that are mixed with the shops are in darkness. I head towards the edge of the village where a majority of the houses are.

"Come play little one, I have a bright red ball," a voice whispers. I freeze, turning towards the small house on my left. I wasn't sure who lived here but the babunook was here.

I had no weapons. I creep closer to the house, sticking to the wall as I make my way towards the back yard. I freeze at the end, not game enough to look around. A shadow falls over the back yard, with a large hunched back and long claws.

"I can't. I was told to not play with you," a little girl whispers back. I squeeze my eyes shut. What am I meant to do? If I screamed, would her parents come out? Would the babunook flee?

"No one wants to play with me anymore, I just want a friend," it cries back. I hear the creak of wood and my eyes fly open. Surely she wasn't about to climb out of the window.

"I have friends, but we play in the day time."

"Can you be my friend? The ball is just over there, near the trees."

The shadow moves as an arm points towards the dark forest, the girl sighs.

"Well, only quickly. Otherwise mummy and daddy will be angry with me for leaving my room." I hear the rustle of clothes as one shadow in the back yard becomes two. I am frozen against the wall.

I peer around the corner, the babunook is holding onto one of the little girl's hands. He towers over her, and she begins asking about the ball and why he wants to play at night time.

I make a choked sound, stricken with fear. The babunook freezes, but the little girl looks back to me.

"What are you doing here?" she whispers, frowning. Her blonde hair is in two piggy tails that just reach her shoulders.

"Get over here." I finally find my voice, although my words shake as I take a step towards them.

"What? Why? We're just going to play a quick game of ball. Did you want to play too?" She looks up at the babunook, tugging on his hand. Its head swivels towards me and those golden eyes flare a bright orange.

"If you don't let her go I will scream with village down," I say, staring right into its eyes. Its mouth opens as a black tongue falls out, stroking the little girl.

"I'm sleepy," she mumbles, before slouching onto his arm.

"What the hell did you just do?" I take a few more steps forward, she is only a few metres away. His other hand comes around and holds onto her shoulder.

"You will not interfere anymore, otherwise your little brother will be the next on my list," he growls. I don't think, I just act.

"LET HER GO!" I scream, the volume of it rips at my throat, but I don't stop. I repeat the words over and over. The light in the house behind me comes on and I hear the back door open, the light illuminates the babunook and the little girl.

"Sophie!" a man shouts, running into the back yard.

I watch in horror as the babunook scoops her small limp body into his arms and leaps over the fence before diving into the forest. The man jumps the fence and runs after them as the mother bursts through the back door. I look over with tears streaming down my cheeks.

"What…what's going on?" she asks, wiping the sleep from her eyes.

I shake my head, not being able to form any words. Neighbouring houses begin to light up as people are awoken, I had to leave, now. They couldn't see me properly from the shadows. As she looks back towards the forest I break free from the spell I felt over me and flee towards home.

I don't stop running until I've reached the front patio. I burst through the door, and lean against the foundation as it closes behind me.

He'd taken another child and I hadn't been able to stop him.

I'd put Kalin on his list, if this child lasted a week for him, it meant I only had a week to find out how to kill this thing.

“What on earth is going on?” Ma asks, flicking the light switch on. She stands at the bottom of the steps in a blue nightgown, Da comes down the steps behind her.

“It…it’s taken another child,” I say between hiccups, I can’t stop the overflowing tears. Ma rushes over and wraps me in her arms, I hold her tight as she pats my back.

“What do you mean?” Da asks, frowning.

“A girl’s been taken, I saw it. I saw it.” I whisper, burying my face in her neck. Da comes over and wraps both of us in a hug.

“Come and sit down and explain, okay sweetie? You’re safe here,” Ma says. Da steps away and Ma drags me to the couch. She sits me down and perches beside me, clasping my hands with hers. Da crouches in front of me, resting his hands on my knees.

“Take a few deep breaths honey,” Da says, rubbing my knees. I do as he says. In and out, repeat. I do this for a few moments, waiting until the tears finally subside.

“I was…I saw something in the forest and I decided to follow it. I didn’t make it to Mike’s, but I had to get some answers,” I begin, avoiding looking at either parent.

“Alright, I’m with you. Continue,” Da assures.

“It went into the forest, so I followed. I saw it…change, and I ran away and I got lost.” While I say this I feel Ma picking a twig from my hair.

“I ended up coming back through the forest near the old school. I was on my way home when I heard something talking to a little girl at one of the houses. I went to see."

"Ravynne…" Ma starts, but Da gives her a look that silences her.

"It was terrifying. It convinced her to go with it, and when I saw her shadow I stepped out from behind the house to try and stop it." My hands are shaking, although I'd seen it in a vision it was definitely more terrifying in real life.

"You could have been hurt!" Ma exclaims.

"Let her finish," Da says firmly.

"I told it to let her go, but it wouldn't. It put her in like a coma and I started screaming. Her parents put the lights on and her Dad came running out and he saw it with her, it grabbed onto her and fled into the forest." I finish retelling them, leaving out the parts of me knowing who I thought it was.

"Oh my…" Ma whispers, shaking her head.

"What sort of creature did it look like?" Da asks.

"Magical…I think it's from the realm of the faeries. I know you might not believe me, but I saw it and I heard it talk. It is nothing of this world. You told me a story about a creature from their world living in our mountains. I think this is it." I look up into his eyes then, and see the worry there.

"You know they're just scary stories to tell around a camp fire Rav," Da says. His lips twist as he looks to Ma.

"I swear they're not!" I exclaim, how could they not believe me?

"I think you need to get some sleep honey, it's been a long night and I think you might be a little confused. Tomorrow morning we'll talk again and see how you feel, okay?" Ma helps me stand, herding me towards the stairs. I sigh and relent, I am tired and could think clearer with some sleep. I know what I saw, and nothing they say is going to convince me otherwise.

I go up the stairs but pause at the top. I strain my ears to listen to what they're saying.

Sick.

Delusional.

Still grieving.

Doctor.

I hurry into Kalin's room, shutting the door silently behind me. Moon light spills into his window, and I quickly look out to make sure the babunook isn't lurking around.

I climb into bed beside him, not minding that I'm far too tall for his bed. He sighs as he wraps a small arm over my waist. I brush his hair back from his sleeping face.

I will do anything in my power to stop the babunook from taking Kalin's soul, even if it means sacrificing my own.

A week has passed and Nyx hasn't returned, and neither has the little girl. No one in the village believes the father about what he saw and even the mother has her doubts. I talked to Kalin to see if he'd heard anything at school, but he assured me he told all of his classmates to not play with the creature. I keep making him drink the potion I'd made, hoping even without Nyx's magic it would still help ward off the babunook. I had been on alert, scared someone would be able to recognise me from the girl's house but no one has said anything.

I spend every night sleeping with Kalin, and I sprinkle a line of salt on the windowsill for a smaller bout of protection. I'll need Nyx to return soon with some answers, because I'm running out of options.

I walk into the kitchen, once again finding it empty. I have a quick drink of water before grabbing a gold coin from the jar and pulling on my boots. We need a few items for dinner so I may as well make myself useful. The babunook couldn't attack in daylight, so the children would be safe.

I set off for the village, wary of my surroundings. I'd wanted to carry around a small weapon, but if someone found it on me I'd be on the whipping pole for being a witch and a child murderer yet again.

I enter the village to find it bustling with people, a thick cloud of anxiousness hangs in the air. I frown as I pause on the outside, watching as people begin to bow down and avoid the centre.

Six guards clad in silver armour march through; the sun shines brightly against them. They each hold a sword in their hand as they make their way through the villagers.

I hide behind the large tree where I usually stop and watch from afar. Their pointed ears are left out of the armour, a statement for us.

Why are the king's guards here? Could he have sent them to help with the babunook?

I lean my forehead against the tree. Nyx had mentioned his father is actively looking for a seer. What if my vision at the funeral had reached him somehow?

I hear someone cry out and I look back around the tree, the guards have Jester pinned to the ground; their silver swords trained on him.

"I don't know where she is!" he exclaims, his hands shake as he holds them up innocently. One guard presses a silver foot onto his chest, his green eyes swirl with blue as he looks up at the others. They can't have been living in the castle, everything about them screams otherworldly.

They are nothing like Nyx.

"You should never lie to a faerie," he growls, tilting Jester's chin up with the sword. His face pales as he bites his tongue, true fear rounds his eyes.

"What does she look like?" he asks.

"B-black hair, long hair, grey eyes," he splutters out, a thin trail of blood begins to run down his throat. He winces, but doesn't make another sound.

"That is a rather bland description," the guard drawls. The other grins down at Jester, exposing fangs. Oh my, did Nyx have fangs?!

"She is bland, that is why. I swear I'm telling the truth, she's as plain as white bread!" He cries out. The guard leans down and sniffs the air. I watch as a dark stain begins to appear at the front of Jester's pants.

"Disgusting human filth," the guard spits as he releases Jester, who curls up into a ball. I don't move a muscle as the guards talk amongst one another. They knew I lived here and were coming for me. This village is only so big and definitely not big enough to outrun their forces.

They continue walking, interrogating other people of the village. I slink between the back of buildings as I go to Ma's bakery. I slip in through the back door quietly. I walk through the cooking area and peer through the archway, Ma is wiping down the counter bench.

"Ma," I whisper, she jolts as she looks up.

"Rav, what're you doing back there?" She frowns, shoving the cloth into her pocket. I gesture for her to come back into the room, as she does I make sure the guards are nowhere near the shop.

"I have to be quick, because I don't know how long I have left. But I need to leave Elderview, now. I can't explain what's going on but the king's guards are here for me. If Nyx returns tell him he knows where to find me, but ask for protection and let him know I will pay whatever the price." I ramble, trying to fit as many words in as I can. If they hurt my family, the babunook is not the only creature I'd be hunting down.

"You're making no sense, this is nonsense Rav," Ma insists. I grab her shoulders and force her to look at me.

"Listen to me for once in your life, there are guards after me because the king wants something I have. If they ask say I've run away and fled for the hills. But Ma, you need to be careful of the creature killing the children. It told me Kalin is going to be on its list and I won't be here to protect anyone."

"Rav…"

"Ma please! I know it's hard to believe, but I have to go. I will be back when the danger passes, but keep Kalin safe. Sleep with him every night and tie him to you if you must. Do not let him succumb."

We both freeze as the front door of the shop opens. I pull Ma back and we stay silent as multiple people enter. The old wooden floor boards groan under their weight.

"Hello?" a voice calls.

"Oh, gentlemen. How can I help?" Aunty calls from her side of the shop.

"We're looking for a girl, black hair and grey eyes. Have you seen her?" one asks, and I look at Ma with wide eyes. She frowns as she looks to me and back to the archway.

"That's a pretty simple description, there're plenty of young women in the village with black hair," Aunty says, but I hear the underlying hint of fear in her voice. She must know.

Ma pulls me back away from the archway and we creep slowly to the back door. She holds it open slowly, gesturing for me to leave. I give her a quick hug before slipping out. The door shuts silently behind me. I wait a few moments, hearing her enter and begin talking to them.

I flee from the village and down towards the farm, I see Da walking towards the house in the distance carrying two large buckets. I jump over the fence and run towards him. He drops the buckets and catches me in his arms as I wrap him in a hug.

"Daddy I have to go, the king's guards are after me. I told Mama I was leaving, but I couldn't go without saying goodbye," I say, clinging to him. He tries to pry me off of him, but my grip is like iron.

"Pumpkin, you never make any sense," he says, finally pulling me from him. I let my arms fall to my side in defeat, if he didn't believe me now I'm sure he would once Ma and Aunty explained it to him.

"I have to go. I love you and Mama, I'll be back when it's safe." I turn and head back towards the house in a hurry, he shouts after me and no doubt is following me. I go inside and grab my saddle bag, stuffing in various items of clothes and the book about potions. I pull off the dress and pull on leather pants and a white long sleeve shirt. I pin my hair up on my head and stuff on a hat, I can't hide my eyes so I have to be fast.

I grab the bag and go back down the stairs, pulling on my riding boots. What I was going to do next would not be one of my proudest moments.

I run into the Densley's back yard, six horses stand in their stables as they nibble on their hay bale. I spot Luna pacing back and forth, and when she sees me she lets out a whinny.

The Densley back yard is huge, the six stables for their horses sit to my left and run along horizontally. An open expanse of grass is in the middle before showcasing another six empty stables.

I climb over the fence and rush through the grass towards Luna's stable. She comes up and nudges the gate impatiently, I fumble with the latch before pulling the gate open. She lumbers out and begins to pick at the grass, swishing her tail.

I pull the bridle off of the rack that hangs along the outside of the pen and walk over to her. She doesn't resist as I slide it on. She wasn't a short horse, and I had no idea how I was about to climb onto her. I didn't have time for a saddle, so bareback was going to have to do.

As if answering my thoughts, I watch in awe as she folds her front legs down; low enough for me to slide my leg over her neck. I do as she suggests, and once my leg is over she stands suddenly and I slide into place at the base of her neck. I gather the reins in my hand and click my tongue.

She doesn't hesitate as she breaks into a canter, flying through the open gate and towards the road. I steer her towards the river and press my heels into her side, the wind threatens to tear the hat from my head so I hold it in place with a hand.

From the first trip we made together, I felt like I'd connected with her on a more spiritual level, and I knew being a seer had something to do with that.

I put the village behind me as we head for the open landscape. I'm not sure if Orrinshire is going to have the answers I need but it's the best place I can start. With any luck, Nyx will be there and I'll convince him somehow to help me.

I just have to hope the help won't be too late.

Two days pass by us in a blur, and once we enter the safety of Orrinshire both Luna and I are dying for a rest and some real food. We head to the only place that will help us, Matt's.

I find the way there easily enough, it's just hit noon when we come to a stop outside of his home. I hop from Luna and my legs nearly buckle underneath me. I'd never ridden bareback before and my butt and legs feel like they'd need replacing.

I lead Luna through the front yard and down to the stable area and unclip the bridle before I open the gate to let her in. She trots happily over to the water trough before heading for the large round bale that now sits in the middle of the small paddock. I leave the bridle hanging on the gate before I head back to Matt's home.

I knock on the back door and peer through the windows, but he isn't home and now here I'm not entirely sure what I'm supposed to do. In the panic to leave, I hadn't thought this plan through at all. What if Nyx just never returns and the babunook kills all the children?

I readjust my hat as I head down the path and back into the main city. My stomach growls and I groan with annoyance. I only have a gold coin, and I doubt that'd get me any good food.

No one gives me a second glance as I walk among the streets; there were no markets on today so the people walking about are more relaxed. Thankfully, there's also no sign of their leader walking amongst them today.

I decide to stop at a small shop and grab a muffin, I leave annoyed with a small muffin and seven silvers left. This muffin is not worth that much money, but I savour it as I gulp it down regardless.

I head towards the library, it seems like the safest place to be at the moment. I brush the crumbs of the muffin from my face as I enter the library, the librarian raises an eyebrow as I enter but doesn't say a word. I head towards the back where Nyx and I had last sat and take a seat, a few random books lay scattered along the table so I pick up a random one and begin to read.

I'm unsure how long it's been when someone wakes me up, I lift my head from the book and wipe away the drool.

"Huh?" I murmur, blinking a few times. I look up to see Nyx frowning down at me. I straighten up; knocking the book from the table. He grabs it before it hits the floor and places it back down.

"What are you doing here?" he asks, leaning against the table. I blink away the last tendrils of sleep and reposition myself in the chair, my back aches from being hunched over.

"What? I'm reading." I point to the book he'd placed back.

"Here, in Orrinshire."

"Oh. Well, funny that. I could ask you the exact same thing." I cross my arms over my chest, and he clenches his jaw. I'm glad to see I can still annoy him, even after not seeing him for two weeks.

"I'm looking for answers. Now, what are you doing here?"

"Well no rush or anything. I saw the babunook take another child and now I have guards sent by *your* father to imprison me. Hence why

I'm here, I didn't think they'd be able to find me here. But if you have, I'm sure it's only a matter of time." I look away from him and back to the front door of the library, a few other people now mill about minding their own business.

"I saw your family, your mother said I'd know where to find you. Here was my best bet."

"How did you get here so fast? It's a two day's journey."

"I'm magic, remember?" he retorts, his fringe falls onto his forehead and almost shields his untamed violet eyes.

"Well I can't return, which means I can't protect the children, which means I may as well just give up." I sigh, drumming my fingers along the table. Every avenue is beginning to look impossible, how could I kill the babunook when faerie guards are turning the village upside down looking for me?

"You can't give up, you haven't come this far to throw in the towel when you come to a problem." He finally takes a seat beside me, although he keeps a healthy amount of space between us.

"Right, so when you see a small child whisked into a dark forest by a creature you know is going to kill her, you can sit here and say don't give up?" I look over to him, he has his head in his hands.

"If you give up, it won't stop killing the children. It's best to say you tried over not trying at all."

"Well I don't know how to kill it. You're no help, at all. My vision has told me more than you have," I snap, before realising my mistake.

He looks up at me, blinking slowly.

"What vision?"

"Wh— I didn't—" I scramble for words but it's no use, I've already put my foot this far into it.

"Don't play me for a fool Ravynne. We may be friends, but do not forget who and what I am." His voice is almost a growl, taking me by surprise. I flinch.

"I had a vision, the one at the funeral. It was the babunook and it was saying something about a soul for a soul. That's all, I swear it." It's not a lie, just a little deception. That's all he needs.

"Did it say anything else?" he questions, leaning slightly towards me.

"No."

He sits back, relaxing into his chair. How his moods can go from one extreme to the next is beyond me. I assumed it's be a faerie thing as no man I've ever encountered has been so temperamental.

"I hate the fact I'm going to offer you this," he groans, looking up at me. I raise an eyebrow.

"One way to keep you going unnoticed by the guards my father sent is to take you to Faerie, which will also be useful if you wish to find more information on the babunook." He grits the words out and I can't help the grin that spreads across my face. This was the break I needed, protected and finding out exactly how to kill the babunook.

"Thank you, thank you, thank you!" The words are joined in one long sentence as I clasp my hands in front of me.

"Don't thank me just yet. You may not leave alive."

"No matter that, when can we leave? Today? Tomorrow?" I stand up and stretch my arms above my head, I hadn't a clue what I was going to tell Matt when I returned. He'd be nice enough to look after Luna while I'm away though.

"Tomorrow evening. I'll come and get you. Where are you staying?" he asks as we begin to walk towards the front of the library.

"Matt's. He lives on the other side of the river, nice little cottage. Luna's in the back paddock, her white hair is hard to miss." Nyx doesn't reply, just gives me a hard nod of his head to let me know he heard. I shrug his annoyance off as we leave the library, the afternoon sun is beginning to turn the blue sky into pink and orange hues.

"I'll see you tomorrow night then. Do I just meet you out the front?" I query, coming to a stop.

"Yes. I'll see you then." He turns and walks back through an alley I'd never been down. I sigh and walk back towards the bridge, once the babunook was dead and gone; my feelings for Nyx would be too. Because when the babunook is dead, I will be alongside it.

19

Explaining to Matt why I'd arrived so suddenly had been the easier part, mentioning troubles at home and it not being safe for me to return. Trying to explain to him that I was yet again leaving and had to keep Luna here was another thing.

"It's hard to explain and God knows I wish I could. I don't want to put you in more danger than you already are now by even having me and Luna here." I look over my shoulder to him, he's leaning against the kitchen counter with his arms crossed over his chest.

"Well I'm already in danger, what's a little more to add to the mix?" he retorts. I bite my lip and look back out the open door, the sun is beginning to set and there's still no sign of Nyx.

"I'm sorry Matt, but I just can't."

"What are you looking for that involves you leaving then?" he insists, coming over to stand by me.

"Information about the trouble that's happening in my town. I can't return and help if I don't have answers. Where I'm going will have those answers."

"I wish you could just tell me more."

"I do as well, but I promise I'll return soon. If anyone comes looking for me, tell them you have no idea who I am. I know how daunting that sounds, but it's safer that way. The less you know, the safer you are." I give him a small, hopeful smile. He struggles to return it, we both turn towards the front yard as we hear the hinges on the gate squeak open.

Nyx opens the gate with a leather clad hand, he's styled his black hair into waves and spikes on his head with a golden tiara of woven branches and golden oak leaves. He's dressed in royalty, his long navy cloak billows behind him as it shows off his dark green court attire.

I am definitely underdressed for this.

"What…" Matt trails off, gobsmacked just as much as I am.
In this moment he is faerie, full blood faerie.

Nyx looks up towards us and gives me an easy, cocky smile that could easily blow the socks and underwear from me if we had been alone. He averts his eyes to Matt and his soft gaze hardens.

"Hullo Matt, it's nice to meet you yet again." He stops half way across the yard, placing his hands in his pockets.

"Uh, yes. Hello." Matt says, looking between us. I rub a hand down my face, he is one for showing off.

"Took your time," I say to him as I gather my saddlebag over my shoulder. I'm wearing my blue dress, the same one from the night he'd saved me from the drunk man and seen me in my undergarments.

"I didn't realise I was on a schedule," he muses as I draw closer to him, sending a wink in my direction. Is he going to be this obnoxious the entire time in his world?

"I know you may be some sort of royalty, but protect her," Matt says, holding onto the door frame tightly. I feel Nyx wrap a cautious arm around my waist, pulling me to him. I press my hands against his chest, debating whether to pull him closer or slap him and scramble away.

"I will always protect her."

Matt nods slowly, his eyes search my face. I give him a hopeful smile, without another word he closes the door as he slips back inside. One moment we're standing in Matt's front yard and the other moment we're standing in a lush forest, with a large uprooted tree blocking our path. I gasp as Nyx lets me go, taking a step away.

I squeeze the strap of my bag as I look from the scenery to him, the forest around us glows brighter than anything I've ever seen. There is no sun, for the light comes from each living thing.

"What…just happened?" I ask, finding my voice. He shrugs as he looks at me with an innocent expression.

"We're on the border of my world and yours, I had to bring you here like so, otherwise knowing you, you'd try and retrace your steps and find this doorway again."

"Obviously. But, what do we do now? I can't see any doors." I gesture around us. I walk around the small clearing, my boots squash the vibrant grass with each step. To my amazement the grass corrects itself once my foot leaves the earth.

So much life flourishes here and I can understand why he wouldn't have wanted to bring me here. Nyx walks over to a fallen tree, gesturing for me to come closer.

"The door way is on the other side of this tree, I'll give you a hand up." He clasps his hands together as a foot hold for me, I hesitate before placing my boot in his hands. I reach one hand up and grapple for a grip of the bark or a gnarled root.

"Go," he whispers and I go flying upwards. I let out a scream as I pivot over the tree and land on the soft grass on the other side. It reaches out and tickles my cheek, weaving pieces though my hair.

I breath hard as I lay there, looking up at the sky that is far too blue to be normal. Landing hadn't hurt me, but a little warning would have been nice. I see Nyx launch himself over the log, landing gracefully on both feet.

He leans over me and looks down, cocking his head to the side.

"Move," I groan, forcing myself to roll over and stand. I brush my hands through my hair, pulling out little blue flowers as I go.

"The tree folk like you," he says, plucking a flower from my hair and observing it.

"What?" I tuck my hair behind my ears and look around. Just a few feet from us sits a toadstool circle, the vibrant red and white mushrooms sit in a perfect circle. We'd been warned as kids not to go near them, as once you enter you never return.

"The tree folk protect the circle, they like you. They're no bigger than a butterfly." He passes me the blue flower, and I look down at it. I decide to slip it behind my ear, it might work in my favour taking something given from their kind to the other side.

"I won't be the same when we enter, not unless we're alone. I need you to remember that." Nyx says.

"Why not?"

"Because the person you see and the person I am are two very different people. Weakness is a sin in Faerie, one that I learnt the hard way. Do as I say and follow my lead, no matter how much you don't want to." He grasps my face in his hands and tilts it towards him, brushing his thumbs against my cheek.

"You will soon see a side to me I wish I never had to show you, but I do hope you can forgive me once we return to this world."

I know this is a serious moment, but I can't help myself any more than he can, "I've seen this side and I'm not sure it gets much worse. Now let's stop the sappy cinematics and get what we came for." I step out of his grip and walk straight for the circle.

"You will be the death of me," I hear him mumble, catching up to me. I keep the small panic I feel surging masked, because faeries couldn't lie, which could very well mean I am going to be the death of Nyx.

He holds onto my hand as we both step into the circle, keeping his eyes on my own. "Don't take your eyes from me."

Once in the circle, the world around us breaks away like a shattering glass. I keep my eyes trained on the violet of his and as we begin to descend, they grow more vibrant and otherworldly.

Around us out of my peripheral vision, I see familiar faces and otherworldly creatures. I squeeze Nyx's hand in my own as he watches me and I wonder what he's thinking in this moment. If he wants to, he could very well keep me down here and no one would know where I'd gone or what had happened to me.

"Look at us Ravynne, why won't you look at us?"

"Come and play Rav, we've missed you."

"Cece is here too, she wants to see you."

I block out the voices that fill the air around us, the descent begins to drop faster and my hair whips around us as we fall but stay planted in the same spot. Surely we'd be near the bottom.

The whispers turn into hateful screams as I ignore them, the faces blur into a mixture of light and I feel myself being tugged in all different directions.

Nyx's hand in mine is the only thing keeping me planted.

Suddenly we're standing in a grass clearing in a toadstool ring, except the mushrooms are pink and white. I take a gasping breath as I look around us, in the distance a large white castle sits. A thick forest spans out around it, and I can vaguely see multiple creatures walking in and out of the forest as well as flying above it.

"That's where we need to go, welcome to Oakwood," he says. I look back from the castle and to him. He's slightly taller and more lean here, his ears are sharper and longer while his face has become more detailed.

"You're beautiful," I whisper, before I can stop myself. He looks down at me and his violet eyes now swirl with gold tendrils. The faerie world has stripped away the glamour he wears in my world, even his voice sounds more crisp here.

"We're going to be in for a lot of trouble. Come, let's get this over with." He takes my hand, with fingers abnormally long that swallow my entire hand. I hide my giggle as I focus on walking ahead. This is so surreal.

Land stretches further than my eye can see, mainly deep green forests but there is the occasional snow-capped mountain in the distance. A large river runs down the mountain to our left, and disappears into the forest we're about to enter.

We don't say a word as we walk through the tall canopy of trees. I keep my grip on his hand as the vines and leaves hum around me and lean in towards us. Either drawn to me, or him.

He keeps his head high and shoulders back, not sparing me a second to glance down. Already he has begun to change, and a small part of me feels afraid.

What on earth would I do if he changed completely and didn't remember me? And trapped me here?

I don't have a chance to overthink as we emerge to a cobblestone footpath littered with rose petals. The forest breaks apart, although grass still grows through the cracks of the path. We walk through an arch way into a court yard, Nyx drops my hand and walks a step ahead of me. I wrap my arms around myself as the fae here and other creatures I'm not sure I'd ever seen before begin to look at us.

The fae here are just as beautiful as Nyx, dressed in similar clothes with darker and lighter colours. The females don dresses and jewellery, their strange eyes focus on me.

A dark green goblin sniffs the air as I walk past, growling when he notices me. I feel my cheeks flush as I hurry to catch up with Nyx, who is now kneeling at the base of a throne. Upon that throne, sits the most stunning woman I have ever laid my eyes on. She's draped in golden silk, concealing the more private parts of her body but leaving little to imagination. Her red hair is curled perfectly around her face, cascading down to her belly button. Atop her head is a white crown, a large carved raven flares its wings at the centre, the wings spread out to become vines and thorns.

"Ah Nyx, what a pleasure it is to finally see you again." Her voice is warm like a harmony of voices and my legs quiver, her white eyes pierce mine and she offers me a wicked smile.

"And you've brought me a treat, how *thoughtful*." Her words snap from whatever spell she'd cast over me, I find myself at the base of her throne; almost about to climb up to her. I scramble backwards and fall on my ass down beside Nyx. He gives me a pointed look.

"Unfortunately your highness, she is mine." His voice causes the others around us to break into whispers and laughter. My cheeks burn as I look down at the blue dress that has no comparison to the female's gowns here. No wonder they thought this was funny.

"Yours? That's a mighty claim Nyx, one that needs follow through." She drums a hand against the stone arm of the throne, humming to herself. I feel her eyes crawl over my skin, poking and prodding; looking for weakness.

"One that I'd be happy to follow through. Ravynne will be with us for a few days before I return her to her own world," he declares, finally rising from his kneeling position. I stay seated, I doubt my legs will support my weight in this moment.

"Why does she come?"

"Because she is foolish enough to believe she is worthy of my love." More laughter erupts from the crowd and it takes all my strength not to bury my head between my hands. I look up to see his face set in a grin, his whole presentation screams cocky and I want to shove my fist in his face. He warned me, yes, but I didn't realise how embarrassing it was going to truly be.

"Very well, I will give her three days and then she must leave. But tonight you are both to come and celebrate with all of us. It has been too long since you've returned home." With the flick of her wrist we're dismissed. The crowd mills around us once again, whispering as they watch Nyx extend me a hand.

I reluctantly take his hand and plaster a smile on my face as I follow him through the crowd. I may as well feign stupidity for them all, best they think me a typical human.

We leave the bustling courtyard and go through a wooden door. I pull my hand from his as it opens up to a large hallway where the ceiling seems to stretch upwards to the sky. There is no real roof, only the illusion of the cool blue sky with the occasional wispy cloud floating in and out of view. I keep focused ahead as we walk along the grass carpet. The right side of the hallway is a glass window that show cases a breathtaking garden. Water pixies fly to and fro, splashing in bird baths, one catches me looking and flies up to the glass.

I pause as she presses a tiny hand against the glass, her wings are a blur on her back and she grins wickedly, exposing razor sharp teeth. Her little thin pink dress is in ribbons, but stays in place as she zips back to the others.

I look up and see Nyx about to turn a corner, I rush to catch up. We round the corner to another grass hallway with a set of stairs at the very end. I stay silent as we ascend the stairs.

It opens up to a large circular room, except there are no walls and only the leaves and branches from clustering trees. He walks over to a curved wooden door. When he opens it, the space shimmers.

"Where are we going?" I ask, tapping a foot against the marble floor. The room is fairly plain, having no decorations. He looks over his shoulder and smiles gently, the mask falls away and suddenly *my* Nyx is standing before me.

"I'm taking you to my room."

"If you think I'm going to share the bed, you have another thing coming," I say as I walk past him, waving a hand as I do. He chuckles as he follows me through.

We enter a spacious room, a lush red and gold queen size bed sits in the middle, against the back wall. The floor is covered in gold and green rugs, while a red mesh net is pinned up against the wooden bed frame. I twirl around the room as I take in its beauty.

There are two archways beside each other, one leads to the bathroom while the other leads to a balcony that overlooks the castle below. The walls are a deep red, someone has been drawing over the walls with a green paint; mountains and rivers.

"Wow, I didn't pick you to be so into red," I finally say, looking over to him. He leans against the closed door, watching me with those sharp eyes.

"There's plenty you don't know about me," he says smoothly, tucking his hands into his pockets. I huff and turn away from him, dumping my bag at the end of the bed as I walk out to the balcony.

The air here is clearer and below I can make out the odd creatures milling around. Were the other faeries cruel like the fairy tales, or are they more like Nyx?

And if not, why is Nyx different to them all?

"The library we need access to is in her highness's chambers," Nyx says, coming up behind me. He leans on the stone railing and looks down at the others. I trace a rose in the stone wall.

"Well, can't we just walk in there?" I question. She doesn't seem like a reader, she seems more…wicked. Books would be a waste to her. I wish he had have warned me how enchanting she was.

"The only way I'd be able to get into her room, is if I'm joining her in bed. No one enters that room unless they're warming her bed and if they do she makes sure they cannot return." His voice betrays no emotion, but I feel myself squirm.

"Wait, so you have to sleep with her to get in there? But that doesn't mean you'll be able to get in the library?" I look at him now, he sighs and runs a hand through his hair; pulling off the tiara and throwing it into the room.

"Yes, that's right. It's guarded by two other faeries, her most trusted. To get legal permission, we'd have to go through lots of formalities."

"Why can't we just tell her there's a babunook on the loose killing children?"

"Because she doesn't care for mortals."

Oh.

"So you have to sleep with her and somehow smuggle me in and then I'll have to try and get past the other two faeries?" This sounds impossible, I can be charmed by them; I'd be no use trying to get into that library.

"Unless…" I trail off, trying to piece my thoughts together. I had three days, she wouldn't be in her room the entire time. I'd need to be sneaky and break into the room and Nyx was going to have to help.

"Unless what?" he looks over at me, his eyes flicker to where I chew my bottom lip. I snap my fingers.

"Unless I walk in there. You can glamour right?"

"Yes?"

"Make me look like her." The thought half delights me, but Nyx doesn't look so intrigued by this idea. His ears twitch as he frowns.

"No. No way, if you're caught you'll be killed." He stands to his full height and crosses his arms over his chest as he looks down at me.

"Oh come on! Nyx this is the only chance we have." I whine, puffing out my bottom lip. "Can we just try now, to see what it would be like?" I reach out and clasp his arm; shaking it annoyingly.

"Rav this is mad."

"I am mad, so please, let's try." I walk back into the room and wiggle my arms out before facing him again. He still stands outside, frowning at me.

"Oh come on, live on the edge a little. If I can come here into this world with you, you can do this for me." I wave my hands around the room, he groans as he walks into the room.

He approaches me and holds onto my face.

"Wha—"

He presses his lips to mine, cutting me off. My eyes flutter shut as I kiss him back, my hands hold onto his arms as he breathes into me through the kiss.

My body begins to vibrate before relaxing again, a warmth spreads through me like liquid honey as the kiss deepens. My head spins as the kiss changes, becoming a bit more aggressive.

I press myself against his chest, his hands drop from my face and find their way to my waist; his fingers dig into the soft skin as I wrap my arms around his neck.

We walk a few steps to the bed, where he slowly lays back while I climb on top. His hands skim my sides, hesitating on the curves of my breasts. I groan in the back of my throat and press myself into him, the hardness of him rubs my thigh and I hear his own gasp.

I open my eyes and break the kiss, his lips are swollen and when he opens his eyes they are wild and untamed. My hair falls around us, and I squeal when I see it's red.

"You did it!" I jump off him, and look down at myself. I am wearing the same dress she had on earlier, with the same red curls. I'm taller and more slender, and I reach up and feel my now pointed ears.

I rush into the bathroom and freeze, star struck. White, glowing eyes meet mine in the mirror and I gasp; touching my lips. I am *her* but me.

I walk back out of the bathroom to see Nyx leaning on his elbows, with his erection pressing against his pants.

Had he only been turned on because I'd looked like her?

Don't think that now Ravynne, you have more important things to worry about.

"Was the kiss necessary?" I ask, my voice is still my own which might be a problem if I was going to have to talk. Nyx's cheeks are flushed red and his hair is dishevelled. He smirks casually.

"No, but I wanted to kiss you."

"So you could have done the glamour without the kiss?" I cross my arms over my chest, pretending to be annoyed.

"Yes, I could do it by just looking at you."

"You're a pain in my ass." I feel my lips twitch into a smile, unable to help myself.

"That's not the first time you've told me that."

"It won't be the last either." I raise an eyebrow at him, "You can take it off now. I just wanted to see."

He begins to unbutton his shirt. I hold up my hands as I feel my eyes widen.

"Woah, woah. I meant the glamour," I squeak. He looks up from his shirt, confused; it was already half undone and I could see the muscles on his chest.

"Oh," he grins, but leaves his shirt undone. He waves his hand in my direction and I feel the same tingling sensation and the warmth. I look down to see my own dress.

"Thanks." I crouch down and open my saddlebag, I desperately need a shower to wash away the ache I feel for him. A hot shower is the perfect thing to clear my head.

"Why do you keep thanking me?" he asks, I look up over the end of the bed. He's laying down looking up at the ceiling. Why did I? I wasn't sure myself.

"It's the polite thing to do." I grab a fresh pair of clothes and stand.

"But you know it means you're in debt to me. Why do you keep doing it?" He looks at me, his emotions open and raw on his face. I struggle with an answer.

"Because maybe I'm not ready for this to be over once we kill that thing. Because maybe you'll still stick around for repayments." *Maybe I'll never be ready for us to be over*. Before he replies, I go into the bathroom. I dump my clothes on the marble sink and go to shut the door.

There's no door.

"I'm showering, if I catch you peeping I will kill you." I shout out into the room, thankful he wouldn't be able to see anything from the bed. A deep chuckle meets my ears as I turn to the large white bathtub, turning the golden handle that sits above it. Warm rain begins to fall from the ceiling and into the bath.

After the day I've had, nothing is strange to me now.

I observe myself in the bathroom mirror. I'd reluctantly pulled on the dress that the Queen had sent to Nyx's room. He's yet to see it. When I'd looked into the bag I'd blushed madly and run into the bathroom, threatening death if he entered.

I'd run a brush through the loose waves of my hair, I'd braided a few blue flowers through the locks. The dress she'd chosen for me screams lust, and I'm not sure if I can bare to leave the room wearing it.

I don't know how I feel about Nyx seeing me in something so…revealing.

The black silk material is feather light, it wraps around my throat before splitting in two, each strand barely covering my breasts. The thin material shows the darkness of each nipple. It clinches above my hips connected to a silver acorn, before splitting down both thighs and exposing both of my bare legs.

The black lace underwear I'd chosen to wear is painfully obvious but there is no way I am going to this party and wearing no underwear.

"Are you nearly ready? By the time we get there it'll be over." Nyx groans, no doubt pacing back and forth in front of the bed. I brush a loose strand of hair behind my ear and look over myself once more. I can do this. Before thinking better of it, I turn and walk out into the bedroom. She'd sent a pair of black flats that wrap up my calf, along with the dress. At least my feet will be comfortable.

Nyx is doing as I predicted; pacing and staring up at the ceiling while playing with a red berry necklace.

"Well?" I ask, crossing my arms over my chest as my heart thunders in my chest. I feel the need to hide my breasts from him, if he sees them…I don't think either of us will be willing to leave this room.

He trips over himself and drops the necklace of berries as he looks me over, his jaw goes slack as his eyes roam freely over me; heating each inch of my skin. I feel my cheeks redden.

"You…look…" he seems to choke on his words, as if there isn't a word to describe how I look. I wave him off.

"Yes, I know how I look." I groan, I reach down and pick up the necklace he'd been fiddling with. I hold it up and look back to him. "What's this?"

"A necklace of rowan berries, it'll stop the other faerie's being able to charm and glamour you. Just don't let anyone get close enough to pull it off. This party won't be like any you've been too and I wanted you to feel as safe as you could…but now…" he trails off, physically forcing himself to look away from me.

"Now what?" I look down at the berries ad undo the small bronze clasp.

"Now I'm afraid nothing will keep you safe when you're dressed so painfully seductive." I feel him come closer. I don't dare to look up. I keep my eyes down cast as he takes the necklace from me and brushes my hair over my shoulder. I shiver as his fingers skim the exposed skin, sending shots of heat through me.

"Done." He steps back and I feel the weight of the necklace press reassuringly against my throat. Only then do I finally look back up at him.

"I guess we should get this over with then." I sigh, extending a hand towards him. His lips quirk into a soft smile.

"Yes, we shall."

We enter the courtyard with my hands clasped around his firm arm. He'd worn dark green loose fitting pants and a button down white silk shirt, the buttons stopped just below his chest; exposing the muscles there.

The faeries pause and look towards us, the males take me in hungrily with their eyes while the females do the same with Nyx. I feel each gaze on me, each stare and each judgment thrown my way.

A large, bathtub size golden cup sits in the middle. Nyx leads us towards it, grabbing two golden goblets that hang from the side of it. He dips each in, passing one to me. I take a look into it, the very galaxy itself is in my cup. The liquid is a dark purple, literal silver stars shine and twirl around with golden tendrils. He chuckles at my awe.

"What on earth is this?" I ask, looking back up at him.

"Faerie wine, you can't have more than one cup so make this one last." Nyx leads us away and through the crowd, finally stopping as a large green leaf unfolds from the side of the cobblestone wall.

I take a seat and lean into the curve of it, leaving enough room for Nyx to sit beside me if he chooses. He takes a sip as he looks around, nodding and offering smiles where he can.

I do the same, finally taking a sip.

My body explodes with light, each cell expanding and growing. I gasp in surprise as it rushes through me, engulfing me in a warm flame. Nyx snaps his eyes to me. I look up at him and both his eyebrows raise.

"How are you feeling little bird?" He murmurs, crouching down in front of me.

"Light," I whisper. I raise a hand and look at it. I do feel light, limitless. The gold tendrils in his eyes swirl faster I as look back to him.

"Rav-"

"I'm so glad you could make it!" A female voice trills behind Nyx. We both look up to see the Queen standing before us, wearing nothing but a necklace of sapphire and diamonds. My eyes traitorously wander down to her perky breasts, pausing at her diamond shaped pink nipples.

Her white skin looks so soft in the glow from the lanterns. What I assume are lanterns. Nyx forces himself to look towards the ground, his jaw twitches.

"I appreciate the invite and lending me the dress." I sit up straighter, fixing where the dress had creased.

"Oh of course honey. Any friend of Nyx's is a friend of mine." Her voice drips with nectar and I feel the enchantment laced in her words, thankfully they do nothing for me. I silently send thanks to Nyx.

"What do we owe the pleasure of your company?" Nyx asks, finally rising. Not on her daunting throne, she's shorter than Nyx, but only just. She reaches out and skims her hand down his bare chest, I narrow my eyes. An ugly emotion rises when he doesn't stop her.

"I simply came to see how my favourite man has been. Really Nyx, it's been an awfully long time since we've shared a bed, you really were the best of the best." She shakes her head sadly and sighs, resting her palm against his chest now. I feel my blood freeze in my veins. He'd slept with her.

I want to vomit.

"Is that all you came to tell me?" His gaze is as hard as steel as he looks down upon her. I silently stand, shaking my shoulders out. Her eyes flicker towards me before she continues to argue with Nyx. He doesn't notice as I slip away and begin to walk around.

I force myself to calm, to see reason. Nyx hadn't known me when he'd slept with her, but I have to wonder; how many of the faeries around me right now has he slept with?

Two drunken males stumble past me, one with yellow skin has the tail of wolf as it wags back and forth; purposefully trying to hit the man beside him. It makes me smile slightly.

I find myself back at the large golden bowl, I peer over the edge of the bowl and gasp. It moves on its own accord, swirling and reflecting the night sky above us. I'm vaguely aware of a soft melody playing in the back ground, before I know it I'm dipping my cup back into its contents and sculling the drink.

I may not be able to be charmed by a faerie, but nothing and no one are stopping me from indulging in this sweet nectar.

It hits me instantly, each cell in my body explodes with light. I can't stop myself. Going back for a fourth cup, a gentle hand wraps around my wrist.

I look up to see a stunning pale blue skinned female faerie looking down at me, her dark blue hair flows around her thin shoulders in waves. She gives me a soft smile, her golden eyes are too large for her face. But she's stunning.

"Dearest, how many cups have you had?" her voice is as soft as silk, wrapping smoothly around me. I keep my eyes on her, noting the freckles that splatter across her nose and cheeks like a constellation.

"Um, three?" I offer, flickering my eyes towards my empty cup and back up to her. She grins and it lights her whole face up.

"Oh my, you humans sure like to party like a faerie don't you?" She leads us away, back towards a large blossomed pink flower. Three other female faeries sit on the petals, talking amongst one another. They all wear similar dresses to my own.

"I guess. I don't really drink much, but this tastes amazing." I sigh in pleasure, remembering the euphoric feeling I'd gotten when I'd been drinking. She brushes her hair over her shoulder, sending a breeze my way; I breathe in the hint of the sea water.

"We'll get along just fine then, come, meet my friends." She stops in front of the flower, which now has glowing petals. She steps away from me, letting me go. I stand awkwardly, resisting the urge to look down at my feet.

"Girls, this is Ravynne." The girl on the lowest petal looks up at me with large light yellow doe eyes. Her blonde hair floats around her heart shaped face.

"I'm Nicolia." She smiles, her voice is high and when she erupts into giggles they turn to a squeak; reminding me of a mouse. Her pale skin is similar to mine, but I know we're nothing alike when I spot the golden glow of her fingers.

"Sarisha," the green girl says, sitting the furthest up on the flower, she lounges on her back and turns her head towards me. Thick dark green dreadlocks spill over and hang down. She looks over me lazily, gold is smeared around her plump lips.

"I'm Blossom, easiest name to remember," the last one pipes in, leaning over the edge of her petal to get a better look at me. Short pink hair hangs just below her chin, my eyes widen when I notice the pig like tail that wraps around her thigh. The end flicks back and forth. She looks down and smiles, "Don't mind that."

"That's so cool," I sigh, wishing I had something special about me. The girl that brought me over here begins to climb up on the petals, settling beside Sarisha.

"Come on, climb up." She gestures to the empty petal beside them and I hastily climb up. I don't know how I manage to make it up without making a fool of myself, but I'm satisfied when my legs dangle over the edge. From here I can get a full view of the court yard.

I'm acutely aware of my blood buzzing in my veins, almost as if it's on fire. My light mood begins to darken when I see Nyx still with the

Queen. She's closer now, with a hand against his cheek.

"Don't worry about it, she's like that with every male," the blue girl says, looking over to them.

"It's not…"

"No need to explain yourself, we all know why you're here. Nyx announced it." She gives me a gentle smile, "I'm Natahila by the way."

"Thank you, by now I feel I'd have climbed into the bowl trying to drown my sorrows." I shake my head and chuckle, already itching to get my hands on another drink.

"Our deepest sorrows are the ones with the greatest lessons, you can only drown them for so long before they demand to be heard." She looks back to Nyx with an almost troubled expression.

"I don't know what you find so charming about him," Sarisha snorts, looking up at me. I feel the heat rise in my cheeks.

"Well, he's kind and caring, smart, and witty. I don't know when I let my guard slip around him, but he's somehow managed to get underneath my skin," I confess, feeling far more truthful than I have my whole life. Is this an effect of the drink?

"Cut him out," Sarisha growls, looking back to Nyx. Natahila slaps her arm, narrowing her eyes at her.

"Just because you think he is vile, does not mean she does," she hisses.

"Why do you think that?" I ask, before she can stop Sarisha talking.

She looks up to the stars above us, not seeing anything as she thinks.

"I have many reasons to think that. Before his mother died he was engaged to my sister. When his mother died we cancelled the wedding. Fae are not affectionate, or have families. We just are. We just exist and then we die." She finally tilts her head back to me, trying to make me understand exactly what she's trying to tell me.

"He is not one of us, even though he may think he is. He has a putrid human heart, it stops him from reaching his full potential. Did you know the Queen offered him a place by her side? As King of Oakwood? He would have matched his father in all things equal, and he refused." She pauses, taking a breath. "Do you know why he refused?" She asks.

"No…" I trail off, Nyx had never told me any of this.

"Because he claimed he did not love her and would not marry into a loveless relationship. Wouldn't form an alliance for the greater good because his feelings would be hurt if he did. Do you know the consequence of his defiance?"

I stay silent, my answer is obvious. The other girls go still, knowing what is to come isn't going to be good.

"They killed my sister. They knew he cared for her and to ruin him they took her."

I go still, looking back to Nyx and the Queen. He's looking at me, even though the Queen has her hand wrapped around his arm. His jaw twitches. I frown. I feel sick.

"We exist and we die, but Nyx does not work like us. He is not one of us. If he was, my sister would be alive and our court would be flourishing." Her voice holds no emotion, as if she's as cold as she seems to want me to believe.

"I'm sorry for the loss of your sister, I know that pain all too well," I say softly, watching as Nyx begins to walk towards us casually. His eyes flicker to the girls around me before settling on the empty cup I'd dropped on my way up to the petal.

"You cared for you sister. I did not. We are not the same."

Before I can hide my shock or reply, Nyx stops in front of the flower, he toes the empty cup and looks up at me. His hands hang casually in the pockets of his pants, gold smears his lip.

"Having fun ladies?" He muses, his lips pulling to a smirk. I feel my blood heat at his words, my heart begins to beat faster. Why did my body react so keenly when he was near me? Why did it betray me when I needed my senses more than ever?

"Nyx, how nice of you to finally join us. We were watching miss poppet here devour cup after cup, but I decided to step in before she drank the rest on us," Natahila coos, sending a wink my way.

"How many cups has she had?" He asks, suddenly concerned.

"Three that I know of if she's telling the truth. I was going to let her have four but I feared for your sake that her liver would fail and then we'd be left to deal with cleaning her corpse up." She waves a hand through the air, scrunching her nose up. She only stopped me because she didn't want to deal with the consequences if I died. Here I was thinking they could be friends of mine.

We are not the same.

"Ravynne darling, please come down." He lifts a hand up, he hides his worry well. But beneath the layers of falseness I can see it, almost smell it in the air.

"You're asking? Why not just come up and grab her?" Sarisha says, feigning boredom. I swallow harshly, suddenly feeling like I'd swallowed a cup of sand.

"She is her own person. Now Rav, I think it's time we got you some food." His fingers wiggle, waiting for my hand. I hesitate. I still had that ugly feeling gnawing at my bones when he'd spent the last however long it had been with the Queen. She's touched him. I can't touch him.

"Go dearest, otherwise Blossom over here will take your place." I look to Blossom, who blushes furiously and looks away. Her tail whips nervously back and forth. I sigh and begin to climb down, shaking and wobbling as I go. Nyx's warm hands come to my waist as he helps me stand on solid ground. I feel the earth tilt and hold out a hand, resting it on his arm. He clicks his tongue.

"How you're still standing is beyond me. Humans usually pass out after their first one." He wraps an arm around my shoulder, I melt into his side and wrap my own arm around his waist. My fingers dig into the muscle of his side.

"You were trying to get me to pass out?" I hiss, stumbling away as he leads us from the girls. I don't get a chance to say goodbye, but a part of me wishes I had stayed and talked with them more.

"If you did, it would give us both an excuse to leave. And well…they would not stop me from taking you back to bed," he whispers, coming to a stop at a mushroom the size of his bed. He gently places me down, I fall back and look up at the stars. The mushroom is soft beneath me, so soft I fear I'll never stand.

"They'd let you rape me?" I ask, the full seriousness of it goes over my head.

"I'm afraid there has been worse things done in Faerie." He sighs, sitting beside me. I draw my eyes to him, watching as his back muscles move as he massages the back of his neck.

"What did the Queen want with you?" I ask. Thankfully only goblins are near us, and all of them are off their heads. I hear a small shriek cut short as one goblin rips a small hare in two. I shiver.

"What she wants every time I visit. To take me to bed, to make me her King, all of that nonsense." He brushes it off like it's no big deal. But I pause.

"If it would benefit the court or kingdom or whatever, why don't you do it?" I lean up on my elbows, feeling more awake.

"Because I only do things out of love, not greed." He finally looks over his shoulder at me, his eyes travel from my legs to my face and I feel my insides turn to liquid lava…the way he's looking at me right now is driving my senses wild.

"So, if I asked you to kiss me right here, right now. Would you do that out of love or greed?" I ask, my voice soft. I would never ask such a question sober, but after the nectar of their world I feel a part of me has been stripped away. Not drunk per say, but something *other* is happening to me. His Adam's apple bobs.

"Both."

I suck in a sharp breath. Desire for him fills me, taking over every inch. My body is screaming for him, needing him to fulfil what I've offered. I couldn't care if the whole world was in this court yard to witness it.

I look over him, his dark hair is dishevelled and the light hits one side of his face; igniting the golden and violet mixture of his eyes. Above looking breathtakingly beautiful, he looks tired. Dark circles have begun to linger under his eyes.

"I want you to be greedy," I whisper and my pulse races. If he rejects me now, I will never live it down. Not until the day I join my sister in the afterlife. To my amazement and shock he turns and climbs onto the mushroom, on top of me. I part my legs as he kneels above me, painfully aware of the way my thighs rub against his and the way my legs wrap around his waist.

He plants his hands on either side of my face and looks down.

"This is the nectar talking."

"No, it's not." I rest both hands on his chest, unsure of what to do with them. My inexperience is obvious, and I feel myself flush red.

"Pray tell, why tell me you want us to go separate ways after we slay the beast?" He whispers, lowering his face to mine. His lips graze my jaw and leave small kisses as he trails to my earlobe. I groan.

"Why act like you don't want this when I see the way you look at me?" His kisses begin to trail down my throat, I'm panting. I don't know how to breath properly.

"Why do you keep me at a distance when I only want to help you?" He pauses at my collarbone, his lips a painful torture.

"Why do you act as though you can't love me, when I know you can? I don't give my heart to others, but with you it landed in the mud the day you did and you picked it up and never gave it back." He pulls back, looking down at me with burning intensity.

"It's selfish of me to think you could ever feel the same way about me." He's suddenly standing, and I'm left a quivering mess.

"Nyx…" I sit up, the front of my dress rubs against my now hard nipples and I squeeze my thighs together. This is unfair. He can't say these things when I'm in this state.

"Don't. I don't want to hear your lies tonight. I wasn't lying when I said you needed food, let's go back to the room and I'll order some." He helps me stand, keeping a hand pressed firmly to my lower back. I avoid looking at the other faeries as we slip out into the hall and head back towards his room.

My mind is a whirl of thoughts I can't unscramble.

I did like Nyx, more than I have ever liked anyone before. If he was gone forever, it would be like losing a limb. Three dangerous words want to bubble from my lips, but I push them away. My confession would not change anything.

I blink and we're in the room, Nyx heads immediately back out and I sigh. I rummage through his cupboard and pull out a white short-sleeve shirt. I run the water in the shower and pull out the blue flowers, undoing the braids in my hair. I watch my reflection, my eyes are almost aglow. I slip from my dress, underwear and shoes. I bathe quickly. I pull on his shirt and walk out onto the balcony. Down below music travels up to me, caressing my ears. I lean against the stone, spotting the large flower and the girls. More creatures have arrived, and I'm glad we left when we did.

The door to the room opens and I look over my shoulder to see Nyx carrying three white, square cardboard boxes. I frown and walk inside, he sits them on the bed and holds two forks.

"Okay that smells heavenly. What is it?" I ask, standing beside him. I take the fork from him and open each one.

"Chinese." We both sit opposite each other on the bed. I pick up one box and he does the other, mine is full of rice mixed with vegetables and small pieces of white meat.

"I don't know what that is but I bet it tastes amazing." I dig in, not giving it a second thought.

"It's one of my favourite dishes. You're eating fried rice, while I'm having curried chicken. The last one is honey prawns." We eat in silence, swapping the dishes until they're well and truly empty. Nyx clicks his fingers and the empty containers and forks disappear. I groan as I lay back on the bed, resting my hands under my head.

"Thank you for dinner, that was by far the best thing I've ever tasted," I say, looking over at him. He gives me a small smile, a pink tinge in his cheeks.

"Rav…why aren't you wearing any pants?" He asks, nibbling his bottom lip. My jaw drops in horror, I squeal as I jump from the bed and pull the shirt down to my thighs. He turns as I pull on a pair of underwear, chuckling.

"I forgot, I swear," I say, climbing back into bed. He looks back.

"So you only put underwear on. You make no sense," he muses, running a hand through his hair.

"I rarely do."

"Are you tired?" He asks. I get under the covers, nodding. My bones ache, my body aches and my soul aches for all the things that are left unsaid between us.

He stands up and comes around to my side of the bed, tucking the sheets around my shoulders. He brushes the hair back from my face and plants a small kiss on my forehead.

"Get some sleep, I'll come to bed shortly." The lights go out and I see nothing, but still feel his warm presence.

"Sweet dreams, my wild bird," he whispers.

It's selfish of me to think you could ever feel the same way about me.

He can't be further from the truth.

I wake to something touching my foot and I blink away sleep as I look towards the end of the bed. A red creature stands at the end of the bed, a gnarled hand pokes my foot. Its parsnip shaped nose touches the bed sheets as its black beady eyes flick up to me. A small tuft of black hair sprouts from the top of its head.

"Um, excuse me. It's rude to touch people without their permission," I say, pulling my foot away from its hand. I throw the covers off and pull my legs up. It sniffs the air and walks around the bed, rocking from one side to the other as it walks around to my side.

"Can you talk?" I ask, trying not to flinch as a hand reaches out to touch my hair. Its fingers are broken in different directions and the skin is wrinkled. A piece of hair gets snagged.

I hiss as it tries to tug its hand away.

"Leif, what are you doing?" Nyx says, entering the room. Leif and I look up towards him and I can only imagine what it looks like, his shirt barely covers my legs and the chilly morning air has hardened my nipples.

"I was just inspecting her," Leif grumbles, her voice is scratchy but smooth. She yanks her hand out and breaks off a few strands of hair. I reach up and touch my scalp, pulling my hair over my left shoulder so it's out of reach.

"She's mortal, they are more reserved with touching than we are." He looks down at Leif as she waddles over to him, she shakes the pieces of my hair from her hand as she encloses her arms around his calf. She only just reaches the height of his knees, her round red belly is covered in a thin green shirt that covers right down to her gnarled feet.

"Why have you brought a mortal girl back here?" Leif asks, looking up at him. He strokes the black tuft of hair on her head and smiles down at her.

"Because a babunook is giving her trouble in her world so I am helping."

"Stupid boy, mortals aren't our business," Leif snaps, shaking her head. She looks back at me and scowls; exposing small sharp rat like teeth.

"She is mine and she's only here for two more days, so be nice. She's a guest." He looks over to me, his eyes wander over my body before he looks back down to her. I remember every word he spoke to me the night before.

"You're lucky I like you," Leif grumbles as she lets him go, she heads out the door leaving us in silence.

"She seems…" I can't think of a word.

"She's looked after me my whole life. When father didn't want me anymore he sent me here, where Leif took me in. She doesn't like strangers." He walks over and passes me a cup of warm dark liquid, steam curls from the top. I eye it warily but take it from him.

"It's just coffee," he says, amused. I shoot him a warning look before taking a small sip, indeed it is just sweet coffee.

"That's nice of you. So what's the plan for today?" I ask, crossing my legs underneath me. He takes a seat in the space my legs occupied and looks out over the balcony.

"Well if you still want to pursue your plan of glamour, which I feel will fall apart, we'll have to do it on your last day. You can't leave any earlier as she's spoken your time here, but on the final day you can leave whenever you please. Not a day later or earlier. So we have two days."

"Two days for you to prove I'm not worthy of you to return my love." I take another sip of coffee and look out to the balcony as well. I feel him turn towards me but I don't look back to him.

"You're definitely not forgetful are you?" he sighs.

"No. So let's go explore, I may as well see some good things while

I'm here. Just don't let me become a stupid mortal and fall for any faerie nonsense?" I finish the coffee and sit the cup on the bedside table.

"Get dressed then." He stands and walks out onto the balcony, giving me some privacy. I dress quickly, deciding on my grey dress. I didn't want to draw unnecessary attention to myself. I keep my hair down and pull my boots on.

"I'm ready," I call out as I adjust the necklace he'd given me. I always forget it is there, and I have to wonder what sort of visions I'm missing out on. The rowan berry necklace still sits smugly against my neck.

"Follow me, remember I won't be the same once I leave this room." His hand rests on the door knob as he looks at me over his shoulder.

"Yeah. Trust me I got the memo yesterday." I grumble, following him through the door. We emerge in the same plain room and head down the steps.

Other goblin like creatures walk the hallways today, I spot Leif talking to another dark purple creature with a nose as small as a strawberry, but eyes as big as an apple.

She scowls as she catches me staring, wobbling off with the other creature. I keep in stride with Nyx as he leads us back out into the court and I begin to feel uneasy. His shoulders straighten and he walks with more *purpose*.

He keeps an easy smile plastered on his face, occasionally winking to the female faeries that lay draped on large green leaves that have been shaped into chairs. I don't see any of the girls I'd met last night.

They're all stunning, and I have to force myself not to look to hard at them all. A girl with pale pink skin approaches us, her pointed ears are covered in silver hoops and studs. Her blonde hair is cut into a bob like fashion with a wispy fringe covering her golden eyes.

"Nyx, it's been too long," she says, caressing his arm. She's wearing a tight corset that exposes a large amount of cleavage and shows how tiny her waist is. It fans out into a thin mesh skirt that covers her long legs.

"Raxanda, what a pleasure." He reaches out for her hand, peppering a kiss onto her palm. Her cheeks turn a soft red shade and she plumps her lips out.

Jealously coils in my stomach like a snake, I'd never been one to be jealous. Apparently here everything and anything is possible.

"Always a pleasure with you Nyx," she giggles, batting her long white lashes at him. I turn away from them and look around, feeling slightly sick at the open display of affection.

Gross.

A group of male faeries sit around a large golden bowl similar to the one I'd seen last night but only the size of a cauldron, scooping out golden liquid with their mugs. Gold smears their lips and cheeks, and I feel tempted to go over.

One with long brown hair catches me looking, his green eyes are vibrant as he tilts his head to the side. His skin is a soft shade of yellow, blending down his arms to a dark orange.

I thought being bland would help me blend in, it was making me stand out more. He whispers something to the other four and they all look over. I turn back to see Nyx still chatting with the girl, throwing her flirty comments and compliments.

"Nyx can we go?" I ask, crossing my arms over my chest. Raxanda looks over to me and grins wickedly.

"Oh Nyx, I forgot you had a little pet following you around." She giggles, but I hear the malice in her voice.

"A pet indeed," he muses, looking down at me. I catch a small glimpse of his kinder self in his eyes.

"Whatever, talk to little miss faerie all you want," I grumble, stalking off. I wasn't sure where I was going but I wasn't going to waste another second hearing them flirt back and forth.

I walk through the large archway we'd entered the day before and out into the forest, rabbits the size of dogs jump past me; giving me curious looks before leaping away.

I continue walking down a dirt path, where the grass has been trampled away. I hum softly to myself, pushing the swirl of emotions I felt earlier, away. I hope Nyx won't say anything to me later, I am in no mood to argue.

I exit the forest and look out over the large expanse of land, no buildings or trees litter it. Only grass that reaches my knees covers the land as far as I can see.

I look over my shoulder, hoping Nyx has followed. But the forest is dark and empty. I am alone. I sigh and trudge out into the grass, the small strands tickle my ankles as I walk through.

I head towards the river, a swim would be nice.

The walk there is shorter than I would have thought, but sure enough I reach the edge of the forest to find a large river running directly into it. The water is a dark blue, and swirls lazily towards the trees.

I walk over and sit down at the edge, I pull my boots off and sit them beside me before bundling my dress up around my thighs. I dip my feet into the water, surprised to find it warm. Usually the river back at home is ice cold, regardless if the sun has been bearing down on it all day.

I swish my feet back and forth, slightly unnerved that I can't actually see them under the surface; it's as if they've disappeared. No other creature lingers around the edge of this part of the forest, I can vaguely hear things walking through or catch sentences from conversations but no one emerges.

I lie back down and rest my hands under my head, looking up to the sky. Large, white clouds hover in the sky above me, offering me some shade from the glow of everything here.

Once I'd left this place, I'd have to write it down and try and sketch out the strange creatures I've seen here. My drawings wouldn't do them justice, but this is something I didn't want to forget.

A sinking feeling weighs down on me as I realise what I have to return to, I could only hope the babunook hadn't struck again. Why would the faeries create such an ungodly creature?

I hear a splash from the river and prop myself up on my elbows to have a look. At the opposite bank of the river, a black horse's head has emerged. Its black mane is tangled with weeds and shells. It watches me with black depthless eyes, breathing water in and out through its nose.

A golden bridle sits securely on its large head, with black crescent moons engraved along the metal.

I hadn't read anything in the books about this, whatever this was.

"Um, hi?" I sit up and quickly pull my feet from the river; a thin blue sheen of goo covers them. I wipe as much away as I can with my dress, still keeping my eyes on the horse.

It doesn't move closer, or speak. It stays in place, watching me with unblinking eyes. I shiver at the thought of it being near my feet.

"Is this your river?" I ask, gesturing towards the forest and up towards the mountains. It nods once, snorting out water.

"It's nice here." I nod a few times, looking around. I feel awkward. I'm never one for small talk.

It begins to float closer to me, and stops once its head is in the same place my feet had been dangling only a moment ago. I itch to reach out and stroke its nose, the hair is slick with water and I want to wipe it away.

"You're far from home," it says. Its voice sounds muffled by the water and gurgles slightly.

"Yeah I know, there's a babunook running rampant in my village and I came here to figure out how to kill it." I give it the truth. It seems harmless if not a little scary.

"The babunook is a beast that lingers on the edges of this world, many of them roam the mountains of your world." It blinks slowly, I look up towards the mountains in the distance. Did they just roam in the wilderness in their beast form since there are no children here to eat?

"I can't let it live." I look back to the horse, and watch in horror and fascination as hands as black as night leave the water and grip the edges of the bank, only centimetres away from my dress.

Its nails dig into the soft earth as the water drips away from it.

"Are you getting out?" I ask, feeling my heart beating as fast as the pixie wings had been. It doesn't say a word. Behind me I hear the crunch of boots on brittle leaves, I look away from the horse and see Nyx come around the corner of the forest.

"There you are. I've been looking—" he freezes as he spots me. He raises his hands slowly.

"Rav, get over here right now." His face pales as his eyes widen, I frown at him and look back to the horse. It seems harmless.

"We're just talking, I finally found someone who wants to talk to me," I snap over my shoulder, clenching my hands into my dress. The horse's eyes stretch at the corners, and I have the distinct feeling it's smiling.

"Kelpie, leave her alone," Nyx growls, taking a step closer. A black hand reaches out and grabs onto my dress.

"Hey, woah hands off." I try to pull my dress from its hand, but its grip is tight and the material doesn't budge.

"Rav get back here now!" Nyx's voice rises and I feel his panic and begin to panic myself. I scramble back as far as I can, the dress strains around my shoulders. Nyx's hands loop under my arms as he tries to pull me backwards.

The kelpie lets out a gleeful laugh, its black hand begins to pull me towards the water. I grab onto Nyx's arms and cry out as my feet hit the water.

"Nyx! Don't let it take me!" I shout, water begins to close around my legs and seep into my dress. I scream out as multiple hands begin to grab at the dress and my legs. I try and kick my feet out at it, but come into contact with nothing. The laughter turns into a howl.

"Fuck!" Nyx shouts, his hands grip tightly into my arms as he tries to pull, hard enough to leave bruises. It yanks again, and only the top half of my body and arms are on the bank. Something smooth twists itself around my waist and I gag as it tightens.

Nyx is sitting on the ground, digging his feet into the earth and trying to pull me out. He looks at me with wild eyes as I feel the kelpie yank again. I break from his grip.

And down I sink.

My scream is swallowed by the water as I'm dragged under. I close my mouth and try to pry the tentacle away from my waist. I open my eyes into the water and see the kelpie's face in front of my own, the bottom of its jaw is rotted with the flesh falling away. Multiple arms are attached to its body, grappling at me.

I shake my head and try and kick out my legs.

There is no bottom here. Only darkness.

A fire begins to ignite in my lungs as my body desperately begs for oxygen

The kelpie's eyes begin to glow a murky white colour as its bottom jaw drops open. Fear sets in.

It's going to *eat* me.

I struggle more, nails break the skin of the tentacle around my waist. Black hands swarm my legs and hold me immobile, forcing me to sink deeper. The dim glow of the world above darkens.

What was Nyx going to tell my family? A horse ate me?

Who is going to protect the children in my village? Protect my brother?

I wonder if this is how Cecelia felt, lungs on fire in the darkness all alone. My vision begins to form black spots, and my lips tremble. Once I part them, it will be over for me.

It knows I've nearly reached my end, I let myself go limp and watch as my hair floats eerily around me. The kelpie comes closer, eyes blazing brightly.

A shadow fall over us, but the kelpie pays no mind to it. I use the last of my strength to look towards the surface, only to see violet eyes coming down towards me.

Nyx.

A smile pulls at my lips as I finally breathe in.

Water floods my lungs and I begin to choke, my body begins to convulse as I try to spit the water out but only swallow more.

Something bright flashes in front of me, dismembering the kelpies hold on me. It roars and the water begins to shake around me.

Warm hands grab onto me and begin to pull me towards the surface.

I was so close…but I let go.

I sink down to the darkness.

One.

Two.

Three.

Black.

"Ravynne, wake up!" A voice shouts in the dark, coming from nowhere and everywhere. I look around but see nothing as I float as soft as a feather. It's peaceful here, warm here.

"Come back to me."

The voice is familiar, and a flash of violet eyes lights up the darkness and I *know* those eyes. I know those eyes.

A girl appears, she walks over to me.

"Cece?" I ask, reaching out for her. She runs into my arms and wraps her thin arms around my legs.

"Ravie, you shouldn't be here," she whispers, looking up to my face. I stroke her face with my hand, why shouldn't I be here with her?

"I'm not leaving you alone again." My voice sounds far away, but she's solid and real.

"I'm safe now, and I'm not alone. But he will be."

Black soft hair flashes before me, pointed ears with a silver hoop.

"He doesn't love me. You do." She begins to evaporate and my hand goes through her ghostly form. We both know I'm lying.

"One's love for another are different things Ravie, look where you least expect it. I forgive you."

She disappears and leaves me alone once again.

"Cece!" I shout into the darkness, but she doesn't return.

"I call you back on a debt you owe me, return at once and fulfil this payment." The familiar male voice surrounds me, and warms my skin.

I am being pulled towards something, I'm unsure of what it is but I keep my eyes trained above me. Light begins to break through the darkness and I hear the sounds of rushing water.

Pain lights a fire through me as my eyes fly open, I'm turned onto my side as water gushes out of my mouth. I choke and spew out more, gasping for air. My entire body shakes, there's warm hands on me patting and rubbing my back.

I open my eyes, the grass is soft on my cheek as I spot the river in the distance. The kelpie's head emerges and I shut my eyes again. I am safe, I am safe.

"Rav?" the warm hands gently turn me onto my back. I gasp for air as if I've run a marathon, I force my eyes open to see Nyx peering down at me. His hands are on either side of my shoulders.

"Safe to say I'm not a strong swimmer." My voice is weak and raspy, but I relax. He saved me. He buries his head into my neck and pulls me up onto his lap. I weakly pat his back.

"Thank you," I say, coughing a little.

"Don't you ever die on me again." He pulls back again and looks worriedly over my face, gently touching my cheek.

"How do I look?" I murmur, raising an eyebrow suggestively. If I didn't find the humour in this situation I don't think I'd be mentally stable enough to handle what had just happened.

"You're a foolish girl." A weak laugh rattles in his chest as he shakes his head. He picks me up in his arms and begins to walk back through the forest. I lean my head against his shoulder and let my eyes close.

"Nyx loves me," I whisper, more to myself than him. He doesn't say anything, just continues walking. I drift into a bleary sleep, dreaming of darkness and the kelpie's face.

Nyx gives me multiple lectures the next day. After we'd returned to his room yesterday he'd had Leif look over me to make sure I was going to be okay. In her words, I was physically okay but mentally stupid. I was starting to like her.

I'm sitting in a large dining hall, at a long wooden table. Nyx has made me a chicken soup with corn, insisting I needed to eat. I don't object, dying really sapped the energy out of me.

I still can't quite believe it. I had died and returned. I'd seen Cece, and she'd forgiven me. She forgives me. I may have died, but I came back feeling more whole than I had before.

I don't leave Nyx's side, not caring if the others think I'm clingy. He doesn't pay attention to the other females that come over, seeking his attention. He only puts his arm around me and steers us in a different direction.

I swirl the soup around in the wooden bowl, Nyx sits beside me; anxiously tapping his finger against the table.

"If you continue to do that you're going to give me a headache," I say, tapping the bowl with the spoon.

"If you being here before hasn't put me on edge, it definitely has now." He stops tapping, but looks up at me, "Tomorrow is not happening. I will drag you kicking and screaming back to your world if I must."

I let my spoon go, "No way, you are not backing out. I need to get into that library Nyx!" I hiss, pressing my palms on the table.

"You died yesterday! There are only so many times luck will be on your side before it runs out. This world is not a lucky place."

"Well it's a risk I need to take. I'll be getting into that library with or without you. You either help me or leave me alone." I point towards the door, raising both brows. He laughs harshly.

"And what? Leave you to your own devices? Were you not present yesterday when I did just that?" he barks, the skin of his neck begins to turn a shade of red and I feel a wave of anger radiate off of him.

"If you weren't so busy fucking around with the pretty appetisers here I wouldn't have gone to the stupid river and talked to the stupid horse!" I yell, forcing myself to stand. The chair scrapes against the floor and nearly topples over with the force.

"So you nearly get killed because you're *jealous?*" He stands as well, prowling around the table to me. I turn and face him, unflinching as I look into his angry eyes.

"When you say it like that it just sounds stupid." I bite my bottom lip. He reaches a hand out and brushes my cheek with his freakishly long fingers.

"You've learnt nothing in your time here Rav, I warned you I was different around my people." His voice is soft, he grips my chin and tilts my face towards him so he can see me better.

"You're just an asshole around them," I whisper.

"They seem to like asshole more than you do."

"Why on earth would I like to see you flirting with other females that look a million times better than I do?" I squeak, feeling sparks of my anger evaporate. He frowns down at me.

"Why would I like to know you spent the night at another man's?" he replies. *Matt's* house the night before we'd come here.

"I didn't sleep with him, I just needed a place to crash and someone to look after my horse."

"I know you didn't, but I can't control the same jealousy. We both do things that nag at one another." His finger trails over my cheek as light as a feather.

"Have you slept with that girl?" I ask. I focus my eyes on his hair; not wanting to see whatever emotions his eyes portray.

"I've slept with many of the females here, yes." His voice is quiet and I feel something snap in my chest. Suddenly I want to cry.

"I refuse to be another one. Let go of my face."

He does as I ask, I turn and walk from the room. I slip into the hallway and will my heart to slow, will the tears to dry up and evaporate. This trip has been a horrible idea, a horrible, horrible idea. I just want to go home.

What was I thinking falling for Nyx?

Stupid mortal Ravynne.

I walk aimlessly down the hallways, not paying attention to where I go. I don't leave the castle, afraid I'll run into trouble if I do. I enter the hallway that leads to the courtyard, but I take a seat on the ground and watch the pixies flitter around the garden.

They dance and chirp and throw what seems to be handfuls of glitter at each other. I press my forehead against the glass. The first pixie that came over to me the first time comes over again. She takes a seat on the branch of the shrub that sits against the window.

She taps a small hand against the glass. I look up at her and offer a weak smile. She shakes her head and her mouth moves, but I don't hear anything. I tap my ear and mouth 'no', hoping she understands. She throws her small hands in the air and seems to huff. She flitters off towards the others again.

Suddenly they all come over, there is ten in total and each unique as the next. They begin throwing the glitter at the glass, and as it hits and sprinkles down to the ground the glass begins to shimmer and become transparent.

I can hear the flitter of their wings and the rustle of the shrubs. My pixie breaks away from the group and hovers over the expanding hole. She gestures for me to crawl through.

I look up and down the hallway, no one apart from me is here. I sigh, what else did I have left to lose? I squeeze through the small space, and once I'm through the glass solidifies again. I crawl through the shrubs and pull myself up once I reach a patch of grass.

"That's kind of you," I say, brushing the dirt from my palms and from my dress. My pixie comes to stand on my shoulder, holding onto a few pieces of my hair to keep herself in place.

"Why are you sad, mortal?" Her voice is high pitched and squeaky, but she means no harm. A small hand pats the side of my face.

"Boy trouble," I murmur, looking around the garden. The other pixies fly around me, watching me with curious eyes.

"You have a beautiful garden," I say. Around me it flourishes with life. Butterflies and small birds linger around the bird bath and the yellow, white, purple and pink clusters of flowers. In the middle of the garden in front of me is a small pond, koi fish swim about lazily under the lily pads.

"Yes, we take good care of our garden," the pixie says proudly, fluttering her wings.

"What's your name?" I ask, peering down onto my shoulder.

"Nelicia. What's yours?" She flies from my shoulder and hovers in front of my face. Her head tilts to the side as her big eyes look over my face.

“Call me Rav.”

“Rav, what are you doing here?” She frowns, wringing her hands in front of her. I sigh as the other pixies come closer, floating behind Nelicia.

“A babunook is eating the children in my village back in my world, so I’ve come to get more information on how to kill it but Nyx doesn’t want to help me anymore. I have to leave tomorrow.” I sit down on the grass, leaning back against my hands. Grass strands caress my hands and forearm gently. The pixies land on my knees, all grappling at my dress to get a spot to sit.

“Not the babunook.”

“Terrible.”

“Scary.”

“Poor children.”

The pixie voices muffle into one as they all jitter back and forth. Nelicia tugs at my dress.

“Are you going to slay it?” she asks.

“I’m going to try my best to.” I nod a few times. I’ve died once before, what’s a second time? Right?

“Silly Rav, but very brave Rav.” One of the other pixies try to move her out of the way and swats their hand away; they tumble to the ground. I reach out and they land on my palm, the pixie is a man with white spiky hair.

He straightens his wings and crosses his arms over his chest, turning away from Necilia. I smile as I sit him on my shoulder, I hear him sigh and take a seat; kicking his feet against my collar bone.

"Do you know if there's any way I can get more information? Nyx said the only way is the library, but I can't get to it as it's her highness's."

"You shouldn't make bargains with the faerie kind miss," the pixie on my shoulder whispers, leaning against my neck.

"I know, but what choice do I have?"

"Many choices. We could help you?" Necilia says.

"Yes, her highness hasn't been very forthcoming with us lately. We wanted a new flower to plant in the garden and she refuses to give us the seed," one of the other pixies grumbles.

"Yes! She keeps the seed in her room!" the pixie on my shoulder exclaims.

"Why won't she give you the seed?"

"It's a sacred seed, allowing those who eat the petals to gain more magic for a small amount of time. Through generations the seed has always been passed along, she chooses not to give it to us simply because she likes us to feel…" the male pixie trails off, squinting.

"She likes to make you feel small." I finish for him, smiling sympathetically.

"Yes, like we are less than our real value." He pats my cheek, watching me with sad eyes.

“Will you get in trouble if she finds you’ve got the seed?” I ask, looking from each one.

“Yes, but once it’s been planted there is nothing she can do.” Necilia assures me.

“If I get the seed, will you get the information I need to kill the babunook?” I ask, looking at each of them. I’d never made a deal with pixies before, but it seems like a fair trade.

They whisper back and forth between themselves.

“Yes okay, is that the deal you want to make?” Necilia asks.

“I will retrieve the seed you want and give it to you in return for information on how to exactly kill the babunook.” I hold out my hand for a hand shake. Necilia takes hold of my finger with both of her hands and gives it a small shake.

“You have a deal.”

☾

“You did what!” Nyx exclaims, leaving the bathroom. A towel is wrapped around his waist, exposing his muscled but lean chest and arms. I gulp as I look away.

“You weren’t going to help me, so I found someone that would. I only have to retrieve a seed,” I say exasperated, why does he have to make it out like it's such a big deal?

"How the hell do you think you're going to get into her chambers to start with? Do you even know what the seed looks like?" He stops in front of me, furiously running his hands through his hair. Droplets of water fall and stick to his chest, running down the divets. I clench the bed sheet underneath my hands.

"Well…no." I mumble.

"You are so painfully human sometimes, Ravynne," he groans, pressing the palms of his hands into his eyes.

"Yeah well you're painfully an asshole nearly all the time so check mate." I cross my arms over my chest. He groans again, I had only told him about the deal I'd made because I needed his help getting into the room. I hadn't said a word to him all day after our argument in the dining hall, the sun has set an hour or two ago and the night sky had erupted with stars.

"Tell me something I don't know." He removes his hands from his eyes. I hold my fingers up in front of me and begin to tick them off.

"You're stubborn, sort of cruel, nice but in that asshole kind of way, you play games with me as if I'm some kind of dog." I hold my four fingers up in front of him, "I can go on if you wish." I raise both brows and wiggle my fingers.

"I didn't mean literally." He crosses his arms and my eyes betray me as they watch the muscle in his chest and shoulder move with that simple movement. I lower my hands onto my lap and clasp them together.

"Oh."

"I told you no one can get into that room unless they're taking her to warm her bed, Ravynne. I refuse."

"Oh so you'll sleep with every other female in this place but not her?" I retort.

"Her and you."

Ouch.

"Ass-hole." I stand and stalk out onto the balcony, taking my deflated ego with me. His mood swings are too much for me. I hear him let out a frustrated sigh.

I look out over the garden and into the court yard, they'd lit a few small bonfires and are dancing around them, I could just hear the whisper of music making its way up to the balcony. Every night here must just be one big party for them, no wonder Nyx was always in my world. It made me question why his father had stayed there too. Why not rule here?

Nyx comes out and leans against the balcony beside me, he's thrown on a loose pair of green trousers and a thin white shirt.

"Come to rub salt in the wound?" I mumble, looking back down to the party.

"No. I wouldn't sleep with you." His words definitely rub salt into the wound, *hell* he's cramming salt into them.

"Yeah. You've said that."

"I wouldn't sleep with you *here*, in this world," he gestures around us, "It may be a home to me, but it isn't to you. Your first time shouldn't be in strange territory where you aren't truly comfortable." He lowers his hand but refuses to look at me. So he would?

"We shouldn't be having this conversation."

"I know we shouldn't, but we always seem to find ourselves here don't we?" He finally looks over to me, the cocky asshole mask he wears is gone, replaced by soft and squishy Nyx.

"That's because you take it there."

"No way, you do." He smirks at me and I huff out a loud breath.

"Well, so what if I do? I like to annoy you." I look back out to the courtyard.

"You're the one that said once the babunook is dead we'd go our separate ways."

"That's because you said you couldn't give me what I need, what else was I meant to say? Beg you to tell me different? I'm not one to beg, Nyx."

"If you would have let me finish my sentence, you would have known but another talent of yours is cutting me off at important times." A smile tugs at his lips as we look back at each other. My heart begins to pick up pace as I see the way he looks at me, with hungry eyes.

"Okay, well…finish your sentence then."

He takes a steady breath, is he nervous?

"Because…I can give you what you *want* and more. But it is complicated, and dangerous. I don't want any harm to come to you, but I also can't steer clear of you. If my father ever finds you, I'm afraid my wrath would not even be close to containable. There's still a lot you do not know about me Ravynne."

I stay silent as I watch him, his lips twist and he looks away with a sigh. He stops leaning on the balcony and straightens up, running a hand through his hair.

"I'm not as fragile as I look Nyx," I say softly. I take a hesitant step towards him and rest my hand on his arm. He looks down at me.

"I know you're not, that's what scares me."

"Have some faith in me, if we've come this far I'm sure we can go further." His hand covers my own and he intertwines our fingers together.

"I'll help you get into the room, using your glamour idea. No way are either of us sleeping with her." I can't help but smile, suddenly my plan seems brighter and more in my reach.

"Alright, let's start planning then."

I take steadying breaths in front of the closed bedroom door, I had one chance to pull this off. If I failed or slipped, both Nyx and I would be in grave danger.

"Are you ready?" He asks, adjusting his tunic as he comes to stand beside me. I catch a glimpse of myself in the mirror, my red hair is in curls and cascades down my back. Nyx had gone that morning to report to her, and had memorised her appearance. Today she wore a deep blue gown, tight at the waist and multiple layers of saffron blue skirts to cover her legs.

Gold bangles cover both of my arms up to my elbow, while the golden choker makes it slightly hard for me to breath. I look exactly like her, I can't see this plan going wrong.

I nod once and face the door once more, he'd last seen her in the courtyard; draped on the throne drinking wine and toying with a few goblins.

We enter the hallway, multiple goblins bow down as they see me. I force myself to prowl ahead, I don't acknowledge any of them. She's a bitch like that.

Nyx links an arm coolly around my waist as he steers us through the maze of hallways, we past a few other female faeries who look at me with envy.

Everyone apparently knows exactly where we are headed and what we're planning to do.

It sort of makes me feel sick.

We round another corner and the grass floor is replaced by white marble. This hall is larger than any other one we'd been in, and at the end two large golden doors sit erect. Two guards stand stoic in front of them, holding a golden sword in both hands in front of them.

"Are you sure this will work?" I whisper. Nyx presses a few kisses to my throat, causing my heartbeat to become erratic. Who knew that would feel so nice? After the other night, I hadn't realised how much I'd enjoyed them.

"No, but we can only try." he murmurs back, tugging at my earlobe.

Oh boy.

I focus less on the warmth of his mouth and take in the details of the wall, the large white marble walls break away at the ceiling; revealing a large forest. It's a mirror of sorts, and my reflection in it isn't her highness, it's Ravynne.

Shit.

We approach the guards, who look at Nyx with caution and envy. I clear my throat as we come to a stop, Nyx pulls himself from my neck and acts slightly drunk, keeping a stupid smile plastered on his face.

"Move aside please," I say gently, in the highest tone like hers that I can muster.

"Are you okay your highness?" the guard on my left asks.

"Are you questioning me?" I growl, taking a few steps forward. He shrinks back and shakes his head, fear clouds his eyes as he looks between the other guard and me.

The other guard shrugs and stands to the side, the other follows. I smile sweetly at both of them as I pull open one of the gold doors. Nyx follows me in and locks it behind us. I look around her room in awe.

A large white bed sits on a dais in the middle of the room, with literal clouds floating above it. The staircase up to the bed is made of white marble. The room is circular in shape, and the walls are littered with all sorts of treasures.

I spot a crown in the corner leaning against a statue of a bear. There's a typewriter tipped on its side, exposing multiple golden cups.

"I didn't realise she's a hoarder," I whisper, moving deeper into the room. Nyx goes to one side, looking through drawers.

"She's a sucker for shiny items."

Clearly.

I find a trinket box and open the small latch, the lid pops open and a tiny ballerina twirls to soft piano music. I shut the lid and place it back down.

Where would she put a seed? The possibilities are endless, and we're running on borrowed time as it is.

"Nyx, where did you say her library was?" I ask, looking over to where he rifles through draws.

"Out there, did you notice the mirror above us stripping glamour?" he whispers, pausing to look over at me. I sit down the gold cup I'd been toying with.

"Yes."

"It's up in there." He goes back to looking through clumps of stuff and I sigh, feeling defeated. I didn't want to think of what would happen if I didn't get the seed for the pixies. Time passes and we come up empty handed, we'd gone through each cupboard and lifted each piece of treasure up. Nothing. No seed.

"Are you sure she has a seed in here?" he finally asks, stopping the fruitless attempt to continue digging around. I give up as well, taking a seat on of the stairs.

"Honestly, no. It's just what the pixie told me." I rest my chin on my palms and sigh. I'm not sure what I'm going to tell the pixies, maybe they'll just chop off a finger in return for my failure.

"Well, it has to be here somewhere," he frowns.

Outside the door we hear a small commotion. Nyx reaches for my hand with wide eyes .As he wraps his arms around my waist and drags me to the back of the room I see a shimmer of glamour fall over us.

The golden doors open and the guards peer in, I freeze when they look directly at us; until I realise they're looking through us. He'd made us invisible. I was glad he'd removed the berry necklace.

"You are both idiots," her highness says, prowling into the room with a cruel snarl on her pretty porcelain face. The male faerie I'd seen the day before with the yellow skin lingers outside the door.

After the guards do a thorough sweep of the room they shrug and exit, taking stand once again outside the door. The male slips in as her highness climbs the stairs to the top if the bed.

"Well? We didn't come here to talk," she purrs down to him. Nyx holds a hand over my mouth gently as she undoes the back of her dress. It falls into a pile at her feet, exposing her slim stomach and perky breasts.

The male faerie can't seem to get naked fast enough as he rushes up the stairs. I feel my cheeks go red as he pulls his pants off, tossing them in my direction.

This can't be happening.

Nyx is as still as steel against my back, I look up at him to see him focused on me. Awh, he could be cute when he wants. I, on the other hand, look back up to where they're having sex.

They are in a position I wasn't even sure is humanly possible, and I can feel my eyes widen. I am glad Nyx hasn't been with her, for that male faerie looks like he's having the best time of his life.

The clouds above the bed begin to darken, and that's when I spot it.

The seed.

Its small brown shell sits plump on the cloud.

I raise a hand and silently point towards the cloud, blocking out the moans coming from the bed. I feel Nyx tense against me, he senses the dilemma we're in.

How the hell are we going to get the seed? It hadn't been there moments ago when the clouds had been white.

I look back down to her highness and see the pure euphoria plastered on her face.

The clouds adjust to her mood. If she left or they finished, the clouds would go back to normal and we'd lose any hope of getting that seed.

I pull myself from Nyx's arms and act as though I'm pulling a cloak over myself, hoping he gets the hint. He frowns. I imitate slapping my forehead.

I try again, grabbing the air around us, and wrapping myself in it. His mouth makes an 'O' shape as he realises what I mean. I feel more of his glamour shimmer around me and I silently make my way up the stairs, I keep my footsteps light as I tread carefully.

As I near the top the overwhelming smell of flowers and sweat chokes me, I silently gag as I turn away; only to find Nyx silently laughing at me.

The bed is large enough for eight people to sleep comfortably, so when I crawl on neither of them notice the dint I make. The clouds are in reach, and the brown seed is taunting me.

I slowly stand on shaky legs and I take a tentative step closer to the sweaty bodies. His leg moves out and nearly touches mine. I bite down on my lip hard as I reach up.

My fingers graze the seed.

I decide to risk it, and do a small jump.

My hand encloses around the small seed, aha!

As I land, I teeter towards them. I reach out my other hand as I stop my fall onto them. I press down on his back, forcing him to go deeper into her.

She lets out a loud moan, encouraging him. I take my hand from his back and quietly climb off the bed. Nyx has tears streaming from his eyes as he bites down on his knuckles. I furiously wipe my hand against my dress as I go back down to him, sliding the seed into my secret pocket.

I mouth 'Let's go,' and point towards the door.

He wipes at his eyes but nods, taking my hand in his as we walk towards the door. It's risky leaving like this, but there is no way I'm staying in this room a second longer. He cracks open the door, wide enough for us to slip out. The guards turn and grumble.

"Shut it!" she screeches and the guards rush to shut the door. We're already half way down the hallway when they close it. We round the corner and break into a run, Nyx leads us back towards his room. The glamour peels away as we enter the hallway that leads us up the stairs.

We slow to a casual walk, the goblins scowl at our clasped hands but no one pulls us up. No one calls on us or accuses us. We'd done it, we'd pulled it off.

We enter his room and as soon as the door shuts behind us I let out a squeal, leaping into his arms. He spins me around the room and laughs along with me.

"We did it!" I squeal as he puts me down. Without thinking I lean up and press my lips to his in the heat and excitement of the moment.

The kiss is brash and rushed, but as I pull away his cheeks are a slight red and there's a hint of emotion in his eyes I can't place.

"Yes we did, lucky for me," he smirks, twirling a piece of my hair between his fingers.

"We need to go to the pixies and then we're getting out of here." I turn from him and gather my saddlebag, "Do you need to take anything with us?" I look over my shoulder at him.

"No, let's go. This holiday is over." He takes my hand in his as he leaves the room, leading us back down the garden hallway. I tap at the glass and the pixies fly over, they sprinkle their glitter again and I slip through.

"I got the seed," I say as Necilia hops onto my shoulder.

"You are a good, brave Rav," she chirps, stroking my cheek.

"There's only one way to kill the babunook. You must be willing to trade a soul for a soul as the babunook is a creature of other worlds. It has to be on a full moon. You must drive a stake through its heart soaked in the blood of a goat, and when you do you must repeat these words, *may I offer my soul for another, as the darkness claims us all in the end.*"

"I like you Rav, please don't do this." She flutters her wings anxiously.

"I'm sorry, but I have to. I don't see any other way. I won't let Nyx die over this." I look out to see him standing on the opposite side of the glass, watching us patiently. If this trip has taught me anything, it's that there are people worth dying twice for.

"Is that all I need to do? It'll be dead then?" I ask, looking down to where she plays with a piece of my hair.

"Yes."

I dig into my pocket and pull out the seed. Three pixies fly over and pluck it from my fingers; they place it down beside the small pond.

"You are a good human." She kisses my cheek and flutters off with the others as they crowd around the seed. I leave silently and find Nyx hand waiting for my own.

He gives it a squeeze as he leads us forward, "Let's go home."

24

We return to Orrinshire, and I'm shocked to find two weeks have passed while we've been gone. Time in faerie is far slower than the time in my world, and I now know why Nyx might worry. We have to get back to my village though, there is no more waiting and stalling. We go to Matt's cottage, Luna spots us from the paddock and neighs as she runs along the fence.

Matt opens the door and is visibly relieved when he sees me come through the gate. In a rush I have strong arms crushing me, I smell wheat and burning wood as I hug him back.

"Thank goodness you're safe." He squeezes me tightly, Nyx clears his throat behind us. Matt drops me and rubs the back of his neck as he looks up to Nyx.

"It's alright, I didn't realise how much time had passed. I've come to pick up Luna and return home, my village needs me," I say, walking down towards the paddock. Matt walks in step beside me.

"Was there any trouble?" I ask.

"Not really, there were royal guards here that I'd never seen before but they didn't stay for long at all. They're the ones looking for you, aren't they?" We pause at the gate and Luna rushes over, swishing her tail back and forth.

I grab her bridal and enter the paddock, she rubs her face against me as I wrap my arms around her, whispering sweet words into her ear.

"Yes, but I swear I haven't done anything wrong. They've mistaken me for someone else." I put the bridal on and turn back to Matt.

"I cannot thank you enough, for everything you've done for me. You are such a good friend." I give him another hug, feeling an overwhelming amount of gratitude. I am worthy of friends, and I am never going to take that for granted again.

"You'd do the same for me."

"Of course I would." We walk back up the house, where Nyx observes a bee buzzing happily around a white dandelion. I can't help but smile as I watch him.

"When will you return?" Matt asks.

"Soon, once the danger has passed in my village." Nyx looks up and takes the reins from me. He leaps onto Luna in a smooth movement, she paces anxiously underneath him.

"Could you help me?" I ask. Matt smiles and boosts me up. I wiggle close to Nyx's back and wrap my hands around his waist. Nyx digs into his pocket and pulls out a small money bag.

"This is for looking after Luna." Nyx chucks it to him, Matt catches it and looks in; I glimpse a fair few gold coins.

"Thank you both. Safe travels Ravynne." Matt waves us off as Luna trots down the road. I wave until I can no longer see him, leaning my cheek against Nyx's back.

"Are you ready for what's to come?" Nyx murmurs, leading Luna through the crowds of people. We receive a few odd glances as we go, but I pay them no mind. Their judgemental stares feel so dismal to me now.

"No, but I don't have a choice. I hope he hasn't struck again." I sigh, tucking my hands into the pockets of Nyx's coat. I'd forgotten its winter here, and I hadn't dressed for the chillier weather.

"We'll find out in a few days. How are you feeling about…everything?" he asks. We'd reached the edge of Orrinshire, and the daunting mountains stand tall in the distance with their white caps beginning to blend down the mountains.

"It's been a crazy few days, let's set up a camp first and then ask me that question again." I shake my head and close my eyes, savouring his and Luna's warmth. He breaks her into a canter as we set off for home.

"As you wish, Ravynne."

☾

We reach a familiar camp as the sun begins to dip below the horizon, going off the path and through a small patch of forest. He dismounts before helping me down, I wander around and begin to pick up small twigs and dry leaves. Luna walks down to the small stream that trickles past the camp site and takes deep gulps.

I shiver at the thought of going near a stream or river that goes deeper than my ankles. I turn back to the charred circle on the ground and sit the twigs and leaves down, positioning the rocks around it.

"Can you use your magic to start a fire?" I ask, looking up from where I'm crouched. Nyx smiles as he twitches his hand. The twigs catch alight and the fire roars, but doesn't eat away at the sticks.

"Show off." I grin, taking a seat a few steps away from it. He comes up to the fire and holds his hands over the golden flames.

"I have to impress a stunning woman, I need to show off." I feign surprise as I look around the clearing.

"It's only me here though." I look back up to him and see mischief in the glow of his eyes. Once we'd left faerie his usual glamour slipped back into place, and I felt bad. He could never truly be himself here because there's no real magic.

"What are you thinking about?" he asks, coming to sit beside me. The sun has dipped down and stars are beginning to speckle the night sky above us.

"You."

"What about me?" He traces patterns on my thigh, I shiver at the parts that tickle.

"That you can't really be you in my world, you look the same but it's not…you. The you you're comfortable in." I run my tongue along my teeth, staring into the fire.

"Rav, you don't need to worry about me."

"I do though, I can't help it." I shake my head and sigh as I lean against him. I rest my head on his shoulder and trail my fingers against his knee.

"I'm more me when I'm with you, not in Faerie. When I'm in this world, you see me better than any other person or creature." He presses a kiss to the top of my head and wraps his arm around me. I lie down and let my head rest in his lap, staring up at him. His right hand rests over my chest while his left one combs out the knots that have formed in my hair.

"That's because I can see you so clearly. When we first met I was a peasant girl with a sad past. You looked past all of that and gave me the benefit of the doubt," I whisper.

"You really don't know how strong you are, do you?" he muses, focusing on a stubborn knot in my hair.

"Apparently not, but when we return back to Elderview that's going to be tested." Do I tell him what I must do? I have too. If that vision becomes true, I had to make the choice.

"You'll have me by your side, I won't let anything happen to you."

"You can't promise that."

"I'm trying to give you comfort woman, goodness." He shakes his head. I puff out my bottom lip but smile softly.

"I'm sorry, comfort isn't something I'm use to." I smile back up at him, I lift my hand up and stroke his cheek softly. He looks down at me and his lips part.

"I'll have to change that."

"I mean, if you think you're up to the task," I smirk and shrug a shoulder.

"It will be a tough a feat but one I'm not afraid to tackle."

We fall into silence. The fire crackles and Luna munches down grass close by. I was going to have to buy her from the Densley's, I couldn't part with her after everything.

"Tell me about your childhood," I whisper.

"There isn't much to tell. After mother had me I was between worlds, depending on father's mood at the time. She died twenty years ago. Her anniversary was only a few weeks ago actually." He clears his throat, looking up to the sky.

"I'm sorry."

"Don't apologise, it was a long time ago. I think she's given me you in return for leaving me behind. The world works in…weird ways. I miss her every day, but I think missing you might feel worse at this point."

I stay silent as I intertwine our fingers and rest them under my chin. I kiss each of his fingers.

"Once she was gone I had to deal with my father, and he's not an easy or kind man; whereas my mother was. She's similar to you in a lot of ways, she would have loved you."

"I'm sure I'll meet her one day." I look up to the stars, is she looking down on us with Cecilia right now? Guiding and protecting us?

"Most likely, she's full of surprises."

"After all the time we've spent together I feel like I know you, but at the same time it's like I've only scratched the surface of who you are."

"A long time ago, I was not how I am now. When I lost my mother I didn't cope with it, faeries are taught to have no weakness and that's how my father had raised me. I ended a wedding with a girl who assumed to love me. I lashed out at everyone, I did cruel things that gave our race the ghost stories. I was not a kind of just man Ravynne." He looks away and focuses on the fire.

"I sort of find that hard to believe," I say softly, still focusing on him.

"I made a man blind in the first week my mother died simply because he looked my way. I turned a young woman into a pig because I didn't like how she was dressed. Little things crawled under my skin and got the better of me every time. If I was the same when you'd slipped over, I'm afraid of what I would have done." His jaw tightens and his shoulders tense. I stroke my thumb over his hand.

"Why did she pass?" I whisper.

"She'd fallen ill nine months before, and grew worse each day. There was no real sickness, she was healthy and well but was deteriorating before our eyes. One night she was there and the next day she was gone." Tears drip from his eyes and land on my cheeks, and I feel my own swell of emotions.

"You said it was the twentieth anniversary recently?"

"Yes. A few weeks ago, it was your birthday," he whispers.

My birthday.

His mother died on the night I was born.

Could…it be linked? In some, magical way? Could his mother's powers have passed to me and given me life? Could I be the seer his father is after?

"I am so sorry Nyx, if I had any idea…"

"It's okay. I don't blame you being cautious around me, I went back to Faerie that day and spent it with Leif." I feel guilty, if I'd just sucked up my pride and spent that afternoon before my birthday with him, maybe it would have helped cheer him up. There's so much that goes on behind closed doors.

"When Cece died I fell apart. No one wanted to talk about it, no one wanted to relive the memories we had with her. I feel as though I'd robbed everyone from getting to know her and watch her grow. I robbed that treasure from myself." Now tears stream down my face, my breathing starts to hitch but I take deeper breaths.

"Mother was the only good thing I had in my life, when I was little she'd take me to Faerie and build castles with me and play make believe. Every night she'd bring me a glass of warm milk and tell me a story. I know what you mean when you say you feel robbed." Nyx looks down at me, he wipes away his own tears and then my own with his free hand.

"Cece always carried a stuffed rabbit around with her, she'd take it to school and sleep with it and do everything with it. At dinner time she'd even have a plate of food ready for it. The day we went to the river I couldn't find it, I think Aunty was repairing a seam that had come undone. The only way to make her stop screaming was to go swimming."

"The days leading up to when mother died I stayed by her bed, and told her stories and would bring her every form of pain relief I could find. Now…I've forgotten how sweet and soothing her voice always was. How delicate her hands were and how she made a room come to life."

"I feel the same with Cece, I remember her face but that's really it. I hate it, I hate knowing I can't even hold onto memories of her because I'm beginning to forget." I feel my heart split open in my chest, and can sense Nyx's do the same. I hadn't talked about Cece with anyone, and in this moment I wouldn't tell anyone else. She is still so precious to me, and Nyx deserves to know the parts of her I can offer.

"Faeries are usually immortal, so I dread to know what I'll be able to remember a hundred years from now."

"You'll forget me," I blurt, unable to control my emotions after delving so deeply into them.

"Rav, I could never forget you," he whispers, tracing my cheeks. It dawns on me that even if I give this a chance, I only have my human years.

"I guess we'll find out in a hundred or so years," I murmur.

"You are so silly. Why focus on such dire things?" he asks.

"Because letting go of you feels like letting go of me, the thought of losing you is beginning to sink in."

"I'm not going anywhere Ravynne."

But I am.

"Promise?" I whisper.

"I promise. Now stop crying because I don't want to start again." His lips tug at the corners as he wipes away the fresh tears that I can't control.

"Fine, but not because you told me too," I say, feeling a sad smile tug at my lips.

"I like your world, I like being here like this with you."

"I like this too." I look sideways to the fire, "You know, we're in my world now." I murmur, looking back at him. He looks down at me, slightly puzzled.

"Mmm?"

"Well…you said you wouldn't take me to bed me in your world, but we're in my world now. We don't know what tomorrow or the day after is going to bring, and I don't want to give myself over to someone who isn't you," I say sheepishly, looking down at our hands. My cheeks flame as he uses our hands and tilts my head back so he can see me.

"I would be honoured," he whispers. I sit up from his lap and sit back from the fire, finding a softer patch of grass. He stands before me.

"Are you sure this is what you want?" His voice has dropped an octave deeper. I squeeze my thighs together and nod.

"Say it. I need to hear you say it."

"Yes. This is what I want." My breath is barely a whisper, but he takes the few steps towards me before he's standing near my feet. He reaches for my hand and pulls me up to him, he shrugs out of his cloak and lays it down on the grass for us.

I take my time as I unbutton his tunic and then the white shirt underneath, his hands undo the ribbon of my dress. He loosens each thread one by one, before helping my arms slip out of it.

The dress pools at my feet, leaving me standing in my undergarments. I help him out of his shirts and sit them beside the cloak.

I step out of the dress and kick it to the side, he guides me down. His muscled arms encase me as he positions himself between my legs.

I feel the heartbeat of his hardness nestle against me and I squeeze my thighs around his waist.

He leans down and kisses me gently, more gentle than we've ever kissed before. I melt into him, letting my hands run down his back; I skim the band of his pants before running them up his chest.

He breaks the kiss and leans his forehead on mine, our breathing hard, I lose myself in his eyes. Nothing has felt more right or perfect then this moment.

"Show me how much you want me," I whisper, threading a hand through his hair. He sucks in a sharp breath before leaning back and taking his pants off. I watch in fascination as he kneels before me completely naked.

"You are so breathtaking." I sit up and undo my bra, tossing it carelessly to the side. He helps me out of my underwear before laying back down on top of me.

"I have never been more caught up in another being for so long," the tip of him sits against me, waiting. I hold his face in mine as I slowly raise my hips.

"I'm glad it's me."

I cry out in pleasure and pain as we connect as one, physically and emotionally on another level. I give myself over to him, allowing him to see every inch of darkness and light inside of me.

We lose ourselves in each over and over again, before emerging as one. Stronger than ever before, and forged on nothing other than love.

Nyx loves Ravynne. Ravynne loves Nyx.

I hold the reins between my hands easily as we walk along the deserted road, Nyx's arms are looped around my waist while his head rests on my shoulder.

I couldn't keep my hands off of him.

My cheeks heat as I think of the events that happened the night before, once hadn't been enough for either of us and as consequence I'd developed a limp and am now extremely sore. If Luna went any faster than a walk but slower than a canter I'd cry out, not used to throbbing pain between my thighs.

At this rate we wouldn't reach Elderview until tomorrow evening, but not one part of me minded. I knew I had to return home and face my family and the babunook, but in this moment I want to spend every normal second with Nyx that I could.

I think he feels the same, as he wasn't in a rush this morning when we woke as the sun rose, or when he'd helped me wash off in the small stream.

It was almost odd being so normal after so long of resisting him and the passion we both so clearly felt for one another. I hadn't asked what was going to happen once we returned or what would come after. Right now, doing what we are doing is enough for me.

"Are you awake back there?" I ask, nudging my shoulder upwards. Nyx groans as he tightens his arms around me, pulling me closer to him.

"Five more minutes," he mumbles. His breath tickles my throat as he takes heavy breaths; indicating he's asleep. I don't disturb him again as we continue to trod along, instead I focus on the scenery around us.

From the main road we're on I can see the mountain peaks of Elderview, the snow has begun to spread down from the peaks and now covers nearly half the mountain.

So we are going to be in for a cold winter this year then.

"Are you hungry?" Nyx mumbles into my ear, he unloops his arms and stretches out behind me.

"Mmm, a little. But we have no food, and I'm not a good hunter." I take a glimpse over my shoulder and feel the butterflies kick in again, his hair is an untamed mess on his head and the top buttons of his white shirt are undone. He wipes the sleep from his face before looking back at me, his violet eyes hold a twinkle in them.

I look back towards the road.

"We could catch a fish?" he suggests, pointing through the forest to our left where a wild river rages. I shiver as I catch glimpses of it between the few breaks in the trees.

"*You* can catch a fish, I am not going near that river." I slow Luna down to a stop and listen to the steady roar of the water, there must be a waterfall down river more or some sort of decline for the water to sound so fast.

"I can catch us a fish then." He swings down from Luna and stretches his legs, making a show to stretch his arms as well. I roll my eyes at him.

"You are so dramatic."

"You love it," he winks at me as he comes over. I rest my hands on his shoulders as he gently helps me down from Luna. I tie the reins into a knot so she won't trip on them if she decides to go for a walk.

"We'll be back, girl." I pat her neck and receive a snort in return. She walks to the other side of the road and begins to pick at the green grass. Nyx holds onto my hand as we begin to walk into the forest, picking our way around broken branches and thorn bushes.

"Are you sure this is safe?" I peer around him and ahead of us, the thin tall trees widen before completely disappearing as we reach a small ledge. It's covered in golden and brown dead leaves that crunch beneath our feet. The ledge drops away to reveal a raging river, sharp rocks stick jaggedly out in the middle as the water storms past it, occasionally rearing up and splashing over.

"For me? Yes. For you? No. You might want to stand back a bit." He squeezes my hand before letting it go. I retreat a few steps, back to the safety of the thin trees, I lean against one and fiddle with my necklace.

"If you fall in I hope you know how to swim," I say loudly over the river.

"If I fall in, I think swimming will be the least of my worries." He begins rummaging through the dead leaves, finding a thick and long broken branch. I watch as his magic comes to life, creating a woodland fishing pole with a small worm on a sharp curved rock. He throws the line in and takes a seat, far enough back to be safe.

"You never told me what the pixies said about the babunook," he asks over his shoulder. I feel my skin go clammy as a wave of anxiety washes through me. I did tell myself I was going to tell him, I had no other choice.

"It has to be on a full moon, the babunook has to be staked through the heart with the stake covered in goat's blood, and when staked a few select words have to be said."

"And those words are?" He looks over his shoulder, his eyes run from my boots up my pants and undone shirt and finally find my face. I'd left my shirt undone for the ride, having only my bra on underneath. It was still warm enough through the day to break a sweat, and the breeze had kept me cool.

I can't imagine what I look like, I'd thrown my hair up into a wild bun and left it at that.

"I'm not telling you." I purse my lips, narrowing my eyes.

"Yes, yes you are. You're not the one staking this creature, I am." He half turns towards me, disbelief colouring his words. I shrug, looking down to where my hand fiddles with the necklace. "Ravynne you can't be serious."

"I am, I'm not telling you those words. Over my dead body. But it'll be alright, we'll just trap it and fight it and when it's weak I'll swoop in and kill it. Easy done." I look back up at him, his eyes are wide and his eyebrows are raised higher than I'd ever seen them go before.

"What? It's a start of a plan, I haven't given it much thought. Although I don't know when the next full moon is."

"It's a week from today, a Friday night to be exact." The line tugs, and he looks back to the river. He stands up and begins to pull it in.

"How do you know the day? I don't even know the day anymore, hell I forgot they even had names," I say, genuinely surprised he knew. He pulls the rest of the line in, revealing a large salmon wriggling at the end. Its pale pink belly shines against the sun, it's large enough to keep us both comfortably full.

"I um can't be here when you kill it." I say, feeling squeamish. He cocks his head to the side as he look at me.

"You don't like it?"

"No, I don't. It grosses me out, I might go wait with Luna. Don't fall into the river." I turn and begin to pick my way back to the road.

"You could only hope not." he calls back after me. I find Luna in the same place we left her, I take a seat under the shade of tree close to her; wincing as I lower myself to the ground. There would be no freaky business for me for a while.

Nyx emerges, holding the now dead, headless and scaled fish. He grins as he holds it up proudly.

"Are we going to cook it?" I query as he comes closer, oil covers his hands as he sits across from me. He holds the fish fillets in one hand and reaches into his pocket, pulling out a small pocket knife.

"No, there's nothing wrong with eating it raw." He begins to slice thin pink strips off, passing them to me as he does. I line them neatly on my hand, the faint stench of fish begins to hang in the air.

"I've never had raw salmon before," I say, lifting a piece up. The strip is tender in my mouth, oil coats my tongue as I swallow it down; grimacing from the taste. It tastes the same as it smells, just more intense.

"Do you like it?" Nyx asks, giving me a lop-sided smile as I gingerly put another piece in my mouth.

"Eh?" I say between bites, it's definitely not something I'd be voluntarily eating in the near future. He finishes cutting the fish fillets into thin strips, wrapping the remaining pieces up in a cloth.

"Food here doesn't compare to the food in my world. Fish is a whole new category in itself." He puts three pieces in his mouth and chews happily, grinning to show me pink bits stuck between his teeth.

"You're so gross," I laugh, handing him what's left on my hand. I wipe both of my hands on my pants before leaning back against the tree.

"You love it."

"Occasionally," I smirk.

"Are you nervous to return home?" he asks, digging into the remaining pieces. His question catches me off guard.

"I mean…no? I don't think so. I'm more anxious about whether the babunook has struck again."

"Should I go ahead first when we get to the village to make sure it's safe?" I wave his concern off.

"I'll be fine Nyx. I haven't been there for almost two weeks. I'm sure by now they've conspired about something else that doesn't involve me," I assure him, offering him a comforting smile. He sighs heavily, but doesn't protest.

"Let's get going then, we have a village to save."

☾

We arrive in Elderview with a few hours of sunlight to spare. Once we reach my home, Nyx helps me dismount Luna. She whinnies in protest as he begins to lead her towards the Densley's home.

I watch as she tosses her head back and forth trying to look over at me, swishing her tail furiously. I wrap my arms around myself and feel incredibly bad, no matter what it cost I was going to buy her and bring her home to me. She lets out another distressing whinny as they disappear behind the house, I turn and trudge over to the fence of my own.

I look up and look over the home, feeling as if it isn't my own. The cream boards are faded from the constant sun, weathered down as the years have passed. No lights are on inside, and I begin to wonder where everyone is.

"Nyx…is it quiet to you?" I ask softly, hearing the crunch of his boots behind me. The crunching stops, but he doesn't say anything.

I frown as I turn around, expecting to see him there but instead see a person wearing all white with a black hood concealing their face.

I scramble back and a scream escapes me, the gate digs into my back as I half fall into it. The hooded figure moves fast, grabbing me by the shoulders and yanking me forward.

I careen into the dirt road, coughing as the wind is knocked from me. I feel rope loop around my ankles, tightening and biting at the soft skin.

They begin to drag me.

My shirt rises and the sharp rocks dig in and cut at my stomach. I cry out as I roll over, letting my back take the most damage.

"*Nyx!*" I try to grab onto something that will keep me in place, anything to stop me from moving. My whole body is erupting with pain and I can feel something sticky running down my back.

"*Nyx where are you!*" I glimpse behind me, and find him no were to be seen. A suffocating realisation dawns on me, what if this was his plan the whole time?

No, no it couldn't be.

Nyx wouldn't do that to me, he loved me.

Does he really though?

He wouldn't have done this, regardless of the person I may be. He's a better man than that, and not cowardly.

That leaves one thing…I am being taken to the burning pole.

"You can't do this!" I cry out at them, trying to wiggle my feet as best as I can in the rope. It's no use, it only bites into my ankles and begins to blister.

The hooded figure says nothing.

I grow panicked, clawing at the earth underneath me as we reach the top of the slope. Lanterns have been lit and set up in a straight path, leading to what I can assume is the forest.

Drums begin to play, thudding like a soft heartbeat. I can hear people mumbling around us, I look around through the lanterns and see other hooded figures.

Where is my family? Had they been in on this as well?
We grow closer to the edge of the forest, and the hooded figure comes to a sudden halt; dropping the rope. I scramble onto my knees, wincing as the broken skin on my back begins to burn. My hands shake in front of me as I sit back on my heels, my shirt is in tethers and barely holding on.

"What's going on?" I ask, my voice soft. No one answers, no one offers any help. I hold back the tears as I press my hands into my pants, rocking slightly. This is not how I planned to return, this is not what I thought was going to happen.

I hear a scuffle and a struggle and look up from my hands, Nyx is being held between five guards, they've managed to put a rope around his neck and pin his arms behind his back. He's snarling at them before he senses me, he looks away from the guards and up at me.

This fuels his anger even more.

"I demand you to release me," he bellows, struggling. The guards begin to press down on him, forcing him to his knees a few metres from where I am.

I want to crawl to him, but I can't bring myself to move. I can feel the warm blood trickling down my back and soaking into the waistband of my pants.

"Enough of that, Nyx," a strong male voice says from behind me. I freeze at the same time Nyx does. He looks up and over me; his anger is wiped from his face and replaced by a blank stare. But I see the fire in his eyes, dancing with the violet.

"Good. Release him, he isn't a peasant." The guards let go of him and undo the rope from his hands. He rises and pulls the rope from his neck, throwing it to the side. He takes a step towards me.

"Uh uh, not so fast my boy."

I take a steadying breath and grit my teeth as I force myself onto my hands and turn towards the King. I hear Nyx growl as I expose my back to him, I spit on the ground as I lean back on my heels. I look up to see the King standing before me, staring down at me.

I don't avoid looking into his eyes, his lips twitch into a smirk.

"Just like her," he states. He turns curious as he crouches down across from me. His hand begins to reach towards me, before he yanks it back.

"Like who?" I ask.

"Veronica."

"I don't know a Veronica," I say slowly, choosing my words carefully. His expressions grows to distaste, his lips pull back over his teeth.

"She was Nyx's mother."

"Don't you dare bring mother into this," Nyx says from behind me. The King's eyes flicker over to him before focusing back to me.

"Did you know, Nyx? Have you known the entire time and kept it to yourself?" he asks. Nyx stays silent and I'm solely confused.

"Silence is an answer in itself." He rises.

"What are you talking about?" I ask, following him with my eyes as he straightens his suit out.

"The night Veronica passed, you were born. I have come to the conclusion her power and a piece of her soul now reside in you. Your abilities have confirmed my beliefs."

My thoughts whirl as I think about what he's said. How could I have been linked with her? I knew Aunty was a seer, but how did that have anything to do with the faeries?

"Such a confused human. Nyx, what was your plan for her?" he muses, grinning wickedly. I look down at the ground again and take deep breaths, this is all too much for me to handle. How am I meant to get out of this situation? The babunook is still out there killing children. I can't let the King get the better of me.

I reach up and undo the necklace Nyx had given me, I shove it into my pocket and lean my hands against the dirt. I don't know if this is going to work, but I'm out of options. I shut my eyes and clear my mind of the jumbled thoughts, looking for peace.

I let the calm wash over me, feeling a grey haze fall over me and numb my body.

I'd never attempted to reach out to other forces before, or spirits. I knew seers could speak with the dead, but I'd never needed a reason too until now. I open my eyes as everything around me goes silent, standing beside the king is a ghostly figure.

Long black raven hair falls over her slender shoulders, exposing two pointed ears. Her violet eyes look from the King and down to me, she gives me a sad smile. Nyx has the same eyes and nose as her, and I know this is his mother.

"Sweet girl, I am sorry you've been dragged into this," she whispers, her voice as gentle as a cool breeze. She unclasps her hands and floats over to me, kneeling down in front of me. She tucks her hair behind both ears, her pale green dress fans out around her.

"Can they see you?" I ask. I look back up to the King; his mouth moves but he's looking over at Nyx.

"No, only you. Why have you called me?" She reaches out and holds my chin up so she can look at me properly. For so long I'd felt like I hadn't belonged, like I was an outsider with my own people. Her touch fills me with warmth and washes away all of my anxiety and concerns.

"I need help. I think your…husband wants to kill me." I bite my bottom lip, my heart races in my chest as I look into her eyes. Her phantom touch lingers as she rubs her thumb over my cheeks, she looks over my shoulder to Nyx.

"Raine Nyx would never allow that."

"I know, but I can't have him hurt in the process. What do I do?" I ask, feeling desperate. I can't run, I can barely stand with the state my back is in. I'd need help more than anything, but everything feels impossible.

"Do what you do best Ravynne."

Pieces of her begin to be swept away with the breeze, I reach out and desperately try to hold onto her; only to have my hand go through her. I don't know what I do best. I hide like the coward I am. I've hidden from everyone for the last ten years.

"Survive."

She's gone and reality slams back into me. I blink and the King's voice fills the space around me, he hadn't noticed I haven't been listening. What did she mean, survive?

"I won't let you harm her," Nyx says, his voice is laced with anger and power. Power I didn't realise he had. I look over my shoulder. He stands with his feet slightly apart and shoulders back, his violet eyes shine fiercely. The air around him begins to churn with darkness, as if he could command the night itself.

"I am your father. I brought you into this world. Do not think I'm afraid to take you out of it." Tension snaps into the air, the wind begins to grow restless and pick up around me; whipping the torn pieces of my shirt against my back. A long gleaming silver sword forms in Nyx's right hand, the tip almost touches the ground.

"I am done being afraid of you." Nyx moves fast, one minute I'm crouched looking over at him and the next I'm standing in his arms. He pushes me behind him, making sure I'm out of the way. The ropes around my ankle begin to wither, falling to the dirt.

"What are you doing?" I hiss, gripping his shirt tightly. His father cracks his neck as he draws his own sword, this isn't going to end well.

"Saving you, now go." He doesn't look down, instead he focuses on his father' sword. I force myself to let go of his shirt and stagger back, the movement tears open the wounds on my back as they begin to bleed again.

Hooded figures move closer to the two faeries, getting a good view of what's to come next. I turn to leave, only to see the guards that had brought Nyx here closing the opening to my escape. I wasn't foolish enough to run through them or the crowd.

"Nyx, I can't," I whisper, looking around at the shadows that flicker over everyone.

"Get back then,"

It's the last words that leave his lips as he moves forward, striking his father's blade with such force the ground seems to vibrate beneath my feet. I turn back to see Nyx and his father circling each other, swords raised and ready for attack. When the King begins to come towards me, I use it to my advantage.

I grab the necklace from my pocket, and bite my bottom lip as I throw it towards him; striking him in the back of the head. He snarls as he looks over his shoulder at me, swinging his sword towards me.

I watch wide eyed as Nyx scores a blow against his side, red blood spills over the sword and onto the ground. His father shrieks in fury as he swings the blade towards Nyx. Nyx raises his sword to block the blow and to my dismay his blade breaks in half.

"Have you learnt nothing of mortals?" his father says, swinging towards Nyx. He jumps back, keeping his eyes trained on his father's sword. His own sword is merely a jagged stump, not nearly long enough to block a hit.

"Have I taught you nothing?" Again, he advances. They move towards the forest, Nyx is light on his feet; never staying in the one spot for too long. This frustrates his father even more. I look down at the broken blade.

I am going to survive. Nyx is going to survive.

I pick up the piece, tightening my hand around the broken end. The blade bites into the flesh of my hand but I pay it no mind, not as I see Nyx fall to ground.

Not as I see his father bringing the blade down.

I move forward, ignoring the pain in my back.

Nyx's small jagged sword is thrown from his hands. His father stands above him, sword resting on his chest over his heart.

"It's a pity I have to do this, you were my only son and you've again disappointed me," He presses the blade down, breaking through Nyx's shirt. He hisses but doesn't say a word; his hands go to the blade and push back against it.

"Once I have her, she'll be as good as dead," his father whispers, and I only hear this because I'm directly behind him. Nyx's eyes widen as the sword begins to go deeper.

I don't think.

I jam the blade through the King's ribs, right where his heart should be. My hands are cut in the process and as I wrench it back out, blood spills from the wound. The King drops his sword and turns around, his face begins to pale as he looks down at me.

"You are Veronica after all."

I step out of the way as he falls face first into the dirt, his skin pales to a sickly green colour. Faeries don't decompose the same way humans do. We're children of the dirt, whereas they're children of the air.

"Ravynne?" Nyx murmurs, I look away from the ever growing puddle of blood and to Nyx. He leans on his elbows, the front of his tunic where the blade had been pressed soaks through with a small amount of blood. I drop the blade and wipe my hands against my pants. People in the crowd scream, some run away.

I fall to my knees in front of Nyx, he sits up and pulls me gently into his arms. I don't know when I began to cry, but now I don't know if I will ever stop. I'd never killed anyone before, and I'd just killed his father.

"I'm so sorry, I didn't know what to do." I sob into his shirt, burying my face into him. His arms wrap around me gently, he's careful not to touch the cuts on my back.

"It's okay, everything's going to be okay," he whispers, stroking the back of my head.

"Ravynne?!" I hear Ma yell and there's a commotion behind us. I lean back and look over my shoulder but stay in the safety of his arms.

Ma breaks through the crowd, wearing no hood or robe. Da and Aunty follow close behind. Ma sees me and runs over, stepping over the dead king. His body has begun to sprout flowers, green moss has begun to form on his skin and has spider webbed to the ground.

"Oh my god I thought we were too late, I thought we'd lose you." She wraps her arms around me and Nyx, also careful not to touch my back.

"What's going on?" I ask, wiping my wet cheeks.

"We'll tell you once we get you home and cleaned up," Ma kisses my forehead, rising. Nyx stands and helps me as well, he keeps a protective arm around me and looks around the clearing for any other threats.

Da and Aunty take up the rear as we head home, nearly everyone has disappeared. Once the king died I doubt they wanted to follow in his path. I look up to Nyx, he looks down as he feels my eyes on him. I still have so many questions I need answers to, but instead I let him press a gentle to kiss to my forehead and lead me home.

I sit in the white bath tub, the soapy water had begun to turn a dull red and brown colour as Nyx washed the wounds on my back and the blood from my arms. Ma had tried to follow us into the bathroom, but I'd asked for her to wait down stairs with the others. Nyx presses the cloth gently to my back, I hiss as he picks out pebbles.

I don't know if I'm ready to go down there and confront them all.

I'm definitely not ready to confront the fact I just killed someone.

"Nearly done," he says, rinsing the cloth and pressing it into my back again. I pick the blood out from under my nails as I look down. I'd put my hair up into a high bun, a few pieces had escaped and clung to the dampness on my neck.

"Can't you do magic and heal it?" I ask, looking up at him. He sits on a stool beside the bathtub, his legs are too long and he's half hunched over leaning towards me. He'd rolled the sleeves of his shirt up and splashed water over his face, the wound on his chest still had to be cleaned.

"Yes, but I need it clean first." I look away and stare at the end of the bathtub. "I can imagine you have questions?"

"Did you know?" I whisper, afraid of the answer. His hand stills on my back. He can't lie to me, but I feel his reluctance to answer.

It hurts.

"I had my suspicions after the second time we'd met. I didn't want to say anything, you wouldn't have believed me if I did. But as I got to know you, I realised I didn't care if you were a seer. I didn't really piece together that you had a piece of my mother's power."

"Were you in the village looking for a seer for your father?" I ask, avoiding looking at him. I'd opened myself up to him, all vulnerabilities and had shared my sister with him. A piece of myself I never shared with anyone.

"I wasn't actively looking for one, but I was looking around for one. When I met you, you were stubborn and cautious but I couldn't get you out of my mind. I tried and then I wrote that song. You were never meant to hear it." He wipes my back again, getting the last traces of soap off.

"Can I even trust you?" I finally turn to him, barely able to contain my true feelings. I'm coming undone, and I still haven't finished what I came back for. He blinks slowly.

"Yes you can. If you don't remember, I just tried to kill my father to save you." He wrings the rag out, sitting it against the side of the bathtub. Its white material is now stained red.

"I'm sorry about that, but I couldn't let him kill you. I'm sorry." I brace my hands on the side of the tub, wincing as I stand. Nyx has a towel ready and helps wrap it around me. I stand on my own and hold onto the towel tightly.

"If you didn't, I'm afraid of what would have happened to you."

"Let me clean the wound on your chest." I grab the wrung out cloth and gently push him back onto the stool. He doesn't object as I unbutton his shirt and push it from his shoulders. I sit it on the sink and look back at him.

The mark isn't as bad as I'd thought, a quick clean would suffice.

"Are you going to clean it or stand there and ogle me?" A high pitched laugh escapes me. He's being serious. I crouch down, careful not to move my back. I lean a hand on his knee as I reach up, gently wiping around the small gash. His eyes trace my movements, and I feel my cheeks begin to heat.

His stomach is toned, and without his glamour I can't imagine what he'd look like. Eatable, probably.

"Maybe I like to ogle at you," I say, letting my eyes drift from his stomach to his face.

"Don't lie."

"You'd like to think I was. If you can't remember the last few days…I can refresh you," I say softly, looking back to the gash. I'd finished wiping the blood away, but found I wanted a reason to continue touching him.

"I doubt I'll ever be able to forget the last few days with you Ravynne, or the last few months of having you as the thorn in my side," he smirks down at me, teasing.

"Even roses have thorns," I say sweetly, standing up. He gently pulls me to him, his hands rest on the back of my thighs as he tilts his head back to look up at me. I drop the rag beside him as I clasp my hands around his neck.

"You're my favourite thorn then."

"And you're my favourite rose," I reply, leaning down to plant a kiss on his forehead. I linger a few moments before straightening, I was too keenly aware of how hot I'm becoming, and too focused on the thumb that's lazily tracing patterns so close to where I ached to be touched the most.

"We're the perfect couple then," he states, lips slightly parted.

"Something like that." I reluctantly step out of his arms, pulling the towel tighter around myself. "So does that mean you're king now?" I undo my hair and let it fall around me, acting as a shield. He runs a hand through his hair.

"Yes, it does."

"Oh." I look down and head out of the bathroom and into my room, I shut the door behind me and lock Nyx out. I lean my forehead against the closed door and take a deep breath, if we couldn't be together before we definitely won't be able to now.

"Go downstairs, I'll be down soon," I say softly, pushing myself back from the door. I drop the towel and pull on a white shirt as well as a pair of plain brown trousers. I block the pain out from my back, building a mental barrier up around it. I wouldn't have Nyx there forever to heal my wounds, I had to get use to looking out for myself again.

I head downstairs and brace myself for the worst, I doubt after what just happened it could get worse. I find everyone in the living room, Aunty and Ma are sitting down while Nyx and Da are standing at opposite ends of the room. Nyx looks up as he hears me enter.

"Where's Kalin?" I ask, looking around for him. I strain my ears to see if he's upstairs.

Silence.

Ma bursts into tears and Aunty wraps her arm around her, pulling her close. I look to Da for answers and find silent tears streaming down his own face.

"Where is he?" I ask again, clenching the hem of my shirt. My heart is like a jack hammer in my chest as realisation begins to set in. Kalin isn't here, and that only means one thing.

"I told you not to let him out of your sight!" I yell at no one in particular.

"Rav we thought it was just-" Da interrupts, but I'm at my wits end.

"I warned you! Keep him with you, tie him to you if you must! Why does no one ever listen to me?" I want to break something, the anger building needs to break something.

"It was one night, nothing had happened in the first week and we thought he'd be safe in his own room," Ma sobs between words, looking over at me. Her eyes are bloodshot and puffy from crying, but I feel nothing.

"So he's been gone for two weeks?" My voice is borderline screeching, and I see Nyx flinch. I forgot his hearing is a lot better than ours. I can't calm down, I have to get out of here and find him.

"Yes."

"If I can't find him, I don't know if I can forgive you," I say, taking a step back. Nyx looks at me with warning, a small shake of his head. Da looks up, a muscle in his jaw twitches.

"You're gone for two weeks, no word. We thought you had died and when Kalin went missing we looked everywhere for him. You were no help, we thought we'd lost all of our children, Ravynne. We forgave you for Cece."

"Don't you dare bring her into this," I snarl, pointing a finger at him. Nyx moves from the window and comes over to me. He blocks my view but I try to look around him. He puts his hands on my shoulders and holds me in place.

"Hey, hey. Look at me," he says softly, his voice as smooth as honey. I struggle against him, craning my neck around him. He's so tall and solid and currently a pain in my ass.

“Ravynne,” he snaps, my eyes go to his. His face is full of worry as he looks down at me.

“We will get him back, the babunook is still in the village. We just need to find its lair. Take some deep breaths, don’t take it out on your family.” He rubs my shoulders, calming me. I do as he says, breathing deeply, it helps calm my heart but doesn’t get rid of the sick anxious feeling.

“We need to go now, I know where it is.”

“You do?” He asks, surprised.

“You’re not the only one with a few tricks up their sleeves.” He drops his hands, but the warmth lingers as he steps beside me.

“I’ll get him back,” I state. Dead or alive I would bring Kalin home.

“Be safe Ravynne, take the faerie with you,” Da jerks his head towards Nyx, and I feel my lips twitch. Nyx rolls his eyes as he takes my hand. I look at my small family once more and without saying another word I let Nyx lead me out of the house and into the night. I take the lead and go towards the river.

“How did you find it?” Nyx asks.

“I followed him, it was the same night I saw it take that little girl,” My feet move fast beneath me, and I’m practically dragging Nyx. We reach the river and all is quiet and still, not even the breeze stirs. I look towards the darkest patch of forest and feel fear begin to worm its way into my veins. I can’t let it take hold of me now, not when I had to find Kalin.

"Let's do this," I say softly, but my feet stay rooted in the same spot. I look up to find Nyx already looking down at me. I lick my lips.

"Together?" he murmurs, reaching his free hand up to cup my face.

"Always," I breathe out, closing my eyes as our lips meet. I let the warmth of him flood through me like a wild fire, igniting every pore and cell I possess. He pulls back too soon and looks towards the forest.

I lead the way again, staying closer to Nyx this time around. It seems to open up for us as the moon lights a path. I stay alert for any noises but only make out the faint chirping of crickets. The forest is dark around us, far darker than it had been on the night I'd followed the babunook in here. A cool breeze ruffles my hair, and I have the sinking sensation that I don't have my necklace on to block visions.

I have no control over them, if one were to happen I'd be vulnerable and put us in even more danger. Could tonight be the night were Nyx and I confront it? He didn't have anything on him, only his bare hands.

Maybe we'd be lucky enough to get Kalin back alive and not have to face the babunook. I'm in no state to fight, and after already killing one person tonight I don't particularly feel like killing another; even though I have to.

"Are you sure this is the way?" Nyx whispers, his breath hits my ear and sends a tingle through me.

"I'm not entirely sure, but the forest seems to think it is," I motion around to the trees and shrubs, and notice they lean in the direction we're walking. As if they want to help save my brother and banish the babunook for good.

"I wouldn't be surprised if the forest itself is part magic," Nyx murmurs back. I stay silent and focus. The path of the moon stops and we're faced with a thicket of brambles. I let go of Nyx's hand and move forward. I get down on my stomach and begin to crawl underneath the thorns, a few branches snag my hair and break off but I keep pushing.

Nyx follows beside me, we make minimal noise as we come to a stop at the edge of the thicket; still protected by the dense leaves. In front of us is the babunook lair, exactly how I'd seen it last. Two lanterns hang from the side of the hut, making the gaping entry darker than any black I'd ever seen.

"I have to go in," I whisper, not tearing my eyes away from that darkness. I'm afraid I'll look away and when I look back the babunook will be there, ready to drag me out.

"I am not letting you go in there," Nyx hisses back, I feel his eyes on me. I gulp, I didn't want to at all. But what choice did I have? I had to save my little brother.

"What if Kalin doesn't go to you? He doesn't know you," I point out, but if Kalin had ended up here I doubt Nyx would have trouble getting him to go with him.

"You can't see in the dark, and I'm magic like the babunook. Magic can battle magic, but mortal and magic don't mix. Not when the babunook's magic is so dark. If it attacks, I'll be the only one capable of escaping alive with Kalin. Your brother is food now. The babunook is extremely territorial,"

He has a point, which I hate.

"I don't want to wait out here, what if you don't come back out? What if it comes out while you're in there and I have no way to warn you? What if it's already out here and finds me while you're in there?" I whisper back, finally looking to Nyx. His lips twist, surely he wasn't actually going to leave me out here. He realises the same thing as well and sighs.

"Fine, let's just get this over with but let me heal your back first. Once we find Kalin you take him, and if the babunook comes, you run and don't look back. Do not come back for me." He doesn't let me argue as he crawls out into the clearing, offering me his hand as I follow. He helps me up and gently murmurs a few words, I feel my back begin to warm and go numb, and suddenly the pain is gone. He pushes me behind him. I hold onto his shirt as we walk slowly towards the open door. I grab onto a stick, it won't do much but I feel better with some sort of weapon. I'd forgotten to bandage my hands and wince as the skin breaks and begins to ebb with blood again.

"Can you make me see in the dark?" I whisper as soft as I dare, he freezes and looks down over his shoulder. He sighs silently as he leans down and plants a kiss on both eyes, when I open them again the dark entry way is washed in soft shades of green and grey. Nyx ducks down as we enter the long slim hallway, the air in here drops to freezing and my skin breaks out with goose bumps.

I don't look over Nyx's shoulder as we walk, instead I watch the ground and look at the hallway around us. It's made of sticks and twigs and some sort of moss has grown and is holding everything together. I feel the urge to reach out and touch it, but as I do I see a fly land on a piece. The moss closes over the fly and flattens out once more.

I keep both hands on Nyx's shirt.

I try to block out the faint smell of decay, far too rotten but far too sweet at the same time. Nyx doesn't seem bothered by the cold or the smell, so I try to put on the same brave face as we go deeper. I chance a look over my shoulder, only a small archway of light sits there; we'd gone deeper than I'd thought.

Nyx stops in front of me, and I bump into him. I'm about to grumble at him when I feel a cold breeze blow roughly against my hair. I peer around his shoulder and feel my mouth drop. In front of us the hallway has ended, leading a rocky stair case spiralling down into a deep cave. A light blue glow shines through the roof of branches and moss, the diamonds in the side of the cave walls glitter. A few trees cling to the cave walls across from us, their bare branches droop towards the bottom while their roots barely hold onto the rock wall, reminding me of skeleton hands.

Nyx takes my hand in his as he begins to walk down the stair case, I stick close to the wall; not letting myself be tempted by the sheer drop that's only one wrong footstep to my right. Nyx is confident but cautious with each step, squeezing my hand.

The stair case is jagged rock beneath our feet, and one slip could result in a handsome gash that would leave me crippled. I let my free hand with the stick trail against the wall, tapping on the diamonds as I go. I'm half tempted to take one for my troubles.

Drip. Drip. Drip.

I can only hope its water and not blood echoing around the cave. The stair case curves around the wall as we go deeper, we duck underneath a tree and I'm careful not to touch any of its branches, it doesn't look stable at all; as if one breeze could have it falling below. I look up to see the hallway we came through above us, no light reaches from the tunnel to here. I decide to take my chance and look down, a thick fog hangs below us and I'm unsure of where the bottom is.

"Are we nearly at the bottom?" I whisper, reaching over a broken step carefully. Nyx helps me right my feet and once I'm safe he presses me against the wall with his body. I focus on the curve of his body against mine. His breath hits my face as he looks down at me, his violet eyes begin to glow and I see his usual glamour fall away. His face becomes sharper, his ears longer. He becomes even more beautiful.

"The fog is glamour resistant," he pants, licking his lips.

"I've seen you like this before," I say softly, resting my hands on the curve of his hips. He leans his elbows above me and blocks off any view that isn't him. I feel something hard begin to press against my stomach, and feel the heat grow in my cheeks.

"Nyx, I don't think now is an appropriate time," I whisper, but it's a weak attempt. My body quivers at the thought of him taking me again, remembering how much pleasure he brings me and the way he touches me.

"I know, I can't resist you and without the glamour…it's hard," his jaw clenches and he breathes heavily through his nose. *Not the only thing that's hard.*

"Well thanks I guess? But after, Nyx, we can't do that here." I search his face. "Would a kiss help sate it?"

"If you kiss me I won't be able to stop."

"Okay well how about I go first?" I wiggle myself out from under him, pushing gently. He gives in with a grunt, letting me escape from his arms. I grab onto one of his hands and begin to walk back down the stairs, finding a strange comfort in the unnatural length of his fingers. The stairs descend into the fog and I feel light headed as I breathe it in. I can't see in front of me, and can barely make out the stairs.

We go deeper and the fog clears, creating a cloud roof above us. I pause on the stairs, Nyx bumps into me; his other hand snakes around my waist and pulls me to him. There are only a handful of stairs left until we reach the bottom of the cave. A thin layer of water covers the floor, going from a light blue to a dark blue in the centre of the room.

The babunook is nowhere to be found.

"It's just an empty room?" I whisper. I have the eerie sense that someone or something is watching us. I look around the area again and come up empty, this was the only way we could have gone. There were no other turns, no secret tunnels. It leads straight to here.

"No, it's not." Nyx keeps a tight hold of me as we walk down the last few steps and into the water. It comes up to our calves, I jolt at the sheer coldness. It's below freezing.

"It goes down there," Nyx points to where the dark water is, but we take no further steps. If I focus hard enough I can faintly see the outline of an opening going down, the ripple of water murmurs above it, indicating a current.

"I'll go, follow me down in five," I say immediately. Nyx is the stronger one of us yes, but if he's hurt down there I have no hope for leaving with me or my brother alive. Before he can protest I wrench myself from his arm. I spin around as I stumble backwards; my arms pinwheel as I begin to fall.

Nyx reaches out, wide eyed. Just before his hand reaches me I'm plunged into the water, I surface and splutter. But I push myself backwards, sinking down into the tunnel. He shouts in protest but once I'm underwater its complete silence. I open my eyes and try to adjust to the darkness that's below. I kick and begin to go deeper, letting the current pull me down.

If the current pulls me down, how am I meant to go back up?
I swim harder, finally leaving the tunnel and finding another cave. On the other side I see a light flicker, my lungs begin to burn as I swim towards the light. I grow desperate, clawing at the water. I surface in another cave, gulping down the air. The cavern's reversed and I'm treading water at the back of a cave. Bones litter the stone floor, white and shiny against the lantern that's been hung along the wall. I pull myself out of the water, shivering. I pause, listening for any noise.

I begin to walk forward, following the curve of the cave. My clothes cling to me, I leave wet footprints as I enter a small room. In the middle, Kalin is cramped in a wooden cage, from here he looks asleep. The cage is almost too small for him, he's curled into a ball with his head resting against the mossy bars.

I pause, underneath him is a circle of white. Similar to the one I'd seen in my dream. I hear his soft breathing, and a slight snore. I feel a small amount of relief, he's okay. Around the wet walls of the cave bones have been strung up in no particular pattern, a wooden desk sits across from me, overflowing with scroll parchment and stubbed out candles. Jars litter the floor around it, holding contents I'm not too sure of.

When I'm sure the babunook isn't in the cave I walk slowly into the room, I step on the white line and the water dissolves a hole into it.

Kalin's eyes futter open, he sees me and begins to cry silently. I rush over and reach up to the bars, trying to pry them apart.

"I'm here to save you," I whisper, losing my grip. I look back towards the entrance before trying again.

"I'm sorry sissy, I didn't mean to go with him," he sobs, grabbing onto me with an ice cold hand.

"How do I get you out?" I ask, looking frantically around the room. I let go of the bars and rush over to the desk, scattering the scrolls and knocking the candles off.

"I don't know," he whispers.

I find a thigh bone and go back over. I'm not tall enough to reach the rope that hangs from the ceiling but maybe I can pry a few bars off so he can slip through them. He squirms back an inch as I wedge the bone into the small gap, it's hard to get a good grip as the cage swings with every movement.

"God damn it," I growl. I hold onto a bar with one hand and push the bone in the opposite direction. For a moment the bar doesn't move, and then it makes a groaning sound before it snaps. I do it to another three bars, drop the bone, pull the bars out and throw them on the floor. Kalin falls into my arms, holding his small arms around my neck and his legs around my waist.

I hold him tight, not hesitating as I head back to the water. I have no idea how I'm meant to get out of here with him being as heavy as he is. We reach the edge of the water and I look down, even though I'm really looking up. I see a few shapes moving, and I pray it's just fish.

"We have to go in the water now, so I need you to hold your breath," I say. He nods.

"One, two, three," I count down, and then we both take a deep breath and I plunge us into the icy water. I kick out, moving slow against the current as I try and swim towards the tunnel opening. Something to my right moves, a dark murky figure. Kalin holds onto me tighter, squeezing my throat.

We're near the entrance of the tunnel when something slithers past my foot. Bubbles escape my mouth as I kick harder, fighting the current with every piece of fading energy that I have. I claw at the rock wall as I pull us through. Nyx's warm hands find mine as he pulls us upwards. We break the surface, gasping for air. Kalin coughs violently.

He takes Kalin from me and wraps his arms around him.

"Thank heavens you're okay, I thought I'd lost you," Nyx says, reaching out for me. I reach for his hand and at the same time I feel something close around my ankle. My eyes go wide as a startled scream escapes me. I'm dragged back under the water, down into the depths again. I thrash against whatever has me and I look down to find a Kelpie. Its tentacle is wrapped tightly around my ankle, its horse like head similar to the one I'd seen in Faerie. Around me others begin to detach from the wall, from brown to white they all have those deathless black eyes.

All focused on me.

I reach down and pry at the tentacle, desperately trying to pull myself free. My hands slip against the sliminess of it. Other black hands begin to reach for me, tugging at my clothes and my hair. My lungs burn in my chest and my lips threaten to open, to take a deep breath.

I can't die again like this.

I pull the tentacle towards my mouth, biting down on the soft flesh. Black blood begins to seep into the water around me, water fills my mouth and I spit it out as best as I can. My mouth is coated in a sheen of oil but I can't worry about that now, the kelpie screams as its tentacle unwraps from my ankle.

Nyx appears above me in the water, his violet eyes illuminating his sharpened features. He grabs my hand, pulling me to him. I wrap myself around his torso, holding onto dear life.

I look over my shoulder to see three Kelpies coming towards us, I ignore the burn in my lungs as I bury my face into his neck. He begins to kick towards the surface, straining against the current.

A sword materialises in his hand, with a forceful swing he cuts through the tentacles shooting towards us. Horrid screams fill the air around us, making my ear drums ring.

Black dots begin to spot my vision as Nyx makes it to the opening, Rocks chip from the wall under the force of his hands as he pulls, they sink into the depths below. No Kelpie's come after us.

We break the surface and I spit out black water but before I even open my eyes warm hands are carrying me out of the deeper water. I open my eyes to see Nyx above me, pulling me to the stair case. Kalin sits on the stairs, crying.

"She's alright," Nyx says softly, looking over his shoulder to my brother. His black hair is flat against his head, divots of water run down his throat. We both look like drenched rats. Kalin watches us with teary eyes as we reach the step. I lean on Nyx as I take deep breaths, spitting as I go. I wipe my mouth and reach for his hand, he helps me stand and then wraps me in a huge hug.

His warmth helps dispel the icy feeling the water has left me with.

"Take us home," I whisper desperately, putting my trust into him. Nyx takes Kalin in his arms and has a hand in mine, leading us to safety. I look back towards the water moments before we reach the fog, six Kelpies watch us from the darker part; the guardians of the babunooks lair.

A chill goes through me, saving Kalin has been too easy.
What is the babunook's plan?

I sit on the couch with a warm blanket wrapped around me and a steaming hot cup of tea in my hands. Ma and Aunty are upstairs with Kalin bathing him and no doubt making sure he's okay. Da stands near the window, looking out every few moments for any sign of movement. Nyx stands across from me, near the now lit fire place. He watches me steadily, with an expression I can't place.

I feel warm on the surface, but deep inside it feels like I've been frozen. There's an uncontrollable chill I can't shake, no matter how many blankets I have around me or how many cups of tea I drink down. On my ankle, there're suction marks from where the Kelpie had its tentacle. I'm not sure if it's bruising or if it will always be there.

Nyx hasn't said anything to me since we left the lair; he whispered to Kalin on our way home but only spared me a few glances. Most likely to make sure I was still there. I knew I'd made him angry, I just don't know how long that anger is going to last.

"Will he be okay?" Da asks, turning to Nyx. He'd been the first to spot us and had come running out, taking Kalin from Nyx and upstairs. Nyx had lead me to the couch and looked after me while the others were busy looking after Kalin.

I feel a pang of loneliness.

"He'll be okay, just shaken from the entire ordeal," Nyx doesn't take his eyes from me and I look away, focusing on the steam that curls up from the pale tea.

"What happens now? The King is dead, this creature is still out there and the entire village want my daughter dead."

"When Ravynne killed him, the power was passed on to me but it's dormant until I go back to Faerie and have my crowning ceremony. I find I don't particularly want to rule over a village," I wince at his last words, this is great news for the village. The people would be free to live how they like, with no care in the world. But if he wasn't going to be a ruler, I'd never see him again. What if he chose to stay in Faerie and rule?

"That still leaves the creature and my daughter."

"Ravynne, may I speak to your father in private?" Nyx asks, finally talking to me. I look up at him and look for any form of scheming, he keeps his face blank but I see his ears twitch. I stand wordlessly, letting the blanket fall from my shoulders. I sit the cup down and head up to Kalin's room to see how he is.

All I want to do is eavesdrop; it's my fate they're also talking about.

I find Kalin's door open, the window is now boarded from the inside. The lantern burns bright, Kalin lays on the bed in a deep sleep with Ma curled up behind him. Aunty gnaws at her nails as she watches, when she hears me she looks up.

"How is he?" I whisper, not wanting to wake him. Ma looks up at me as I speak, she strokes the hair from his face. I stand beside Aunty. I feel a small amount of relief seeing Kalin in bed asleep. But I still have to kill the babunook, I still have to figure where I stand with Nyx.

"A lot better, he can't remember any of it thank god," Aunty murmurs, going back to chewing her nails.

"What now?" Ma whispers. Kalin stirs a little before falling back into a deep sleep.

"I kill that thing," I murmur, thinking of what I needed.

"We can't lose you too," Aunty says, placing a hand on my shoulder. I look up at her and put my hand over hers.

"You won't. But I can't let Nyx do this."

"You love him, don't you?" Aunty asks, and I freeze.

"Yes." I'd fallen in love with a faerie.

"Then do what you must, just come home to us in one piece."

I slip out of the room, heart thundering in my chest. I knew vaguely what that feeling was, but now that I'd admitted it out loud it seems like the only thing I can feel. They say love is a lot like fear, and now my steps falter at the top of the stairs. Nyx is down there, my Nyx. He doesn't know I love him, but now I feel as though I'm keeping far too may secrets from him.

I go down the stairs, head high and stop when I see Nyx and Da standing beside each other, whispering back and forth. I clear my throat, causing them both to jump. What were they talking about?

"So, what's the plan?" I ask. Nyx looks over at me and I feel the heat rise to my cheeks. I stop myself from nervous twitching. He knew me far better, and any sign of nerves would give it away.

"Tomorrow night we're going to kill the babunook," Nyx says. Da looks at him evenly. Something's happened between them, what have they schemed up?

"Well I'm coming. No if's or but's." I cross my arms over my chest, raising an eyebrow.

"Yes, you will." Nyx says, but there's a shine in his eyes. Oh. *Oh.*

"Are you staying the night?"

He nods, it calms me down knowing he'll be here. So if anything happens or goes wrong, he can help fix it. Da yawns and rubs the stubble on his jaw.

"I'm going to head up and get some sleep. Nyx, I appreciate it." Da nods towards him before walking towards me. He pulls me into a quick tight hug, "I love you Rav,"

"I love you to." I say, squeezing him back. He let's go and heads up the stairs, I watch as he goes. Once he's gone I look back towards Nyx and the room fills with tension. I take a seat on the couch and lean back. He leans against the side of the fire place, head titled to one side as his eyes trail over me.

"Are you angry at me?"

"Yes." His answer is clipped and he twists his nose. I bet he wishes he could lie to me right now.

"I'm sorry. I couldn't let you go down there, not when it could have been there."

"Do you listen to anything I ever tell you?" he asks, a muscle in his jaw ticks and I look down, I pick at a thread on my pants.

"Yes, but—"

"No Ravynne, no excuses. You could have died down there, again, might I add if you've so foolishly forgotten what happened in Faerie." He comes over and crouches down in front of me, his hands rest on my knees and I slowly look back up at him.

"I do what I do and say what I do, to protect you and keep you from harm. I am here to help you, and your village. You wanted my help and you've got it, but stop going against me. You're going to put both of us in danger." His voice is soft but his words are sharp, and I feel terrible.

"I…I didn't look at it like that," I whisper.

"I know you didn't and it's okay, but promise me you won't do anything like this again. I cannot lose you to the babunook, Ravynne. I couldn't live a thousand years knowing I'd lost you." I inhale a sharp breath.

"Okay, I promise."

I am so glad I can lie. I feel like the worst human being in the world.

"Are you hungry at all?" he asks, his thumb rubs over the material on my knee. I shake my head but lick my lips, I don't like arguing with him. He's going to hate me once we come face to face with the babunook, once he realises what I'm going to do. I lean forward and press my lips to his, winding my hands into his hair.

We have one last night to act as though things will be okay. One last night to feel his skin against mine before I ruin the bridge I'd built between us.

He kisses me back hungrily, his hand trail up my legs and slip under my shirt; resting on my waist. I move forward and knock him backwards onto the rug, he goes down smoothly and positons me on his lap. The fire is our only source of light, it throws shadows across his face.

I pull my shirt off and toss it onto the couch, his hands roam up from my waist to my breasts. He watches me with amazement, he makes me feel amazing. I lean back down and kiss him again, bracing myself on my elbows.

In a flurry of movement and broken kisses, we get the remaining clothes off. I stay on top as I straddle him, lowering myself slowly onto him. He covers my mouth with his to catch the gasp that escapes, if anyone in my family walked down stairs we'd both be in a lot more trouble than the babunook.

We move as one, and I'm overwhelmed with pleasure. Three words linger on my lips.

Three words that have the power to unravel us.

I love you.

I drown them out with his tongue, losing myself in the man I'd come to love.

In the man I'm going to betray.

We both fall over the edge at the same time, his fingers sink into the soft skin on my lower back while my nails rake down his own. I roll off of him, a panting mess. He intertwines our hands and I move my head so it's pressing against his shoulder. We lay like that for so long I think he's fallen asleep, I look up to see his eyes still open.

"What are you thinking about?" I whisper.

"A lot of things."

"When do you have to go back and be crowned as king?" I unclasp hands and move so I'm cuddled between his arm and body, I draw patterns on his bare chest.

"Sooner would be better than later, but I'd like to get rid of the babunook first." He massages my shoulder, sweeping my hair back.

"Will I see you again?" I tilt my head back and look up at him, he focuses on the ceiling but I see the mental struggle behind his eyes as he waits to answer.

"I want to say yes, but I'm unsure." He looks down at me with his lips pressed tightly together. I don't know what he expects me to say back, I told him I wouldn't beg and I'll stick by it.

"Can I make you a deal?" I lean on my elbow so I can look down at him, he brushes the hair back from his forehead as he looks up at me with a raised eyebrow.

"You want to make me a deal?"

"If we both survive the babunook, I want to come with you so I can see you crowned. If you want me to leave you alone after that I will, I just don't think I'm ready to give this up yet," I say softly, speaking from my heart. I press my hand onto his chest, feeling his heart racing.

"And if I refuse?" he challenges, looking at me with a fire in his eyes.

"Then I'll let you. I just thought that maybe you weren't ready to give this up so soon either. My mistake." I go to roll off of him, wanting to put space between us. He grabs my hand and holds me in place.

"You aren't mistaken Ravynne, I don't know if I'll ever be ready to give this up willingly. I'm unsure if we'll see each other again because I don't know if I'll be forced to stay in Faerie. I couldn't ask you to stay there with me." He brings a hand up to my face and wipes away a stray tear, I feel my eyes sting.

"You wouldn't have to ask Nyx, I'd stay because…" *I love you. I'd go wherever you went if it meant being by your side.*

"Because?" he asks.

"Because I'd rather be by your side than be without you. If it meant sacrificing a few years in Faerie then so be it, what're a few years to you anyway?"

"A few years are barely the blink of an eye for me, but for you Ravynne…you're mortal, I don't want you wasting your precious life on someone like me. Even if I want you to." I sigh as I tap my fingers along his chest.

"That's not for you to decide and you know it."

"I know, but I'm only—"

"Trying to protect me, yes, I know." I groan, letting my forehead fall against his chest.

"Someone has too," he says, pressing a kiss into my hair.

"I'm glad it's you." I lay back down and roll over. He spoons me from behind and wraps a protective arm around me. I reach up and grab two pillows off the couch, putting them under my head and his. I hold his hand in mine as I snuggle back into him, he fits perfectly around me. Even without blankets, the fire keeps us warm.

"Goodnight Nyx," I mumble, letting my eyes flutter shut. We'd need to be up early to make sure no one catches us naked on the floor, but that is the last thing I'm worried about. He peppers kisses on my shoulder and up my neck before nuzzling into me.

"Goodnight Ravynne."

I would make a deal with any faerie, fight any creature and drink any potion if it meant being able to fall asleep in his arms like this every night for the rest of my human years. Unfortunately, I'm out of luck.

I don't think I had any to begin with.

☾

The day passes by in a blur, I spend it with my family and Nyx. We go over strategies and Nyx carves a stake out of a piece of wood that was caught in the weeds along the river bed. The sun is already beginning to set and I feel as if there's not enough hours in a day. Nyx follows me into the back yard to Millie's pen, she bleats and buts her head against the gate.

"Don't kill her, okay?" I say again, wringing my hands together. All day I'd made him promise not to kill her, we only needed the tip of the stake to be covered in it.

"I won't. Do you have what we need?" he asks, looking down at me. I grab the knife from my pocket, along with a strip of bandage and a white lily. He nods once and lets us into her pen, she skips over and nibbles at my pants. I scratch behind her ear as I crouch down.

"Will it hurt her?" I hold onto her collar and pass Nyx the knife. He doesn't answer, and I bite my bottom lip. I wish we didn't have to do this, but we have no choice.

"Just be ready to press the lily onto the wound and the bandage, okay? Wait until I say." He stoops down beside me, and nicks her neck with the knife. Blood spurts out and the metallic smell fills the air, I watch in horror as she struggles against my hold. There's so much blood. Nyx coats the stake thoroughly.

"Now," I move fast, pressing the lily and then the bandage. Blood flows freely through my fingers. Nyx presses his hand over mine and mumbles a few words in his language, I feel my own hand heat up and when he pulls our hands away the bandage has dissolved into her skin; revealing a lily shape scar.

"I'm sorry girl," I murmur, scratching her head. She bleats and buries her face into my chest. I give her a quick hug before pulling the few oatmeal cookies from my pocket and tossing them to the other side of then pen. She goes over happily, already forgetting about what had happened.

Nyx and I go inside and wash our hands, he has a brown satchel that carries red mushrooms and white chalk. He places the stake in there as well, and double checks to make sure we don't need anything else. I look out the kitchen window and see the full plump moon beginning to rise in the sky, glowing a rich cream gold.

We have to do this tonight.

"Will she be safe?" Da asks, coming into the kitchen. I turn and see Nyx adjust the satchel on his hip.

"I can't promise that, but she's incredibly brave so I have no doubt she will return. She won't be going near the babunook." Nyx looks over to me, and I hold his gaze. He believes this to be true, and I don't wish to give him any sign it isn't.

"Keep her safe, no matter what you have to do. I need to have her home," Da extends a hand, which Nyx takes. They stay clasped like that for a few moments, a silent conversation going on between them.

"Are we in time?" Ma asks, coming into the kitchen with Aunty and Kalin in tow. He runs over to me and wraps his small arms around my legs. I run a hand through his hair and squeeze him to me.

"We're nearly ready to go," I say, looking over to Ma and Aunty. Aunty comes over and frowns, her mouth turns down at the sides. Does she know, has she seen what's going to play out tonight?

"Be brave Ravynne, tonight will change you, for what I can only hope is the better," she whispers, wrapping me into a hug and squishing Kalin between us. I pat her back.

"I have no doubt about that." If I'm going to survive this, I'd need some serious therapy. No normal human could face a faerie creature and come away unscathed. She doesn't say anything more, just takes Kalin in her arms and leaves the room. Ma comes over then, wrapping me in a hug.

"Know your odds Ravynne and make sure you know if they're in your favour. I know it was hard growing up with everything that's happened in your life, but this battle isn't yours to fight, and if it's too much for you, fall back and let him finish it. There's no shame in sharing the weight." she steps back and runs a cold hand over my cheek, observing every slant and shadow on my face as she does.

"I'll come home Ma, I promise." I give her a kiss on the forehead, she moves around me and begins to boil a pot of water. I look over to Nyx who observes me oddly, I brush it off and walk over to him.

"Now or never, right?" I bump his shoulder with my own, forcing a smile.

"I'll meet you out front." He nods once more to my father and mother and leaves, silence falls over the room. A lot hasn't been said between us all, but it will have to wait.

"Bye Da," I give him a hug, breathing in his usual workman smell after a hard day.

"Be safe pumpkin." He kisses the top of my head and I step back, tucking my black button up shirt into my beige pants. I already had my boots on, all that was left to do is track down the babunook and begin.

"I love you all, and I'm sorry I've made things hard the last few months. When I return, I promise that will change." I leave the room, not giving them a chance to reply. With my head high I go down the front steps, spotting Nyx bathed in moonlight on the dirt path.

His violet eyes glow otherworldly as he looks over to me, I pull my hair back into a high pony tail as I walk over to him. I link my arm with his as we set off for the river, ready for this to be over.

"You must stay in the circle Ravynne, no matter what happens to me or around you, that circle will protect you," he says softly, giving my hand a squeeze.

"I know, stay in the circle and let you do all the work," I snap.

"Yes, exactly that. I promised your family I would bring you home."

Yes. A promise you shouldn't have made.

We reach a clearing, the moonlight shines down brightly down; making the thick forest even more daunting and dark. The shadows try and leak towards us, but have no luck. Nyx begins to set up the circle, pulling the chalk from his satchel. He passes it to me, and as he turns and begins to draw the circle I slip the stake into the back of my pants, pulling my shirt over it.

I hope he can forgive me.

Clouds cover the moon, for a terrifying moment the world around me is washed in darkness.

"Do you need the mushrooms?" I ask, looking around the dark clearing. Nyx finishes drawing a white circle, I silently pass him the mushrooms and watch as he sprinkles them around it.

"Once it arrives it won't be able to touch you in the circle." He stands and shoves the chalk in his pockets. I look up at him and clench my jaw.

"What about you?"

"I'll be fine," he sighs, watching me. I step into the circle and cross my arms over my chest as I look around the dark clearing, the moon breaks the clouds and illuminates me.

"I would feel better if you were in here with me," I say softly, looking back to Nyx. He tugs his bottom lip between his teeth before reluctantly taking a step into the circle. As soon as he does the world around us seems to go still, not even the crickets chirp.

I reach out and grab his hand, squeezing it tightly. I keep my eyes focused on the darkest part of the forest that sits in front of us. I hear a twig snap.

"Don't move," Nyx whispers, slowly stepping in front of me and holding me behind him.

I watch in horror as my vision begins to come to life around me.

The shrubs move away as a tall, dark figure comes towards us. Its hunched back is covered in black thin skin as it walks in the shadows and watches us with those taunting golden eyes. An old, ragged cloak hangs from it weakly, giving off a putrid stench.

"You will leave this village alone," Nyx says, staring at it. The babunook's head seems to tilt to the side as it stops moving. I feel my heart beating as wild as a rabbit in my chest, and this small circle didn't help my worry.

I'd lived this before and have somehow still managed to end up at the same place. I take a deep breath.

"Raine Nyx," I begin, my voice wavers and he looks down at me; shocked. I continue, "I command you to stay in the circle of protection until either myself or the babunook have perished. You may not leave this circle until one of us is dead, nor may you try and stop me." I feel my words slide over him, and hold him to the circle. I drop his hand, and look towards the babunook.

I can think of being a foul traitor later.

"Well, it looks like you've been doing your research, little mortal. How did you figure out his true name?" Its voice croaks, as if in desperate need of a glass of water. I drop the satchel to the ground, feeling the comforting dig of the stake in my back.

"You told me it actually, in a vision." I knew the moment I left this circle it would strike. But being so close to Nyx and *feeling* his anger radiating off of him, I almost want to get out of the circle now. I'm a coward, I can't look at him.

"I'm guessing our little king didn't know that." The babunook's black tongue moves as it speaks, nearly spilling from its mouth. Its gold eyes shine with delight.

"No," I say painfully, finally admitting it out loud. Nyx breathes deeply and I see his hands turn to fists out of the corner of my eye.

"You've taken something that is mine."

"My brother is not yours to take." I finally pull the stake out from my pants and toss it between my hands, getting a feel for it. I'd never fought anything before and I can't say I'm skilled in up close combat. Maybe I should have let Nyx do this.

"Anything in this world is mine to take," it hisses, surging forward. Nyx automatically puts an arm out in front of me, as if to protect me.

My heart splinters in my chest, I promised myself and his mother I wouldn't let him get hurt from this.

"Not the children from my village and I've come to show you that," I say, although I don't move away from Nyx's arm. "Tell me, are you the teacher?"

"A teacher? Ah, yes. One of my many faces I wear. A challenge you say?" It hums, beginning to walk around us. Its cloak billows behind, exposing a rat-like tail as long as a horse. I gulp.

"Yes."

"A soul for a soul. You would willingly sacrifice yourself for children that aren't yours? To never bear your own? That is, if you manage to kill me, but from the odds I know you will be dying tonight." It pauses, standing taller than Nyx, black matted hair hangs from its thin long arms. Its clawed hands are in front of it, while its wolf like skeleton face bobs gently.

It's from Faerie, which means it can't lie. I don't think it can lie, I never checked with Nyx. So I will die tonight, regardless of how this turns out. I finally look at Nyx, his eyes blaze with pain as he watches me. His arms twitch by his side, and I know he's fighting against the invisible chains I've locked him in.

"It's okay, I knew this would happen," I say softly, licking my lips. I'd strangely accepted that tonight I would finally take a stand and leave this world, even if it means leaving so much behind me. Nyx has shown me there are things worth dying for, and I would die a thousand deaths if it means saving him and my family.

"Why didn't you tell me?" his voice cracks, and I feel my heart split in half.

"Because I promised your mother I wouldn't let you get hurt," I whisper, flicking my eyes to the babunook. It seems bored, watching us.

"My mother?"

"I saw her, before your father died. I called and she came, I made a promise." I hold the stake tightly in my hand.

"You're mortal, your word means nothing," he says desperately, taking a small step towards me.

"It means something to me." In a hurry I close the distance between us and press my lips to his. I don't linger as I step away and out of the white circle.

The warmth I'd felt a moment ago dissipates and gives way to the cold, as if the hands of death already have a grip on me. Nyx rushes to the edge of the circle and as he tries to reach out, a glimmer of light flashes; caging him in the circle. My word meant something, my word is far stronger than I thought. He bangs his fists against it, looking frantically between me and the babunook.

I stay close to the circle, I could always jump back in if I needed a break or if I was losing. It would be delaying the inevitable, but it could buy me enough time to get the stake to hit its target. The babunook begins to walk, dragging its feet in the dirt. True fear grips my heart as it moves towards me, but I don't cower.

"Very well, I will feast on your flesh and suck the marrow from your bones once I'm done with you," it growls, flying towards me. I leap sideways, its hand just brushes past my sleeve. I fall to the ground and quickly stand again, only to be knocked across the clearing.

I slam into a tree and sag to the ground, my back explodes with pain as I curl into a ball, still cradling the stake.

"I warned you. I told you what would come if you didn't keep your nose in your own business," it says, walking slowly towards me. I blink away stars as I look up, I pull myself back up and lean against the tree.

"How boring would that have been?" I cough once, trying to ignore the pain. The fight's barely started and I'm already losing. Nyx is pacing frantically around the circle, mumbling to himself. He keeps his eyes on me at all times.

He is going to see me die.

"It would have been safe, but yet again you've shown me just how stupid mortals are." It stops a few feet from me.

"I was thinking brave," I say softly. I push myself from the tree and run towards it. I hold the stake out and as I come close enough to make out the dry blood in the hair of its arm I'm thrown to the side again by its large rat tail. I roll a few times through the dirt, but I pull myself up on shaky arms.

“This is going to be an easy fight,” it muses, swivelling its head towards me, “Here I was thinking you’d be a challenge.”

“You’ve seen the least of what I can do babunook.”

“Being a mortal is a weakness.” It lurches towards me, and I stay in the same spot. Running at it wasn’t getting me anywhere, and trying to avoid it wasn’t either.

“There’s nothing wrong with being weak,” I growl. It swings an arm out towards me and I hold the stake up as a shield as it collides hard enough to rattle my teeth.

Its other hand swipes out and I look down in surprise at the four rips in my shirt and the now bubbling blood. My hand goes to the wound instinctively, and while distracted the babunook snaps its large jaws towards me.

Nyx is screaming behind him, banging hard enough to break the skin of his fists. The world seems to lurch around me as I fall to my knees, I keep my hand pressed to my stomach but keep my eyes on the babunook. If I look down at the blood it will be the end of me.

“Oh little mortal, you tried and failed,” it coos, coming closer to me. Its gnarled feet show underneath the cloak, covered in hard wrinkled skin and dark toenails reminding me of the oak wood table at home.

I never had hope of defeating this creature.

“Ravynne!” Nyx screams, over and over. My name.

I feel dizzy and cold.

I’m so cold.

"You will perish as nothing and be no more than dirt and worms, you are a creature of the clay and will go back to the dirt from which you've been pulled." Its head hovers near my own, its rancid breath blows on my face.

Its black tongue falls from its mouth and touches the side of my face, I feel faint. This is how he took the little girl, lulled her to sleep.

I want to close my eyes, if only for a moment of relief.

"Prove me right mortal, give up."

I do as he says, I fall to my back and move my legs to a comfortable position. Its tail comes around and wraps around an ankle, tugging me roughly towards the babunook. I let my head fall to the side to look at Nyx, he kneels against the barrier. Tears stream down his face as he screams, but I can't hear his words anymore.

The babunook falls on top of me, and as I wait for impact I find he floats above me. I watch in horrified amazement as its jaws open and a golden light begins to spark at the back of his throat. I'm aware of the blood pooling around me.

"Can I say one more thing?" I whisper, feeling weaker than ever. It pauses, allowing me. I position the stake towards its chest, hoping it's aligned with its heart. I stop pressing against my wound and hold the stake, I feel the gush of blood spill out.

"*May I offer my soul for another, as the darkness claims us all in the end.*" As I whisper the words, they form a silver string and fly into the babunooks mouth. It screams in rage and falls on top of me, its large body crushes me; its jaws close around my face.

It plunges onto the stake. I feel the flesh tear and bone break as the stake find its mark, driving into the babunook's heart. Its jaws squeeze my head and I scream with it, I scream through the pain and anger and I offer my soul to whoever needs it.

My world goes black.

I stand on the outside of the clearing, watching the babunook slumped over my own body. From here, I can see we've both perished. Blood has formed a nice red pool around me, and now the babunook's black blood is mixing with it.

I don't take my eyes away as its large form begins to shake and convulse, its chest caves downwards as the cloth is burnt away. To my amazement, black butterflies begin to flutter up towards the moon; beating their black wings strongly.

They only get a few metres before disintegrating and turning to ash, being swept away by the wind. A movement across the clearing catches my eye and I see the babunook emerge from the trees, in a ghost-like shadow like my own.

Nyx runs across the clearing, screaming and crying as he falls down beside me; pulling me into his arms. My skin has turned even paler, my eyes have closed. He presses his lips to my own, my forehead, my cheeks.

"You must come," the babunook says, reaching a hand out towards me. Behind it in the forest creatures scream and growl. Where it's taking me isn't going to be anywhere good. Red and gold eyes flutter open in the darkness behind the babunook and watch on.

"A soul for a soul. You never said which soul must come with you," A female voice says from beside me. I turn to see Nyx's mother standing there; looking regal in her dark blue gown with a silver crown nestled in her hair.

"Veronica…" I say, baffled. She looks at me and then looks at Nyx.

"That boy has lost so much in his life, far more than anyone should endure," she says softly. Her guard drops and her face shows the love she feels for him.

"I promised I wouldn't let him get hurt." I look back to where he holds me. I hadn't told him a lot of things, I hadn't told him I loved him. I couldn't now and I'd never get my chance to again.

"Losing you will break him more than anything in this world." She stands beside me, taking my hand in her own.

"I wish I'd told him how I feel," I say sadly, giving her hand a squeeze.

"You and I are connected in ways neither of us will understand, so I give you this, Ravynne. Make me a promise. Promise me you will stay by his side until the earth swallows him and bursts with violets and marigolds. Promise me that you'll watch out for him, looking after him when he needs it and on days when he doesn't." Wind begins to whip at my hair and clothes, the babunook waits on the opposite clearing but the watching creatures grow restless. She makes me look at her, her eyes blaze with determination.

"Wh—"

"Promise me you'll continue to love him," she cuts me off.

"I promise." How can I promise these things when I'm going to turn over my soul to the babunook? A dog like yip begins to fill the clearing and large black creatures emerge on four legs. Similar to a dog, although their black hairless skin is far too tight over their skeletons.

"Live Ravynne, live." She lets go of my hand, puts her silver crown on my head and pushes me towards where Nyx still cradles me. I stumble towards us, feeling a tug towards my body. I look over my shoulder to see Veronica face the babunook.

"A soul for a soul and I give you mine. The girl is spared," she says clearly, her voice ringing with the authority she had taken to the grave. The dogs come closer, beginning to snap at her with meaty jaws.

"The bargain is upheld." The babunook offers a hand towards her, she gives me one last look; smiling as she crosses the clearing and placing a pale hand in the babunook's clawed one. The tug grows stronger and the dogs begin to snap at me.

"Go now!" she yells over her shoulder, now struggling against the babunook's pull. Other black hands reach out of the darkness and grab at her dress and her arms.

I close my eyes as I fall into my body. The phantom bite of the dog is on my heels as I plummet through my body and into darkness. I fall, towards a bright violet light. I feel myself change as I grow warmer, and feel my soul merge into one. Veronica had offered her soul in place of my own, and in doing that she's given me back the piece of my own that has been missing.

I grab at the violet light as I'm slammed into it, it threatens to slip between my fingers but I hold on tight. I have to get home to Nyx. I promised.

My word is everything.

Tears hit my face as my eyes flutter open, I take a gasping breath as my body convulses. My head falls to the side and I throw up thick chunks of dirt and clay, coating my throat with the sweet taste of earth.

"Ravynne?" Nyx asks, shocked. He pulls me back to him, crushing me.

"Nyx," I gasp, breathing. I can breathe, I can hear, I can see.

I'm alive.

His eyes are blood shot and red rimmed as he looks down at me, still tears stream down his cheeks. His eyes wander to the side of my face and the top of my head, disbelief shocking him into silence. I close my eyes and relax, my stomach stings and I still feel light headed and cold. But I'm alive.

I had lived.

"I'm sorry," I whisper, my throat is raw and when I open my eyes he's stopped crying. The moonlight shines down on us, and I feel safe.

The babunook is gone, we'd done it.

"I'm just glad you're alive," he whispers back, pressing his lips to my forehead.

"But we need to—" I try, needing to talk and explain myself. If I came back from the dead for him to never forgive me it will have all been for nothing.

"Later Rav, later. Can you move?" I curl my toes and wiggles my fingers. I can move everything.

"I think so." I hold onto him tightly as he helps both of us stand, to my surprise I'm taller than before and now that I think about it a lot of what has happened isn't making sense. I look down at my stomach to see the four gash marks, but there's no more blood.

"Wait, how am I here?" I ask, rubbing my throat. I look around the clearing, there's so much blood. Regardless of what happened with the babunook, with all that blood I can't possibly be standing here.

"I'm waiting for you to tell me that." I look back to him. His lips hint at a ghost of a smile as he looks over me, keeping a protective arm around my waist.

"I saw your mother, she said she'd go in my place." I feel the tears well in my eyes, she'd given her soul for my own. She'd saved my life, and Nyx's.

"I told you she'd like you," he murmurs, kissing the tears away from my cheeks.

"I feel…whole now. Like I returned with something, like I've returned with my entire soul and not just a fragment of it," I whisper, looking into his eyes. He takes my hand in his own, and ever so slowly brings it to my face. To my ear.

To my faerie pointed ear.

Epilogue

Kalin runs screaming around the living room, with Aunty chasing behind him. I finish the final touches on the roast, sprinkling rosemary over the lamb leg. Ma sets up the kitchen table with plates and decorations, Da is out on the farm gathering the few lettuces we'll need for dinner.

Hands wrap around my waist, warm lips press onto the top of my bare shoulder. I grin as I look up, finding Nyx standing there. His dark hair is neatly combed, exposing his golden oak leaf crown and pointed ears. He reaches up and twirls a strand of loose hair behind my ear, not wanting to disturb the effort I'd put into my bun. I'd woven violets through the strands, wanting to put effort into how I looked for the Yule celebration.

"There you are, took you long enough to find me," I say, wiping my hands on the tea towel. He breaks into a grin, but I feel his fingers dig into my hip.

"Far longer than I liked," he looks over to where Ma is doing the final touches to the table. I grab onto the tray of roast and move out of his arms, putting it in the oven. An hour and we'd all be sitting at the table, eating roast dinner and celebrating Christmas.

"Do you need any more help, Ma?" I ask, stepping back beside Nyx. She smiles over at us.

"No, no. It's all done, can you head into the village and grab a few more dessert items? Surprise me." She begins to adjust the tablecloth again and I shake my head with a smile as I take Nyx's hand in mine; pulling him out of the house with me.

He intertwines our fingers as we begin to walk up into the village, the trees on either side have been strung with faerie lights and red ball bulls with a light coat of snow covering everything. I hum to myself as I lean my head on his shoulder, feeling happier than I have ever been.

After we'd returned from killing the babunook and I'd shown everyone I was now like Nyx, Aunty had given me a knowing smile. I finally knew what she had whispered before we'd left, that I'd come back changed.

It had been six months since I was faced with killing the babunook, since I had betrayed Nyx in the most awful way. He'd been furious, but since I'd returned in one piece it wasn't hard for him to forgive me. Even now, feeling the warmth of his hand in mine, I'm not sure I deserve it.

I lied, schemed and had used his biggest weakness against him. I was a foul mortal, but now I'm working on being the best possible version of me that I can be. With him by my side, I think anything I dream is possible.

"What're you thinking about?" he murmurs as we reach the edge of the village. After word had spread that I'd killed the babunook, I was looked upon as a god instead of a witch. I'd been blessed and had people coming up to thank me. Nyx nods politely as we pass them, heading to one of the other bakeries that are still open. The sun is beginning to set and all the lights and decorations are being turned on.

"Everything. You, mainly," I wink up at him. I wasn't able to outright lie anymore. I was glad for it, I don't know how Nyx would have felt if I still had that ability. I doubt I'd ever be able to earn his trust again.

"What do you wish to do once Yule is over?" he asks. We go into the small bakery and I put off his question. I grab six slices of chocolate cheesecake coated with strawberries and hand over a gold coin. We leave and begin the walk back to my parents. I link my arm with his.

"I want to do a lot of things. I'd like to travel. I'd like to learn how to sing, I want to visit Faerie again. What do you want?" I ask, looking up at him. He smiles down at me, making my heart ache.

"I want to be wherever you are."

He hasn't returned to Faerie yet to be crowned king, I think he's waiting until I'm more comfortable with my new sense of self. Although I am looking forward to wiping the smirks off all of the female faeries faces that once laughed at my mortality.

"Awh, aren't you the romantic." I bat my lashes up at him, smiling sweetly.

"It is one of my many talents."

I enjoy the silence between us. I've had Nyx by my side nearly sun down to sun set. He'd only left my side to attend the castle and begin to push things into motion. He was giving the village to the people so they no longer had to offer what little they own. Which means the priest will be the main leader, but he's something I can deal with if the time comes.

"After Yule, we should return to Faerie," I say, surprising him.

"Why?" he asks, pausing us just outside the gate to my home. I look up at him, searching his face.

"Because it's also your home, and I'd like to be able to call it mine as well. I'm sure Faerie is larger than what I've glimpsed and it might help me adjust more." I reach up and touch a pointed ear, still feeling surreal they were now my own.

"Only if you're comfortable with it, I don't want you to push yourself," he says softly, cupping a hand to my cheek. I press my own hand over his, looking into his violet eyes that sparkle from the faerie lights.

"I know and I won't. Maybe we can stay for a week or so and then explore Akrania a bit more. This world is large Nyx, and I wish to see all of it with you." Soft snow begins to fall, snowflakes stick to his hair and shirt.

"It would be my honour."

I press my lips to his, sliding my arms around his neck while the snow falls and the moon begins to rise. If someone had told me when I'd first met Nyx that I'd fall in love with him, I would never have believed them.

I pull back and take his hand, heading into the warmth of my home. My family smiles warmly as we go inside, Kalin puts a paper crown onto Nyx's head as we take a seat at the table. We laugh and talk, enjoying Yule together.

If I knew back then what I know now, I can happily say I would do it all over again.

For being mortal wasn't a weakness, it was my greatest strength of all.

ACKNOWLEDGMENTS

Ravynne came to me, almost like it was a dream, while I was at work unloading fruit. I was transported from the back room and placed on a muddy slope, rain pouring down around me with a heavy bucket in my hands.

This is where the seed was planted and oh how I've loved to watch it grow and now bloom. Writing *Enchantment of Darkness* was almost as easy as breathing and the encouragement from the writing community and my friends and family is what helped me continue and see this to an end.

I spent countless hours with my head in my laptop. I want to say a special thanks to a few of my author friends, Brittany Matsen and Catherine Labadie. I can always count on them to help with encouragement and to be there in general when my brain turns to mush from writing so much.

A special thanks to my friends, although most of them aren't readers your support means more to me than you'll ever know. Thanks for letting me become a hermit crab for a few months.

Tara Routley, you've done it again. You've turned my sloppy writing into a story that is more than readable. I can't thank you enough for editing my novels for me, I know they wouldn't be nearly as good if it wasn't for you. It's always terrifying handing over each story but I know they're in safe hands and your patience and love for them is amazing. Lots of love.

A special thanks to my beta readers, I appreciate and value every comment and piece of feedback I was given to bring this story to you all in the best form it can be in.

Franz (coverdungeon) I love the cover you created for this novel, it is exactly what I imagined and it has been amazing working with you. I am so in love with the outcome.

And thanks to you, the reader, if it wasn't for your support I wouldn't be here now writing this. I am grateful for every one of you.

Also thank you to the team at NoShelfControl Bookbox and Ariel, thank you for giving my stories the chance to reach readers. I love you and so does Ravynne, words can't explain how thankful I am that you've given me a chance.

Books by Shana J. Caldwell

Immortal Series

Immortal Awakening
Immortal Suffering
Immortal Reckoning
Behind the Immortals

Enchanted Series

Enchantment of Darkness

Shana J. Caldwell is an Australian self-published author, who is either knee deep in reading or crouched over her laptop with her trusty cat, Luna, as her writing companion. When she's not writing she's got her nose stuck between the pages of a book or can be found with a coffee in hand.

Follow Shana on:

Connect with her online:

Facebook.com/shanajcaldwell/
Twitter.com/ShanaJCaldwell1
Instagram.com/shanajcaldwellbooks
https://shanacaldwell03.wixsite.com/website

www.ingramcontent.com/pod-product-compliance
Lightning Source LLC
Chambersburg PA
CBHW020916310726
48980CB00011B/906/J